Ahab's Bride

LOUISE M. GOUGE

RiverOak®

Good News in Fiction

An Imprint of Cook Communications Ministries • Colorado Springs, CO

All scriptures are taken from the *King James Version* of the Bible.

Published by RiverOak Publishing
RiverOak® is an imprint of
Cook Communications Ministries, Colorado Springs, CO 80918
Cook Communications, Paris, Ontario
Kingsway Communications, Eastbourne, England

AHAB'S BRIDE

First printing, 2004
Printed in the United States of America
1 2 3 4 5 6 7 8 9 10 Printing/Year 06 05 04

Editor: Jeff Dunn

Agent representation by Les Stobbe Literary Agency

Library of Congress Cataloging-in-Publication Data

Gouge, Louise M. (Louise Myra), 1944-
  Ahab's bride / Louise Gouge.
    p. cm.
  ISBN 1-58919-007-6 (pbk.)
  1. Ship captains' spouses—Fiction. 2. Ahab, Captain (Fictitious
character)—Fiction. 3. Nantucket Island (Mass.)—Fiction. 4.
Women—Massachusetts—Fiction. 5. Loss (Psychology)—Fiction. I.
Title.
PS3557.O839 A77 2004
813'.54—dc21
                                    2003012439

Acknowledgments

I am indebted to Dr. Ed Cohen, my thesis advisor
at Rollins College, for his encouragement, wisdom,
and advice as I wrote Ahab's Bride. I am also grateful
to my husband David for his support
and for his patient reading of what I wrote each day.
Thanks to Patti Haley and Pat Grall at the Olin Library at
Rollins College and Betsy Lowenstein and
Elizabeth Oldham at the Nantucket Historical Association.
Very special thanks to my agent, Les Stobbe,
and my editor, Jeff Dunn, who believed in my story
and brought about its publication.

Chapter One

ဆာ

$\mathcal{N}$ ever again!" Hannah Oldweiler muttered through clenched teeth as she marched along the street. The heels of her boots scuffed up clouds of dust from the hard-packed ground onto the hem of her yellow linen dress.

The breezes of early autumn brought a contradictory blend of floral fragrance from nearby gardens and the rancid smells from New Bedford Harbor far away at the bottom of the hill. Ordinarily, Hannah did not notice the odors of the whalefishery, ever present to some degree throughout her hometown. But today the stench seemed particularly rank to her, and even the sweet perfume of late-season roses failed to soothe her annoyance over today's luncheon social.

The next time Lila Gantvort invited her to dine, she would find an excuse, any excuse, not to go. All the young ladies in attendance came from the best New Bedford families. All had received a worthy education and should have been eager to participate in enlightened discourse. Instead, Hannah found their company stifling and their conversation trivial.

Could they discuss Coleridge, Wordsworth, or Shelley? No, of course not. It must be fashion, parties, and engagements, for the only thing her childhood friends ever cared about was matrimony. Hannah would have enjoyed an afternoon curled up with a good book more than all their silly babble. She went to make Papa happy, or rather to appease his idea of what should make her happy.

Poor, dear Papa. He was deeply concerned about her, but there was nothing she could do to ease his worries. Even she did not understand her sense of estrangement from her friends or her reluctance to accept society's assertion that marriage was a woman's ultimate happiness. Perhaps it was because too often she had watched as some vain and pretty acquaintance accepted the proposal of some vain and wealthy man, only to discover after marriage that vanity was all they had in common. Though Hannah was considered a beauty, she refused to play beauty's games. And despite her father's best efforts to make her happy, she felt a restlessness that refused to be pacified.

Her musings about her father softened her mood and slowed her pace. She did not wish to arrive home in a temper, for it would only grieve him. Somehow, she must improve her thoughts.

The distant sounds of the harbor floated up the hill on the friendly breeze: wagons and horses' hooves clattering on the cobblestones, whalers and dockworkers shouting to one another as they performed their duties, and sea gulls calling out to demand a share of the sea's bounty newly arrived in port. The cries of the gulls always seemed to sing out, "Come away and see the world." One day Hannah would answer that siren song.

She glanced across the street at the large Greek Revival house being built for Mr. Blain. Set back from the street some twenty-five feet like many of the County Street houses, its ample front yard would provide Mrs. Blain with plenty of room to plant a variety of flowers. If it were Hannah's property, she would choose rhododendrons to line the semi-circular drive in front of the columned porch. She liked the contrast between the woody branches of the rhododendron bushes and their colorful trumpet-shaped blossom clusters. But whatever flowers Mrs. Blain chose, the house would be a lovely addition to County Street, where many whale ship owners and captains were building their residences.

Hannah's father, Amos Oldweiler, inherited his stately Greek Revival house. Built in 1810, some twenty-seven years earlier, the structure stood out from the Federal-style homes popular back then. With the Blains' choice of architecture, their home would no longer be unique on the street.

Along with the house, Mr. Oldweiler also inherited a small fleet of whaling vessels from his mother's childless brother. Receiving this propitious bequest as a young man of twenty-five, he promptly left his labors on an older cousin's Indiana farm for proprietary concerns on the Massachusetts shores. He had not been brought up in the whaling trade and possessed no aptitude for wise investments. Still, he tried for twenty years to increase his modest inheritance, or at least to keep it intact. Unfortunately, by the time his only child reached eighteen, she had become aware that her father was simply struggling to keep up the appearances of wealth until she married into one of the more financially secure New Bedford families.

Though he never said anything, Hannah could see it dismayed him when she declined proposals of marriage from agreeable suitors. But he would never press her to accept someone she could not love, merely for security's sake. He was never one to demand his own will, and in this matter he had long ago adopted an attitude of resignation, trusting Providence for both their futures.

His lack of business acumen notwithstanding, the amiable Oldweiler had cultivated a number of friendships in the growing community, and his fondest wish was for his daughter to find happiness there as well. But since she did not aspire to be a belle in New Bedford's society, Hannah was content for the time being to manage her widowed father's household and to subdue her restlessness through reading her favorite books and dreaming of travel to distant lands.

The autumn day was warm and bright, so Hannah held her parasol close to the broad brim of her bonnet to shield her face from the sun's browning rays. Although she eschewed most displays of vanity, she did wish to avoid developing freckles. One of her governesses—she could not remember which, for none stayed long enough to leave a serious impression—managed to persuade her that her ivory complexion was an attribute worth preserving. That notion became reinforced at Miss Applegate's school in Boston, where Hannah spent several years. Finally, the envy voiced by friends and the compliments paid by suitors prompted her to guard her fair coloring, though often the exercise proved bothersome.

As she mounted the front steps to her white, two-storied home, Hannah's mood improved with the memory that Jeremiah Harris would be coming to supper tonight. The handsome minister was the youngest son of a New Bedford merchant and a close friend to both Hannah and Mr. Oldweiler. Jeremiah decided at an early age not to follow his father's line of work or that of his maternal grandfather, a successful whaling captain, but rather to enter the ministry. He spent several years in Andover Seminary near Boston and was now back home again. To Mr. Oldweiler's delight, he agreed to spend every available Friday evening at their home.

That evening as they sat around the dining room table, Hannah was once again grateful for the encouragement his visits gave her father. Whenever Jeremiah called, Mr. Oldweiler's face glowed with enthusiasm during their stimulating conversations.

The younger man gave his host sincere and respectful attention, but he often gazed at his hostess.

"Hannah, this was an excellent supper, as usual." Jeremiah touched his napkin to his lips, and then laid it beside his plate. "My compliments to Mrs. Randolph and to your menu."

"Thank you, Jeremiah, or should I say, Reverend Harris?" Hannah replied. "Papa and I are so glad you could come tonight. You must make this your second home now that you are settled for certain back here in New Bedford. I still marvel that there was an opening for an assistant pastor at our very own church just as you finished your seminary studies. I could not have borne it to see you sent who knows where. I was so afraid you might decide to be a missionary to India or Africa, and we would never see you again."

"Hannah, what a thing to say," Mr. Oldweiler said. "Our Jeremiah has chosen the greatest happiness possible in life by serving God, no matter where that takes him."

"Yes, but wouldn't we miss him dreadfully if he were to go away again?"

Jeremiah smiled. "You need not worry. I feel no call for southern climes. We've plenty of sinners right here in New Bedford who need saving."

"And you're just the man to do it, my boy." Mr. Oldweiler stood and nodded to them. "Now, if you young people will excuse me, I will go have my after-supper pipe. Hannah, why don't you show Jeremiah those rose bushes you've been cultivating all summer?"

"Oh, yes, please do." Jeremiah stood politely as his host left the room. Almost six feet tall, with a stocky, muscular build, the young man would have made an excellent whaler, had he chosen that profession. His clear blue eyes, unlined face, and sandy brown hair cut just below his ears made Hannah think more of

John, the New Testament disciple, rather than of the Old Testament prophet of doom for whom he was named. Though he ministered in a Calvinist church, Jeremiah's gentle countenance and kindness never made one think of hell fires or damnation.

She grasped his hand and drew him out the dining room door to the terrace. The early September sun still shone above the western horizon, casting its rays on the colorful garden. The clamshell pathway crunched beneath their feet as they wandered among the bushes, she pointing out the different varieties, and he nodding in admiration at her success in growing them.

"The growing season is long over for most roses, but I've managed to discover a few varieties that can endure the summer heat. This is my favorite." She touched the stem of a single, soft bud on one bush. "I call it Ivory Rose after my mother. Her name was Rose, you know. Papa tells me she had the fairest ivory complexion, with just a blush of rose on her cheeks. When this one blooms, its petals are ivory-colored, but a soft pink tint seems to glow near the edges. It's a lovely effect."

"As the mother, so is her daughter. What a beautiful tribute to her."

"Yes. I think it good always to remember she gave her life so I could live."

"Just as Christ our Lord did."

Hannah smiled up at him. "Always the preacher, Jeremiah?"

He grinned self-consciously and stared down at his feet, then glanced toward the end of the garden. "Could we go into the arbor and talk?" Not waiting for an answer, he took her arm, led her into the shady arbor, and sat beside her in the white wooden glider suspended by chains from a sturdy frame.

"You're so very serious this evening, Jeremiah."

"Yes, I am. I have a very important question to ask you."

"Oh?" Hannah turned away. She had not expected him to propose so soon. It would be impossible to refuse without hurting him, and she dreaded causing him pain.

"We spoke a little about my calling a while ago. The truth is, I have been called to be a missionary, but not far away. My mission field is here in New Bedford, most especially among the whalers. You know my grandfather was a whaler, so it's not as if I have no understanding of them. But you will need to have that understanding too. I know your father has protected you from the roughest of the lot who sail on his ships, and I don't fault him for that. It was fitting that as his daughter you should move among only the highest of New Bedford society."

"Oh, I wouldn't say—"

"Please, allow me to finish. I don't want to draw you unprepared into a situation that will be uncomfortable for you."

"Jeremiah, I—"

"What I propose, if you would permit it, is that I would like to bring to supper next week a certain whaling captain whose soul, I fear, is in deepest peril. He's an older man, and while he is not coarse, he is rather rough, although he certainly has manners enough in polite society, or I would not ask you to entertain him."

Hannah giggled with relief. Proposing marriage was not what he had in mind after all, at least not tonight. "Silly dear, of course you can bring a friend to supper. Is that the question you wished to ask me?"

"Why, yes. It will serve a most important purpose in regard to our future."

"Our future? In what way?"

"If I am to minister to men such as this captain, I must help you become comfortable in ministering along with me. I want you to become accustomed to—"

"But, Jeremiah," she could not let him continue, "you speak as though our futures were one."

"Of course. Haven't we always known that?"

Hannah tried to think of the kindest possible words to deny his assertion. But no matter what, it was best to face the matter and be done with it once and for all.

"Do you mean to tell me," he teased, "that hope chest of yours is being filled for some other man's home?"

"I have no hope chest. And if I did, why would you think … why would you assume—"

"Is this my ever-candid Hannah Oldweiler playing the coquette now? After all, it was you who proposed to me."

"I? I did no such thing."

"But when you were ten years old, and I was sixteen, we sat in this very swing, and you vowed that you would allow me to marry no one but you."

"But I was only a child, and you nearly a grown man … a family friend, like a dear brother to me. Oh, you. You're joking. I demand that you stop."

Jeremiah gazed at her fondly. "Yes, I suppose I should. But as I've watched you grow up so beautifully, I've known it was not enough to be your friend and brother. I've come to realize your childish proposal was my heart's desire as well. I've always felt we had an understanding that we would serve God together." He paused and frowned. "Oh, dear. Now I see that I have failed to honor you by true courtship. It's only fair that you should play hard to get."

Hannah searched his eyes. How often through the years had she gazed into those gentle eyes that never condemned her childish antics? But with all his understanding, how had he failed to observe the deepest changes in her?

"Oh, dear."

"Let me mend my ways. Will this do?" He knelt on the ground in front of her and took her hands. "Dearest Hannah, I love you with all my heart. Would you do me the great honor of becoming my wife?"

She stared down and bit her lip. If she looked into his eyes again, she feared she would do whatever he asked. He was so good, so gentle, so persuasive. But marry him? No. Now that he spoke the words she long feared, she knew she could not accept him.

"My dear friend, I know that as a pastor, you need a wife to stand by your side as a helpmeet. But I'm only eighteen and not yet ready to marry. Besides, Papa isn't well, and I cannot leave him alone."

"Your father has already given his blessing. I would never propose to you without asking him first. As to your age, my darling, you have managed his house for four years with great skill, far better than women twice or thrice your age might do."

"Managing a house is not what I was referring to. I long for something else in life. We live in an amazing world, and this is a time of great discoveries, like the Rosetta stone, the pharaohs' tombs of ancient Egypt, or the site of the Trojan War. Think of how exciting it would be to actually see those artifacts and places we've only read about. I want to see Europe—England, Italy, France. Oh, and of course I want to visit the place where William Penn set sail, bringing with him my ancestor, Peter Oldweiler. I want to see all the places Shakespeare wrote about. I cannot think of being chained to duties and responsibilities far beyond my age and aptitude. I would not serve you well for a pastor's wife."

"But of course you would. Is this my capable Hannah thinking so ill of her own abilities?"

"Weren't you listening to me? I wish to travel."

"Perhaps some day we can—"

"I don't believe in perhaps. I believe in planning."

Jeremiah slowly stood and brushed the grass and dirt from his trouser legs. Hannah could see the hurt in his eyes, but she would not change her mind. A moment of being persuaded by his endearing charms would condemn her to a life she had long ago known she could not live. After a few moments, he sat back down and gave her a sad smile.

"I hope you will forgive me for taking you for granted. I didn't mean to. Honestly."

"You may always take my friendship for granted. But ...," she looked away for a moment, then turned back to him. "Next to my father, you are my dearest friend, but I will not, I cannot, be your wife."

He was quiet again and deep in thought. When at last he spoke, there was no rancor or censure in his tone, only melancholy. "I don't understand why you want to travel. What use will it serve? It seems so selfish just running off to see the world with no purpose in mind. I have never thought you selfish. Why, you're the most unselfish woman I know. And what better way can a woman serve God than by working beside her husband in the church?"

"Indeed! May we forget serving God for a moment?"

"Hannah!"

"No, I mean it. Young men often go on all sorts of travels before they settle down to their life's work. Even you. And if you had decided to become a whaler after your voyage as your grandfather's cabin boy, who would have told you no? Or if you had decided to work in your father's store or become a professor or anything other than a pastor, who would have said you were out of God's will? There were no pastors in your family. No example you were forced to follow. You felt it was God's calling for you, and so you made your decision to enter the ministry."

"Yes, but for a woman, her great work in life, the very highest calling is—"

"To be a wife? Why?"

He thought for a moment. "If you have not been called to be my ... to be a wife, then what are you thinking of? You're far too spirited to live an idle life. Other than caring for your father, what will you do?" He waited a moment, his expression open to whatever she would say. When she gave a little shrug of indecision, he leaned toward her. "You see, you're uncertain yourself. What you need is someone older and more experienced to be your guiding hand, a loving husband to help you find the right occupation for your time."

Hannah gave an exasperated sigh. "What you mean is a husband who will tell me what to do and what to think, as if a woman could not find a proper occupation for her life. That's nonsense. A woman should not feel that she must marry in order to be useful. And if she does marry, may it not be to someone her own heart chooses?"

Jeremiah winced, as if he had been struck. "Ah, now I understand. You're in love with someone else." He was quiet for a moment before whispering, "May I know my rival's name?"

"There is no one. Truly."

"Then I still may win your heart?"

"I would be very sad to lose your friendship, but I cannot promise anything more."

Jeremiah took her hand once more and kissed it. "I will be content with friendship for now, but I cannot promise to cease my quest for the owner of this lovely hand."

She smiled, but gently pulled her hand away from him. Thank goodness this difficult interview was over. Now perhaps she should offer some token of her good will. "You may bring that ship's captain to supper next Friday evening. Until you do find your wife, you will need a home where you can bring these reprobates as you try to save their souls." She noticed with dismay that her invitation pleased him far more than it should have.

Late that evening, Hannah sat on the footstool beside her father's chair, packing his evening pipe, as was their custom. She lifted the elegantly carved pipe to him and struck a match while he inhaled the fragrant tobacco smoke. After the pipe was securely lit, Mr. Oldweiler held it thoughtfully and gazed at his daughter.

"Hannah, I know it's the fashion among your friends for a young lady to decline a gentleman's first proposal, even when she loves her young man. I've not said anything to you regarding your rejection of previous suitors because I was hoping that when Jeremiah returned home from seminary, his boyhood fondness for you might blossom into love. And so it has. He loves you most devotedly. But I must warn you," he said with a twinkle in his eye, "there are numerous other eligible young ladies whose regular church attendance has been assured by, oh, shall we say, a newfound piety that, you may have noticed, coincided with Jeremiah's investiture as our assistant pastor. You'll not want to risk their attracting his attention by waiting too long to accept him."

"But—"

"I've been such a poor businessman, and I have so little security to give you, my dear." He ignored her attempt to interrupt. "You may think his father's wealth, with his eventually inheriting a share of it, is the reason I have always favored Jeremiah. But I must assure you it is his excellent character that has made him dear to my heart, as well as to yours, though sometimes I question whether you or I benefit more from his visits. Just talking with him gives me so much comfort and pleasure. Oh, the faith he has. You don't find many young men his age with such great faith. Do you recall that, even as a child, he possessed that unusual gift for spiritual insights which still astounds us all? He was one of those rare children who seemed filled from his earliest years with a peace so deep and genuine, it affected everyone around him."

Hannah nodded. "I remember your telling me of his childhood." Her father rarely spoke at such length on any subject. She must permit him to present his whole argument in Jeremiah's favor before dashing his hopes.

"Did you notice, when he gave the sermon two weeks ago, how he seemed to tower above us all, like a prophet of old? His voice is so resonant, so confident and compelling. His eyes seem to reach into the very soul of each person in the congregation and at once convict us of sin and assure us of God's loving mercy. Do you see how perplexed and grieved he becomes over those who do not understand God's love as he does? You do see it, don't you, Hannah? Why, if there is any fault in the man, it's his devotion to God. And who could call that a fault?"

Hannah gazed at her father, her heart aching over the disappointment she was inflicting on him. As he spoke, she began to realize that he knew. Somehow, with his wonderful father-wisdom, he knew she would not marry Jeremiah. Yet still he would try to persuade her. How it pained her to break his heart. "That's true, Papa. Loving God and preaching His love to others could never be called a fault."

"Do you recall, dear, when he returned from his three-year voyage with his grandfather, how he had grown? Sailing away as a boy of eleven and returning at fourteen, almost a man. In your excitement at greeting the ship in the harbor, you slipped and might have fallen to your death between wharf and vessel if he had not reached down to save you."

Her little accident was not nearly as serious as her father thought, though Jeremiah received a deep gash on his hand, and her white frock was ruined by the mishap. But Mr. Oldweiler insisted on making Jeremiah the hero of the event. Even then he must have been hoping they would marry. "And you've never allowed me near the docks since that day. I was certainly a naughty little girl, wasn't I?" She spoke lightly, trying to redirect the conversation. "Someone was always getting me out of trouble."

"Naughty? Oh, I never thought so. You were merely curious about everything. And so full of energy. No, not naughty. Lively, perhaps."

"You couldn't keep a governess for me."

"Mm." He gave a little shrug and pursed his lips at the memory.

"And my escapades at boarding school appalled my teachers."

"Ah, well, none of them had any understanding of your temperament." He relaxed back in his chair with a sigh. "Hmm … and perhaps I am guilty of the same failure."

"You? You're perfect in every way, dearest."

He set his pipe on the table and took her face in his hands. "My dearest. I will not press you any further about Jeremiah."

Hannah smiled at him, her heart overflowing with tenderness.

"But," he said as he sat up abruptly and wagged a finger at her playfully. "I will pray!"

Chapter Two

சு

Hannah stood before her wardrobe, considering which dress to wear for the evening. Jeremiah liked the green because, he said, it made her green eyes glow like emeralds. She would not wear it, or he would be staring at her all evening. He said the pink one brought roses to her cheeks, so it would not do either. Ah, yes, the white. When she had worn it last, he had asked more than once if she were feeling well. She pulled the gown over her head, adjusting the whalebone stays beneath her full, graceful breasts and around her slender waist, then spreading the wide skirt evenly over her three petticoats, finally fastening the dress under her left arm. The buttons would chafe her underarm all evening. But with no lady's maid to help her dress, she was forced to have all her gowns made with side buttons rather than more fashionable back closures, simply so she could dress herself.

Surveying herself in the wardrobe mirror, she shrugged. Tall, classical figures like hers had passed out of vogue some years before, replaced by a shorter, fuller look. Still, she was comfortable with herself, and tonight something else was more important than looking attractive. The cleverness of her choosing the white dress was confirmed as she sat before her dressing table to touch up her hair. The neckline was low cut, though modest, and the white lace trim almost disappeared against her ivory chest and arms. As she brushed a few stray hairs into place, she noted with approval that her dark auburn locks did indeed emphasize the paleness of her complexion. She could do nothing to reduce the natural tint of her dark pink lips or to lighten her black eyelashes. But, after all, her intention was not to look ill, simply uninteresting.

Her toilette complete, she went downstairs to the kitchen to be certain Mrs. Randolph had supper under control. The capable old servant, a widow of a whaler who had died many years before, endured Hannah's fussing about with good humor. She finally settled the matter by giving her employer a taste of the dessert pudding and sending her on her way to bother another member of the household staff. It was a ritual they both enjoyed.

After checking the settings on the dining room table, Hannah went to the front parlor where Sally was filling the oil lamps and trimming their wicks. The housemaid was Mrs. Randolph's only child and a whaling widow herself with a twelve-year-old daughter. The Oldweilers employed her several days each week, partly as an act of charity and partly because they could no longer afford a full-time staff. The arrangement benefited both families.

The spacious front parlor was beautifully decorated, though not by Hannah or her father. Neither had any inclination for such undertakings. The work had been done by Mr. Oldweiler's uncle, who at the height of his wealth had built and furnished the house to display his success. After the custom of the time, he had purchased solid furniture, elegant draperies, and exquisite accent pieces, including several Persian rugs. In the twenty-seven years that had passed since the day the old man had first occupied these rooms, the quality of the furnishings had been proven in that most items were only a little worn. More often than not, the furniture was draped with sheets to prevent fading.

Such conscientious care by the elderly butler, Carson, in addition to some skillful repair stitching by Sally, hid the signs of age and kept everything in a sufficiently presentable condition to please the Oldweilers, who seldom entertained.

The parlor was papered in a pale floral pattern that contrasted with the dark mahogany woodwork. In front of the marble fireplace, an oak divan with red velvet upholstery faced two floral print chairs, with a low table in between. Behind the divan was a black lacquered chest from China, inlaid with ivory and painted with colorful designs. Beyond that was another grouping of a divan, several chairs, and some occasional tables. During daylight hours, the sun streamed in through a tall window in the southeast corner, one next to the fireplace, and another in the front of the house. In front of the window was a cushioned window seat which provided a striking view down the hill to the New Bedford harbor just over a half-mile away.

Sally had already laid logs in the fireplace to be lit as the evening grew cooler. Seeing that everything was in readiness for guests, Hannah fluffed the pillows on the red divan, then sought her father in his study. He was seated at his desk, bent over his open Bible with head in hands, a posture he often assumed of late. Hearing her enter, he quickly put on a smile and stood to greet her.

"My dear, you look lovely ... almost like a bride in that white. If you're trying to discourage Jeremiah, I don't think this gown was the best choice."

"Oh, I hadn't even thought of that. Should I go change?"

"No, no." He laughed. "I'm only teasing. Whatever you wear or do or say, he will only see perfection. That surely must endear him to you a little."

"He couldn't be any dearer. But not for a husband."

"Hmm. What shall I do with you then, Daughter?"

Hannah laughed. "And what shall I do with you, Papa?" She nestled into his outstretched arms, savoring the comfort they always gave her. He was only an inch taller than her five feet eight inches. As her arms easily encircled his slender, almost bony frame, she ached to soothe the worry that was harming his formerly robust health.

She brushed back his thinning hair with her hand and gave him a peck on the cheek. "What did Mrs. Brown want this afternoon? Another advance on her husband's earnings?"

"Yes. She has three children to feed and clothe, you know. It's my responsibility to care for them as her husband cares for my ship."

"And did you write down the loan in your ledger?"

"Hmm. No, I forgot to do that ... getting ready for our guests, you know."

"Why don't you write it down right now?" She wanted to scold him for his too-generous treatment of Captain Brown's family. But these acts of charity were second nature to him. He could no more cease to share what he had with those less fortunate than he could cease to breathe.

"Yes. I should do that." He started to reach for the ledger, then turned toward the door. "I think I hear Jeremiah arriving with his friend. We'd best not keep them waiting."

With a sigh of resignation, she followed her father down the passageway toward the grand entry hall where Carson was greeting Jeremiah and his guest. She glanced in a hallway mirror to review her appearance, lingering behind her father long enough to make a casual but effective entrance. However, her thoughts did not remain on her own presentation for long.

From the instant she saw the older man, her eyes could not leave him. Every aspect of his appearance was startling. He was more than half a head taller than his young companion, with broad shoulders and noble posture that were enhanced by his elegant black suit. Through the left side of his neatly trimmed black hair ran a stark white streak from which descended a pale, narrow scar that cut through his sun-bronzed complexion and black chin-curtain beard, disappearing at last beneath his high starched collar. His long, well-formed legs could not be disguised by the straight cut of his trousers. Despite the scar, the classic features of his handsome face caused Hannah to feel as if she were gazing upon Homer's mighty Greek warrior, the god-like Achilles. Why had Jeremiah called him old? The man was ageless. And he was the most magnificent man she had ever seen.

She could barely mask her wonder before he turned, at Jeremiah's direction, from shaking her father's hand to meet her. As his gaze took in her tall, slender form, his dark eyebrows arched with obvious approval. His crooked smile was charmingly roguish, and as he bent forward and took her hand to kiss it, he murmured, "Aphrodite lives."

Had any other man greeted her thus, she would have drawn back, insulted ... or at least confounded. But his compliment seemed so appropriate in the light of her own appraisal of him that she could only smile in return and respond, "How nice to meet you, Captain Ahab."

They proceeded to the front parlor, trading pleasantries. But Jeremiah took Hannah's arm and held her back a moment. "You seem pale, Hannah. Are you sure you are well enough for company this evening?" He appeared quite puzzled when her reply was a merry laugh and a gentle pat on his arm.

While Captain Ahab and Mr. Oldweiler enjoyed a glass of sherry, and Hannah and Jeremiah sipped tea, the captain stood by the fireplace studying the large framed painting above the mantel. It was a violent seascape. A whaling ship had lowered its boats, and the harpooners were busy at their work. Among the various depicted contests between man and beast was one of a whaleboat crew luring a sperm whale cow to her death by harpooning her calf. On the mother ship, men hauled in their kill. In another place, an unfortunate crewmember dangled by one leg from the mouth of an enraged black bull. It was this last scene that held the captain's attention.

"What do you think, Captain?" Mr. Oldweiler asked.

"Quite true to life. Where did you get this remarkable work of art?"

"It was left here by my uncle, and I never thought to remove it," said his host. "It seems to suit our trade, don't you think? I must say, sir, it is a pleasure to have you in my home. Your reputation for successful voyages precedes you. But what brings you to New Bedford, since your home port has always been Nantucket?"

"Aye, I've shipped from Nantucket since I was a lad of eighteen, having been born and bred there. After thirty-two years of sailing, it was time for a change of scene before I lay down my harpoon."

"Well, then, if you take a ship from here and bring it back with your usual full cargo, you're sure to improve our standing. New Bedford is eager to replace Nantucket as the world's whaling capital."

"You do well enough hereabouts," the captain said congenially.

Supper was announced, and after they took their places at the table, Mr. Oldweiler asked Jeremiah to return thanks for the meal. As they all bowed their heads and the young minister prayed, Hannah could not resist glancing up at the handsome captain. She opened her eyes and was startled to see him staring at her. She quickly looked down, then back up again. His head was now politely bowed, and his eyes were closed, but there was a shadow of a smile on his lips. Hannah was accustomed to being admired, but it had never given her quite so much pleasure.

Conversation around the table involved more whaling business. When asked, Hannah made a few polite comments, but her reserve was not due to diffidence. As she listened, she wondered if her father were thinking the same thoughts as she. This very successful captain seated at their table might be looking for a ship. Of Oldweiler's two remaining vessels, one had been at sea for more than two years. The other was in port, but as yet, he had not been able to sign an experienced captain. Although he did not subscribe to the superstitions of the whaling community, he had begun to wonder privately to Hannah if his perpetual lack of good fortune were keeping the best men away. If offered the *Hannah Rose*, would this extraordinary man with the extraordinary name harbor the same misgivings as the others? Hannah guessed that he would not.

The captain's manners were impeccable, almost courtly. His sea-toughened hands moved with surprising grace, and he used the proper utensil at every course. Why had Jeremiah thought him rough? Everything about the man was pleasing to her.

As the main course was served, Captain Ahab turned to Hannah. "Miss Oldweiler, I'm surprised that, unlike most young ladies in New Bedford society, you have not yet asked me to tell frightening tales of my encounters with ferocious cannibals or deadly pirates."

Hannah frowned and shook her head. "Our painting reminds me daily of how so many lives are risked and lost that we may live well, Captain. How then shall I ask such a frivolous question to obtain an amusing and artificial fright, when what I truly feel is gratitude toward all our brave whalers?"

His eyebrows once more arched with approval. "The young lady is not only beautiful but also wise."

"And compassionate," Jeremiah put in. His eyes glowed with a pride that seemed to bespeak his possession of her, and Hannah fidgeted uncomfortably.

Neither look nor movement was lost on the captain. "Well, then," he said, his dark eyes lit with mischief, "out of gratitude to this old whaler, would you consider giving me a horseback tour of your fair countryside before the leaves begin to turn?"

"Hannah has no horse," Jeremiah said quickly.

"Oh, but she has the use of Mr. Williams's stables while he is traveling abroad," Mr. Oldweiler said. "In fact, it would be good to exercise a couple of the saddle horses."

"But what says the young lady?" asked the captain.

Hannah glanced at Jeremiah, distressed to see the alarm in his face. But surely if her father approved, he could find no fault in her riding out with the captain, a man he himself had brought to her home. This might be her opportunity to influence the captain to take their ship. Before she could answer, however, Carson appeared in the doorway and approached his employer.

"Mr. Oldweiler, sir, there is a messenger here for Reverend Harris. The senior pastor sends word that his services are required immediately."

Jeremiah rose at once, disappointment clouding his face for only an instant before concern replaced it. "No, please. Everyone stay seated. I was expecting this. One of our elderly church members ..."

"Take our regards and prayers with you," Mr. Oldweiler said to the departing young pastor. "Captain Ahab, there's no reason for you to leave. Please stay for dessert and join me for a smoke. There's nothing like a good pipe to finish off a good meal."

"Aye, I find great comfort in my pipe, as well."

The captain remarked that he found it interesting when Hannah later accompanied the men into her father's study.

"Most young ladies of society avoid the smoking rooms, Miss Hannah. Once again you surprise me."

"Isn't it scandalous?" she said pleasantly. "I must confess I love the smell of my father's pipe. Perhaps it's because the happiest moments of my life have been when I have sat here on his footstool after supper."

"And for me, as well," said Oldweiler, "for here we've spent many evenings discussing history, philosophy, the classics, the many new archeological discoveries being made all over the world ... and reading to each other, often late into the night."

"And you were interested in all these subjects?" Captain Ahab asked Hannah.

"Oh, yes. I've received a far better education from my father's library than ever I obtained at Miss Applegate's boarding school."

"What more could a man ask for than to have such a loving daughter?" Oldweiler said. "Do you have children, Captain Ahab?"

"I never married. Or, I should say, my bride was the sea."

"Ah, and one with such a remunerative dowry."

"Indeed. My greasy luck always seems to hold." The captain chuckled with satisfaction. "But, Miss Hannah, you have not answered my earlier question."

"Question? Oh, of course. I would consider it a privilege to take you sightseeing around New Bedford. I always enjoy showing off the beauties of our burgeoning town."

"Tomorrow then, at ten o'clock?"

"Papa?"

"By all means."

"Ten o'clock then, Captain Ahab."

The next morning, the captain called for Hannah at the appointed hour, and together they walked the long block up County Street to Abel Williams's stables. Earlier, Sally had been sent with the request, and the riders found their mounts ready and waiting. The groom greeted them enthusiastically as he led two saddle horses from the stables.

"Miss Oldweiler, this is a good time for you to take Samson and Bonnie out. Miss Peach's foal is expected within the next few hours, and they were restless in their stalls."

"We're so happy to be of service," she said. "If we come back in time, may we watch the foaling?"

"Miss Oldweiler," the man said. "What would your father say if I should let you do such a thing? And in the company of a gentleman?"

"Since he was raised on a farm, he would say it's not much different from watching a cat have kittens, only on a larger scale."

Captain Ahab laughed heartily at her answer. "Miss Hannah, I believe we should begin our tour. Allow me to assist you." He grasped her by her waist and with no effort lifted her up on Bonnie.

While he set her left boot securely in the stirrup of the sidesaddle, Hannah placed her right leg around the upright pommel and arranged her skirt comfortably. Having known that she would be riding the chestnut mare, she had chosen to wear her fawn summer riding outfit, with its aproned skirt, military-cut jacket, and matching bonnet, because of the lovely effect the colors created together. Leaving her parasol at the stables, she pulled a heavy gauze veil down from her bonnet and over her face and neck, then tugged her long sleeves over her riding gloves to shield every inch of her skin from the sun.

The captain was handsome in his black morning suit, tall hat, and boots. It was not a formal riding ensemble, but understandably a man who spent his life at sea would have little use for one. So long had it been since he last rode, it took him several moments to get comfortable in the saddle, but soon he had remastered the skill and was seated regally on Samson, the stallion.

Hannah hoped he could not see that, through her veil, she had watched him mount and had noted once again his muscular legs. She wondered, as she had the night before, at the sensations that pulsed through her body as she observed his form. Those pleasant but bewildering feelings were the only thing about which she had never been able to ask her father—and certainly not Miss Applegate. Those feelings that had something to do with men and women. Those feelings that she had never felt for her dear Jeremiah. But just looking at the magnificent Captain Ahab… At these thoughts, she felt her face grow warm and was glad for the veil to hide her uncharacteristic blush.

"What heading, Miss Oldweiler?"

"I suppose you're familiar with the docks. Shall we venture toward the countryside?" She pointed toward the west with her riding crop.

"That will suit me well."

As they kept their horses at a walk on the tree-lined streets, she glanced in his direction every few moments, trying to decide how to begin a conversation. She did not want to speak to him too quickly about the ship. There surely must be some way to warm up to it. She was grateful when he spoke again.

"You're not afraid of life, are you, Miss Oldweiler?"

"How's that, Captain?"

"You seem to face things more honestly than other—"

"Oh, yes, those other young ladies of New Bedford society," she said with a laugh. "No, I'm not much like them. I don't know why."

"It's a pleasant change."

"I didn't realize you had been here that long."

"No, not long at all. It didn't take long to tire of them."

"That's not a very gallant thing to say, Captain Ahab."

"But it's honest, Miss Oldweiler. And I can see that smile through your veil, so I know you agree with me."

They rode in silence for several minutes, enjoying the fresh air and scenery.

"This Samson is a fine horse," the captain said. "He has a good mouth and even gait. Were I a landlubber, I'd offer a tidy sum for him."

"Mr. Williams keeps a fine stable, doesn't he? But since his wife died last year, I have rarely seen him out riding. It's a shame." She chewed her lip, trying to think of a businesslike way to bring up the subject of the ship, to no avail. "My father gave me permission to ask you if you would be interested in taking command of the *Hannah Rose*," she blurted out at last.

He nodded and continued to look straight ahead. "I thought he might ask me. I'm honored."

"So you will?" Hannah tried to contain the happiness rising in her heart. In an instant, visions sailed through her mind of a successful voyage, of her father's health improving, of her own unexpected potential as a ship owner. Just as quickly, he scuttled her hopes.

"Unfortunately, I've agreed to take the *Sharona* in just a few weeks."

"But perhaps you haven't signed the articles yet?"

He reined his horse to a stop, lifted his chin, and stared hard and unsmiling at her.

"My word is sufficient until the signing, Miss."

Hannah felt a violent blush spread across her cheeks, and she bowed her head. "Of course. I... I didn't mean..."

He looked away. "No, of course not."

They resumed their ride in silence. His dark scowl at her unintentional affront had mortified her. To think that one small, unconsidered sentence had dashed to pieces his growing admiration of her. Perhaps Jeremiah had been right about her needing someone to guide her opinions—or at least her foolish tongue. It seemed she was always saying something she regretted. But then, why should this particular man's high regard matter so much?

"Do you like Shakespeare, Miss Oldweiler?" His unexpected breaking of the silence startled her, and she could only nod her head. "Then be 'happy in this: she is not yet so old but she may learn.' Are you familiar with it?"

"*The Merchant of Venice.*"

"Well done for such a short passage."

He smiled again, and her spirits revived. How astonishing that the lines he had chosen were from Portia's engagement scene. He could not have known that at Miss Applegate's school she had played Portia in the annual play. A light-hearted laugh escaped her as she remembered the lines that followed: *Happiest of all is that her gentle spirit commits itself to yours to be directed.* How happily she would commit her spirit to this man for direction. She swatted Bonnie's flank and trotted away to keep him from seeing her all too obvious joy over regaining his good esteem.

They rode through the rolling hills above the city, where the wooded areas were beginning to show the first hints of autumn color, coming at last to a rocky overlook that provided a panoramic view of the New Bedford harbor. Here they dismounted and rested on large boulders, enjoying the morning breeze.

As they watched the ships in the harbor, Captain Ahab studied them with interest. "That ship's done well," he said, pointing to a newcomer maneuvering up to the docks. "The *Piper*. Canst thou make out the one I speak of? We gammed on my last voyage,—Captain Nelson and I—a good man. See how the ship sits gunnel deep in the water? The crew will be celebrating for some time to come." He glanced at Hannah. "What thinkest thou of the whaling profession, Miss?"

"Why, I've never considered what I think about it. It's all I've ever known, except for some five or six months I spent at my cousin's farm. Do you know, I think the two professions are really quite similar. Both require a strong body and great determination to glean a profitable harvest, usually against difficult circumstances."

"Ha, what an answer. Thou dost not respond as one would expect. But what thinkest thou of whaling?"

Hannah stared at the captain, a little surprised at both the repeated question and his seemingly unconscious lapse into the Quaker mode of speech. He was leaning back comfortably against the rocks, and his expression was one of open curiosity. He was not asking an idle question nor seeking an idle answer just to make conversation. He truly wanted to know what she thought.

"It's an honorable profession. One need never apologize for being attached to it."

"But…?"

She smiled and looked down. Her voice had betrayed her. "I only wish that whaling had done better for my father," she said sadly.

"Aye, he has the look of a man who has been … disappointed."

"Disappointed? You're too kind. He looks ill, and that's because he is."

Captain Ahab nodded. "Aye, he is. It's not good for an active man to cease his activity, whether whaler or farmer. He may live in a fine house now, but methinks he would have been better off to stay on the farm. What he lacks is exercise. I would suggest that he walk a few miles every day, or at least ride one of these fine horses."

Hannah gasped. "Oh, never say so in his hearing. The doctors have warned him that he must not engage in any vigorous activity. His heart will not take it."

He frowned briefly at her vehemence, but then shrugged. "Methinks these doctors may have much to learn. But now, look at the sun. The morning's nearly gone. I'd best return thee to thy father."

Hannah's uneasy thoughts regarding her father vanished when the captain lifted her back onto her horse. Gripping his arms for support, she could feel his muscles through his coat sleeves. His strong touch once again generated those pleasant feelings, which she decided to define as—lacking a better term—admiration.

Their tour complete, they lingered at the stable for a short while until it became clear that Miss Peach's coming foal was not in a hurry to be born. Despite the groom's remonstrance, Hannah felt no discomfort at watching the mare in her foaling, even in the company of her guest.

"What a disappointment," she said as they walked back home. "I hope Miss Peach will be all right."

The captain chuckled. "Your interest is quite unusual."

"Do you think so? I do seem to have a prodigious amount of curiosity. When I was eleven, my father sent me to visit his cousin's farm in Indiana. I was there for most of the spring and all of the summer and saw all kinds of birthings... and other things that the animals did as well. When I came home full of questions, Papa packed me off to Miss Applegate's school in

Boston, where I didn't learn anything at all, at least nothing that answered my questions."

It was not what she had meant to say. Hannah pulled her parasol low over her face. For the past hour, her conversation had been improving, and now she had ruined things again. And for the third time this morning, she was blushing—she who could not recall ever blushing—over unconsidered remarks that had seemed to tumble out of her without a thought about how they might sound. Since growing up, she would never have said such a thing to any person of her acquaintance, not any woman, not Jeremiah, not even her father. No decent person seemed to speak of such things or even hint of them.

"I'm sorry that your afternoon appointment will keep you from dining with us," she said quickly. "Mrs. Randolph prepares an excellent noon repast."

"Having tasted her roast mutton, I'm not likely to disagree with you. Another time perhaps?"

At his genial tone, she ventured to peek up at him and was gratified to see no judgment or shock in his face, though she did not quite understand the expression she did see. Was he suppressing a laugh?

"Yes, another time. You're welcome any time."

Chapter Three

ဆ

*H*annah, it grieves me deeply that you have been receiving this captain so often. You've only known him two weeks. It's ... well, it's shocking that you're receiving him every day. If he must come here, could you not discourage daily visits and restrict him to our Friday night suppers?" Jeremiah stood by the front parlor window, with the early afternoon sun shining in around him like a halo.

"But he doesn't visit me," Hannah said. "He's here to advise Papa in business matters. We expect great improvements as a result of their consultations. He has advised Papa to invest our anticipated income from the *Ivory Rose* in certain land-based enterprises which have histories of securing profits. And he may even be able to influence another equally capable man to captain the *Hannah Rose* for us."

"It's his influence on you I'm concerned about. Are you telling me you have no private conversations with him while he's here?"

"It's not like you to ask such rude questions."

"As your pastor, I have the responsibility of guarding your spiritual influences. I told you from the start that Captain Ahab is a godless man, and that—"

"Not so. I promise you. Although he is not a Congregationalist, he was raised in the Quaker community of Nantucket, and there are no more godly people than they."

"Just because he reverts to an occasional 'thee' or 'thou' in his speaking does not mean that he has maintained their beliefs— which beliefs I would question as a true Christian faith."

"Just because the captain has a broader range of experiences than you does not mean that he has forsaken those beliefs— which beliefs I consider just as valid as yours."

"Mine, Hannah? Are they not your beliefs as well?"

"Oh, please don't look so hurt and shocked. Your anxieties are entirely misplaced. It's true that I am examining what I believe, but surely that is no sin. If I don't question what I am taught, how can I claim it as my own? I would merely be reciting a catechism without an honest thought as to its veracity."

"Would you question that the Scriptures are the Word of God?"

Hannah frowned, thinking. "Why, no. I hadn't really thought that. I simply believe there are many other books to read and think about. Captain Ahab suggests that I read—"

"Then you *have been* talking with him. And look how wickedly he's influenced you already." Jeremiah threw himself down on the couch beside her. "Oh, my dearest Hannah, I am filled with fear for your eternal soul. Please, I beg you, don't receive this man any more."

"Oh, stop this, please. You must not fear for me. If God is good and makes all things happen for our good, He will not direct my path astray."

"But don't you understand? Don't you recall what the Scriptures say? It was Eve who was deceived in the transgression, not Adam. How can you think that you, being a woman, will be able to recognize the serpent's lies? To look to foreign ideas, to unchristian writings, is to risk being led away from God."

"But since my childhood my father has read to me, everything from the ancient classics to the more recent works of Byron, Shelley, and many others, despite their being 'unchristian' writings. You have known that and never disapproved. If all little girls were encouraged to reason, as he taught me, they would go astray no more often than men do when confronted with new ideas. But women are taught from childhood that they are silly ornaments. Is that what you want me to be?"

"Your father is a devoted Christian who has always guided you wisely. This worldly captain cannot be trusted to do the same. I despair to the point of madness to think that you will turn away from God, and it will be my fault for having introduced him to you."

Poor Jeremiah, Hannah thought, her heart filled with compassion. It was his love for her that caused this torment. But though she longed to comfort him, she knew that she had to be true to her own heart. "If I turn away from God, was I ever His to begin with? Faith which cannot be tested is not faith at all."

Jeremiah stood and walked across the room, flinging himself into a chair with his head in his hands. He would never have behaved so familiarly in the home of any other friend. Despite their disagreement, she could see that he still felt he belonged here. She hoped he would always feel this freedom, but under happier circumstances.

"I would guard your mind, Hannah. I would protect you," he mumbled so softly she could barely hear him. She went to him and sat on a nearby chair.

"Then examine me."

"What?"

"Examine me. Let me tell you what I have been reading and thinking, and you can challenge my ideas, as I will challenge yours."

He pondered the suggestion for a moment before nodding solemnly. Then he sat up, nodding again. "If this is the only way I can protect your mind—your very soul, in fact—then I accept your challenge." The lines of worry around his eyes softened. "There may be hope for us after all."

She walked him to the front door, her arm looped in his, and soon a gentle, hopeful smile had replaced his worried frown. But the frown returned when, through the glass panel beside the door, they saw Captain Ahab climbing the front stairs.

"Perhaps I should stay …," he began.

"Jeremiah Harris, you are the limit. Go home." Hannah laughed.

Her playful tone, which only a few weeks before would have brought from him a teasing response, made him scowl even more. Hannah refused to acknowledge his distress, for the captain's appearance had caused her pulse to quicken, and she wondered how she could now maintain her composure. She opened the door and gently nudged Jeremiah forward.

"Reverend Harris." Captain Ahab shook the minister's hand genially. "Good to see you. Just leaving, are you?"

"I'd be happy to stay if you would like to talk with me." Jeremiah glanced toward Hannah as he spoke.

"No, no, not at all. I'm sure you must be about the business of saving souls bound for perdition."

"Good-bye, Jeremiah. Thank you so much for coming." Hannah smiled sweetly at him. The young man put on his hat and slowly walked down the porch stairs, glancing back once more. Hannah gave him a last nod, then turned her attention to her new guest. She had been grateful for the brief moments as the two men greeted each other, for it gave her the opportunity to take a few deep breaths to calm her suddenly quivering emotions.

"I hope I find you well, Miss Oldweiler," the captain said as he entered the house.

"Quite well, thank you. And you?"

"Oh, quite well. It's a fine day to be out."

"Yes, I know. I was working in the rose garden this morning."

"Your roses are exquisite, a credit to their gardener."

"Thank you, sir."

Hannah's mind would not inform her of anything more to say. She was aware that they were still standing by the front door, that the captain had hung his hat on the hall tree and was now looking at her with an indefinable gaze, and that her own heart was pounding so loudly she wondered if he could hear it. And if he heard it, surely he would only laugh. Despite their daily chats and his pleasant attentions to her over the past two weeks, how could she think that this man of the world would have the slightest interest in her? But still he gazed, his dark eyes calmly searching hers, as though to stand here thus was exactly what he wished to do. For her part, she could have stared up into his handsome face for an eternity.

"I'll tell my father you're here," she breathed out at last, turning to go.

He touched her arm lightly. "In a moment. I brought thee ... I brought you something."

"Oh, how very thoughtful of you."

"It's only a book, something by an anonymous author. I hoped we might discuss some of his ideas. They're quite interesting." From the pocket of his suit coat, he pulled a small brown package tied with string.

"Thank you. You're so kind." As she took the package, Hannah could not suppress a happy giggle, then chided herself for it. He would think her just a child if she could not cease her silly giggles.

"May we sit down and take a look?" His eyes sparkled with amusement, and Hannah felt her cheeks grow warm.

"Forgive me, Captain. I'm so sorry. Where are my manners? Shall we go to the front parlor?"

"That suits me well."

Carson appeared, and Hannah ordered tea and told him to inform her father of their guest's arrival. She took a seat on the divan nearest the fireplace to unwrap the package and was disappointed when the captain sat on a chair opposite rather than sitting beside her. But she could hardly have invited him to do so. Her foolish thoughts made her cheeks grow hot again, and then she was angry at her blushes. Blushes and giggles. Why did she always blush and giggle in his presence? She fumbled with the string around the package, finally making a hopeless knot that made it impossible even to slip the twine over the edge of the book.

"Allow me." The captain moved to the cushion beside her and pulled a folding knife from his pocket to cut the offending cord. As he took the package, his tanned, callused hand brushed hers, sending a pleasant sensation up her arm and down her spine.

"My, I'm so clumsy," she said, not apologizing at all.

Captain Ahab chuckled as he removed the paper wrapping. "Here it is at last. What do you think?" After slitting several of the bound pages with his knife, he placed the reddish brown volume in her hands, then sat back to study her reaction.

"Nature. It sounds harmless … I mean, interesting, though just the fact that the author wishes to remain anonymous gives it an air of mystery."

"Nothing mysterious at all. Just another way of looking at things. A philosophy."

"Indeed. And do you subscribe to this philosophy?" Hannah thumbed through several pages. As her eyes lit on one or two interesting phrases, her giddiness vanished, replaced by curiosity.

"I'm not looking for converts, Miss Hannah. I'm not one to hand someone a book and demand that he believe it in order to keep my good opinion. No, these are merely interesting ideas worthy of consideration and discussion."

She glanced up and was gratified to see no malice in his expression. He had on another occasion expressed disapproval of the behavior of certain missionaries in the Pacific islands, but it was not his intention to disparage them today. The book once again claimed her attention. She wanted to find a significant passage immediately, discovery of which would make him think her clever, but her eyes darted over the pages randomly. "Oh, I can't do it justice this way. I must begin at the first."

"You needn't read it all just now." His tone was pleasant, and his look was one of amused indulgence.

"Captain Ahab, how good to see you." Mr. Oldweiler entered the room and shook hands with his guest, who had stood to greet him. "Hannah, have you been keeping our guest entertained?"

"Look, Papa. The good captain has brought us a book of philosophy."

"How very generous. Thank you, Captain. Please sit down."

"It is my pleasure, sir. Your daughter has a remarkably keen intellect which should be encouraged."

"Yes, Hannah always has been precocious. What does one do with such a daughter?"

"Why, what would you do with a remarkable son? You'd let him learn all that he wished to about the world. Why not the young lady as well?"

"That's a very progressive idea, Captain, and not one to gain general approval, though I suppose that's exactly what I've done with Hannah."

"Then we're of the same mind. Perhaps my thinking is influenced by the women of Nantucket. With the majority of their menfolk at sea for years at a time, they must keep the community running smoothly. One cannot do that without a keen, well-educated mind."

"Yes, I've noticed a few wives of whalers developing businesses here in New Bedford as well." Mr. Oldweiler chuckled. "Soon the women will be taking over. Think of it, Hannah, you may end up being the mayor of our city."

"A woman mayor, when women don't even vote? Papa, please. Although Miss Applegate is an advocate of women's voting, she never won me as a convert. Besides, since it's my interests we're talking about, I would find my greatest happiness in stimulating my intellect with an extended tour of Europe. Captain, have you visited that continent in your travels?"

"Only a few short visits. I have often thought I should take the time for an extended tour." He sat back on the divan and gazed thoughtfully at the picture above the mantel. "So many years traveling the oceans after the whales … so many trips around Cape Horn. Perhaps the time is coming—perhaps after this next voyage—when I should think of land travel for a change."

"Well," Hannah said, "perhaps you and I will cross paths in our European travels."

The captain regarded her with interest. "Yes. Perhaps." With apparent difficulty, he pulled his gaze from her and looked at his host. "Ah, I'm forgetting the principal purpose of my visit today. Mr. Oldweiler, I have good news for you. I've spoken to Captain Lazarus, an able whaling captain who would welcome the opportunity to discuss the *Hannah Rose* with you."

"Lazarus? Yes, I know him, but I didn't know he had returned from his last voyage for the Gantvorts."

"In port just two days ago. But you know how we whalers are. Can't let the grass grow up around us. By the time the *Hannah Rose* is fitted for her voyage, he should be ready to sail again."

"I'm most grateful to you, my friend. I'll look for Captain Lazarus tomorrow morning at the counting house, if his voyage was successful. At the tavern, if not."

Captain Ahab chuckled. "You can be sure to find him at the counting house, sir. As I said, he is an able captain. From what I saw them unloading, I would estimate his cargo at about twenty-three hundred barrels of sperm oil, not to mention a goodly haul of whalebone and baleen."

"How can we ever thank you?" Hannah said. "You're a dear friend, Captain. A dear, dear friend." She resisted the urge to reach out and grasp his hand in gratitude, as she would have done had he been Jeremiah.

"I'm glad to serve you, Miss Hannah."

"How long until the *Sharona* is ready to sail?" Mr. Oldweiler asked.

"The hull is newly renovated, and work on the masts is progressing. That will take another week. The provisions are being readied, and my mates and harpooners are shipped. We'll be setting sail before the second week in October, if the winds remain favorable."

Hannah's heart seemed to stop. That was only about ten days away. Although she had known from the day they met that he would be sailing soon, the imminence of his departure was suddenly a cause for inexplicable alarm. She hardly remembered any of their subsequent conversation of that afternoon. The captain was dining with the owners of the *Sharona*, so she and her father were forced to bid him a reluctant good-bye, for that day at least. Then Hannah found herself languishing about the house like one of those habitually sick women of her acquaintance with whom she had no patience. But remembering the book he had given her, she decided to read as much of it as she could so as to astonish him with her insights. Then perhaps he would, if nothing else, remember her from time to time on his voyage.

And perhaps that would give him a reason for making it a short one.

Chapter Four

♊

All through supper, Hannah tried not to fidget as her father visited with Captain Ahab over business matters. It should have been enough for her that the captain was providing so much encouragement for her father that he actually looked healthier than he had for months, maybe years. It should have been enough that the captain had personally negotiated with Captain Lazarus to take the *Hannah Rose*, that Lazarus would arrange provisions and find the best crew available, and that Captain Ahab had even invested in the ship himself. But these were not enough. Hannah wanted to discuss the book. He was sure to find her, or rather her insights, interesting. At least she hoped so.

From time to time during their lively conversation, her father included Hannah by a word or nod, or the captain glanced at Hannah and smiled his charming smile. At one point, she wondered if he knew how eager she was to have him all to herself. Perhaps some would think it shameful if he did know, but she did not care. What mattered was that her father understood her interest in discussing books with their guest. For some time, even before the other day when the captain had given her the philosophy book, Oldweiler had begun to find an excuse to retire to his study after supper, allowing them a chance to chat alone in the parlor before the captain returned to his rented cottage on the south side of New Bedford.

"Will you join me in my study to enjoy your pipe, sir?"

Hannah stared at her father with consternation. How could he have said that? If the two men retired to the study, even if she went with them, it would make it awkward for her to invite the captain back out to the front parlor to have him all to herself.

"You really need not be exiled to your study, Papa. I give you my permission to smoke in the front parlor."

Although she was looking directly at her father, she could tell from the corner of her eye that the captain was amused by what she had said. By now his gestures and facial expressions had been carefully logged in her memory. Still, she was not put off. If she was going too far, if he thought her scandalously bold, he would be leaving in less than a week, and she would manage to live down her shame and disappointment. But if he cared for her at all, as he seemed to by all that he was doing for her and her father, then she must not allow him to leave for this lengthy voyage without some understanding of their feelings for each other. After telling Jeremiah that she did not believe in "perhaps," she had found herself saying that word all too often to Captain Ahab, and he to her. It was time now to make plans, if plans were to be made.

Hannah saw with gratitude the understanding that flickered in her father's eyes when he blandly said, "Why, very well, my dear. Captain, I'll retrieve my pipe. Will you and Hannah adjourn to the parlor?"

"Of course, sir," the captain said.

As they walked through the hallway toward the parlor, he offered his arm, and when Hannah took it, he laid his other hand on hers in an intimate fashion. She had ceased examining the lovely feelings his accidental touches created in her; now she simply enjoyed them. But this was a deliberate gesture on his part, as though he meant to capture and imprison her hand. Or was it just her wishful thinking that made it seem so? Either way, she wished it could go on forever.

Still holding her arm in his, the captain paused before the fireplace, staring thoughtfully at the seascape above the mantel.

"Are you thinking of how soon you'll be out chasing the whales again?"

"Aye, that and more."

"What else?"

He turned and faced her, now enfolding both her hands in his. "I've led a rough life, Miss Hannah, and not always a good one." He glanced back up at the painting. "Dost thou see this ill-fated man, the one hanging from the whale's mouth? It was prophesied against me some years back that I would be dismasted thus for some supposed evil I was thought to have done to the prophesier and his people."

Hannah stared up into his dark eyes. For the briefest moment, she had seen something indefinable in them. Not fear, but not scoffing either. No, it was a wildness, a rage, a deadly challenge to any creature that would try to wound him so. She lifted her chin to copy one of his sterner expressions.

"What nonsense. What man or beast would dare strike Captain Ahab?"

"Ha." He threw his head back with a laugh, his dark mood broken. "Child, thou art ever a marvel to me. Thou never sayest what I expect. Now, shall we look at that book?"

She took the volume from the coffee table, and they sat together on the divan. Over the captain's shoulder, she saw her father enter the room, observe them, and then quietly withdraw. Oh, how wise he was. How good and understanding. In his gentle way, he was allowing them to be alone. If he trusted this man to court her—for it was undeniable that the captain was courting her—then there was no hindrance to her receiving him, despite Jeremiah's fears.

"Didst thou find anything in here of interest?"

"Oh, there were many things. From the very first, I found thought-provoking ideas. And though I am not persuaded by the entirety of it, the introduction puts forth one of my own favorite themes. Allow me to read. Speaking of foregoing generations, the author says, 'Why should we not have a poetry and philosophy of insight and not of traditions, and a religion by revelation to us, and not the history of theirs?' This provokes me to tandem thoughts. First, although I have never attended a Quaker meeting, this seems to allude to their custom of seeking an inner light for guidance. Second, this has long been a notion of mine. I cannot receive as my own the religious traditions of my forefathers until I examine them and find my own revelations as to their truth."

Hannah paused. Surely she was talking too much. Yet the captain did not seem to think so. He leaned back and considered her words for a moment.

"Yes, we must surely examine the ideas and beliefs of our teachers before accepting them as our own. But must we necessarily discard all that we have been taught?" He leaned forward and challenged her. "Must we not first have a port, a compass, and a destination? Some reality from whence to proceed and some instrument of direction? Otherwise, we're a ship caught in a calm, not able to sail west or east, north or south, and not even knowing which direction would best lead us to our objective."

"That is why Mr. Emerson suggests that we look to nature," Hannah responded, pleased with herself for meeting his challenge.

"Emerson? Who is this thou speakest of? Hast thou discovered the author of this work?"

"I cannot take credit for discovering him. It was Jeremiah who told me. When this book was published last year, all the Andover Seminary students were warned against Mr. Emerson's transcendentalist ideas. Jeremiah is quite alarmed that I'm reading it. He doesn't trust me to think for myself."

"Your Reverend Harris, eh? That young pup with the audacity to try to convert an old rogue infidel like me?"

Hannah was dismayed to see Captain Ahab scowling. Did he really dislike Jeremiah so much?

"Jeremiah means no harm. Quite the opposite. He wants to convert everyone. And he's the kindest, most loving man I know, next to my father, of course."

"Fond of him, are you?" Abruptly, he stood and walked to the fireplace, there taking a poker and stabbing at the low burning logs until flames roared up the chimney.

He's jealous, she thought with delight, then distress. What should she say now?

"Oh, yes, very fond," she said quickly. "He's as dear as any natural-born brother could be."

The captain grunted and continued to stir the fire. "Many such brothers have found themselves wedded to their sisters in like circumstances."

Ah, he thinks I am using him to make Jeremiah jealous.

"Poor Jeremiah. It hurt him deeply when I declined his proposal."

He looked at her sharply. "Indeed?"

She nodded, gazing at him with a gentle smile.

He set the poker in its stand and walked to the corner window. Pulling back the sheer curtain, he stared down toward the docks where his ship waited to sail in only a few days.

"It was fortunate that Captain Lazarus was available to ship the *Hannah Rose*. I would have liked to ship her myself. But he's a good and trustworthy man who'll do well by thy father."

"I'm ... we're so very grateful to you. I think this will be the beginning of good things for us. You've brought us good fortune."

"I'm glad to be of service to thee."

"And I'm also grateful for all the time you've given to the improvement of my mind. I'll miss our visits dreadfully when you leave." She felt her eyes brimming with unexpected tears, and she tried not to blink. But it was no use. Against her will, her eyelashes fell, sending a flood down her cheeks. What if he saw them? What if he hated women's tears? But he was still staring out the window.

"And art thou truly improved?" Now he turned his head and, seeing her face, smiled ever so gently.

"I ... I believe that I am improving."

He faced her fully. "What else is it that thou wantest from me, child?"

Something in his eyes made her aware that she had, at least for this moment, some kind of power over him, even as she felt his power over her.

"I believe the question should be, what is it that you want from me, Captain?"

He pulled his gaze away and looked out the window again. "I had never thought to marry." He was speaking almost to himself. "But now ..."

Hannah could hardly breathe, and her head felt light. If she gave vent to the giddy laugh of happiness that wanted to escape her, he would think she was laughing at him. With a slow, deep breath, she stifled the laugh.

"Oh?" she managed to say. She knew her teary eyes were wide with childish wonder that he was even broaching the subject and hoped desperately that he would continue to stare out the window. Instead, he turned back again and smiled at her, that crooked, unguarded smile that curled his stern lips with sensuality and made him look so youthfully roguish—the smile that always made her heart pound with excitement and her body tingle with those mysterious sensations she feared and longed to explore.

"Dare we go beyond this friendship?" He stared directly at her. "Beyond this intellectual stimulation? Wouldn't such a delicate rose cease to bloom in my savage garden?" He sighed deeply and crossed his arms, leaning back against the wall. Then he shook his head and whispered softly. "Could this ... nay, should this cold, ancient David take the beautiful young Abishag to warm his bed?" The deep rumble in his voice sent another wonderful shiver through the center of her being.

"Oh, not at all," she said breathlessly. "But mighty Caesar will find his equal in this Cleopatra." She met his gaze without wavering.

In an instant, he strode across the room and knelt before her, touching her face with his rough hand. "Ah, Hannah, child, dost thou know what thou art saying?" His eyes revealed his unguarded heart, and she felt her power over him growing.

"I most surely do, Captain."

"Dost thou know how thou blessest me?"

"I hope always to bless you." She stopped trying to hold back her tears, for her heart was fully unguarded too.

He bent close and his lips brushed hers, making her body tingle with his touch. Her first kiss ever! *Oh, kiss me again*, her heart cried. But he held her back and stared into her eyes.

"Oh, Hannah, Hannah. What hast thou done to Ahab? Thou child-witch, send me away now, for both our sakes."

"I am not a witch at all, but simply a lone siren, singing my love song to Odysseus to lure him away from the sea." The wonder in his eyes made her bolder. "And no child, either, but fully a woman. And if you ask me, I will marry you and be your siren, your Cleopatra, and your everlasting love."

He stared at her still, a grin playing at the corner of his mouth. "Well, then, Miss Hannah, I am already on my knees. I pray thee …" His voice broke. "Oh, God, I've faced death a thousand times on land and sea, but my heart has never feared as it does now. Is it for me or thee that I fear most? Don't answer. Be still." Another gentle kiss, then … "Miss Hannah Oldweiler, wilt thou marry me?" he whispered in her ear.

"My dear Captain Ahab," she sighed, savoring the pleasure his close whispers sent through her body. "I most certainly will."

"Think carefully before thou answerest, child." He gazed into her eyes and caressed her cheek.

"I have answered you."

"But how can I do this to thee? How can I ask thee to wait? This voyage will be long, perhaps four or five years."

"How can we not do it, my love, seeing that there is no one who fills my heart and soul and mind as you do?"

"I am an old man … older than thy father by half a decade."

"You masquerade well as a youth then. And if you insist that I am so terribly young, remember that just this past June a woman of my age became Queen of England and now rules countless subjects. I wish only to be queen of your heart and to rule only one subject: you."

"Ah, sweet Hannah, think carefully of all that is before thee."

"I have thought. As for you, you've only just proposed, and now you're trying to back out. Shall I sue you for breach of promise, you whose word is sufficient until the signing?"

"Hush, thou little chatterbox," he said with a growling laugh. "Thou'lt have thy way. May God help thee never to regret it!" He stood and pulled her up into his arms, kissing her passionately … fiercely, almost as if he meant to frighten her. But with each fiery touch of his lips on her mouth and neck and shoulders, she savored the delicious sensations pulsing through every part of her body until her knees grew weak, and she almost collapsed in his arms. At this complete surrender, he stopped abruptly. He lowered her to the divan and sat down beside her, holding her against his broad chest until they both breathed more easily.

"I swear to thee, Hannah, I will never betray this sweet trust thou givest me."

"Nor I yours, my dear Ahab."

"Precious child, thou makest pleasing the sound of my accursed name."

He had never spoken of disliking his name before. How unfair that he had been branded with the name of an evil biblical king. What torments and wounds it must have caused him as a child. She would spend the rest of her life healing them. She rested in his embrace until her heartbeat slowed, then sat up and gazed into his dark eyes. "We must speak to Papa," she murmured.

"Aye."

Leading him down the hallway to her father's study, Hannah tapped lightly on the door. When he did not respond, she opened it. Oldweiler sat at his desk, bent over his open Bible with his head in his hands. When they entered, he quickly stood and greeted them.

"Here you are. How have your studies gone this evening? Well, I hope."

"Mr. Oldweiler, I have asked thy daughter to marry me, and she has accepted." Ahab's tone was firm but not challenging.

Oldweiler nodded. "Yes, yes, of course." His smile was genuine, but his eyes were sad. He shook Ahab's hand warmly, then embraced Hannah, sighing as fathers do, "My little girl, all grown up. You must take care of her, Captain."

"It will be my privilege, sir. My only regret is that we must wait to marry until I return from this voyage. I must ask ye both to understand—"

"You have no need to be concerned. This business of whaling has its own unique complications for families that we have only observed until now. I'm sure Hannah can manage to fill her time, just as the other women do when waiting for their whaling men."

"And then as soon as you return, we'll have our wedding and take a nice, long tour of Europe for our honeymoon, won't we, my love?" Hannah held Ahab's arm and smiled up at him.

"Thou makest a persuasive argument in favor of it."

Hannah squeezed his arm and rested her head against him. Somehow, knowing that he would be coming home to her soothed her pain about his leaving. She would pray every day that the voyage would reap a successful, hasty harvest.

As he took his leave of her that evening, Ahab's kiss was gentle and controlled, though his eyes burned with desire. Yet when Hannah pressed close to him in response to his longing gaze, he stepped back and held her hands firmly in his. "There will be a time for this, my dear. Be patient."

She laughed softly to cover her embarrassment at his rebuff. "No. I refuse to be patient. I will fret and stew the entire time you're gone," she teased.

"Hmm," he murmured, brushing her cheek with the back of his hand. "Then before I sail I must give thee something to occupy thy time. It won't do for thee to worry thyself into illness."

She laughed again, intoxicated by the happiness of this tender moment. "I wouldn't mind if you gave me an occupation. But I promise to keep myself well for you, my love. Will you do the same for me?"

"Aye, my Hannah, I will." He gave her another quick kiss. "Now, I must go. Tomorrow morning early I must be aboard the *Sharona*, but I will come to call in the afternoon."

Reluctantly, she allowed him to leave. Then she lingered by the door wishing he had forgotten his hat ... or anything that would bring him back to her. At last, seeing he would not return, she sought her father in his study. Seating herself on the familiar footstool, she badgered him with her happy chatter until he stopped his reading.

"Do you know, Papa, that Ahab can make a compass from shipboard tools and a sailmaker's needle? Isn't that remarkable? He knows how to mend anything that breaks and even how to remedy almost any injury. Once he has even had to ... to cut off a man's arm when he developed gangrene after an accident at sea." She shuddered as she said it. "But the amputation saved the man's life. Have you ever known anyone who knows as much or can do as much as he? He has been all around the world countless times and can name all the southern constellations as well as the northern ones we are familiar with. He's so well read that if you name a book, he can tell you all about it. And yet he's not boastful about it, and he never makes me feel foolish or inferior because I'm so much younger or because I'm a woman. He says that—"

"Yes, yes, my dear Hannah," Mr. Oldweiler said, laughing. "He is remarkable. All these whaling captains are quite brilliant. They have to carry their whole world with them on their ships. Whatever crisis arises, it is the responsibility of the captains to see to the safety of their crew and cargo. They must always be in command of themselves, for they may be forced to invent a life-saving solution in the midst of a violent storm or on an unfriendly shore."

Suddenly thoughtful, Hannah gazed up at her father with adoration. "You could have refused to let me marry him."

He nodded, returning her look with equal affection. "Yes. But I know my Hannah. I know that you love him as you have never loved anyone before. I only wish—no," he interrupted himself, "I'll not spoil what's been decided. Ahab is a good man, generous and truly brilliant, not to mention financially secure. He'll take good care of you when the time comes." He leaned back in his chair and studied her with amusement. "In the meantime, don't you think you should start filling that hope chest you've always scorned to supply ... you who had no plans to marry? Your mother's old trunk is in the attic—"

She tossed her head with mock annoyance. "Not at all, Papa. When my fiancé returns—oh, how good that name sounds!— we'll be traveling to Europe. We'll get what we need then."

"You set great store by that trip, don't you?"

She stared at him with curiosity. "Of course I do. Why?"

"Haven't we always said 'If the Lord wills it'? God may have a different path for your life when Ahab returns."

Hannah frowned. "No, I don't think so. I'm sure God wouldn't spoil our plans. We both want to travel, so travel we will. Besides, I'm not really certain that Ahab ... I mean, he hasn't really talked much about ... that is ..."

Oldweiler sighed deeply and worry lines appeared on his brow. "You're not certain that he's a Christian, are you?"

She looked down at her hands, shaking her head. "No," she said softly. "But then, I'm not certain that I am either."

He was quiet for a moment, then he sighed again. "I know, my dear, and it troubles me. I have searched my mind and heart to discover if there was anything I could have done differently in raising you that would have assured your belief in God. But telling you what to believe never would have persuaded you. From your earliest childhood, you have questioned everything. What else was I to do?"

"Oh, my dear Papa," she cried, laying her head on his lap, "you have always been perfection personified." She looked up into his face as tears began to slide down her cheeks. "If there is a God, He must be as good and kind and gentle as you are. I don't know why I still wonder about Him. I often wish I still had the faith I had as a child."

He caressed her cheek, wiping away her tears. "Perhaps you do and don't realize it. The coming years of separation will give you plenty of time to think about it."

"Why?"

He gazed at her with fondness. "Will you not pray for your intended's safety and his hasty return?"

"Of course I will."

He chuckled softly. "Then, my dear daughter, you do have faith, after all. Why would you pray if you had no faith that there is a God who will answer your prayers?"

Hannah gave him a sheepish grin. Perhaps he was right. Praying was as natural to her as breathing. Maybe she had been playing a game without even realizing it, pretending not to believe so she could prove to herself that she'd arrived at faith on her own. Yet she had so many questions. Not so much about God as about religion. For some time she had felt a growing resistance to things of the church and the Christians she knew, all except her father and Jeremiah. In fact, until Jeremiah had returned from seminary, she had begun to use any possible excuse to avoid attending services with her father.

But now the important question was what would Ahab think? What if he was disappointed in this seeming change of mind about religion? With sinking heart, she realized that she must tell him, even if it made him angry with her. Would he think she had deceived him? Once or twice, he had spoken of missionaries and preachers with disdain, yet she had never heard him speak ill of God or even curse. But what did he really believe? Was there time to find out before he left? Late into the night, Hannah pondered her dilemma, finally deciding that whether or not Ahab was a Christian, she loved him and would marry him.

That is, if he would still have her when she told him of her own struggling, finite faith.

Chapter Five

∾

She slept little that night and brooded all morning while waiting for Ahab. When he finally appeared, there was a sweet desperation in her embrace that brought forth even more tenderness in his gaze at her. They sat together on the divan before the fireplace, reading aloud from Emerson's book, but not really paying attention to the thought-provoking concepts written there. Ahab was studying Hannah's face and form, as if to imprint them in his mind for their long separation. Hannah was trying to think of some way to bring up the subject that worried her. Finally, though she felt it was a cowardly ploy, she invited him to attend Sunday services the next day.

"Jeremiah will be delivering the morning sermon because the senior pastor is in Boston for the week. He's really a very good preacher. Papa and I always enjoy discussing his exegesis afterward, and I'll treasure your opinion of his message."

"I would much rather spend the time alone with thee, seeing that, if the winds and tides remain favorable, we'll sail Tuesday morning."

"Oh."

He slipped his arm around her waist and whispered in her ear, "Dost that disappoint thee?"

His embrace quickly changed the focus of her thoughts. Perhaps she was taking all this too seriously. With a happy laugh, she stood up and after adjusting her skirts, she sat down on his lap and looped her arms around his neck.

"There. I've been wanting to do this since you arrived this afternoon. Do you think I'm scandalous?"

He laughed heartily and held her close. "Prodigiously. Now, I think we should continue our discussion of Mr. Emerson. And if thou must sit on my lap, child, belay thy squirming. Thou makest me … uncomfortable."

She nestled into his embrace, staring up at the left side of his face with adoration.

"Hast thou only now discovered my scar? Does it not frighten thee?"

"Not at all," she said. But when she tried to trace its path down the length of his face, he took her hand.

"Belay that," he said, suddenly cross.

She stretched up to kiss the white streak through his beard. He moved his head away, frowning.

"Hannah …"

"Tell me, Captain Ahab, where did you win this mark of courage? Did you once ride into battle as a Cossack or hussar in service to the czar? Were you a Prussian officer defending your prince in a sword duel? I must say, it's a most handsome, noble badge of honor." She freed her hand from his and stroked the blaze of white hair above his temple.

He grasped her hand once more and glared deep into her eyes. But at her smile, he softened. "Noble badge of honor? This vile disfigurement? Oh, what rosy lenses cover the eyes of the lover. It was indeed on a battlefield that I won it, a sea battle some eighteen years ago. Hmm. That would have been the year thou wast born. Think of it, Hannah. Perhaps it was God's wish to strike me dead to keep thee safe from me."

"Nonsense. What happened?"

He chuckled. "What indeed, my dear? See how thy sweetness coaxes me away from my worst thoughts." Then, with a sigh of feigned weariness, he began. "It was in the midst of a storm that tossed our ship about violently—not unusual for any whaling voyage, though we do our best to avoid them. I was at the wheel, holding us on course while lightning and waves crashed around us." He paused to study her face, then laughed. "Oh, child, I wish thou couldest see how thine eyes grow round with wonder when I tell thee my sea tales."

"Yes, I know," she sighed. "It's why you still call me 'child.' I'm not the slightest bit sophisticated, am I?"

"I would not have thee thus. Thy wonder at life's mysteries revives my soul."

She smiled and kissed his cheek. "What happened next?"

"The second mate came up from the hold to assist in striking the sails and informed me that some of our cargo was lost. Broken barrels were leaking precious whale oil all over the lower deck. If lightning were to strike us just so, the ship would have gone up in flames and all of us would have been lost in a watery grave. It was a cargo hard won by a worthy crew. I implored the heavens not to take it from us. In the midst of that prayer, I was struck by the lightning wrath of God! But, by God, when the sparks were cleared, I still stood firm, my hand fast on the wheel, and the ship steady on course! I vowed that moment that I would no longer perform the sacramental act of pleading with so unjust a God. And I defied Him still to take away what my hands had toiled for. To neither love nor reverence is God kind, and the only right worship is defiance. As for that night, my only remembrance of it is this repulsive—ah, have it thy way—this noble badge of honor."

Hannah bowed her head and nestled close to him again.

"What troubles thee? Dost thou not believe my tale?"

"Oh, yes. It's what I would expect of you. But promise me, dearest, don't defy God again, not on this voyage. I would not wish to be a widow before I am a bride."

He kissed the top of her head and held her tightly. "Nothing, not even God Himself, shall prevent me from returning to thee." His vehement assertion sent a chill through her. He should not try to prove the fervency of his devotion to her by challenging God. Or was she just being superstitious to fear that God might accept that challenge? She wanted to scold him, but it would not be a good beginning to a conversation about faith. His embrace soon warmed her heart, however, and she once again read from their book.

"Tell me what you think of this: 'Every natural fact is a symbol of some spiritual fact ... An enraged man is a lion, a cunning man is a fox, a firm man is a rock, a learned man is a torch ...'"

He pulled the book away from her and continued reading, "'A lamb is innocence ... flowers express to us the delicate affections.' Thou art my innocent lamb and my Hannah Rose, the flower of my heart."

She laughed with delight at his compliment, but pulled the book back. "'Man is conscious of a universal soul within ... This universal soul, he calls Reason: it is not mine or thine or his, but we are its.' Hmm. We are its. If that is so, then I think, rather, that the universal soul is God, not Reason. And I cannot think we all have that universal soul within us. Otherwise, would not all men agree on everything? After all, if that soul were truly within each of us, would not reason, if it is honest, draw all men to the same conclusion? But mankind has always been riven by disputes. Nor am I sure I like to think of God as It. No, I don't think I can ever call the universal soul 'It,' but rather He is God and very much a separate being, above and apart from us." Hannah was delighted with how easily the words came out. She had not needed to force her talk of faith into the conversation at all. She looked at Ahab. "What do you think?"

"I think thy course of thought has merit and deserves further consideration. But I would question thee, who is this God? Is it the God of the biblical tales that is the object of thy beliefs?" There was no antagonism in his tone, only interest.

"My mind continues to question, yet sometimes I think my heart believes without my mind's consent. Do you think me foolish?"

"When I brought thee this book, it was not my intention to quench thy faith, child. I only insist that thou'rt honest with thine own heart and mind, no one else's. Never forsake thy questioning."

"But though I question many religious practices, I still find the gospel story endearing."

"Thou findest the wrath of God endearing?"

"Oh, I never think of God as wrathful, only loving. Perhaps, as with you, my experiences have formed my opinions about the nature of God. To me, He seems like a devoted Father, and I believe He loves everyone in the world. I believe He loves you."

"Hmph. It is thine own loving nature that sees love in thy Creator. It is not merely my own experiences that have formed my opinions. Thou hast not seen what I have seen, child. There is too much suffering in this world to convince me of God's kindness. And do we not hear confirmation of His lack of justice from the pulpit, that the wrath of God is unleashed upon the evil and the righteous man alike, with cruel impartiality?"

"You've yet to hear Jeremiah preach."

Ahab sat back and lifted his chin. "Speak not too kindly of my rival, Hannah, else I will brood on it while on my voyage," he said crossly.

"If you truly thought him a rival, you would marry me today and forsake your voyage," she said with a pout. "Oh, don't frown at me like that. I know you must go." She stared down, aware once more of the gaping chasm of loneliness awaiting her in only a few days. "I know you must go," she repeated softly.

He once again held her close, somewhat appeased by the sincerity of her sadness. "I will attend services with thee tomorrow and hear how thy good friend preaches. Perhaps I, too, will be won to the gospel by this famous persuasiveness of his."

Sunday morning services at the Trinitarian Congregational Church of New Bedford were always well attended. The popularity of the new assistant pastor brought this day's crowd to overflowing when word was circulated that he would deliver the message. However, it was not only Jeremiah's sermon that increased the assemblage. A number of the men in the church had signed on as crewmembers of the *Sharona*, and it was considered advantageous for them and their families to attend services just before a voyage. Though these Christian men seldom needed encouragement to be faithful to their spiritual duties, they were further influenced by this being their last chance to worship with their loved ones for years to come. And perhaps, it was well understood, their last chance forever to pray in their home church. For as hopeful as all might be at the outset, it was a rare voyage that incurred no tragedy, whether large or small.

Seated between her father and Ahab as they waited for the service to begin, Hannah found herself looking about the room like an inquisitive child. For the first time in her life, she was beginning to understand the somber mood that always prevailed among the whalers and their families before a voyage. Until now, she had gone so far as to be annoyed at the teary-eyed prayers of men and women alike. How could she have been so heartless? she wondered. One day, would she sit empty of heart and soul, like the dozen or so widows throughout the room, and stare despairingly at the cross in front of the pulpit? She shuddered at the thought.

Both her father and Ahab turned at her involuntary movement.

"Are you ill?" her father asked.

"Art thou chilled?" Ahab said at the same moment.

In an instant, Hannah saw an unusual expression in her father's eyes as he looked beyond her to Ahab: mild surprise, followed by a slight smile and nod of acquiescence. He was surrendering her care, at least for the moment, to the man who had captured her heart. She gave her father a quick smile of gratitude, then looked up into Ahab's eyes.

"I'm quite comfortable, thank you," she whispered. She looped her right arm in Ahab's left one and laid her left hand on her father's right forearm. With these loved ones beside her and Jeremiah in the pulpit, her happiness was complete, at least for the coming hour.

During the hymn singing at the beginning of the service, which was led by one of the elder lay ministers, she noticed that Ahab maintained a placid exterior. But then, she had never seen him without firm self-possession. "A firm man is a rock," Emerson had said. Ahab was the firmest man she had ever known, just like a rock. And since he did not seem uncomfortable being in church, she was able to sit back with a contented sigh and listen to Jeremiah's sermon.

The young minister stepped up into the pulpit with no ceremony. He bowed his head for a moment, praying silently. When he looked up, he seemed surprised that there were nearly two hundred faces staring at him with hushed anticipation. His boyish face was sober, in keeping with his spiritual responsibility of the moment. But it was also open and honest, revealing the sincere heart within. His listeners gladly submitted their wills to him for the next few hours, knowing he would use no tricks to manipulate them, no threats of retribution to strike fear into their hearts. Rather he would seek to persuade them through the love and mercy of God.

Hannah wondered at his calm demeanor. How could he stand before so large a crowd without nervous trembling? She gazed at him proudly and smiled, in case he looked her way and needed encouragement.

Glancing about the congregation, Jeremiah did see Hannah and Mr. Oldweiler, and his eyes brightened. Then his gaze took in Ahab, and his brow furrowed involuntarily for the briefest instant. He forced his eyes down to the pulpit, cleared his throat, and began to read his prepared sermon.

"My friends, the time of departure has come for many of you. Though I cannot claim to have sailed on more than one voyage, and that as a boy, I do know something of the hardships facing you for the next few years. In addition to the mighty battle that pits man against beast as you wrest your living from the storm-tossed seas, there will be another battle, this one waged within you. Evil influences as strong and as wild as the fiercest hurricane will seek to tear your hearts and minds away from God, family, and home. Not only is this true for those of you who will weigh anchor this week, but it is also true for those of us left behind. How are any of us to remain afloat when so many around us are shipwrecked? Often all that is required to save us from the shattering shoals of corruption is the example of someone who has faced similar tempests, yet without being drowned in the sea of sin.

"Let us consider two such examples, both of whom were great leaders of Israel. One chose to serve God through humble obedience. He died at a ripe old age, leaving behind a legacy of honor and piety to his children, his nation, and to all future generations. His name, Joshua, has come to be associated with great faith, and he is listed in the book of Hebrews with the mightiest Old Testament saints. The other man served God as a youth, but after a time grew proud of his exalted position and chose his own way. He and his sons died together on a battlefield, leaving a legacy of eternal loss. We cannot think of his name, King Saul, without being reminded of his pride and his willful disobedience to God. The result of this disobedience was madness that destroyed both him and his army because he refused to accept God's healing grace. What can we learn from these two men?

"Let us first turn to the book of First Samuel, chapter nine, where the story of Saul begins. Here is a magnificent young man, well favored and standing head and shoulders above his fellows, with all the noble bearing of a mighty warrior. Yet he is a humble man whose only responsibility is to care for his father's flocks and herds. Even after the prophet Samuel anoints him as king, he hides himself, fearful of taking on the greater responsibility of caring for God's flock, the nation of Israel. Despite this reticence, once he is raised into leadership, we see in chapter eleven that Saul becomes a mighty leader who courageously defeats many of Israel's enemies. With the power of God on his side, who can defeat such a man? Surely no enemy can stand before him.

"With the passage of time, however, Saul grows proud. In chapter thirteen, observe how he begins to think his victories are the result of his own strength. Then God, seeing Saul's pride, withdraws from Israel, allowing their enemies to defeat them. Do you see this lesson, my friends? Do you see how the people suffer because of their leader's sin? But how does Saul respond to God's withdrawal? Rather than waiting on Samuel, God's anointed prophet, rather than repenting, rather than begging for forgiveness and mercy, Saul takes it upon himself to further sin by assuming the priestly office. He offers a sacrifice, which duty belongs only to those anointed to perform it. Thus, this king, this leader, this captain, who should set a pious example for all whom he leads, breaks God's immutable law, as if he knew better than the very God to whom he offered the sacrifice. Fathers, mothers, if you teach your children no other lesson of Scripture, let them learn these words which Samuel spoke to Saul: 'Hath the Lord as great delight in burnt offerings and sacrifices, as in obeying the voice of the Lord? Behold, to obey is better than sacrifice, and to hearken than the fat of rams.' Simple obedience is all that God asks for, my friends. Obedience to His benevolent, guiding hand. And yet, Saul continues to disobey until at last God rejects him as Israel's king and promises his crown to another.

"Is it any wonder that after the spirit of the Lord departs from Saul, he is overcome with madness that torments him until the end of his life? When we turn away from God, when we reject His goodness, which is madness itself, what else can we expect? But still God extends His grace to Saul. Look in chapter nineteen, verse six. Here God gives Saul a moment of sanity wherein to repent, as he promises his son Jonathan that he will not kill David, his anointed successor. Or here, chapter twenty-six, verse twenty-one, when Saul cries out to David, 'I have sinned. I have played the fool.' God always sends these bright moments to the tortured mind, when the clouds disperse and Truth comes shining through. Perhaps it is when the suffering soul looks into the eye of a faithful friend and sees a reflection of the Savior. Perhaps it is when he recalls a joyful moment spent at home with pious parents or devoted wife and child. Perhaps it is when he looks back upon his own wasted life and grieves over his rebellion. My friends, do not let these moments pass you by. Repent of your rebellion. Grasp God's loving mercy. Do not return to wickedness. Do not be like Saul.

"And what of Saul's family, his soldiers, his nation? Such a man does not suffer alone. He causes anguish to many hapless souls, dragging them down with him to perdition or leaving them abandoned and helpless before the face of their enemies."

It was Jeremiah's custom as he read his sermons to glance up from time to time and survey his audience. Often, despite the serious tone of his message, as his gaze took in the face of a suffering parishioner, a look of godly compassion would briefly illuminate his eyes. No recipient of such a gaze would lightly dismiss the comfort it imparted, which was as though an angel of God had whispered in the ear of the sufferer, "Peace, be still."

As Hannah watched him throughout his message, she could read his thoughts. Poor Mrs. Tilsbury had lost her husband and elder son to whaling. Now her only living son added to her grief by wanting to follow their line of work. Old Mr. Bailey had lost his right arm and eye last time out. The once powerful harpooner could no longer ply his trade and had no way to support his motherless children. One glance from Jeremiah reassured them of God's keeping in their difficult days to come. How they all did hang on his every look and word.

"Now, with whom is one to contrast Saul, seeing that we must find an illustration of righteous obedience to countervail his pernicious example? Turn with me to the book of Exodus, chapter twenty-four, where we meet Joshua, the humble servant of Moses. It is Joshua who goes with Moses up into the mount of God to receive the Ten Commandments. In Exodus thirty-three, it is Joshua who sits in the tabernacle of the Lord, listening to

God. It is Joshua who, along with loyal Caleb, declares that God's people can indeed defeat their enemies, no matter how powerful they seem. It is Joshua who wholly follows the Lord. It is Joshua, full of the spirit of wisdom, who leads the nation of Israel into the Promised Land, that land flowing with milk and honey. Only Joshua and Caleb, of all the thousands whom Moses led out of Egypt, are permitted to enter the Promised Land because they believe God and obey Him. Listen, my friends. Would you be joyful? Would you find contentment? Would you secure God's richest spiritual blessings? Then strive to be a Joshua.

"I hear someone ask, 'Who could be so righteous?' Make no such mistake. God understands our frailty. Joshua was not a perfect man. Read in the book of Joshua, chapter nine, the story of his prideful error regarding the Gibeonites. Yet, unlike Saul, he repents of his pride and, in the future, listens all the more closely to God. How can we be like him? We must become as little children and listen all the more closely to God. How shall we listen? Saul had Samuel to give him the word of God. Joshua had Moses as his teacher. We have the Holy Scriptures for our instruction. My friends, hold fast to the written Word.

"As you embark on your voyage this coming week, whether setting sail for heathen waters or struggling to navigate the currents of life on these shores, who will be your example? Will you follow Saul, who served his own prideful self-will, bringing upon himself madness and destruction? Or will you follow Joshua, that great captain of Israel, who fell on his face in humble obedience and served the living, loving God. As he prepared to depart this life, Joshua charged the children of Israel to remain faithful. As I leave this pulpit, I likewise charge you: 'Choose you this day whom you will serve. But as for me and my house, we will serve the Lord.'"

How proud Hannah was of Jeremiah's wisdom. Though she had failed to communicate God's love to Ahab, surely he could see it in Jeremiah's manner of speaking. When she turned to smile at her fiancé, however, she was dismayed to see a scowl on his face. She questioned him with her look, and his responding frown suddenly annoyed her. She pulled her arm from his and sat through the rest of the service with her hands folded tightly on her lap. In like manner, Ahab seemed to move away from her in the pew and continued to glare at Jeremiah, which further irritated her. He had no reason to be angry at this lovely sermon.

After the service ended, Ahab accompanied the Oldweilers home for dinner, during which time conversation was strained. No matter what subject Mr. Oldweiler brought up, neither Ahab nor Hannah gave him more than a short response. As she toyed with her food, Hannah glanced at her father and saw in his expression a curious mixture of distress and hope. Was he happy about her obvious quarrel with Ahab? No, not her dear father. He could not be so cruel as to wish they would end their engagement. Still, the fear these thoughts produced caused her to quickly reevaluate her annoyance. But must she apologize to Ahab when she had done nothing wrong? She could not think straight with him sitting so near wearing that dark scowl.

"I'm going to the garden," she announced, then stood and marched from the room out to the terrace. No further explanation seemed necessary.

Looking up at the autumn sky, she savored the warmth of the sun even as a cool breeze blew through her thin sleeves. In her haste to escape the dinner table, she had forgotten both shawl and parasol. But she would not go back. She wandered among the rose bushes, which had ceased to bloom and were now pruned for the coming winter. However, on one small bush, which heretofore had shown no promise and thus had received little care, a small bud bloomed out of season. Its crimson color seemed to bespeak the fervency of its life force, and Hannah felt a sudden kinship with it. Her love for Ahab had bloomed out of season too, and it was every bit as fervent. Had she met him at a more convenient time, they would not be facing this impossible separation. Surely it was their anxiety over his leaving that caused them to quarrel. But how was she to reconcile with him? She knelt to touch the stem of the rose, pulling back quickly when a hidden thorn almost pierced her finger.

"My rose also has a thorn, but her fragrance and beauty have ensnared me."

She had been too deep in thought to hear him approach. Yet here was Ahab, pulling her to her feet and into his arms, wrapping the forgotten shawl around her as she shivered in the wind. She rested her head against him and let him warm her body as his thoughtfulness had warmed her heart.

"I wish to marry thee, Hannah."

She nodded, not lifting her head away from his chest. "Then you must hurry back to me," she murmured.

"Nay. I mean I wish to marry thee before I sail on Tuesday."

She stared up into his eyes, tears springing to her eyes and hope blossoming in her heart. "Oh, could we, my love?"

"We must. I cannot leave thee without sealing our promises with marriage vows. Could either of us bear such a separation? I think not."

"Then we shall marry," she said, with a giddy, tearful laugh. "Come, let's tell my father. He will help us with the arrangements." She tried to turn toward the house, but Ahab held her still.

"We will marry tomorrow at the Whaleman's Chapel, where my old shipmate Father Mapple mans the pulpit. I will see to the preacher."

"Very well," she said with some hesitation. Why could they not marry in her church? But perhaps this was best, seeing that his discomfort in her church that very morning had caused their rift. And since the senior pastor was out of town and Father Mapple was known to be a good Christian man, her father would approve of his conducting the marriage. "And I will set Mrs. Randolph to preparing a fine wedding supper for us. Oh, my dear, you've made me so happy!"

Heedless of anyone who might be passing by, they shared a tender lovers' kiss in the bright sunlight of that October afternoon.

Chapter Six

ℰꙨ

*W*ith his customary resignation, Amos Oldweiler accepted the news and entered into the preparations. When Ahab expressed concern about obtaining a wedding ring on such short notice, he offered his late wife's small gold band. It fit Hannah quite snugly, but could be enlarged later. And while the mother's twenty-year-old wedding gown, preserved in the old trunk in the attic, was too short for the daughter, her veil was easily freshened by Sally's skillful workmanship. Hannah's white lace dress would have to do for her bridal gown. In the flurry of the activities, Hannah managed to send Carson with verbal invitations to some of her friends. Hasty weddings were not unknown in the whaling community, though most were not as sudden as Hannah's. Still, by Monday afternoon at three o'clock, a number of wellwishers had gathered in the Whaleman's Chapel to witness the event.

There was no music or bridal procession. Hannah and Ahab simply stood by the front pew of the chapel, waiting for the appearance of Father Mapple ... or so Hannah assumed. She gazed adoringly up at Ahab, barely aware of anyone else. It was not until she heard Jeremiah's voice, soft and strained, that she turned to him in surprise.

"Dearly beloved, we are gathered here today in the sight of God and these witnesses ..."

His face was pale, his white lips trembled as he spoke, and his eyes stared at the page of his prayer book. Tears sprang to Hannah's eyes, and her heart sank. Where was Father Mapple? Surely he had not been available. Otherwise, Ahab would not have asked Jeremiah to marry them, would he? Since he must sail tomorrow, they must marry today. They both wished it. Yet she could see how Jeremiah was suffering, and throughout the short ceremony, she could barely think of what was being said.

"Do you, Hannah, take Ahab to be your lawful wedded husband, to have and to hold from this day forth, in sickness and in health, so long as you both shall live?"

Jeremiah's expression was calm now. His sad eyes looked into hers with encouragement. If this is truly what you want, Hannah, I give you my sincerest blessing, they seemed to say.

"I do."

"I now pronounce you man and wife." He cleared his throat. "You may kiss the bride."

Now Hannah gazed up at her beloved Ahab. For a brief moment, there seemed to be an inexplicable look of triumph in his face, but as his eyes met hers, triumph was replaced by tenderness. He kissed her gently, then turned to Jeremiah.

"Parson, wilt thou go back to the house with us to celebrate at our wedding supper?"

Jeremiah shook his head, his eyes filled with disbelief at the question. "No. Thank you. As soon as I sign your ..." he cleared his throat again, "... your Bible here, I must attend to other duties." He signed the large family Bible that Mr. Oldweiler had brought to the chapel. After Ahab and Hannah had also signed, he faced the couple one last time. "God bless you both.

Good-bye, Captain. Good-bye, Hannah." Then he turned away
and left them in the small company of wellwishers.

The wedding supper was a pleasant affair. Mr. Gantvort was
full of compliments for Ahab, whose every voyage had resulted
in a full harvest of whale products, thus earning him wide
acclaim. Miss Lila Gantvort confided to Hannah that she, too,
would soon be wed to the widower Abel Williams, who had
recently returned from his year of mourning in Europe. Carson,
Mrs. Randolph, and Sally bustled about, enjoying the celebration as much as the guests whom they served, for they all had
helped to raise their Hannah.

Mrs. Randolph had produced a grand feast, despite her short
preparation time. Roast lamb, ham, chicken, her specialty of
smoked eels, new potatoes, and a variety of newly harvested
vegetables covered the two dining room buffets. A large white
wedding cake provided the centerpiece for the table and at the
end of the meal was consumed to the last crumb.

After supper, when the men adjourned to Oldweiler's study to
smoke their pipes, the women gathered in the front parlor to
advise the bride. Hannah endured their teasing, hoping for some
tidbit of usable advice, but it was not forthcoming. Though
several matrons spoke in generalities and nodded to each other
knowingly, the presence of unmarried young ladies in the room
precluded any talk of the most intimate of marriage duties. But
then, Hannah doubted that any of them would have been likely
to address such a subject even in private. She decided it would
be best if she could simply be alone with her husband and find
out at last what all the mysteries of marriage were about.

All the guests had left by ten o'clock—none too soon for
Hannah. Then Mrs. Randolph and Sally helped her pack a small
bag for her wedding night at Ahab's cottage. As she began to

descend the stairs, Hannah heard her father below and, arrested by the strain in his voice, she stopped to listen.

"Sir, I must admit this has all been quite overwhelming, so much so that I hardly know what to say. But difficult as it is, I must do my duty by my daughter." He cleared his throat. "You see ... that is, you are aware that Hannah has grown up without a mother to advise her about ... about marriage responsibilities and—"

"Sir," Ahab interrupted, "don't concern thyself. I am devoted to thy daughter's happiness."

Her father breathed a sigh of relief. "Yes, yes, of course. Thank you for your understanding."

So even the men spoke vaguely of such things. Yet her husband—oh how she loved the word!—was devoted to her happiness. What more could she ask for? Hannah thumped her foot on the top step to signal her presence, then skipped down the staircase into Ahab's embrace. After Hannah's blushing farewell to her father, the couple walked out into the night toward Ahab's cottage.

Ahab seemed unaffected by the cold evening wind, but Hannah shivered in her cloak. He pulled her close, slowing his long stride to accommodate her as they walked the blocks to his cottage. The clear sky was resplendent with a thousand sparkling diamonds strewn across its black velvet expanse. Hannah tried not to think beyond this night, but she could not help but remember that he would soon be viewing very different constellations in the southern hemisphere. To soothe her sinking spirits, she glanced up at Ahab and was rewarded with a loving gaze.

"Hast thou thought any further of something to occupy thy time whilst I am gone, Mrs. Ahab?" His eyes twinkled as he used her new title, and she laughed with delight.

"Well, Captain Ahab, I do think I'll be sufficiently occupied with managing my father's household; though love him as I do, I look forward to being mistress of your ... of our Nantucket home."

"But, child, for thine own good, thou must set thyself to some task. Perhaps thou couldest take up cooking under the tutelage of that excellent Mrs. Randolph."

"Cooking?" Hannah stared up at him, slowing her pace. "You can't be serious. Not one lady of my acquaintance cooks. Won't we always have servants to do such things?"

"Thou wilt always have the best of care, my dear," he said. "My wealth assures that. Yet I have worked with my hands from childhood. Though I am captain, it is still my hands on the iron that earns my bread. Art thou above any labor, even that which is for thine own good, if not thy livelihood?"

Hannah stared down at the dark, hard-packed dirt street before her. "I think I do far better than most of my friends. I've never even had a lady's maid."

To her dismay, Ahab chuckled. Oh, they must not quarrel this night. How could she defend herself without causing an argument?

"I arrange my own hair and see to my own mending ... usually ... sometimes."

Now he laughed out loud. "Never mind, child. I only think it fitting that every young person should serve an apprenticeship of some sort to learn about the hardships of life. Perhaps being married to me will be hardship enough for thee."

"Don't say such things," she cried. "You are my happiness, and when you return from your voyage, we will never be parted again."

They had arrived at his cottage near the corner of Acushnet Avenue and Russell Street, a small house set in a row with several others like it. He opened the door, tossed her bag inside, then turned to her.

"Mrs. Ahab, welcome to my home." He lifted her into his arms and carried her over the threshold. After setting her down in the parlor, he lit an oil lamp and set it on the mantel where it would give the most light to the room.

"Art thou hungry? I would prepare thee something." There was a hint of amusement in his tone, but she ignored it.

"I'm not hungry, thank you. Show me the rest of the house."

Carrying the oil lamp to light the way, he led her through the four rooms of the first floor: the small parlor, an equally small dining room, a kitchen, and a tiny chamber sufficient to board one servant. The steep flight of stairs that ascended from the front entry led to an unenclosed sitting room from which opened three bedchambers. The cottage was equipped throughout with well-made furnishings, from tables, beds, and chairs to draperies and lamps. It had been the home of a whaler who, having ascended through hard work to the rank and modest fortune of first mate, had been lost at sea a few years before. His mother now rented it out as he had left it, unwilling to take with her any remembrance of her bitter loss.

"This is our room, my dear," Ahab said, opening the door to the largest of the bedchambers.

Hannah entered and looked about critically. It was a nice little room, but she wondered aloud how such a large man as Ahab could endure its restricting size.

"It's four times the size of my shipboard quarters," he said. "And the bed is far more commodious than my hammock. There's even room to share."

She smiled at him, her cheeks flaming. The time had come. Her heart seemed to skip a beat. Not knowing what else to do, she took her hairbrush from her bag, sat down at the vanity table beside the bed, and began brushing her dark auburn tresses over her shoulder. She could see in the mirror that he was watching her and that her own eyes were large and round as they always became when she was alarmed. She looked down quickly, hoping that he would not misunderstand, not think she was afraid of his most intimate embraces. She must tell him. They had agreed to be honest in every way, about everything. That meant even those things about which ladies never spoke, things about which unmarried girls could only guess, things which brides were expected to endure. And yet her every thought of those things was a happy anticipation.

Now he was behind her, taking the brush from her hand and sweeping her hair back over her shoulder. As he brushed with one hand, the other touched her neck lightly, making her skin tingle with pleasure. After a few moments, he bent down and murmured in her ear, "Art thou then affrighted to share my bed after all, my dear?"

The rumble of his deep voice produced a new wave of pleasure that surged through her entire body. With a soft gasp, she glanced up, and her eyes met his in the mirror. "Oh, yes, my love, but not as you think."

His puzzled brow and almost-smile gave her courage.

"You will think me evil ..."

He knelt beside her and turned her around to face him. "Never."

Still hesitating, she folded her hands tightly in her lap. Then with a sigh, "Since as long as I can remember, I have felt ... have felt these feelings. Oh, how can I say these words?" Her cheeks felt on fire with her embarrassment.

Ahab sat back on his heels and regarded her with amusement. "Go on."

"But I've been told ... no, never really told, but given to under-stand ... that good Christian ladies not only do not speak of certain ... uh, marriage practices, but must surely be wanton and even wicked if they happen to, happen to … enjoy … or should I say, wish for … and most certainly do not pursue, even from their husbands … satisfaction for certain … longings that she … that she might just … long for." Cheeks once again on fire, she stared down at her folded hands.

"Ha!" Ahab threw back his head and laughed one loud, explosive roar. "Great heavens, girl, good Christian ladies must suffer unending martyrdom at the brutish hands of their holy husbands! If God made us, and if Christ be God, why would He give pleasure to the pagan girls of the South Pacific islands and not to His own daughters in Christendom?"

"But I—"

"Hush. Dost thou enjoy thy supper? Dost thou enjoy thy tea? Are those sins? Of course not. Then why shouldest thou not enjoy the embraces of thy loving husband, which thine appetite for is as surely from thy God as eating and drinking?" He leaned close with a teasing grin and whispered, "Dost thou think I would have married thee if I had not seen smoldering embers in thine eyes, just waiting to be stirred into a hot fire?"

Hannah gazed at him in wonder. She could not argue with his logic, nor did she wish to.

"Wilt thou come to me, my ivory goddess?"

His husky voice sent waves of pleasure through her body. She unclasped her hands, reached out to him, and smiled. He swept her up in his arms, laid her on the bed, and began to teach her some customs he had learned in the South Seas islands.

A dim light began to infringe upon the darkness outside their window. Hannah's back was turned to Ahab, but she sensed that he was awake. Now her body reminded her of last night as an intoxicating mixture of pleasure and pain pulsed through her. He was impatient with any sort of weakness, so he must have been pleased that she had not cried out at the unavoidable discomfort that first time they had joined together as one. The ache would soon go away, leaving memories only of the delicious sensations she had freely enjoyed at his hands. He had caressed her in ways she could never have imagined, had given her pleasure in ways she could never have dreamed. At last she understood what her own heart and body had been longing for with all those unsettling feelings, feelings which God had created in her as surely as He had created all good and beautiful things. This wonderful gift He had given them was intended to bind husbands and wives together in a lasting commitment. And by this loving demonstration of their passion, she knew that Ahab would be hers forever, and she would be his.

Wide awake now with these pleasant thoughts, she rolled over to find him propped on his elbow, watching her. Even in the dark room, she could see the light of love in his eyes.

"Awake at last, my dear?" he said.

She smiled and nestled close to him. "Good morning, my love."

He enfolded her in his arms, kissing her forehead, nose, and lips. But when she began to return his kisses, he gently pushed her back and leaned against the headboard.

"What hast thou done to me, thou little vixen? I don't even know myself this morning."

With a short giggle, she moved close to him again. "I'll do it again and make you my slave, you blackguard."

"Easy, easy, my dear." He took her hands in his and kissed them, gazing at her fondly. "Not too much, too soon. We've the rest of our lives to enjoy marital bliss. Let's be up and take a walk before I must sail." He arose from the bed, lit the lamp, and began to dress.

Hannah watched him with worshipping eyes. It had been a skillful dance they had just executed. She had wanted to please him despite the pain. He had wanted to protect her despite their mutual desire. She would trust him. She would let him lead. As with everything he did, Ahab led very well. But even as she was affirming her trust in him, she despaired at the great gaping darkness that lay before her. She lay back on the bed and put her hand over her mouth to suppress a sob and to keep from begging him not to leave.

"Get thyself up, child. We must be on our way." He was still dressing and only halfway glanced at her.

Using the top sheet, Hannah wiped at the disobedient tears that insisted on covering her cheeks. Then rising to her knees on the bed, she held out her hands to him. "Husband, come here … please."

He looked at her and frowned. "Belay that, Hannah. Thou must not—"

"Come here." She feigned a cheerful tone. "I must ask you something."

Though his expression was distrustful, he came, and she flung her arms around his neck. "Now that I am your wife, completely your wife, will you please stop calling me 'child'?"

He laughed with relief over the simplicity of her request. Holding her close, he said, "Dearest wife, thou art truly a woman. But since thine every look and gesture bespeak such innocence, I may forget."

"Just don't forget last night, no matter how long your voyage," she whispered.

"Hannah, I will never forget last night. And yet," he said, suddenly thoughtful, "I fear that, stirring up in thee such passion, thou mayest …" He paused, his brow furrowing. "I have great pride in my Nantucket house. I wish for thee to live there as befitting my bride. Before sailing, I'll quickly write a letter to my housekeeper so that she will receive thee."

"Oh, dearest, shall I be bereft of both you and my father? Please allow me to stay in his safekeeping until you return."

He pushed her back and held her at arms' length. "And is there none other than husband and father whom thou wouldest yearn for in Nantucket?" His eyes were narrowed, his mouth grim.

"What?" She stared at him in disbelief, then with understanding. "Oh, how cruel for you to still be so jealous. Don't go away from me believing that I could sin against you and God by being unfaithful. If I had wanted Jer... anyone else but you, I could have married long ago. And had we not married, I would have waited for the rest of my life for you to return from your voyage and married you then, even if you returned a broken man. Don't you realize that you are all that I ever wanted or ever shall want? Oh, Ahab, how could you?" She held him desperately as the tears she had tried to check over his departure now poured forth, disguised as anger.

"Shh, don't cry. Don't cry. I see how it is now. What madness put that yellow-eyed demon in my thoughts?" He held her and caressed her hair. "Perhaps our hasty wedding was not needed after all."

Hannah choked back her sobs, trying to forgive him, though he had not asked to be forgiven. "Oh, yes, it was. I had to be sure you would come back to me."

He chuckled and gazed at her fondly again. "Then let us doubt one another no more, dear child ... umm, dear wife."

She impatiently brushed away her tears, trying once again to put on a brave face. "And will you promise not to make any stops on your voyage, stops on those infamous South Pacific islands, since you will be coming back home to me?"

He laughed. "Mr. Stuart has given me a very Christian crew, and every man but my cabin boy has a wife or intended awaiting him here in New Bedford. We'll be making no unnecessary landings, my dear, or we'd all have a very cold hell to pay upon our return. Now, get thyself up with no more delay, woman. Thou must walk me to my ship."

A crewman arrived to take Ahab's sea chest to the ship. Hannah had hoped that with his hands free, her new husband would stroll with her to the docks, his arms about her waist, lingering with her as long as he could. But Ahab's lengthy stride was quick, his gaze toward the harbor expectant. While his words were jovial and affectionate, with a hint of regret that he was leaving her, it was clear that he was eager to get under way. Hannah was forced almost to run to keep up with him, and her somewhat breathless responses were nearly lost in the wind. But then, by the time they reached the docks where her father waited to escort her home after the *Sharona* departed, there were no more words to be said.

When Ahab held her close and kissed her one last time, she wished desperately that she could melt into one being with him and thus never be parted. How could she live with him gone? Would he feel only half a heart in his breast as she would feel half of her heart was at sea? As he shook hands with Mr. Oldweiler and walked toward the gangplank, she hoped not to shame him by weeping aloud as she wept within. A handful of other wives and sweethearts were there, some shedding more than their share of tears. But she was the captain's wife. Instinctively she knew, though she had never before watched a ship depart, that she must set an example of courage. As the *Sharona* began to sail out of the harbor, Ahab turned and waved one last time. His proud smile confirmed that she had not failed him.

Chapter Seven

80

There were times when Hannah thought that her marriage to Ahab, in fact Ahab himself, was all a dream. Having no portrait to remind her, she feared she would forget his handsome face and magnificent form. Even her mother's ring on her left hand was not convincing evidence, for often as a child she had made a game of wearing it. But then her body would remind her of love's fulfillment on their wedding night, and she knew the ache within her heart and flesh was for a real man. Her man. Her husband.

After all her protests against marriage, what an amazing surprise it was to find herself wed. But how could she not have married Ahab? He was unlike any other man she had ever known. She could not have risked losing him. Still, she wondered how other whalers' wives endured these separations. To console herself, she wrote to Ahab each month, proclaiming her love for him and informing him of things of interest, then posting the letters by way of whatever whaler was setting out to go around Cape Horn.

She also took consolation in her father's fellowship as they looked forward to the return of the *Ivory Rose*. They discussed making investments, as Ahab had suggested, and she found herself attracted to the intricacies of finance. Though she never would tell her father, she felt certain she could be more capable than he in monetary affairs. When the profits from the *Ivory Rose* were secured, she would encourage him not to deviate from Ahab's recommendations.

Other than attending Lila Gantvort's wedding, which Hannah thought entirely too lavish, they spent a quiet winter with few visitors. To her dismay, she discovered several days after her marriage that Jeremiah had resigned his position and had left New Bedford. He had not even bid her father farewell, much less her. But under the circumstances, she could hardly blame him. Poor, dear Jeremiah. She would always miss the warmth of his friendship.

Shortly after Christmas, Mr. Oldweiler suffered a mild, though lengthy bout of influenza, and with no Jeremiah to lift his spirits, his recovery was slow. By the time the trees began to put forth their new leaves, Hannah had become so eager to get out of the house that her father had to caution her not to begin too soon to cultivate her roses or else her work would be in vain.

One new custom had been incorporated into Hannah's life since the previous autumn: climbing the narrow stairs above the attic to their railed roof walk. From there she watched for the signal flag to fly above the harbor. Hoisted by the harbormaster to signal the return of a whaling ship, the flag brought many women scurrying to the docks in hopes of greeting their husbands, sweethearts, or sons. Though Hannah realized it was foolish to think the *Sharona* would be returning after only six months or the *Hannah Rose* after only four months at sea, she was eager for the profits from their other ship so they could begin investing. When at last in early April the harbormaster identified an incoming vessel as the *Ivory Rose* and sent word to them, Mr. Oldweiler was hard put to keep Hannah from running to greet the ship. Rather, he insisted that, because of the rowdy atmosphere of the docks, he would go and bring her word as quickly as he was able.

As she stood and watched him from the front window, he limped down the street, leaning on the cane he had recently begun to use, yet cheerful at the happy prospects before him. Although Hannah had yielded to him on this occasion, he would not be able to keep her from the docks when it was the *Sharona* that arrived. How often she dreamed of that day. But for now, she would not embarrass her father by violating social constraints. After several long hours, she saw him limping up the street again, stopping after every few steps to catch his breath from the uphill climb. As he drew closer, she ran out to meet him and was dismayed to see his ashen color.

"Papa, what is it?" she cried. "Oh, why didn't you let me go to the docks? You've made yourself ill again despite our good news."

He shook his head, unable to speak. She led him to a chair in the front parlor and called for Carson to bring water.

"Papa, please, what is it?"

"Oh, Hannah, my dear, the best laid plans of men ..." he whispered.

"What? Oh, what? Tell me."

As he sipped the water that Carson brought, he gazed toward the front window. "Such a beautiful spring day for such bad news," he murmured. "Only two hundred barrels, my dear."

Hannah gasped. "No, no. You mean two thousand."

"No. Two hundred. Not even enough to pay back the investors or give a living wage to the crew."

"But why did they return with such a small cargo? What kind of whaling crew is that? They should have stayed out until they filled every cask." Even as she said it, she realized how much it contradicted her own thoughts about Ahab's voyage.

"No, my dear. There's no fault in their early return. They lost their drinking water in a storm on their way out. The water casks were weak. I must have chosen poorly. While they were replenishing on one of the Cape Verde Islands, several of the men contracted scarlet fever from the crew of another ship. Almost the whole crew was stricken. By the time they got around Cape Horn, seven out of the thirty-one men had died and were buried at sea, one of them Captain Brown. The first mate, Mr. Tobias, took command and tried valiantly to continue, but it was no use. The majority of the men were far too weak to hunt the whales." His report was punctuated by pauses as he endeavored to catch his breath.

Horrified by his news, as well as its effect on her father, Hannah anxiously watched as he rested against the back of his chair, his eyes filling with tears.

"Four men left widows and children, and one left a fiancée," he continued in a raspy voice. "Every lost man had mother or father, loving sister or brother, who will suffer from this tragedy until the day they die."

She glanced across the room where Mrs. Randolph stood dabbing her eyes and nodding in sympathy. Icy fingers seemed to grip Hannah's heart as she thought of Ahab out on the very seas that had taken those seven men. But as she watched her father's suffering, she feared that this calamity would claim yet another life. Still, her voice was calm as she spoke to Carson.

"Please go for Dr. Hastings. Tell him my father is ill."

Mr. Oldweiler did not protest, but he did seem to rally. "I have a thought, Daughter. It's the only right thing to do. We must sell the *Ivory Rose* and use the money to help all those families. I'm certain that Mr. Stuart or Abel Williams will give us a fair price. Someone will." His voice trailed off, and he continued to stare out the window.

"Yes," Hannah said. "That's the right thing to do. Let's get you to bed now, dear. It's been a trying afternoon."

Dr. Hastings prescribed constant bed rest for the patient. He also told Hannah to hold back all distressing news from her father, saying that he could not give her any hope for Mr. Oldweiler's recovery if he were to receive any further blows.

The meager cargo of the *Ivory Rose* still had to be sold. Putting on her most cheerful face, Hannah told her father—in tones she had overheard Ahab use—that she was capable of obtaining the best market prices for the whale oil and ivory. She also promised to speak to both Mr. Stuart and Mr. Williams about buying the ship. But while her brave assurances encouraged him, she herself was filled with doubt. In keeping with rules of propriety, she had not taken a step near the docks since her childhood, except to bid Ahab farewell. And, of course, she'd had no business experience. Both Carson and Mrs. Randolph offered to accompany her to the counting house, but she declined.

"Thank you, good friends, but I must learn to conduct this business on my own."

"Then you must be firm, just as you've seen me bargain firmly with the butcher," said Mrs. Randolph. "Even men claiming to be Christians will cheat you out of your profits to line their own pockets. They will try to take advantage of you because you are a woman. Oh, do let me go with you, Miss Hannah."

"No, dear. If they think I am weak or uninformed because I am a woman, that may work to my advantage. I will speak to Mr. Williams before going to the counting house. He can tell me the latest prices for the oil and ivory." As she said the words, Hannah felt a surge of excitement. Ahab had wanted her to find an occupation for her time. What would he think if he came home to find her an accomplished businesswoman? However, her more immediate goal concerned her ailing father. If she received a good price for both cargo and ship, it was sure to revive his health, or at least his spirits.

She decided to wear her light green dress to visit Abel Williams. Like Jeremiah, he had often complimented her eyes as she was growing up, and this dress made them sparkle. She arranged her hair loosely around her face to emphasize her youthfulness. It could do no harm for him to find her a pleasing sight, but she would be certain that Lila was present before consulting with her husband.

It was fortunate for Hannah that the couple was at home after their short honeymoon trip. They welcomed the chance to assist their friend and neighbor. Mr. Williams informed Hannah of the current rate for whale oil, baleen, ivory, and ambergris, and he offered to write the prices down lest she forget them. She thanked him, but said she could remember without assistance.

As Lila walked her friend to the door, she took her hand and held it for a moment. "I could not say this in my husband's presence, dearest Hannah, but I must give you a warning."

"Warning?" Hannah tried not to pull away, but Lila's attitude seemed somehow unbearably condescending. "What on earth must you warn me about?" No matter what Lila said, Hannah would go to the docks.

Lila glanced back toward the parlor where they had left Mr. Williams. "My dear," she whispered, "you have had no mother to advise you, and I would not be a good friend if I did not tell you what my own mother has taught me about overburdening your mental faculties."

"Overburdening my mental faculties?" Hannah began to laugh.

"You mustn't laugh. Such arduous use of a woman's mind as applying it to business matters is known to damage her ability to become a mother. My mother has this information from the best medical authorities."

Somewhat sobered, Hannah stared at her in confusion. Could this be true?

Lila sniffed, her feelings offended by Hannah's doubts. "I simply wanted you to be aware of the danger. As for myself," she looked down, blushing, and placed a hand at her own waistline, "I am already expecting a happy event in late autumn, and I only wish all my married acquaintances the same joy."

As Hannah left the Williams house, she experienced a small twinge of envy over Lila's impending motherhood. Oh, how wonderful it would be to bear Ahab's child. But she decided that if using her mind truly threatened her ability to one day become a mother, it was a risk she would have to take. Her father's health, indeed, his very life, was at stake.

She returned home and changed into her black dress, then pulled her hair back into a matronly bun and put on her black coat and bonnet. Studying herself in her wardrobe mirror, she practiced an uncompromising expression, lifting her chin and furrowing her brow as Ahab did when he was displeased. She decided that her brow lacked the necessary severity for intimidation, though her unusual height for a woman might provide some advantage in the negotiations. But would the men at the counting house find her a formidable client, she who felt like a trembling child within? All she could do was try.

The warm April sunshine filled her with optimism as she wended her way down the hills of New Bedford toward the wharves. By the time she reached the dock where the *Ivory Rose* was anchored, she was forced to remind herself of the serious nature of her errand. Whaling men of every description and race swarmed over the docks, some working, some seeking work. Their salty language assailed her ears, and the ogling stares of some assailed her dignity. Charging through the unpleasant hubbub, she at last found the ship's first mate, for the time being its captain, and commended him for his skillful handling of their mutual tragedy.

"Mr. Tobias, my father sends you his best and wishes me to thank you again for all you've done," she said, using her most authoritarian tones. "I'm sure you could see that your news struck him quite hard yesterday. He regrets that his health prevents him from managing the arbitration over the sale of the cargo. I will take his place. Have you completed unloading?"

"Nearly completed, Miss Hannah. We should be finished by late tonight." Mr. Tobias, an experienced whaler about thirty years of age, nodded politely as he spoke, but his expression was one of amusement.

Hannah was annoyed, then disheartened, by his demeanor. However, lifting her chin, she frowned at him. "Would you please advise me as to the proper person at the counting house with whom I must negotiate the sale?"

"Miss Hannah, may I suggest that you allow me, your father being ill and all, to manage the sale?"

"No, Mr. Tobias. I am well equipped to see that we all receive a fair portion of the profits, little though they may be."

"Miss Hannah—"

"Mr. Tobias, must I find the buyer myself, or will you take me to him?"

The mate's indulgent expression was replaced by an angry scowl. "See here, Miss—"

"No, sir. You see here." What a wonder. Her voice held firm. "I have my father's power of attorney in hand, and I am his agent. As such, I will handle the negotiations. You can be assured that you will receive a fair portion. You should also know that I will make certain that every widow, orphan, and dependent mother will receive their share as well. Now, may I have the tally sheet?"

Mr. Tobias glared at Hannah for a moment, and then relented. He produced the document from the ship and gave it to her. "Come with me."

He took her inside a large building next to the dock where workmen were busy hauling about casks of whale oil, some new ones being counted, others being moved out to market. The noise and disagreeable smells had begun to annoy Hannah, and she hoped her annoyance would work to her advantage. Mr. Tobias took her into the office, introduced her to two gentlemen, and stood beside them facing her.

"Mr. Lamech and Mr. Elihu, this is Mr. Oldweiler's daughter. She has come to negotiate the sale of the *Ivory Rose* cargo." He traded a knowing look with the two men that Hannah did not fail to see. She decided it was time to take charge.

"Gentlemen, I won't waste your time with useless haggling. Mr. Tobias assures me that although our products are limited, they are of superior quality. Therefore, these are my prices: two hundred twenty-seven barrels of whale at nine and a half dollars per barrel; twelve hundred eighty-six pounds of baleen, at three dollars per pound; one hundred thirty-one barrels of sperm, fourteen dollars per barrel; one hundred forty-nine pounds of ivory, two dollars a pound. I will accompany you while you determine that Mr. Tobias's weights agree with yours, and then we can each calculate the total amount."

Mr. Lamech and Mr. Elihu exchanged shrewd smiles and turned to Hannah with courtly bows.

"Miss Oldweiler, it is a pleasure to meet you," said Mr. Elihu. "We have always enjoyed doing business with your father and are quite distressed to hear of his illness. Sometimes it is difficult to understand the will of God in these matters, but we must trust that He is our Sovereign Lord and always knows what is best. Of course, we will give you a fair price for your cargo, but you must understand that, at the present, due to last year's economic depression, prices are down considerably from those you quoted. That must be taken into consideration."

Mr. Lamech nodded vigorously. "Yes, indeed. We cannot forget all those souls who are dependent on us at both ends of this trading. Just as your people will suffer from this disappointing payload, our people would suffer if we were not diligent to set a more reasonable price. As good Christian stewards, we must do our duty by all concerned. Surely your own Christian heart bears witness to that principle."

For the briefest moment, Hannah felt herself being swayed. Perhaps it was God's will that the families of the *Ivory Rose* whalers should learn some spiritual lesson through this loss. Who was she to argue or to interfere with His plan? Why did she ever think she could negotiate with these experienced businessmen? Had her foolish pride made things worse? If Mr. Elihu had given her only a few more seconds to consider it, he would have been the one to fix their prices.

"You will also understand, of course, that at present, our funds are low and that we will be forced to delay payment for some weeks, Miss Oldweiler," he said, taking on a paternal tone that further stung her pride.

"Mrs. Ahab," she said.

"I beg your pardon?" Mr. Lamech said. All three men stared at her.

"Mrs. Ahab. I am Mr. Oldweiler's daughter, but I was recently married."

Mr. Elihu cleared his throat. "By any chance, is your husband Captain Ahab? Of the Nantucket Ahabs?"

"Captain Ahab who recently sailed on the *Sharona?*" added Mr. Lamech.

Mr. Tobias took a firm step to Hannah's side and faced the other two men with her.

Hannah lifted her chin, amazed at her own calm. It must have been due to a clash of emotions settling for a median, for just as much as she wanted to laugh at their obviously fear-filled respect for Ahab, she wanted to weep that it might require the power of his name to sell at the price she had named. What fools these men were. There were no Ahabs of Nantucket. Ahab had been orphaned at twelve months and had no living relative but her. But whatever they knew or did not know of Ahab was not important, as long as their absurd dread of him won her an honest price for the cargo.

"Why, yes. Do you know my husband?"

"Only by reputation." Mr. Lamech's eyes were wide with amazement.

"I've met him briefly," said Mr. Elihu. Hannah was certain she saw a slight shudder pass through him.

"Now that I think of it, Mrs. Ahab, I do believe we might manage a better price for your cargo," said Mr. Lamech.

"Yes, of course," added Mr. Elihu. "I seem to recall that market prices are expected to go up sharply very soon. We can speculate on that, considering that your father has always been such a dependable supplier for us. Well, that is to say, what he lacked in quantity, he made up in quality."

"And there's no finer Christian man on the face of this earth, no sir," Mr. Lamech added.

Hannah leveled her gaze at them and spoke in firm tones. "Mr. Tobias has provided me with a list of our cargo. Are you ready to count and weigh with me, or would you like to accept his accounting and just give me my price today?"

Mr. Tobias stared at her for a moment, his mouth agape. "Perhaps I should recount," he said at last. "I would not like it on my conscience to have unknowingly overcounted and cheated these good gentlemen."

Hannah glared at him, certain that he meant just the opposite of what he said. He probably had undercounted, with plans to privately sell the uncounted products for his own personal gain. And they probably were all together in the scheme.

"I will count with you, Mr. Tobias," she said.

"But Miss Old ... Mrs. Ahab. How can a lady of your breeding endure the rotten smells and coarse atmosphere of the docks a moment longer?" Mr. Tobias asked.

"Never mind, sir," she replied. "Let us waste no more time. I will not leave until the tally is affirmed, though it take us a week to count and weigh." *It's the stench of corruption here that demands my presence*, she thought.

At final counting, the numbers were up almost by half, but it was still a disappointing sum. It was two o'clock in the morning when a weary Hannah trudged home with Carson, who had come to find his tardy mistress. Tired though she was, she lay awake for some time, wondering at the day's events. How had she developed so much insight so quickly?

In the morning, she would take great delight in telling her father about her experiences. But then it occurred to her that she could not reveal the whole truth to him. By exposing Mr. Lamech and Mr. Elihu, not to mention Mr. Tobias, as conniving thieves, she would be telling her own beloved father how gullible he had been all these years, thus heaping on him more anguish. His tender heart always believed the best about everyone. No, she would simply tell him that prices were up and that, weakened by the difficult voyage, Mr. Tobias had undercounted.

Then there was the business of disbursing the profits to all the crewmembers and the families of those who had died. For this she would depend upon her father's advice ... and his generous nature. Her own heart was so distressed by the actions of the accountants that she hesitated to show kindness to the seemingly most pious of the new widows and orphans, lest they, too, find a way to cheat her father.

Unaccustomed as she was to financial management, Hannah took many days to calculate what percentage was owed to each crewmember. The matter of paying wages by lays confused her somewhat, but in time she began to understand. Although her father should have received one-third of the entire ship's income, he refused any profit until the others were taken care of. To Captain Brown's widow and children, they paid twenty-three hundred dollars. Mr. Tobias received twelve hundred, and so on down to the least experienced crewmember. Hannah wrote letters seeking relatives of the two lost seamen who did not live near New Bedford and was rewarded with responses directing her where to send the dead men's meager wages.

In keeping with her father's instructions, she cut by half the amount owed back to him for loans made to families of the crew to tide them over during the voyage. In the end there was very little left and numerous creditors still to pay. She and her father had agreed that taking care of the whalers and their families came before repaying their suppliers. It was their hope that by selling the *Ivory Rose*, they could settle all those debts.

No bargaining was required in that sale. Mr. Stuart, owner of the *Sharona*, demonstrated both his respect for Mr. Oldweiler (and perhaps Ahab as well) and his own Christian charity by offering a price proportionate to the old vessel's condition and the current market value. All creditors thus being satisfied, Hannah and her father hoped to manage on the scant remainder until the *Hannah Rose* returned.

Hannah did not cultivate her roses that spring, but left them to grow wild about the garden while she tended to her father's needs and helped the servants around the house. That summer when she noticed that Carson's footsteps had slowed and his back was bent even more than before, she gave him leave to retire to his son's small farm in Maine. With help from Sally and Mrs. Randolph, she covered the parlor furniture with sheets and pulled the aged draperies over the windows to prevent further sun damage to the fading Persian carpets.

In the early autumn, near the first anniversary of the day they had met Ahab, the Oldweiler household was visited by a Captain Floyd who had recently returned from a successful voyage to the Pacific. Although his call alarmed Hannah, she uncovered two chairs in the parlor and asked Mrs. Randolph to serve tea. After their initial pleasantries, the captain's agreeable manners seemed to assure that he brought no bad news of her husband. But as he continued to speak vaguely of whaling, his thankfulness for a good voyage, and other topics in which she could not be expected to have any interest, she finally interrupted.

"Sir, I'm most grateful for your kind visit, seeing that you have been acquainted with my father. Since he is ill, I hope you will forgive me for not presenting you to him. I must confess your presence gives me some mild alarm. Have you news of the *Sharona* or of my husband, Captain Ahab?"

"Captain Ahab? Ah, I did not realize Old Thunder had married. What a fortunate man to have such a lovely young wife. Forgive me for alarming you in that regard. I assure you I did not encounter him on this voyage. No, I'm afraid my news is of another sort, yet perhaps equally as distressing. Now you must understand that this may only be a rumor. And you must understand that we whalers, while sometimes a superstitious lot, are loath to bring unnecessary worry to our fellow whalers and their families. Still, we must inform you when there is any information ... we feel it is cruel to give you hope for that which is not to be ... that is to say ... I have news of a possible sinking."

Hannah took a deep breath. "Go on, sir."

"Am I correctly informed that your father is the proprietor of the *Hannah Rose*, which sailed from New Bedford last December with Captain Lazarus in command?"

Unable to speak, she nodded.

"Then I have the unfortunate duty to inform you that she may never have made it to the Pacific waters. The Nantucket whaler *Cherbourg*, which sailed soon after the *Hannah Rose* and was on her way around Cape Horn, came upon evidence of a sinking: numerous items of equipment identified as belonging to your ship, some of which bore her name."

Hannah felt as though her head were detaching from her body. She gripped the arms of her chair to keep from swooning. "Are you certain? I mean, was the *Cherbourg's* captain certain? Could it not have been merely extra items thrown away to lighten the load or—"

"Madam, I would gladly spare you this news, if at all possible. But it was the main mast, two shattered whaleboats, even some personal items and clothing. The mast and personal items could have been lost in a storm or perhaps belong to another ship. But the whaleboats, identified by her name, would not yet have been lowered, since they had not reached the whaling waters. Nor could securely attached boats be torn away from the ship in such a manner. At least that is what captain of the *Cherbourg* determined."

"Dear God, have mercy!"

Hannah jerked about in her chair. There stood her father in the parlor doorway, leaning on his cane. She quickly rushed to his side.

"Papa, dear, please return to bed. It's only a rumor. Captain Floyd says so. Isn't that true, Captain?"

The captain hurried to Mr. Oldweiler's side. "Sir, allow me to assist you."

The sturdy whaler lifted the faltering invalid in his arms and carried him upstairs to bed. Then, at Hannah's request, he went to call Dr. Hastings. That errand complete, the good captain was filled with remorse as he took his final leave of Hannah.

"Madam, if there had been any way to spare you, I would have given my last breath to do so. Is there anything further I can do?"

"Thank you, sir. I only ask that you tell the senior pastor of the Trinitarian Congregational Church that my father has taken a bad turn."

That evening after both doctor and pastor had come and gone, Hannah spooned broth to her father's unwilling lips and continued to murmur assurances to him. "I'm certain it's just a rumor, Papa. Ahab would not have recommended Captain Lazarus if he were not competent to command the ship wisely. We must not assume it's truly lost."

"Oh, my dear child," he said softly. "It was never the ships that burdened me. It was the men, the lost whalers and their poor families. Oh, to have the power to save them all. But I have done nothing but fail in every endeavor. Poorly chosen equipment and supplies. Incompetent captains. And I, the most incompetent of all. God forgive me, forgive me." His eyelids closed, and his breathing became shallow.

"Papa, don't leave me," she whispered. "What shall I do if you leave me?"

He opened his eyes and smiled. "Why, Jeremiah will care for you, of course."

"But—"

"He loves you, you know. You must marry him soon. Don't keep him waiting, my dear." Again he seemed to sleep.

"Papa, please. Wake up. You're dreaming. You must eat. Let me read to you."

Amos Oldweiler looked up once more, staring at the ceiling above the bed with a gentle smile. "Listen, Daughter. God is singing."

"Papa, please ..." Hannah shook him, trying desperately to think of some way to stop his too-willing submission to death. But his eyes closed again, and soon his chest no longer moved. She stared at his lifeless form, unable to comprehend what had happened. After all, the doctor had been certain that a good night's rest would revive him. The senior pastor had said a suitable prayer and assured her that God, in His great goodness, still had earthly work for this dear saint. But her father was gone. Dead. Forever.

"Nooooo," she moaned and pounded her fists against the bed. "Why wouldn't you fight? Why would you never, never fight?" she cried.

Then she cradled his beloved body in her arms and wept.

Chapter Eight

ഇ

*E*veryone had been so kind. Mr. and Mrs. Gantvort, along with the senior pastor, had arranged the funeral. Other friends had visited and offered condolences. Mrs. Randolph and Sally, recalling their own tragedies, had stood on either side of Hannah and supported her through the ordeal. Afterward, the two servants had washed Mr. Oldweiler's bed linens and thrown open the windows to air the room, despite the autumn chill. When the house seemed to echo with its emptiness, they would recall to Hannah and each other some fond memory of their employer.

Many fall and winter nights, Hannah wept at her father's desk, where he had often sat reading with her or finding consolation in his Bible. Many days she slept from dawn till evening in his bed. When she dreamed of her father or Jeremiah, she awoke with a heavy heart. Only when she dreamed of Ahab could she grasp any measure of peace. Still, with an unknown interval of loneliness stretching before her until his return, she could feel little hope for the future.

She did what she could for the families of the lost crew, and by spring her money was nearly gone. But rather than discourage her further, this inspired her. In the midst of her regrets over not being able to give Sally and her new husband a wedding gift, she decided to remedy the situation by selling her home. Lila had always admired the Oldweiler mansion far more than her husband's older house, one of the first built in New Bedford and expanded as far as its original property would allow. Abel Williams welcomed the chance to purchase the adjoining property to provide room for his growing family. He and Lila gave Hannah as much time as she required to vacate the only home she had ever known.

With the help of Mrs. Randolph, Sally, and her husband Aaron, Hannah spent the spring and summer sorting through all her belongings, selling most, and packing up her father's books in wooden crates. The Williamses had agreed to store them in the attic until she could claim them sometime in the future. She only took what would fit in her mother's trunk: her clothing, a few mementos such as a small pencil sketch of her father, several books, and a sixteen-dollar Ecuadorian gold piece her great uncle had long ago tucked into a corner of his desk. She would give it to Ahab when he returned to her.

Aaron Mathes proved himself to be a good friend. For years, the whaler had courted Sally in the short intervals between his voyages. His decision to retire from the sea finally won him his bride. Strong of body from his life of hard labor, he helped Hannah pack and move with Mrs. Randolph into a small rented cottage. It was the same cottage where she had spent her wedding night nearly two years before.

On Hannah's first night there, snuggled into the bed where she and Ahab had become one flesh, she slept in peace at last. Waking up refreshed the next morning, she was ready to consider ideas for using the money from the sale of her house. How proud Ahab would be of her if she could prove herself a wise investor. Although the economy had changed over the past two years so as to negate his specific recommendations, there certainly must be principles of finance to use as guidelines. She lamented not listening more closely when he had advised her father. But then, she had been so much in love that all she had thought about was winning his love in return. To succeed—and to make him proud—she would have to be very careful in choosing what investments to make. But who would advise her? Mr. Stuart and Mr. Williams put all their whaling profits back into their ships. Hannah could not bring herself to sink another dollar into the sea. She decided to put her four thousand dollars in the bank until she could learn more about financial matters.

By delaying action, she found that her initial enthusiasm was cooled by growing apprehensions about the possibility of failure. Despite her success in bargaining with the oil merchants (had it truly been a year and a half since that day?), she wondered if, like her father, she would be doomed to make poor choices. What if she chose the wrong advisor? What if, despite careful planning, her chosen investment failed? With each passing day, her fears grew. Perhaps it was best simply to leave the money in the bank, where it could draw interest. It was a tidy sum that would supply everything she needed for a long time to come. Still, Ahab had been right. Restless as she was, she needed something to occupy her time and energies.

Because of Mrs. Randolph's devotion to Hannah, she adapted to being the only servant to reside in the household, managing duties far beyond the kitchen. Sally was busy taking care of her own new home, but once a week she sent her fourteen-year-old daughter Kitty to help with the dusting. Despite her age, the girl was already smitten with a deep affection for a young whaler. But her mother and grandmother discouraged marriage, hoping to spare her the grief they had known during their husbands' long voyages and their own eventual widowhood.

As Hannah observed the relationships among these three women, she realized how much she had missed by not having a mother's influence. No woman had ever filled that void in her life. Not Jeremiah's mother, with her gentle but other-worldly ways. Not Mrs. Gantvort, who was benevolent but distant. And certainly not the resolute Miss Applegate, whose unauthorized attempts to turn her charges into suffrage seekers would have appalled their parents. Through the years, it had been Mrs. Randolph who had provided more nurturing than any other person beside Hannah's father.

The older woman's practical nature appealed to Hannah as well. Since Mr. Oldweiler's death, she had often stepped in with timely advice when it was needed, always with the respect due one's employer. Hannah came to treasure her wisdom and wanted to repay her loyalty. The woman had simple tastes and desired no embellishments for her life, her only joy being her family. In this, Hannah found the answer to both her problems. To demonstrate her gratitude, she would buy a business for Sally and Aaron, investing some of her money to benefit them all.

Aaron Mathes had been a whaler since his teens and had risen as high as second mate on his last two voyages. However, due to the system of paying by lays, in which owners and captains reaped the lion's share of all profits and crewmembers were paid decreasingly by rank, he had little to show for twenty-one years at sea. With the two-hundred-dollar wedding gift Hannah had given the couple after the sale of her home, they had bought a small house on the west side of New Bedford. Aaron then hired himself out to do odd jobs and heavy work for the numerous women whose husbands were at sea. In a little shed behind the house, he repaired everything from wagon hitches to water pumps. With Hannah's five-hundred-dollar investment, he bought the vacant lot next door, built a larger shed, and bought more equipment. And he enticed Kitty's young man to accept an apprenticeship upon his return from the voyage for which he had recently signed.

In light of the benefits they received, both tangible and intangible, Hannah understood the gratitude the family lavished on her. She decided that this first investment was just the beginning of her financial ventures, and she was particularly proud of it. Like Ahab, she had done what she could for her friends. She was only just beginning to prove herself.

The bitter winter of 1839–40 was made worse by a severe smallpox epidemic that devastated New Bedford. Because Hannah had survived a mild bout of the disease in her childhood and had no fear of contracting it again, she offered to watch by the bedsides of sick friends and minister to their needs. To her sorrow, among those stricken was the pretty five-year-old daughter of the late Captain Lazarus of the ill-fated *Hannah Rose*. After the death of her only child, Eliza Lazarus seemed to lose heart for living. She too became ill. With Hannah sitting nearby, she spoke of the joy of joining her husband and child in heaven. Then, with a resignation that dismayed Hannah, she slipped away.

Not all of Hannah's stricken friends succumbed to the disease, however. Among those whom she helped to nurse back to health was the youngest son of Mr. Stuart, the owner of the *Sharona*. Mr. Stuart demonstrated his gratitude by promising to increase Captain Ahab's share of the ship's expected profits.

After that grievous winter, one unseasonably warm February day inspired Hannah to consider planting roses that spring. The landlady did not object to improvements, so Hannah walked up the New Bedford hills to her former home. The Williams's gardener would soon begin reviving Hannah's rose bushes, and perhaps Lila would allow her to have some cuttings. The young mother, who was already expecting another happy event, was draped across her large new divan in front of the fireplace. She had redecorated the interior of the house to such an extent that Hannah was able to quickly overcome the homesickness that had threatened her as she came up the front steps. After a pleasant chat and the requisite praise for Lila's eighteen-month-old daughter—who was allowed in the parlor only in the firm grasp of her nursemaid—Hannah secured a promise that the gardener would bring the requested cuttings as soon as they were available.

Back home, she studied her small, bare yard, pondering where to put the roses and wondering if she should plant other perennials too. Geraniums or chrysanthemums might grow well. Forsythias were a must. And if she made a flowerbed along the north fence for annuals, they would get plenty of sunshine. Now that spring seemed imminent, the possibilities seemed endless.

As the afternoon wore on, she sat on the stoop and leaned back against the doorjamb, her gaze drifting lazily over her surroundings. It was not a bad place, this humble little street. Not as impressive or as well kept as her old neighborhood. Yet housewives planted flowers here as well as there. Dogs roamed the neighborhood, cats kept mice and rats at bay, and children played outside, no matter what the weather. Whatever had been so grand and wonderful about that other section of town? She would gladly live in even humbler dwellings than this if only her father were still alive and if only her Ahab were safely home from his voyage. In fact, it was strange how detached from the old place she had felt while visiting Lila. Though she did miss watching the ships come into harbor each day, for this house had no roof walk, it was home now—at least until Ahab returned and took her to Nantucket, then to Europe. She drew her shawl around her, hating to give in to the cold wind that would soon drive her inside. This pleasant scene was prompting such happy thoughts.

After a few warm days in February, spring seemed to change its mind about putting in an early appearance. Then March winds reaffirmed their reputation with enthusiastic vigor, keeping Hannah indoors and restless. She had spent the winter exercising her mind through reading the books that Ahab had given her, especially the one by Emerson. She had also exercised her fingers, learning to embroider from Mrs. Randolph. In lieu of growing a rose garden, she had found relaxation in stitching colorful flowers on white cotton squares. Now she longed for the greater exercise of gardening. But it would be useless even to try to turn over the frozen soil until it thawed. So, as she had every day for months past, she sat in a cozy chair by the parlor fireplace and read, waiting for Mrs. Randolph to return from the market.

When the woman returned, she bustled into the room with uncharacteristic haste. "Miss Hannah," she said breathlessly, "it's the *Sharona*! She's been in port for three days!"

Hannah marked her page in the Emerson book and casually looked up. "You must be mistaken. As much as I wish it could be so, it's impossible. You yourself have always told me that a successful voyage takes at least three years. That means we've at least six more months to wait. Besides, if he were here, Ahab would have looked for me the moment the ship reached port."

Mrs. Randolph shook her head with enthusiasm. "No, ma'am. No matter how eager he may be to see you, he's still the captain. It's his job to settle all accounts before he can go home."

Hannah sat up, allowing herself a moment of hope. "But would he not have sent word for me to come to him?"

The older woman again shook her head. "Do you think a fine gentleman like Captain Ahab would wish for his lady wife to come to the docks or that he would wish to greet her with the smell of the ocean and dead whales still on him? No, no, dear. Don't you know how it's accomplished? After the unloading comes the counting. After the counting, there's the paying of the crew. After the paying, he'll go to the bathhouse to bathe and shave, perhaps even have his hair trimmed. But never you mind. He'll be here shortly, I'm sure. The harbormaster knows to tell him that you've moved here to this house."

"Oh, no. If the *Sharona* is truly in port, I must go to him. That is, unless ... unless something has happened."

Using her privilege of intimacy with her employer judiciously, Mrs. Randolph now assumed her most maternal posture. "Miss Hannah, you must never think it, despite all your recent sorrows. But if evil has befallen your Ahab, you must be strong. Some men return sick or maimed and yet, unlike my beloved Charles, they do return. Your future happiness with your husband lies in your response, no matter what has come to pass. Many a foolish and weak young wife has further injured her man by hysterical tears or disgust or pity for his condition. A man cannot live with that. No, you must trust Providence and accept with courage whatever comes."

Hannah drew in a deep breath and shuddered. "If only I can. But if something has happened ... Oh, I must go find him!"

"But, dear, don't you recall how your father forbade you to go to the docks? You saw how rough it can be down there in that business with the *Ivory Rose*. Captain Ahab truly is in port, but he may be on his way here now. If you run to meet him, what if you take a different street? You'll miss him, and he'll come home to an empty house. Oh, do wait here."

Hannah was suddenly overtaken by giddy laughter. "And where was Mrs. Randolph when her Charles sailed into port?"

The old woman embraced her, then took her face in her hands. "Why, I was on the docks, of course."

Hannah grabbed her shawl from the hall tree and hugged it around her shoulders. The stiff March wind cut through her light wrap, but once out the door, Hannah would not go back inside. She started down the cobblestoned street toward the docks, studying every man who came within her sight. One moment, she wondered if she would even recognize Ahab. The next, she thought she saw the familiar figure of her father or Jeremiah walking toward her.

The loneliness that had for so long been her companion jealously suggested that she had no right to look for happiness to return to her life, that she must expect disappointment. Perhaps Ahab had forgotten her or now regretted their short courtship and hasty marriage. Would he still find her beautiful? Would he still desire her? Or would she find him changed and be the one with regrets? No, never! If there were no other good quality she possessed, at least her heart was constant. But did she love a phantom?

Over the past two and a half years, Hannah had often feared that it had all been a dream, that there was no Ahab, and that she was truly and forever alone in the world. Just as often, she had imagined seeing him walk up this very street to come back to her. He would walk firmly, urgently, like the tall gentleman dressed in a handsome black suit coming her way now. That magnificent man with the long, powerful legs striding up the street, his gaze fixed on her as though she were his very destination.

Ahab. Ahab! It was he, with his stern face and piercing black eyes. Ahab, with his open, crooked grin and possessive determination. Her Ahab. He had returned. Relief, happiness, joy, and desire combined to strike her dumb and immobile. Hysterical laughter froze in her throat. She trembled violently as he came nearer and halted before her.

"Hannah!"

And she was once again in his arms.

There was a fierceness in his love that night, a ravenous hunger as in a starving man who at last finds food. And so she fed him. But she hungered, too, and she demanded that he satisfy her as well. She had buried her memories of passion beneath the reality of recent sorrows. Now his burning kisses and possessive embrace resurrected those passions, reclaiming her body, refreshing her spirit, restoring her heart. After an explosive consummation of their pleasuring, she lay in his arms and wept while he murmured comforting words.

"Ah, my dear Hannah, this old whaler has never had a sweeter homecoming," he said, his voice husky. He touched her cheek and studied her in the dim candlelight. "Thy face has grown thinner, more womanly, I think. Yet I'm distressed that all thy sorrows have creased thy brow this way. To think that none of thy letters reached me, and I knew nothing of thy bereavement. Would to God that I could have spared thee thy suffering or at least consoled thee in thy grief."

She gazed up at him through her tears and caressed his face. His sun-bronzed complexion seemed devoid of lines. His dark eyes were lit from within by joy so transparent that she could not doubt his love. His hair and beard seemed blacker than ever in contrast to the stark white streaks blazing through them. And his scar … When they had last shared this bed, she had not noticed how far the lightning had wounded him during that long-ago midnight storm. Now she could see that the scar extended straight down from his face and neck, ending on his breast in a round pock just above his heart, the whole white line of it set startlingly against his sun-darkened skin like a mark of exclamation. She pressed her lips against the scar and gently moved her hands down the length of his body.

"Then you must console me now, my Ahab."

Chapter Nine

✍

*A*hab's pride in his beautiful young wife was rivaled only by his pride in his characteristically successful voyage. Despite their short time at sea, the crew of the *Sharona* had managed to fill the hold—and many other assorted spaces on the ship—with sperm and ivory. They had even been rewarded for their labors with more than forty-five pounds of rare ambergris. No one could dispute that Ahab was a brilliant captain and that his "greasy luck" was extraordinary. Therefore, the ship owners of New Bedford, Mr. Stuart in particular, were astonished and disappointed when Ahab refused another ship. No, he had informed them, he had no plans for another whaling voyage at present. After setting things in order at his Nantucket home, he and his bride would be sailing to Europe for a belated honeymoon.

Before they took the packet to Nantucket, however, he must complete all business regarding this last voyage and his other mainland investments. When the crewmen who unloaded the *Sharona* finished their job, all that remained was for them to remove their personal belongings before the ship went under repair for its next voyage. As the only one who was permitted to fully furnish his onboard quarters, Ahab had two sea chests and some other items to unload. With the help of two crewmen, he

lugged the chests home, storing them in one of the spare
bedrooms. He also insisted that Hannah replenish her wardrobe,
as she had not bothered to acquire any new clothing since before
her father's death. Sally and Kitty were engaged to make dresses
and petticoats, hats and coats, for the coming year of travel. This
great undertaking would require several weeks, but they were in
no hurry. After their long separation, Hannah and Ahab relished
the opportunity to learn more about each other. Spending that
time in New Bedford was as agreeable to both as Nantucket.

How little she knew her husband was brought home to
Hannah when they had their first misunderstanding less than a
week after his return. As the couple sat before their evening fire,
Ahab had chanced to mention that his housekeeper was an
excellent cook and would be the only staff they needed, considering their imminent journey. Hannah, feeling that she could
not do without Mrs. Randolph, had taken it for granted that this
last remnant of her childhood nurturing would continue to serve
them in Nantucket.

Her entreaties and sincere tears at his announcement had
brought from him a frown, a calm remark that his decision was
final, and some focused attention on cleaning his pipe. For the
remainder of the evening, Hannah brooded in silence over the
situation. Of course it made no sense to take the older woman to
the island only to leave her there in a few months. But she could
not accept Ahab's assuming authority over her realm of responsibility or his dismissal of the matter, especially after she had
cried. Not given to tearful ruses for the sake of manipulating
others, she nonetheless would have been pleased to see him
moved a little.

Mrs. Randolph unknowingly solved the dilemma when she
approached the younger woman a few days later and expressed
her desire to live with Sally and Aaron to assist with their

coming baby. She would, of course, stay with her employers until they moved to Nantucket. Hannah received her friend's resignation, albeit with regret. But though she put on a happy countenance for her husband, it was several days before she could surrender her hurt feelings over his behavior. She loved him beyond all words of expression, yet his authoritarian behavior, while appropriate and indeed essential when shipboard, simply would not do in their marriage. How could she make him understand that?

If Ahab was aware of her heartache, he made no mention of it. As they took daily walks about town, however, he would point out a pretty parasol or beaded reticule in some shop window, and he seemed surprised when Hannah showed no interest. During their evenings beside the parlor fire, he spoke of the exotic ports the ship had visited for supplies, and he referred to the gifts bought by some of the men for those at home. He commented on the exquisite scrimshaw many of the crewmembers had carved from whalebone for their loved ones, lamenting that he had never taken up that seaman's hobby and therefore had no such artwork to present to her.

"A carved jewel box, perhaps, or a busk for thy corset, or a bodkin for thine embroidery. Even an ivory candlestick or lantern to hold our bedside candles. What thinkest thou, my dear? What would delight thy heart?"

Hannah glanced up from her embroidery, and was struck by the expression in his eyes. He seemed eager to please her. Perhaps this was his way of making amends to her for his peremptory behavior. With a smile, she put down her stitching and went to sit on his lap. Looping her arms around his neck, she kissed him tenderly. "I have no wish for anything other than what I already have. You came home to me safe and sound. That delights my heart. You are my gift, my love, and I will never let you go."

He chuckled. "Ah, my dear wife, thy loving words spoken in private warm my heart. But when thou findest thyself with other women, wouldest thou not like to exhibit what thy husband hath brought thee?"

"And if he has brought me a more elegant gift than all the rest, does that make me a woman more worthy of love? Or does it prove that he is more loving than the other men? I fear that such a display would actually demonstrate a very shallow love."

He gazed at her with such warmth and, it seemed, gratitude as well, that her heart was stirred. He stroked her cheek, careful not to scratch her delicate skin with his sea-roughened hands. "Such a sentiment is all that any man could ask for, to be loved not for what he giveth but rather for who he is." He sat back and stared into her eyes, wrinkling his brow thoughtfully. "But wouldest thou despise a humble gift from a devoted heart?"

Hannah sighed with gentle impatience. "I would never despise your gifts, humble or grand. The value of the gift is the love that prompts its being given."

It was his turn to sigh with exasperation. "Wife, I confess I am unused to giving gifts to women. I know not what to give nor how to give it. I would give thee the world if I could. And indeed I will soon enough. But for now, wilt thou accept what I have brought thee or not?"

His annoyance explained it all. He had been trying to coax her into demanding a present, like a child on its birthday. Indifferent as she was to receiving a gift, he was nonetheless passionate in wanting to bestow one. Now perhaps she had spoiled his delight in giving.

"Oh," she cried, exerting what enthusiasm she could. "Did you bring me something, then? I thought we were speaking in concept only."

He shook his head, but smiled. "Hannah, Hannah, belay this attempt to fool thy old husband. If thou hast no wish to—"

"Stop teasing," she said with a giggle. "What did you bring me, and where is it?"

"Nay, nay. I would not wish to burden thee with my gifts."

"Oh!" She stood and stamped her foot, then held out her hand. "Give me the key to your trunk. I want it now!"

Laughing, he grasped her wrist and pulled her back down on his lap, then held her close and murmured in her ear. "Oh, God, how I missed thee all these long months and years, Hannah. There were times when I thought our marriage to be all a dream. Then there were times when I thought I had done a great evil to marry thee, then leave thee alone, a bride and yet a widow."

"Not to have married me would have been the evil thing. But now all the loneliness of my waiting has been forgotten in the happiness I feel. Dearest love, kiss me again so that I may truly believe that you're here in my arms."

Ahab complied with her request, kissing her again and again until she knew and felt in every particle of her being that he had in fact returned to her.

It was not until the next morning that he opened his sea trunk and presented her with several bolts of colorful Chinese silk and a Jade necklace, with earrings and bracelet to match. Her heartfelt astonishment at the beauty and value of his choices proved to his satisfaction how much she appreciated them. In return, she presented him with the sixteen-dollar gold piece from Ecuador. Pleased with the unusual and unexpected gift, he studied the design of the coin for some time before placing it in his trouser pocket, which place he stated would now be its permanent home.

Despite this pleasant diffusion of their misunderstanding, Hannah still felt discouraged that Ahab made all their decisions.

He sometimes asked her opinion, but only after he had made whatever arrangements a situation required. Further, after she proudly told him of her investment in Aaron Mathes's workshop, he laughed.

"My dear little Hannah, such charity is not an investment. A true investment brings thee a return of money over and above what thou hast put in. This was merely a gift to thy friends. For as handy as Mr. Mathes may be, he will never derive enough income from his work to care for his family and pay thee dividends as well. Thou wouldest not wish him to pay thee money and leave his own family destitute, wouldest thou?"

His words had stung less than his condescending attitude.

"No, of course not. But what shall I do then? I have no idea where to invest my money." She tried not to pout as she said it.

"Why, I will manage it for thee, my dear. I had already planned to do so. Unlike the women of Nantucket, thou hast had no financial training. Wisdom in these matters comes over time."

Though relieved that she would no longer have to worry about her money, Hannah was dismayed at his autocratic behavior, a behavior that extended to all their activities. Having always planned her own days, she now found herself required to keep Ahab company on every venture. She loved to be with him and was pleased that her presence was important to him, but it was beginning to exhaust her. As the days went by, he seemed to be walking faster. Despite her height, his longer stride obliged her almost to run in order to keep pace with him.

"Step lively, woman," he would say with a jolly laugh, seemingly unaware that her long skirts and petticoats—not to mention her dealing with her parasol—further made obedience to that order difficult. She could not bear to start an argument with him. Nor did she wish to dampen his enthusiasm. But she longed to gain some foothold of equality in decision making, even if only about the pace at which they walked.

On a bright morning in late April, when he had been home from his voyage for nearly six weeks, they took their usual daily walk up and down the hills of New Bedford. Hannah, who would be planting no flowers this year, wanted to stop and admire the blossoms breaking forth on numerous bushes about town. When Ahab continued his energetic stride despite her attempts to slow him, she slipped her arm free from his and paused to study a particularly lovely forsythia bush. He stopped and turned back in surprise.

"Come along, my dear." His tone was cheerful, but it was clearly an order.

"No, my love. You go on. I wish to stroll this morning and enjoy the flowers."

He frowned briefly, then walked to her side and said in a pleasant tone, "The flowers can be enjoyed another time. Thou needest thy exercise after a long winter indoors."

She bent closer to the bush as if to smell the blossoms, though of course forsythia have no fragrance. "Hmm. Lovely."

"Come along, Hannah." His tone was firm. "I am concerned about thy health in view of our coming travels. A vigorous walk in the fresh air each day will improve thy stamina."

She gave him a sidelong glance from beneath her parasol, then resumed her study of the flowers. "Do you realize how ridiculous I look having to practically run to keep up with you? Not that I care for the opinions of others, but you're exhausting me. Rather than increasing my stamina, I get more tired every day." If they had been in a more private place, she would have added that her corset constricted her breathing almost to the point of strangulation.

When he did not respond, she glanced up at him and was surprised at the tender concern in his eyes.

"A slower gait, then, my dear. I must recall that thou lackest the hardiness of Nantucket women. Yet methinks with practice thou canst increase thy pace."

From that time, he took an early morning walk at his own pace, then accompanied her on her daily stroll. His consideration endeared him to her even more than ever, and she decided that all her concerns had been for naught.

In turn, she had an opportunity to set his mind at ease. One evening, he looked up from reading the *Morning Register* to casually inquire about "that young Reverend Harris." Hannah kept her eyes on her embroidery as she just as casually remarked that Jeremiah had left town the same day as he, and that neither she nor her father had ever heard from him. Ahab gave a grunt of satisfaction and resumed his reading. She wondered what had prompted the question, but decided not to ask him, lest another misunderstanding arise.

By the middle of May, Ahab's mainland business was concluded, and Hannah's new wardrobe was finished. Arrangements were made for the shipment of Mr. Oldweiler's library to Nantucket, along with some rose bush clippings. When Hannah made a trip to her old house, she was surprised to see that its pristine white exterior had all been painted pale blue. It seemed an odd choice for Greek Revival architecture, but Lila would have blue. The landscaping was also being redesigned, truly making the place no longer her home. After a final visit to her father's grave and tearful farewells to Mrs. Randolph and her family, she was free from every former tie. In happy anticipation of her new life, she accompanied her husband to a small Nantucket-bound packet schooner moored at the New Bedford wharf.

It had not occurred to Hannah to tell Ahab that she had never been on a boat of any kind. Her father had always feared so much for her safety that he had sheltered her not only from the docks but from everything that had to do with the ocean, even excursion boats. Now that she was walking up the gangplank to board the *Moss*, however, the prospect of actually being out on the water began to unnerve her. Her husband did not fail to notice her hesitation. As they boarded the sturdy little schooner, he put a reassuring arm around her waist. Then he found her a comfortable place to sit among the motley group of passengers. She watched in amazement as he stood nearby, his hands in his pockets, not bothering to steady himself by gripping railing or post, despite the vessel's pitch and roll in the choppy waters.

As sails were hoisted and the *Moss* glided down the Acushnet River, Hannah gazed up at New Bedford's terraced landscape. Flowers and trees were in full bloom, and it seemed to Hannah that they were waving their good-byes to her in the soft spring breeze. Shortly, however, her focus was diverted to some uncomfortable feelings in her stomach. Despite her excitement over their coming adventure, she had devoured a hearty breakfast, which now threatened to repay her in a most unpleasant way. She laid her head back against her chair and held her breath. It only made matters worse. To add to her misery, when she looked to Ahab for sympathy, he seemed amused at her distress.

"My dear, thou wilt have need to adjust to the ship's motion if we're to sail for Europe in the fall. Come, let's take a stroll around the deck and strengthen thy sea legs."

Standing up did not alleviate her queasiness. As Ahab tried to steer her around the deck, she made it known to him through indistinct and clumsy gestures that she felt an urgent need to seek the railing. As the warm May sun beat down upon her, she struggled to shield herself from its rays with her parasol while eliminating the source of her stomach's discontent. One job superseded the other in importance, and she was dismayed to see the parasol descend into the churning sea foam along with her breakfast.

Resting once more in her chair, she sipped with reluctance the ginger tea—provided by the boat captain's wife—that Ahab pressed her to drink. But as the aromatic liquid slid down her throat and appeased the raging of her inward parts, she was once more aware of her husband's ability to solve any problem. She gave him an apologetic smile to reward him for his wisdom and patience.

"Never mind, my dear," he said. "I'll buy thee a fine new parasol. That was an old one and due to be replaced."

His gentle tone warmed her heart far more than his words. She would not tell him that the old parasol had been a gift from her father and, therefore, could never be replaced.

After several hours, she forced herself to stand by the railing again. There, leaning against Ahab with his strong arm supporting her, she watched the port of Nantucket come into sight. How she had longed for this day. At a distance the island seemed flat, a stark contrast to New Bedford's terraced hills. For a moment, she wondered if the island's heavily vegetated heathlands might come to bore her. On further inspection, however, she saw that the land beyond the harbor was higher and had more hills than she had been led to believe. But whatever the landscape, it was enough that Ahab had been born here on these very shores and from here he had embarked on countless voyages. Here she would meet all his friends and live as mistress in his house. And after their upcoming voyage, it was here where she would spend the rest of her life making him happy.

After they had disembarked from the *Moss*, Ahab arranged for their baggage to be brought to his house. Scorning the horse-drawn hacks available for hire, the couple walked from the harbor up Main Street, passing several blocks of whaling supply stores. Turning south, they walked the long block to Ahab's sturdy, two-story house, which was located at the highest point on Orange Street among numerous other houses owned by whaling captains.

The house was much larger than their rented cottage, but smaller than Hannah's childhood home. The house front was white clapboard, freshly painted in anticipation of Ahab's homecoming. The sides of the house were covered by gray shingles with white trim and shutters around each window. Inside, the downstairs consisted of an entry hall, a large parlor on the north side of the entry, a small parlor on the south side, an elegant dining room, a kitchen, and a bedchamber for the housekeeper. One large chimney stood in the center of the house. Imposing fireplaces warmed the north parlor and dining rooms and had their counterparts directly above in the master bedroom suite on the second floor. Each floor could be paced in a circle through the rooms and hallways that surrounded the chimney. The narrow, square stairway was protected by a heavy oak balustrade. From the first landing, the stairs descended in one direction to a small hallway leading to the kitchen and in the other direction to the hall outside the parlor. Upstairs was the master suite, which consisted of two rooms: the large bedroom and a sitting room that also served as Ahab's library. The door to the attic stairs and roof walk was across the hall from the suite. Finally, there were three smaller bedchambers, one of which had a door leading to an outside staircase.

Every item in every room—whether chair, bed, table, carpet, drapery, or candlestick—was like new. The elegant china bore no chip, the freshly polished silver no patina. Neither was there a trace of lace or brocade in the house. It was clearly the residence of a bachelor who had spent less than two years out of the past thirty-six in homeport. While he had purchased the finest furnishings, as befitted a prosperous whaling captain, there was a noticeable starkness to the house of which even its owner was aware. When he carried Hannah across this second threshold and set her down in the center of the north parlor, he exclaimed, "Ah, at last. This house now has a light brighter than any lamp or candle."

Chapter Ten

ʬ

*H*annah's first encounter with the housekeeper was less than felicitous. After Ahab had set his bride down in the north parlor, she had spun herself about in excitement to take in the details of her new home. Unaware that the woman had appeared like a shadow to greet them, she had slammed into the servant, who stood firm while Hannah fell back into her husband's arms with a cry of surprise. Feeling like a foolish child, she stammered her apologies before remembering her position and her dignity.

Ahab calmly introduced Abigail to her as though nothing had happened, but to Hannah it seemed that Abigail's eyes bespoke disapproval. Further, the woman was not at all what she had imagined from Ahab's description of "his old housekeeper."

Almost six feet tall and somewhere near Ahab in years, she possessed that same ageless quality as he. Her eyes were dark and comely, and she had inherited the slender grace and handsome countenance of her mother's people, the Indians of Gay Head, on Martha's Vineyard. Perhaps it was her ancestry that fused Ahab's loyalty to her, for some of those indigenous people who had lived for years on Nantucket Island had had much to do with his upbringing. But it was the woman's easy manners with him that bothered Hannah at present. He touched the woman's arm, with only his eyes seeming to smile, and they spoke together quietly, familiarly, as if … as if what? Hannah was slow to dislike people, but Abigail made her more than a little uncomfortable.

On that first night in Nantucket, Hannah suggested to her husband that he give Abigail a pension, after the custom of English lords, so that the faithful old servant might retire from her labors. Ahab stared at her as if she were a stranger. Then, in a severe tone she had not heard before, he instructed her never to make that request again. All the joy of her new home vanished. She sat at the foot of the bed, hugging the bedpost and staring at the floor. How could he be so cruel? He could release her servant but refuse to allow her the same privilege with his. Should they not be starting their household afresh, with new servants? Who was this woman to him that he would deny his wife her wish? And how could he speak to his wife as if she were a disobedient member of his crew?

"Turn in, wife. Our little cruise has wearied thee." He put out the oil lamp beside the bed and settled beneath the covers.

She bristled that he could dismiss her concerns with such ease. No, she would not "turn in." She went to the window and stared out into the night. Despite the brightness of the rising moon, the spacious lawn behind the house was shrouded in darkness … just like her new life … just like her marriage. In truth, she knew nothing about Ahab, his island, or his friends. Her dim reflection in the glass revealed the pout on her lips, but even that seemed fitting. A childish expression on the face of a woman who was being treated like a child by her husband.

She heard him stir, and her spine stiffened. Would he try to appease her with a loving embrace? If so, she would refuse him. She would not be reconciled to him until he listened to her concerns. But he did not come to her. Soon weariness began to overtake her, and she wondered if she should try to sleep in another room. Even the divan in the sitting room seemed preferable to lying beside him. But it proved too short for comfortable sleeping. Without lighting a candle, she could not wander about this unfamiliar house to find a bed. Reluctantly, she felt her way back to the large four-poster and slipped beneath the covers.

"She will do thy bidding. I will see to it." His tone was patient, even kind. He was meeting her halfway. But she could not respond without tears, so she stared into the darkness until sleep overtook her.

A residue of seasickness made it difficult for Hannah to get out of bed the next morning. She was not helped by Ahab's enthusiasm at the prospect of introducing his bride to his friends. When she grumbled that it would have to be put off until another day, he laughed and instructed her to "turn out to meet the day." It was not until she proved her point through her body's involuntary rejection of breakfast—ginger tea notwithstanding—that he relented. He set off by himself to renew old acquaintances.

By afternoon, her health seemed restored, but her spirits were still depressed, for Ahab had not returned. Abigail's quiet attention to housekeeping seemed a rebuke to Hannah's idleness, something Mrs. Randolph's duties had never been. After preparing a large breakfast, the woman had unpacked Hannah's trunk, placing her dresses and accessories in the bedroom wardrobe in an orderly fashion. She had dusted and swept where needed. And she had prepared a luncheon broth, which alleviated Hannah's abdominal ills.

Early that afternoon, Hannah received two visitors: Mrs. Charity Coffin, a middle-aged Quakeress, and her young daughter Kerenhappuch. Aunt Charity, as the widow insisted on being addressed, was a lean woman of medium height and indefatigable spirit. Though her face appeared severe in repose (it was seldom in repose), her cheerful nature was evident in her eyes and smile. Kerenhappuch, a slender, pretty girl of sixteen, was not as outgoing as her mother, but her sweet temper was equally evident in her countenance.

Hannah noticed that Aunt Charity had a way of intruding into people's lives without offending in the slightest way. She had come on a mission to welcome the new resident and to ensure that the notorious, albeit well-liked Captain Ahab was treating his young bride properly. Within minutes of taking her chair in Hannah's parlor, she had ascertained the tension between her hostess and the woman who served them tea. Once Abigail left the room, Aunt Charity leaned toward Hannah and informed her that there was no finer housekeeper on the island than this Gay Head woman, or any friend more reliable in time of need.

"Never mind those astonishing eyes of hers, Mrs. Ahab. Though they seem to bore into the very center of thy being, it's only her way of scrutinizing character. She means no harm, and her heart is in the right place. Now what's this thou hast gone and done by marrying our Captain Ahab?"

Her tone was so pleasant and her face so congenial that Hannah was compelled to respond in kind. "Why, I just found the most splendid man available and claimed him as my own."

"Indeed, indeed," the Quakeress said. "Many a woman has set her cap for that one without success. I suppose the time was ripe for a pretty young thing such as thee to snap him up. He came back sorely wearied by his last voyage out of Nantucket. I suppose he told thee of his travails off Cape Horn some three and a half or four years ago when God so mercifully spared him?"

"Yes, he told me of his illness," Hannah replied, leaving out that Ahab had given no credit to God for his recovery, but rather, felt that he had withstood God's attempt to take his life. "He had a dreadful fever and nearly died. He took a long time to recover, during which he pondered the sum of his life. He decided to make some changes, if only to ship from New Bedford rather than Nantucket. He had no idea that marriage was also in store for him in my hometown."

"How didst thou meet him, Mrs. Ahab?" Kerenhappuch asked with eager curiosity.

"Through a friend. Why do you ask?" She smiled at the girl's sudden courage to speak.

"Oh, thou must forgive my daughter. She is determined to hear every story of fair love won. Methinks she is overeager, in fact, to find her own true love, while her poor mother longs to hold this last child at home." Aunt Charity was laughing at both her own and her daughter's foibles.

"Well, then, Miss Kerenhappuch, I will tell you the whole tale," Hannah said, enjoying this woman-to-woman conversation as she never had with her old friends at home. "My dear friend from childhood, Reverend Jeremiah Harris, was seeking my father's and my assistance in ministering to a certain whaling captain. The two gentlemen were invited to supper, and in a very short time, I became Mrs. Ahab."

Both guests started at the mention of Jeremiah.

"Could this be the young pastor newly come to Nantucket that introduced thee?" Aunt Charity asked.

It was Hannah's turn to be startled. "Jeremiah here?"

"The new pastor of the First Congregational Church is a young man named Jeremiah Harris of New Bedford," the woman responded. "Thou understandest, of course, that we Friends do not make use of titles of position or rank, but those in his church call him Reverend Harris."

Kerenhappuch nodded with enthusiasm, her eyes so wide with admiration for the party being discussed that Hannah could hardly refrain from laughing. If Jeremiah truly was here, this young woman was probably just one of many Nantucket maidens whose eyes were lighted by the mention of his name. But more than that, the prospect of seeing her old friend brought great joy to Hannah's heart. She quickly stifled it. This innocent Christian girl's open esteem indicated that he was still unmarried. How would Ahab react to his presence in Nantucket? Hannah harnessed her haphazard thoughts and declared that if this pastor was indeed their old friend, it would be a pleasure for both her husband and her to renew his acquaintance.

After her two guests left, Hannah felt a flurry of confused emotions. She could not deny that the possibility of Jeremiah being in Nantucket was thrilling. She longed to know where he had been for the past two and a half years. And, of course, he would want to know about her father's death. Yet because he had loved her and lost, she was not so certain that he would wish to see her. Did he still love her? Could he face her without pain? Moreover, the potentiality of inciting jealousy in her husband further tempered her eagerness. Still, should she be denied the connection to her childhood that Jeremiah's friendship would provide?

In a moment of annoyance, she thought of Ahab's lifelong association with Abigail. Her own relationship with Jeremiah had been completely innocent. Would she discover one day that Ahab and Abigail's had not been so? After all, for many years before Hannah's marriage to him, her husband had been a man of the world.

Her musings were interrupted by Ahab's noisy entrance. "Hannah, my dear, look whom I've brought to see thee." He pulled into the parlor a somewhat reluctant Reverend Harris.

In a matter of seconds, Jeremiah's face told Hannah what she wished to know. Hesitant at first, he had to force himself to look straight at her, as though he feared his own feelings. But as his eyes met hers, they glowed with all of his characteristic gentleness and affection, yet without any of his former ardor. He seemed to breathe a small sigh of relief, and with a boyish grin, he stepped forward and grasped her hands.

"Hannah, it's so good to see you. You look wonderful. More lovely than ever." His smile was true, his tone cheerful. "I can see that marriage agrees with you."

She glanced beyond him at Ahab. His expression was almost inscrutable, but not quite. A brief flicker of triumph was followed by a satisfied smile, which dissolved into bland composure. The changes were so quick that she almost missed them. Yet his bringing Jeremiah for this confrontation and his reaction to seeing them together seemed to put everything in place for him.

"Jeremiah, how wonderful to see you." She squeezed his hands and gazed at him. "And what a wonderful surprise to find out that you're ministering in a church here in Nantucket. Mrs. Charity Coffin informed me only this afternoon."

"Are you surprised? I thought you might have seen the notice in New Bedford's *Morning Register*."

Hannah once again glanced at Ahab, but his face was a mask. At least she now understood what had prompted his question about Jeremiah those long weeks ago. "No, I must have missed it."

"Ah, Hannah how good it is to see you looking so well. You can imagine my astonishment when Captain Ahab came to see me this afternoon and invited me to supper." Jeremiah's brow wrinkled. "Please accept my condolences in your father's death. I could never hope to know a finer Christian man than he."

She nodded her thanks. Despite the sadness it invoked, the mention of her father seemed to change the atmosphere, making it possible for them all to feel more comfortable with one another.

Over supper, Jeremiah responded to all her inquiries regarding his disappearance. At the time in question, he had decided that life had been too easy for him. First growing up in his sheltered

New Bedford family. Then going whaling under the watchful eye
of his devout grandfather. Next attending conservative Andover
Seminary near Boston. And finally taking the position at his
own home church. Certain circumstances (here he cleared his
throat) had caused him to doubt his calling to the ministry and
even his ability to discern the will of God.

Deciding that he must see more of the world, he had gone to
New Orleans, not to serve in a church but to take on the challenge of working on a steamboat. He made several trips up and
down the Mississippi and Missouri Rivers in the company of men
who had not been raised in Christian communities. That opened
his eyes to their view of life. He could now return home confident in his new understanding and more able to minister to those
of different upbringings. Of course the assistant pastor position
had been filled in his absence. But he was soon hired to fill the
pulpit of the First Congregational Church in Nantucket.

As he talked, Hannah studied his face, making certain that she
glanced at her husband frequently and smiled. Jeremiah had
matured both in character and appearance. His face was leaner
and more tanned, and he had grown a beard and mustache.
There was even a small, jagged scar on his left cheek. When
Hannah asked him about it, he admitted with some embarrassment to participating in a "rather nasty fight." Though he promised he had not struck first, he did admit to having found cause
to repay his opponent.

Ahab laughed heartily. "Merely self-defense, of course. Thou
didst nothing to warrant it."

Jeremiah shrugged and grinned sheepishly. "After a strenuous
day of labor, I found myself provoked by a certain, eh,
gentleman's remarks over ... well, never mind over what. In any
event, I responded with an ill-advised comment to which he
likewise took exception, demonstrating his feelings in a rather

forceful manner." He touched his scar, shrugging again. "Then, of course, I felt it necessary to give back a portion of that which I had so generously been served."

"Jeremiah, how could you?" Hannah cried.

"Oh, don't be alarmed. At the end of it all, we became fast friends."

Ahab laughed in appreciation of the story. "Thou wilt do well in Nantucket, Parson. Thou wilt surely do well."

Hannah masked her horror over Jeremiah's admission of such uncharacteristic and violent behavior. These two men meant the world to her, each in his own way. To have their former ill will replaced by this new camaraderie brought her great peace of mind. She would overlook the foolish conduct that had helped to bring it about.

Hannah had always marveled at Ahab's determination to solve every problem and to conquer every adversary, even his own jealous nature. That night as they lay in bed, she realized from his mellow demeanor that he was no longer concerned about her lifelong friendship with Jeremiah. In return, she gave evidence of her own tenacity by stating that she would not rest until Jeremiah had married the lovely Miss Kerenhappuch—after giving the young lady another year or two to mature, of course.

"I think they would make a handsome couple. And I would love to see Kerenhappuch as happy with Jeremiah as I am with you." She snuggled close and with her finger traced his beard along his jaw line. "What do you think, my darling?"

He took her hand and began to kiss her fingertips, then her palm and wrist, moving his lips slowly up her arm. "I think that if thou wishest to be a matchmaker, there is precious little I can do to stop thee," he murmured as he kissed her shoulder.

"But ... but ..." Her breathing had become almost a pant. She was losing her ability to concentrate. "Don't you think ... don't you think ..."

He placed a finger over her lips and gazed at her in the dim evening light. "Methinks I have married Aphrodite." His kissing proceeded downward from her neck, and whatever they had been discussing no longer seemed important to Hannah.

Aunt Charity's visit had prompted in Hannah an eagerness to meet more of her new neighbors. The next morning, however, she was no more able to accomplish it than the previous day. Once again Ahab set off without her. When on her third morning in Nantucket she was still not able to arise without feeling ill, she suggested to him that there must be something in the island's night air that did not agree with her. He, on the other hand, expressed some annoyance at her malady.

"Thou must master these internal stirrings, my dear. Our voyage will be intolerable if thou givest in to every small complaint."

If she had been able to lift her head from her pillow without retching, she would have assured him that her complaint was not small. She could only gaze up at him in misery and let her eyes express her regrets over spoiling their day. She did not even possess the energy to be bothered by his words, but rather was pleased when he ceased harassing her and left for his morning walk. In a short while, she pulled herself up to a sitting position and tried to drink the ginger tea that Abigail had brought earlier. Despite being tepid, it seemed to soothe away most of her nausea.

With one ill eliminated, another took its place: bruised feelings. Why had Ahab been so harsh with her? She had never been one to complain or to take to a sick bed over trivialities. And she really had tried to get up these past three mornings. It had to be the night air of Nantucket, a miasma perhaps, just as she had told him. Otherwise, why would she feel so much better every after-noon? Besides, they could visit his friends later in the day just as well as mornings. He was being unreasonable and selfish, and she would tell him so as soon as he returned. That is, whenever he decided to grace their home with his presence.

In the middle of these thoughts, she heard the front door slam-ming and her husband's hurried footsteps on the staircase. She would have preferred to look more attractive during their confrontation, but she would manage despite her unbrushed hair and unwashed face. She was more than ready to scold him. But when Ahab threw open the bedroom door, his expression caught her off guard. Not since he had returned to her from his voyage had she seen such overwhelming adoration in his eyes. Somehow, however, instead of mollifying her, it increased her annoyance. If he planned to apologize, she would not easily forgive him.

"Hannah, my dear!"

He strode to the bed, sat beside her, and pulled her into his arms. Against her will, her head rested against his chest, but she still could not relent. She would make certain he could not ignore her displeasure.

"My dear," he murmured, "something has just occurred to me. Hast thou noticed that since my homecoming thou has not suffered thy monthly, eh, discomfort?"

She pulled back and looked up into his eyes. "I ... I hadn't thought of it, no. Why?"

He chuckled. "My innocent bride, knowest thou nothing of women's ways? Dost thou not know that these are the things that happen when a child is expected?"

She felt a renewed surge of anger at his patronizing manner. But in truth, she knew very little about what was involved in the arrival of children.

"No," she snapped. But in an instant, the possibility of imminent motherhood came home to her, and she gasped. "No, I didn't know. Am I … will we …?"

Ahab caressed her cheek, as he did in his most tender moments, and she now allowed herself to enjoy the light glowing in his eyes. "I would not wish to give thee false hope, for only time will tell the truth of it. But I suspect that by Christmastime, we will have a son."

A mixture of joy, fear, and amazement struck her heart. She pressed once more into his strong embrace, grasping him in return. As he stroked her back and brushed her hair with kisses, a gentle peace crept through her, along with a reaffirmation of her absolute trust in her husband. When she was in his arms, anger disappeared and their hearts seemed bonded by unconstrained devotion.

"Dear wife, thou hast already brought me more happiness than ever I expected or deserve in this life. For long, long years, my path has been so lonely. Then to find thee in my old age. Past fifty was I when we met, child. Perhaps to pursue thee was a great mischief, yet I won thy love despite thy tender youth. When I sit with thee at our hearthside, there is a contentment in my soul that I never knew to be possible. And now, that thou couldest give me a son in my old age heaps such happiness upon me that I scarcely know how to bear it."

She started to tease him that she might decide to give him a daughter. But when she saw a hint of tears in his eyes, her own eyes became moist. Ahab was not a man to speak of his deepest feelings this way. As they gazed at each other in this moment of joy, their souls seemed more tightly interwoven than ever before.

"Do you love me so very much, then, my Ahab?"

"Aye, my Hannah. Thou art my very life."

Chapter Eleven

&

When Ahab consulted with Abigail about Hannah's morning sickness, he was given a simple remedy: she must eat soda crackers with her ginger tea before rising. Although this settled the most disagreeable part of her condition, she still felt too weary to venture out until after her noon meal. Ahab was glad to readjust his routine, taking his own brisk walk in the early morning as usual, then later accompanying Hannah for her exercise. She would have preferred not to walk as much as he insisted, but their trips around Nantucket also provided her with the opportunity for socializing with his numerous friends.

Having been sheltered from New Bedford's whaling community by her father, Hannah had not been aware of the intricacies of its human relationships. But even if she had been familiar with the whalefishery and its people, she still had much to learn in Nantucket. This remote island was a society—and a world—within itself. Here she discovered that with hard work and good fortune, a boy from the poorest home could grow to be a wealthy captain or ship owner. Here Ahab had been raised, partly by the Gay Head Indian woman, Tistig, in whose care his dying mother had left him, and partly by generous Quakers who had seen to his education and religious instruction. Always mindful of his duty, he had attended college to demonstrate gratitude to his benefactors. Then at eighteen he had shipped his first whaling voyage as a harpooner. Though this position was usually reserved for more experienced men, his prodigious strength and accuracy soon had made him a legend.

Many whalers had come and gone from the island since Ahab's boyhood. And those who were of his generation more often than not had retired from the active hunt. Most had taken their profits and settled on some mainland farm or plied a trade in town or subsisted on investments made in others' ventures, for few could claim to equal Ahab's physical stamina and enduring good fortune. Then there were a few others whose financial success rivaled his who could not resist the lure of the sea and the wealth it produced. With a cry of "Just one time around Cape Horn," they would bid resigned wives and weeping children good-bye for another three or four years. For as long as the oldest inhabitants could recall, women outnumbered the men on Nantucket Island by four to one. When Hannah heard some of their tragic stories, she was grateful that her husband would never go whaling again.

Among her favorite new friends were, of course, Aunt Charity and Kerenhappuch. She was soon introduced to Charity's brother and Ahab's old acquaintance, Captain Bildad. Bildad had not been to sea for some years, but he still retained his title and owned several whaling ships. A tall, gaunt, severe, and apparently righteous man, he and his wife were leading members of the strict orthodox Quaker faction of the divided denomination. Aunt Charity, who leaned more toward the Hicksite views, had little patience for the church schism. She simply went about her labors of Christian charity, which her name so appropriately prophesied of her. It was her custom to stock her brother's ships with homemade treats such as ginger-jub to reward any successful harpooner and yet keep him sober for his next lowering. To minister to each man's soul and to further demonstrate her liberal Quaker views, she placed hymnbooks and tracts by the Congregationalist Isaac Watts on every berth. And she carried on board with her own hands other homey items to encourage the crew of any ship belonging to her beloved brother Bildad, and in which she herself had invested a few dollars. This aggressive kindness and open-mindedness endeared the woman to Hannah.

Aunt Charity was not the only Nantucket woman who visited the house on Orange Street to plumb the mystery of Captain Ahab's choosing an off-island bride. Without exception, every woman who called left satisfied that their native son had chosen well. Several indicated that she was welcome to join their particular circle of friends. Ahab assured her that it was not his reputation but rather her own charming ways that had merited these invitations.

Hannah felt especially privileged to be accepted into the society of Mr. and Mrs. Joseph Starbuck and the couple's many children and grandchildren. Mr. Starbuck was a Nantucket ship owner and visionary who, in addition to his business ventures, had recently completed building three stately brick homes on upper Main Street for his three sons, the first brick homes on the island. Although the senior Mrs. Starbuck was not in the best of health, she did not let that prevent her from attending book reading and music groups in the new homes of her daughters-in-law. At last Hannah had found women whose intellectual interests were similar to hers. And Ahab took pride in his young wife being named a part of Mrs. Joseph Starbuck's circle.

Pleasant afternoons drinking tea with the ladies gave Hannah an appreciation for the company of other women that she had overlooked when she was younger. She also discovered that most of the women of Nantucket were more independent than her limited group of acquaintances in New Bedford. Many of them were required to manage both businesses and homes, as well as raise children, while their husbands were at sea. Therefore, not all of her new friends were wealthy.

While Hannah was welcomed by the people of Nantucket because she was the wife of one of their most successful whaling captains, she was also the subject of good-humored teasing any newcomer must endure. Nantucketers had their own language, with many unique expressions, and they often regarded off-islanders as somewhat ignorant when they did not get the drift of their conversations. Hannah had often heard Ahab use the word "gam" to mean a social visit, whether between ships at sea or friends on land. If people came for a visit, he would invite them into the house with "Come aboard." "Scud" meant to hurry. And, of course, "greasy luck" referred to a voyage that brought in a good cargo of whale oil. But though she was confounded by such everyday expressions as "astern the lighter," "splice the main brace," or "kettle halyards," Hannah could discern that when anyone said Mrs. Ahab had "sat in the butter tub," she knew it was a compliment of some sort, either to her or to her husband. And no one dared to call her a "coof," at least not in the hearing of the captain.

Ahab made a point of introducing her to the wife of Captain Stoddard, a former shipmate. Mrs. Stoddard ran a dry goods store in her husband's absence, and his employer, Mr. Lyons, saw to it that she had the best wares from Boston to sell. Like most other ship owners, Mr. Lyons made certain that his captain's wife did not go hungry while her husband took care of Mr. Lyons's ship. Ahab encouraged Hannah's friendship with the woman. With a troubled frown, he told Hannah, "Mrs. Stoddard is an off-islander like thee. She may require thy friendship some day." Though he offered no further explanation, Hannah sensed that if she were to meet Captain Stoddard, she would not care for him.

Hannah saw nothing unusual in her husband's introducing her to his acquaintances. In New Bedford, it had been the custom of women to become friends with the wives of their husbands' associates. In the isolated community of Nantucket, however, it was the women who formed the social circles, with their seldom-at-home husbands following them about to socialize when the men were in port. Therefore, in keeping with the Nantucket custom, Ahab endeavored to give Hannah every opportunity to choose her own friends.

His actions were in keeping with the Quaker tradition of equality that continued to influence Nantucket affairs long after that religion had ceased to be the dominant spiritual force. Nantucketers had a history of forming their own opinions apart from the mood of the rest of the country. Return visits by Nantucket natives and popular speakers Anna Gardner and Lucretia Mott made the island a seedbed for the abolition and woman's suffrage movements. And Maria Mitchell, who was only two years older than Hannah, enjoyed her father's encouragement in her studies of astronomy and mathematics.

With these examples before her and with a view toward their impending trip, Hannah revived her own favorite studies of European history. She visited the Atheneum Library, perusing maps and travel journals. She felt that she had to make arrangements around the baby's arrival so that they would miss none of the historic sites she had longed to visit since childhood. When they sailed to England in late September, they would be able to see numerous points of interest and still be comfortably settled in London long before Christmas. There they could await the child's arrival and be assured of care from the best doctors.

Before the trip, some of her wardrobe would have to be altered to accommodate the anticipated expansion of her figure. But there was no shortage of hard-working women in Nantucket to take on such a well-paying job for the wife of Captain Ahab.

Not all of Hannah's socializing was in Nantucket town. In June, Ahab rented a horse and buggy to take her for the three-mile drive to the island's annual sheep shearing at Miacomet Pond. The three-day event brought throngs of people from all over the island and even from the mainland. The widely varied assemblage included members of other cultures within the whalefishery, such as Chinese, Portuguese, South Pacific islanders, Africans, and many others. Following the primary activity of shearing some fifteen thousand sheep, music, games, and feasting abounded, with each of the diverse groups finding entertainment within its own enclave. To Hannah, who had never seen such an event or so many different races of mankind, it seemed like bedlam. To Ahab, it was a cause of great celebration, for he had seldom been home to enjoy the festivities. As with everything else, he took great pleasure in introducing Hannah to the new experience, as well as showing off his beautiful young wife.

In addition to visiting with Ahab's old friends and making new acquaintances, they ate mutton and oysters, smoked eels and codfish, puddings and pies, washing it all down with flagons of lemonade. Ahab tried his hand at the dice table for a short while, but quit in deference to Hannah's wandering gaze. When a dance platform was laid down and a small band of musicians struck up a lively jig, he grasped her still slender waist and spun her around in time to the music until, with breathless laughter, she begged for mercy.

It was she who took the lead for their next activity. Seeing a fortune-teller sitting in a small tent on the outskirts of the other activities, she insisted they have their fortunes told. Ahab agreed to the exercise with indifference. He'd had his fortune told many times before, always with the same results. The prognosticator would make dire predictions of doom for him, and Ahab's good fortune would invariably increase. Rather than hold to the customary superstitions of most whalers, which superstitions were held even by those seafarers of strong religious beliefs, he had little regard for such foolishness.

On land, his view was the one most accepted, especially among churchgoers, though not because he was counted among their numbers. Although the power of the Quaker religion was waning on Nantucket, other denominations flourished. In every church, fortune-telling was denounced. But with the influx of people from different cultures, different customs also arrived. Though righteous citizens might decry the seers, those enterprising individuals would claim it was all a game and thereby avoid being driven off the island.

Hannah had never seen a fortune-teller before, nor did she believe one could indeed see the future. But she felt compelled to needle her husband for his insistence that their child would be a boy. "Why must it be a son? May I not have a daughter to dress in frills and spoil with trinkets?" she said with a laugh. "That old woman over there will set you straight, husband." She dragged him to the shady booth where a gray-haired Portuguese woman sat reading palms.

After paying a generous amount of silver to the woman, Hannah lifted her hand to be read. The crone studied its lines, nodding with approval.

"You have long lifeline, pretty lady," she croaked. "There be times of happiness and times of sorrow. Three great joys to lift you to ecstasy. Two great sorrows to tear your soul. No more to tell you."

"But what of my child?" Hannah asked, dismissing such a vague forecast for her life. After all, every person had joys and sorrows. The woman was an obvious fraud if she did not even know Hannah was expecting. "What of my daughter?" She gave Ahab an impish grin.

"Ah." The woman waved her hand impatiently. "It is boy, of course."

Hannah frowned and would have pressed her for more information, but the woman stared up at Ahab. "Now you."

She reached for his hand, but he shook his head. "I've had enough of prophesies."

"Oh, dearest, do play," Hannah begged. He complied with reluctance.

As she studied his callused palm, the woman's face contorted in sympathetic spasms. "Oooh," she moaned, "there is pain here. So much pain. As you have done to others, it shall be done to you, and more so. You think you escape old prophecies by making new life, but old life pull you back hard. You laugh at prophecy, but one day you see. You see then."

"Stop it, you old witch!" Hannah hissed. She grasped Ahab's arm and pulled him away from the booth. "What a dreadful woman. I'm sorry for making you do that."

"Never mind, my dear," he chuckled. "Perhaps we will have a daughter after all."

"But …" She started to tell him that it was his fortune she was protesting. But when his eyes met hers, the light therein told her there was nothing to fear, and she laughed with him.

On the trip back to town, Hannah chattered about what fun it all had been. "You never cease to surprise me, my love. To think that you can dance such a merry jig. Will you be able to dance something a little more refined when we're in London?"

"I think with our delay I will have plenty of time to learn. What fancy steps are being executed by the gentry these days?"

"Delay?" she asked, not hearing past his first few words. "What do you mean 'delay'? Are we not leaving in September?"

"Why, no, of course not, my dear. Thy condition prohibits such rigorous travel. I thought thou wouldest realize it. It will be some time before we can plan to—"

"No. Don't be silly. I'll be fine. I'm already over my morning sickness, and my energy has returned. Why should we delay?"

He grew quiet and seemed to direct all his thoughts toward the uneven road ahead so as to rein the horse around holes and rocks. She did not fail to notice, though, that his chin lifted ever so slightly and his shoulders straightened by an almost imperceptible degree, as they did only when he was implacable. Her heart felt as though it had been struck. She stared out across the grassy plain, trying to think of some way to soften his resolve. Petulance was deceitful and would never work with him anyway. Angry words always reinforced his silence. Beside that, her disappointment was so profound that she felt more hurt than angry.

"Ahab," she whispered, praying that she would not cry.

"Aye." His tone was flat.

"Will there ever be a time when you listen to what I want? A time when you honor my requests?"

He continued to stare at the road. "Aye. When thou hast seen enough of life to make wise decisions."

But if I never go anywhere, how can I see anything of life? If I'm not permitted to make decisions, how can I become wise? Her thoughts screamed inside her head, but she could only ride in silence. Just as he now guided the horse over the country road, he steered the course of their marriage. She was only a passenger.

Presently, he reached out and pulled her close to his side, kissing her forehead. "'Tis for the best, Hannah. Thou must trust me."

Only Hannah seemed to regard the postponement of their voyage as a tragedy. Aunt Charity declared that she had prayed for the delay on account of the baby. Mrs. Starbuck observed that Captain Ahab could always be relied upon to make the wisest decisions. Kerenhappuch confessed her desire to assist with the infant's care from the moment of birth, as she had with numerous other babies since her own childhood. But it was not until Ahab began to talk of a spring departure that she could welcome him back into the secrets of her soul.

In mid-summer, she began to feel the reality of her coming motherhood. One day, when she was struggling to lace her corset over her expanding waist, Ahab instructed her to dispense with it for the sake of the growing baby. For once, his autocratic tone brought forth a giggle of relief. She tossed the uncomfortable garment into the back of her wardrobe with a vague and futile hope that by the time her child came, corsets would no longer be in fashion.

Another day, as she lay on her bed on her stomach watching Ahab dress for his early morning walk, she felt a tiny movement inside her. Startled and a little frightened, she rolled over and pressed her hand against the spot. Ahab embraced her and did his own search for the cause of her concern. Though he could not find the object of his probing, he assured her that in the next several months there would be many more and much stronger stirrings, and that it was indeed a good thing.

With the help of Aunt Charity and Kerenhappuch, Hannah began to apply herself to the baby's practical needs. She purchased what items the local stores sold, but there were few of those. Some other mothers promised to pass along some barely used items to her. But as the wife of Captain Ahab she would be expected to provide an infant's wardrobe worthy of his wealth. She and her friends made patterns and hand-stitched baby clothes from the finest, softest cotton or knitted sweaters from Nantucket wool. When she arranged the little booties, gowns, and diapers in the nursery bureau, her heart overflowed with love for the tiny, unknown person growing inside her who would soon wear them. With Ahab's help, she found a good carpenter and ordered furniture to be made for the nursery. Then she had the room freshly painted.

She also involved herself with exterior changes. Like most Nantucket houses, Ahab's was set close to the street and had no front yard. In the back, however, the large, sloping, grassy lawn invited improvements. With a man-of-all-work hired to help her, Hannah set to work to accommodate the need. She begged clippings of flowering plants from neighbors who were pruning. In the fall, she would bury iris, tulip, and daffodil bulbs. A friend across town brought two chrysanthemum bushes to be transplanted. Hannah had set out her New Bedford rose bushes soon after their arrival, but just as with her other perennials, it was too late to expect them to bloom this summer. She talked Ahab into having a trellis built at the end of her garden for a new variety of climbing roses. And she planted annuals that, though started late, brought a rainbow of color. There were multi-colored sweet peas to adorn the white ship's rail fence, daisies to line the stone walkway, and marigolds to blossom in planters about the yard.

By late September, she had managed to diffuse her disappointment over the postponement of their trip through cultivating her new garden. She had never bothered to replace her white lace parasol, and veils had proved too cumbersome in her gardening chores. Though she wore a hooded bonnet, her once-ivory skin had become quite tan. No one, not even Ahab, seemed to notice. In Nantucket, many women did not bother with any form of umbrella.

Hannah tried to use her busyness in gardening, sewing, and socializing as an excuse to avoid the daily walks Ahab obliged her to take. Some days she was more successful than others. Yet once out the door, she always enjoyed herself. As they walked along the cobblestoned street, he would hold her elbow protectively, ready to catch her if she stumbled. Glancing up at him from time to time, she could see the pride in his face as he called out to acquaintances they passed along the way. Many of these friends commended the old captain for his luck in securing such a lovely bride and for his impending fatherhood. She was as proud of her popular husband as he was of her, though she could not understand why people called him old. Not only did his lightly lined face and black hair belie his age, his energy and enthusiasm for life outshone many young men half or a third his age.

As their third anniversary drew near, he still required her to walk, despite a chill in the October wind. One day, he showed mercy and shortened their usual route. They were only a block from their house on Orange Street when he stopped, his attention directed toward a tall, gray-haired woman striding toward them.

"Tishtega!" He hailed her, and the woman raised her hand to greet him in return. "Tishtega, this is my bride, Mrs. Ahab. Hannah, this is Tishtega. She is a full-blooded Gay Header from Martha's Vineyard. Nantucket's her home now. Her grandmother was my nursemaid, Tistig."

Hannah nodded politely. "How do you do, Tishtega."

The woman nodded a short greeting, but her eyes were on Hannah's abdomen. Without asking permission, she placed her long, bony fingers around the protruding belly and bent her ear close. Hannah gasped and tried to step back, but Ahab held her firmly in place.

"Tishtega is a midwife. She's delivered many a Nantucketer safely into his mother's arms, as her mother and grandmother did before her."

"Oh, how ... how nice." Hannah tried to engage her in eye contact, but the woman's attention was on the business at hand. Hannah glanced about her, dreading the thought that perhaps Mrs. Starbuck or Mrs. Coffin might see her being thus examined right here on the street.

When she had completed her poking, Tishtega ignored Hannah, looking instead into Ahab's questioning eyes. "In two and a half months you will have a son. He will be strong, like his father. She must walk more." She jerked her head in Hannah's direction, and then strode away, her long gray hair flowing freely behind her in the breeze.

"Well," Hannah said, "that was quite an experience."

"Thou must walk more, Hannah. It will affect the birthing." Ahab had resumed walking, almost pushing Hannah along beside him.

"But Dr. Gayer said I need more rest. Don't you think he's the one—"

"No."

Ahab lifted his chin and stared straight ahead, indicating that any argument would be futile. She would have to find another way to beg off these daily forced marches.

Though she resisted the exercise, she had taken to heart Ahab's assertion that she needed to see more of life. At every opportunity, she talked with Aunt Charity about the coming event. The older woman would explain what she could in all delicacy, then would assure her that nature had a way of taking care of itself. Of course Hannah had never seen a human birth, and her recollections of kittens and lambs on the farm were hazy, so Aunt Charity obtained permission to bring her along to her niece's confinement. It was the custom in Nantucket during times of lying-in that the women of the family would gather at the birth home to pray and to assist where needed. This was an opportune time for Hannah to see what would happen in her own near future.

In late October, as Hannah and Ahab sat by the evening fire in their parlor, Kerenhappuch made a brief stop on her way to Mrs. Coffin's delivery, then hurried away to assist in the birthing. But as Hannah prepared to follow, Ahab intervened.

"Thou mayest not attend, wife." His voice was calm, and he did not look up from his reading.

She stared at him. "Of course I can. How can I know what to expect if I haven't seen it happen? Why, even young Kerenhappuch will be there, and she isn't even married." She walked to the front entry and took her coat from the hall tree.

"Hannah!" His voice was stern, yet still he did not move.

She stood in the parlor doorway, watching in annoyance as he continued to peruse his book.

"Stow thy coat and come sit down."

She glared at him, flung the coat around her shoulders, and started toward the front door with her bonnet in hand. Before she could open it, he was at her side, gripping her arm firmly.

"Thou wilt not go," he growled.

Never before had his touch been devoid of gentleness nor his words so harsh. She could see in his eyes that he was struggling with his anger. Would he strike her? The question must have been written on her face, for his expression quickly softened.

"Hannah, thou must trust me," he muttered.

She jerked her arm free and flung down her bonnet and coat. "Oh, you are impossible!" she cried, and lumbered up the stairs to bed. It was not until the next afternoon that she learned that young Mrs. Coffin had died in childbirth.

"She was sickly, my dear. It would have given thee useless fears to watch her struggles."

"What of the child?"

"They were able to take it safely."

It was all he said, and his brooding silence precluded further questions. A few days later, however, the grieving Aunt Charity explained that Dr. Gayer had been forced to cut into the dead mother to save the child. Hannah shuddered in horror. Something similar had happened at her own birth, to her own mother. Was this what lay ahead for her? Seeing her distress, Charity stated that the fault did lie in her poor niece's weak constitution, just as Ahab had said. Hannah would do well, she declared, for she was strong and robust.

In bed that night, Hannah clung to her husband. In tearful whispers, she reaffirmed her trust in his wisdom and promised she would try not to argue with his decisions in the future.

Chapter Twelve

ஐ

When icy November winds began to sweep across the island, Ahab took pity on Hannah regarding their daily outdoor walks. He kept a watchful eye on the temperature, however, and if it was warm enough after their noon meal, he still would pull her out the door for a short stroll just at the time she was wishing for a nap. However, if bitter weather prohibited such an outing, he would walk her about the house several times a day, pacing through the circle of the rooms or up and down the stairs. She endured it with resignation, exhausted but trusting. Her reward came at night when he would fall asleep snuggled against her with his hand resting protectively on her belly. Despite her discomfort, she had never felt safer or more loved.

Weather did not prohibit Ahab from sallying forth each day to gam with his friends. In the company of Captain Bildad and his partner Captain Peleg, both former shipmates he had known all his life, he squandered many hours reminiscing about the glories of their youth. Bildad no longer sailed. But Peleg, retired for several years, had begun to speak of returning to the active part of their trade. After those visits, Ahab would return home with some newly recalled story of his past glories in the hunt of the whale or some escapade on foreign shores. It seemed to Hannah that with each story his thoughts seemed focused more and more on some unseen exultation in which she could have no part. He began to grow restless and spent hours on the roof walk, no matter what the weather. Back inside, he scanned his ocean charts and tinkered with his quadrant. To Hannah's dismay, his talk was all of whale hunting.

"Never mind, my dear," she said one evening, when his eyes seemed to gleam with too much nostalgia. "We'll be sailing soon enough. What would you think of our taking Kerenhappuch along with us as a nursemaid for the baby?"

He did not answer right away, but began to clean his pipe with more concentration than necessary. Something in his movements, or perhaps his expression, struck fear into her heart.

"I will need a nursemaid, you know. And Aunt Charity, for all her brother's wealth, has very little money. Kerenhappuch has cared for babies all her life and—"

"Aye," he muttered, "thou wilt need help. The girl will do for a nursemaid. We'll add a berth to the nursery for her."

Hannah studied his face, her stomach churning, but he would not meet her gaze. "And we should help with her wardrobe for the trip. We can't take a shabbily dressed nursemaid with us, can we?"

He nodded, puffing on his freshly filled pipe. "Thou mayest provide her some clothing."

Hannah stared at him, her eyes wide and filling with tears. At last he looked up at her and frowned. But he said no words of comfort, nor did he inquire about the cause of her distress. For a moment, his eyes narrowed, as if he would defeat her with a glare. But it was his eyes that fell first. He cleared his throat and studied his pipe.

"The child will appreciate the trip more when he is older. It will advance his education."

She struggled to control her trembling voice. "We can go a second time when he's older."

He was quiet for a moment. "Unknown diseases abound on foreign shores."

Her response was quicker. "Nantucket children have their share of illnesses."

Once again his eyes met hers, but the sight of them seemed to seal her doom. This was his captain's face. Surely many a sailor had quaked under this stare. Worse than autocracy. Worse than anger. He sat there like chiseled stone—a god who could not be persuaded or appeased.

"I have agreed to take the *Pequod* around Cape Horn as soon as she is fit."

"No!" she cried. "No, you can't do this to me … to us!"

"The articles are signed. We sail after the first of the year."

Now that the words were said, he was ready to dismiss the subject. He picked up his book to resume reading. But Hannah would have none of it. She pulled herself out of her chair, snatched the book from his hands, and flung it into the fireplace. Then she grasped the lapels of his suit coat and stared into his face.

"You will not do this to me! You will not! We were to have a life together, not apart. The whaling life is unnatural. It destroys families. Would you have me a widow while you yet live? Would you have our child fatherless while you play your seafaring games?"

He set down his pipe, then gently but surely gripped her hands and removed them from his clothing. "Thou hast never spoken this way to me before. We have always understood each other, have we not?"

She yanked her hands from his and stood glaring down at him. "Understood each other? I thought so too. But it was you who broke our heart bond. You made the decision to sail without even so much as discussing it with me."

"Nantucket women understand what their men must do."

"I am not a Nantucket woman. If you had wanted a Nantucket woman, you should not have married me."

"Perhaps thou speakest more truth than thou knowest."

The wound was effective, but she would not relent. "What do you know of truth? After all your prideful talk about your word being sufficient bond, you've lied to me since the day we met. You promised there would be no more whaling voyages. You promised that we would go to Europe together. You promised that we would travel as soon as the child is born. But you always intended to go out whaling again."

"Thou heardest what thou wished to hear. I have never lied to thee, nor did I make thee such a promise regarding whaling."

"You made me believe it then. That's the same as lying."

"Thou hast never had a tantrum before, Hannah. 'Tis well, for it doth not become thee." His casual tone and renewed involvement with his pipe enraged her more.

"You will not go! I forbid it!"

For the first time, he lifted his chin, then leaned forward and spoke with a calm, menacing voice. "I am the captain of this ship, woman, and wert thou not with child, I would show thee what is done to the insubordinate under my command."

"Oh, how very clever, Captain," she said, trembling with rage. "If you cannot win the argument, if you know you're in the wrong, then just threaten me. How absurd. This is not a ship. You are not my captain. You are my husband, and I am your equal. Isn't that the Nantucket way? And for all your talk, you would never dare to hit me. But even if you beat me till all my bones were broken, I will never forgive you for taking on this accursed voyage. If you go, it will destroy everything we have planned and nullify everything you have promised me. Don't say you didn't promise!"

"Words like that cannot be spoken of a whaling voyage. Even thou shouldest know that. Wouldest thou place a curse on us?"

"Oh, is Ahab suddenly superstitious? How convenient. You who have always scoffed at curses and prophecies."

He stood and walked to the fireplace, pulled out the book with a poker and snuffed out its heat with his hands. Satisfied that it was not burning, he tossed it aside and glared down at her. "It is carrying the child that makes thee speak thus. I'm going out for a walk. See that thou art calm and collected by the time I return." Then, grabbing his hat from the hall tree, he walked out into the winter night.

Despite an icy wind, Hannah stood in the open doorway and watched him disappear down the street. Tears froze on her cheeks, and soon her trembling rage became a trembling chill. She was barely aware of Abigail, who wrapped a warm blanket around her and pulled her inside the house. Without a word, the woman guided her up the stairs and undressed her for bed. She placed a bed warmer at Hannah's feet and pulled the down comforter up to her neck. Assured that the chill had abated, she finally spoke in dark tones.

"Mrs. Hannah, you cannot change him. Ahab is Ahab, and will be till the day of his death."

Hannah stared up at her, seeing her as a person rather than a servant for the first time in all her months in Nantucket. "You know him well, Abigail." She could not read the woman's face.

"As one knows a brother." Abigail turned to go, then turned back at the doorway. "You should sleep now. Remember the child."

Lying on her side, Hannah felt the baby kicking within her, but for the first time, it brought her no joy. Hot tears burned her cheek and dampened her pillow. She tried to stop, but it was no use. The sobs she tried to suppress broke from her like a thunderstorm, great gulping sobs that racked her body, interspersed with anguished wails. Her whole marriage had been a lie. She had believed every word he had said. She had forced herself to trust him when her instincts countered his decisions. Now he was betraying that trust in the worst possible way. How could he claim to love her? How could he say that he was devoted to her happiness? How could he say that she was his very life? Lies! All lies!

In time, weariness overtook her, and she lay exhausted on the bed. She could not sleep, but her hysteria had subsided, and her breathing had become normal. Hours had passed—she did not know how many—when he came to bed. She pretended to sleep, fearing she would begin to sob again if he touched her. But soon she felt him move, felt his arm slide across her body, felt his large, callused hand against her swollen belly. At his touch, she could no longer keep quiet. Jerking away, she buried her face in her pillow and began to wail again and to pound the mattress with her fist.

"Shh, wife, belay this weeping. Thou wilt harm the child. Be still." He drew her up into his arms and held her, rocking her and placing gentle kisses on her hair until her violent sobs had once again subsided into small, involuntary shudders and soft sniffles. "There, that's the way. I know this is hard for thee, but thou canst learn. This is the way things must be."

She lay in his arms, enraged at his words but too exhausted to protest any further. Moving away, she slid under the covers again, her back to him. But he was not done with her. He nestled beside her and covered her with his protecting arm. This time, she allowed his embrace to comfort her, despite the anger in her heart.

She thought that in the morning he would leave her alone. But he acted as though nothing had happened. After their noon meal, he announced that it was warm enough for a walk. The sun indeed was bright, and its heat seemed to bore into her breast, as if to melt the ice that had replaced her heart. She walked beside him in silence, accepting the support of his arm only for the sake of her child. Today he led her down toward the Brant Point shipyard where the *Pequod* was being refurbished for its next voyage.

It was an old ship, as old as Ahab himself. But unlike its captain, the *Pequod* showed her age. It was rather small, compared to any of the vessels her father had once owned, or to the *Sharona*. Severely weather-battered, with well-worn decks, the sun-darkened whaler nonetheless commanded attention by several startling features added over the years. Captain Peleg, before he bought into the ship, had been its chief mate. During his voyages on it, he had replaced many essential parts with carved ivory when they chanced to be damaged or broken. Perhaps most startling of these parts was the ship's steering device. Rather than a turnstile wheel at her helm, she sported there a tiller carved in one mass from the long narrow lower jaw of a sperm whale.

As Ahab gazed at the vessel, his face was lit by excitement. "Aye, it's a noble vessel," he said, more to himself than to her.

The look in his eyes was such as she had never seen in his most tender gaze at her. Not more fervent, simply different. Yet she hated the sight of the ugly little ship and hated him for loving it.

When they turned back toward town and she thought he would have taken her home, he continued to walk, directing her past the cottages on the wharves and up a narrow lane. He guided her at last to a small cabin, almost a hut, where a grizzled, ancient man sat staring out at the sea. Spittle covered his unruly beard and a disagreeable odor pervaded the place. He probably had not bathed for some time. He held a knife in one hand and a piece of wood in the other, but he did not whittle. Ahab pulled his reluctant wife in front of the man.

"Captain Paddock," he said, raising his voice.

The captain looked up, attempting to focus his eyes on his uninvited guests.

"Captain Paddock, this is my wife, Mrs. Ahab. Mrs. Ahab, meet Captain Paddock. We began as shipmates together when we were lads of eighteen, my dear."

"How do?" the man mumbled, nodding absently. Then his eyes hazed over, and he looked out toward the sea again.

Responding to Hannah's attempt to break away from this disturbing scene, Ahab turned her back toward the path. "Farewell, Captain Paddock," he said heartily. The old man did not answer.

They walked home in silence. By the time they reached that erstwhile pleasant haven, Hannah was deeply exhausted and deeply troubled. What had been the purpose of taking her to meet that poor old soul?

As if reading in her eyes the question she refused to ask, Ahab asked, "Is that what thou wishest for me, Hannah, that I should grow old and infirm sitting by our front door? To remain the man thou married, I must be about my work. It keeps me vital, girl. It would have been better for Captain Paddock had he been swept into the sea than to sit there like an imbecile, alive only in his own dreams of the past, a target for children to mock and younger men to pity."

"Who could pity Captain Ahab?" she spat out. "He has his fine house, his young wife, and soon a child. And now he will set sail on his fine, noble ship for another successful whaling voyage, for he isn't rich enough, it seems."

"The money has no value to me. It's merely a useful tool. I am a whaler, girl. Whaling is what I do."

Weary of the discussion, she gave him a sad stare. "And what am I, Ahab? Merely another useful tool? One that you can set aside whenever you no longer want or need it? No, not a tool … another … another whale." She patted her huge belly. "Something to conquer, to bring home and exhibit to all your friends. Well, you certainly did conquer me, Captain Ahab. I am defeated. I am your prisoner."

He held her in his arms and gazed into her eyes as he often had before, the gaze that had always joined their spirits and confirmed their love. "I will make it up to thee. When I return—"

"No!" She jerked away from him. "Don't promise me anything. Don't you ever promise me another thing!"

When rational discussions were no longer possible, an uneasy truce developed. Rather than argue, they spent most of their time together in silence, speaking only of mundane necessities. Hannah tried to think of anything that might dissuade Ahab from his course, but she had few weapons in her arsenal. As a last resort, she began to invite Jeremiah Harris to supper on Friday evenings, for all their other acquaintances were involved in one way or another with whaling. Their sympathies would surely be with Ahab. Perhaps Jeremiah could help her. By mid-December, his weekly visits had become a habit for them all.

The young minister was filled with enthusiasm for his new church. The congregation commended his sermons and was responsive to his ideas. Even some of the older members, all Nantucketers whose ideas were deeply entrenched, admitted that Reverend Harris had the makings of an excellent pastor. With his focus on spiritual matters, he spoke freely to Ahab and Hannah, as to old friends, about his plans for the church's future.

In response, Hannah expressed interest in Jeremiah's personal future, asserting that he must consider taking a wife.

"Have you noticed the lovely Miss Kerenhappuch Coffin? She's just sixteen, but you can't imagine how mature she is," she said.

Jeremiah pretended to be annoyed. "Please permit me to have an evening free from matchmaking. Every mother in my congregation has a daughter for me. And think of the discord it would create if I married a Quaker girl rather than one of my own church members. Besides, her mother would surely not permit her to marry someone outside her faith."

Hannah laughed. "You don't know Aunt Charity. She's full of 'thees' and 'thous,' but she's very liberal-minded and admires anyone who is truly spiritual. Now, Jeremiah, listen to me. When my husband has gone on his voyage, we will need a man to check up on us from time to time. And what better person than you? Kerenhappuch comes from a good family, and since she is going to be our baby's nursemaid, you can meet her here."

It had not been a good day for her. Feeling miserable, she wanted to lash out at someone or something. Teasing Jeremiah seemed a harmless enough game and would not bring the difficulties that targeting her husband would. She glanced at Ahab, who was listening to the conversation with a bland expression on his face. Feeling reckless, she might have been more blatant as she teased Jeremiah just to goad Ahab. If she had not been with child, she might even have found a way to flirt with him. But if she had not been with child, she and Ahab would now be in Europe. But then again, she would never wish her dear child away.

Every thought and every thing seemed to increase her misery. Despite the two men's opinions to the contrary, she thought the supper tasteless and could not eat it. The wind was strong, and snow was falling at an increasing rate. The smells of the fireplace seemed oppressive, but its heat was ineffective to warm her. And the abdominal cramps that had become her constant companion for over two weeks had become more severe as she sat at table. Then, after a strong surge of pain—during which she endeavored to keep a pleasant face—Hannah was filled with an unfamiliar serenity, an unfamiliar certainty. She laid her spoon beside her plate and addressed her husband.

"My dear, would you please send Abigail for Dr. Gayer? I do believe our son has decided to put in an early appearance."

Jeremiah's immediate look of alarm was replaced by decisiveness. "I'll go. Captain, please allow me."

Ahab nodded, his expression calm. "Thou hast my thanks, Parson. Come, Hannah. We'll go to thy bed."

Hannah waited until Jeremiah had grabbed his coat and plunged out into the driving snow before attempting to stand. She must be brave ... must not cry out. Refusing Ahab's assistance, she tried to stand, but pain ripped through her body.

"Ahh!" she cried, falling back into her chair. She glared up at him. "You're going to be ashamed of me. I can't do this without crying out in pain. Why don't you leave?"

"Belay that nonsense, Hannah. Come. I'll carry thee. Abigail," he called out. "Step lively! The child is coming!"

He lifted her from the chair and carried her up the stairs as though she weighed no more that a kitten. Setting her on her feet, he swept the quilt and blankets from the bed, then laid her on the white sheet. Abigail appeared at the door, ready to help.

"Fetch water and rags. Thou must keep her head cool." Ahab removed Hannah's clothing and replaced them with a white gown, then threw a top sheet over her. He sat beside the bed and would have held her hand, but she pulled it away.

"Don't touch me," she said, turning her face from him. But as her body was seized by a powerful contraction, he gripped her hand and let her dig her fingernails into his palm. When the pain subsided, she looked at him with gratitude.

"I'll not leave thee," he said. "We will do this together."

Abigail had returned with a pan of melting snow and began to dab Hannah's forehead. Minutes, many long minutes stretching over an hour, dragged by as the pains grew longer, more intense, and closer together. Hannah began to anticipate each new contraction by tightening every muscle in her body.

"Easy goes it, wife. Remember the animals giving birth. Thou must breathe lightly and relax into the pain. Recall the foaling mare—"

"How can I relax?" she responded through clenched teeth. "It hurts so bad."

Before Ahab could answer, they heard the slamming of the front door and footsteps running up the stairs. Jeremiah burst into the room alone, throwing his coat off and surveying the scene with dismay.

"The doctor is at the elder Mrs. Starbuck's. She's suffered a stomach attack of some sort. They fear she's dying. If he can come, he will … as soon as possible."

"Oh, no," Hannah began. But Ahab shushed her.

"No matter. Childbirth is natural. We will manage. Parson, shouldest thou not attend the dying patient?"

"Her own pastor is there, I'm certain," Jeremiah answered. "I can help here if I'm needed."

"Um, um … very well," Ahab responded calmly. "Then hold the damp cloth to her brow. Abigail, fetch … more snow for her relief." He stared into her eyes and nodded. The old woman returned a nod.

"Aye, Captain." She hastened from the room.

"Hast thou seen a childbirth out on the frontier, Parson?" Ahab asked.

"Not directly. I have been in the next room—"

"Then prepare thyself to obey my orders when the time comes."

Jeremiah stared at him. "Aye, Captain," he whispered.

Though Jeremiah dabbed Hannah's face, she was barely aware of him as each new spasm ripped through her body. So far, she had not screamed out in pain. But now, the outrage of it all seemed to burn in her heart.

"Let go of me!" she shouted at Ahab. "Quit that!" She shoved Jeremiah's hand away. Flailing her hands about helplessly, she seemed to be trying to get up. "Leave me alone! How dare you do this to me?" she screamed at her husband. "I hate you, Ahab! I hate you!"

"Hannah, for heaven's sake ..." Jeremiah began.

"Hush, lad," Ahab said. "This is a good sign."

"Good sign!" shrieked Hannah. "You monster! I'm dying with pain! Why don't you do something?"

"Easy, Hannah, easy. It will be over soon."

But it was not over soon. Her labor continued well into the night. Then there was a long pause between the pains, and Hannah lay quiet and exhausted. Able to think with a clear head for the first time in hours—indeed, in months—she grasped her husband's hand and pulled it to her lips.

"Husband, listen to me. I'm so very weak. I cannot push any longer, and the child is not coming."

He could not mask the concern in his eyes. "Aye, I know."

"You must take him."

"No. Not yet."

"What are you talking about?" Jeremiah said.

"You must. If you don't, it may be too late," Hannah whispered.

"I'll go again for the doctor," Jeremiah said. "I'll make him come."

"No," commanded Ahab. "I'll need thee here. Do as I say."

"Where is that blasted Abigail?" said Jeremiah, suddenly remembering the servant who should have been there to help.

"Ahab, take the child. Please."

"I cannot do that to thee, Hannah. Not just yet."

"Yes, you can. My mother died so I could live. She made her choice. I'm making mine. If you don't take him, he may die, and you will lose both of us."

"Oh, God, Hannah, I cannot bear to lose thee."

"Do it!"

Ahab looked at Jeremiah. "Go to the kitchen and fetch a large knife. See that it's a sharp one. Now!" he ordered when Jeremiah hesitated. Reluctantly, the younger man obeyed, returning in a few moments with a gleaming blade.

"We must pray first, Captain," he said.

"Whilst thou art praying, hold her down, Parson." Ahab drew back the sheets and stared for a moment at his wife's swollen belly. With focused concentration, he probed for movement beneath the quivering surface of her abdomen, trying to decide where to pierce it.

"For God's sake, Ahab, how can you cut her?" Jeremiah cried.

Ahab reached across the bed and grabbed Jeremiah's collar. "Shut thy mouth and hold her down."

"No. Do not cut." The command came from a tall, sturdy old woman standing in the doorway. Abigail stood behind her, and they both were wet with snow.

"Tishtega," Ahab cried with relief. "Thou hast come at last. Canst thou save her ... and the child?"

"Move away," the woman responded. "Give me the knife." She took the blade and placed it under the bed. Glancing at Jeremiah, she added, "It will cut the pain."

Jeremiah frowned his disapproval of the ritual, but made way for Abigail to take his place.

Tishtega probed Hannah's belly, feeling for movement. "Has the water come?" she asked Ahab.

"Nay. No water."

Giving orders to Abigail in their native tongue, Tishtega took a small blade from a pouch at her waist. Holding the blade against her long, bony finger, she gently pushed it between Hannah's legs into the birth canal. While Jeremiah knelt in prayer in the next room, Ahab and Abigail held Hannah down, despite her screams and writhing. Tishtega pulled her hand from Hannah's body, bringing forth a gusher of blood and water. Within seconds, a tiny head appeared.

"Push," the old woman ordered, and Hannah found strength to push once more. The child plunged into the world, all blue and red. Again, Tishtega gave orders to Abigail, who began to tend Hannah. Tishtega cleared the infant's mouth of mucous and breathed into him, then held him upside down and pressed his back until he began to wail at the indignity of such treatment. Next, she produced twine from her pouch and tied and cut the infant's cord. Last, she pulled out a packet of salt and began to rub him vigorously. Giving Ahab a sidelong glance, she nodded toward the door.

"Go have a smoke. All is well here."

Instead, Ahab sat down close to the bed and caressed Hannah's face. "Thou didst well, wife. Thou hast given me a son." His voice was husky, and his eyes were moist. "Thou hast never been more beautiful than at this moment, nor have I ever been so full of happiness. Oh, Hannah, my dear, brave Hannah, splice thy heart with mine once more. Let us be divided no longer."

His eyes told her all she wished to know at that moment. He did love her, truly love her, after all. She gave him a weak smile and pulled his hand to her lips.

"Oh, my dear Ahab, my heart is bound to yours forever, forever," she whispered. *But don't you remember that it is you who would divide us?*

Chapter Thirteen

ℰ

*E*ven though the delivery had been difficult and Hannah continued to feel its effects, the joy of her son's birth softened the pain. Ahab was pleased that she refused to hire a wet nurse, and in a few days her milk came in abundantly for her ever-hungry baby. When she held him to her breast, she experienced a feeling of wellbeing such as she had never known. Ahab was at her side every possible moment, and his eyes shone with unhindered love and pride.

"He's a fine, strong boy, wife. Thou hast surely done well," he said more than once in the days after the birth.

"Do you think he is like you, my love? Yes, I think even now he shows your noble brow."

Ahab grunted with satisfaction. He placed his large finger in the baby's hand, then lifted. The baby held tight and seemed to pull himself up. "Ha, see how strong my son is,"

"Like his father."

"Aye. But I'll not burden him with my name. We will call him Jacob."

Hannah fussed with her son's blanket and said absently, "No. His name is Timothy."

"That name is too soft for my son. He will be called Jacob," Ahab repeated. "'Tis a fine, strong name for a fine, strong boy."

Hannah laid her head back against her pillow, closed her eyes, and expelled a weary sigh. "It is I who went to death's door to give him life, husband, and it is I who will name him. He will be called Timothy."

There was an edge of annoyance in Ahab's chuckled response. "He will be called Jacob."

Hannah opened her eyes slowly, as though from a long sleep, and smiled sweetly at her husband. "Only when you are in port, Captain Ahab."

"Woman, dost thou defy me?" he barked, rising to his feet and standing above her. The infant jumped at the sudden noise and began to cry.

Hannah shushed him softly. "There, there, Timothy, don't be frightened. Your father is throwing a tantrum, but he will get over it soon enough."

With a muttered oath, Ahab stormed into the sitting room, returning in a moment with the family Bible. "His name will be written here as I say."

In the embrace of her maternal euphoria, her heart overflowed with love as she gazed up at him. "Then I pray you, husband, write there 'Timothy Jacob,'" she whispered.

He stared down at her, scowling. But his scowl gradually softened, and for the first time in their lives together, Ahab surrendered. He set the Bible on the bed, then sat beside her and caressed her cheek. "Ah, wife, thy loving gaze bespeaks such devotion and tenderness of heart such as I have not seen there in many a day. I am persuaded by thy fond look to do thy will as no words could ever move me." He looked at the Bible. "A strong boy can stand firm, no matter what his name—as well I know. I will write 'Timothy Jacob.'"

So wondrous to Hannah was Ahab's acquiescence that, in the coming days, she wondered if she might be able to persuade him

from his voyage through a similar display of love. Yet, as he
began to spend more time at his ship, she could see once again
that light glowing in his eyes that had nothing to do with marital
bliss or paternal delight. She, on the other hand, began to grow
more despondent over their coming separation. If she had not
had the companionship of Kerenhappuch, all her days would
have been spent weeping. As it was, a heavy heart had
supplanted her sense of wellbeing so that even nursing her son
brought forth tears. Try though she might to entice Ahab with a
loving gaze, he would only brush her cheek with a kiss, then
continue to pack his personal effects in his sea chest, leaving her
to weep once again.

She was thankful that he did not seem wearied by her melancholy. In the evening as he sat by the bedside reading to her, he
might glance up with a look of concern if she sniffled back a
renewed bout of tears, but he made no comment. She decided
that their arguments had been as painful to him as they had been
to her, and he was merely avoiding any further disagreements. It
was not that she wanted to mope or cry. She would have done
anything to prevent it, anything to show him a brave face. But
the tears sprang unbidden and without warning. Oh, how glad
she was for his patience. Each night as her silent tears fell, he did
not refrain from his custom of holding her in his arms. With this
demonstration of his devotion, she resigned herself to cherishing
the few weeks that remained until his departure.

Ahab had reluctantly allowed Hannah to keep to her bed for
eight days after their son's birth. But as her moodiness continued,
he announced that exercise was the cure for her despondency.
On the ninth morning, after Kerenhappuch took their well-
nourished infant back to the nursery, Ahab announced that
Hannah must leave her bed. Walking, he assured her, would
refresh her both in body and spirit. He himself supervised the

event, giving proper consideration to the physical necessities of a new mother. As weak as she felt, Hannah endured the regimen, trusting that Ahab knew what he was about.

The snow-covered ground and bitter winds precluded outdoor activity for her. But to Ahab, who always exercised at sea by pacing the confines of the ship deck, the circle of the downstairs rooms provided more than ample space. Each morning he would take Hannah for a stroll, making the circle several times, then taking her up and down the stairs to increase the strength of her legs. Home from his afternoons at the docks, he would again bring her downstairs for supper at the dining room table. Then he required her to sit with him by the parlor fire. Two weeks of these practices did make her feel stronger, encouraging them both. But tears were still and always close to the surface.

When she did in fact cry, he studied her with a thoughtful gaze for several moments before taking her into his arms in a futile attempt to console her. Yet he expressed dissatisfaction with Dr. Gayer's diagnosis that young mothers, especially ones whose husbands were about to set sail, often indulged themselves in excessive crying that should be scolded away. Not so, declared Ahab. Rather, there was a difference between petulance and a true ailment. His Hannah was not given to petulance. Therefore, he himself would find a solution for the problem before he sailed. Where he searched for that solution, Hannah never discovered. He simply came home one afternoon some three weeks after the birth and gave his instructions to Abigail. She was to serve Mrs. Ahab calf's liver twice a week, along with yams and a thick porridge of oats, until Hannah regained her health. Confections were to be kept at a minimum.

Nearly a month to the day after her son's birth, Hannah was surprised, on waking, to find herself feeling, if not happy, at least enjoying a certain contentment. And she had more energy than she had felt in a long time. That day she allowed Kerenhappuch to teach her the art of changing diapers. She visited Abigail in the kitchen, much as she used to visit old Mrs. Randolph in her New Bedford kitchen, but without the familiar jesting. She looked out the dining room window at her frozen flower garden and began to think of spring improvements. And that evening in the parlor, she waited until Abigail and Kerenhappuch had retired, then playfully sat on her husband's lap, much to his delight.

"Well, Captain Ahab, I think you have a healthy wife again." She snuggled close to him and planted a kiss on his cheek.

"I'm glad to hear it, my dear. I do not like to see thee feeling ill." He gave her an affectionate squeeze and nuzzled his face in her neck. "But sad or happy, I always treasure having thee in my arms."

She gazed into his eyes. "Then how can you bear to leave me? Won't your arms ache with emptiness? Won't your lips hunger for my kisses?" She was as surprised as he that she could say the words without tears. A frown of concern appeared on his brow, but she soothed it away with her fingertips and continued. "Won't your body burn with longing for mine? I know that mine will long for yours." She moved closer, her lips slightly parted. His eyes questioned, and hers affirmed. He brushed her lips with a tentative kiss. Then the warmth of her response ignited his long suppressed desires. Sweeping her up in his arms, he carried her upstairs to their bed, bolting the bedroom door lest a hungry infant and its nursemaid come calling.

That night, once again, Hannah marveled at the gift God had given to His children, a gift to be unwrapped in only blissful marriage. When at last they lay quiet in each other's arms, she continued to caress his powerful chest and arms and legs.

"Ah, Hannah, I would give thee the world." He touched her cheek.

"Oh, would you?" she whispered. "The whole wide world?"

"Aye." He gazed at her with adoring eyes.

She nuzzled her face against his shoulder. Why had she not thought of this before? It was the solution to their coming separation.

"Then take me with you," she breathed into his ear.

Ahab groaned, a long, tormented, fervent, wishful groan. She could hear the rumble of it deep in his chest, could feel his entire frame shudder with violent contemplation and indecision, and then, sadly, could see granite resolution settle on his face.

"It cannot be done."

"Other wives go."

"It cannot be done!"

She bowed her head against his chest with a sigh and said no more. Why had he sounded angry with her so soon after his declaration of love, so soon after their wonderful lovemaking? She would never understand his swiftly changing moods. She would not push him now. Perhaps the morning would bring a softening in his disposition. But if not, would she be able to smooth things over before he sailed away?

Ahab spent the next day at his ship and said little over supper that evening. Hannah was disappointed but not surprised when he looked at her distrustfully as she sought his lap again that evening. This time he held her at arms' length and would have put her off if she had not affected such a happy countenance.

"I've been a wicked, wicked wife, my dear." Her playful tone belayed her words.

He grunted his agreement. "Thou truly hast been difficult. I will have no more of last night's troubles from thee."

She gave him a saucy grin. "It wasn't all bad, was it?"

He moved his legs restlessly. "Sit still, girl. I'll not be deceived by thee again."

"Oh, Ahab, my darling husband," she cried. "I never meant to deceive you. In fact, I wasn't speaking of last night at all."

"Well?"

She sighed, staring deep into his dark eyes. "You love the sea so much. You love the whale hunt. I don't understand—"

"Hannah ..." he warned.

"But I want to." Her expression and tone seemed to mollify him, so she went on. "I've never asked you why you're so devoted to whaling, why it means so much to you. You're so very brilliant, so clever in every way. You could have done anything with your life. Yet you chose whaling. And despite all your love for me and our son—and I do believe with all my being that you love us— yet you still cannot escape the call of it on your heart. If my poor father could have been as devoted to whaling, or any other calling, for that matter, he would still be alive."

Ahab's eyes bored into hers as she spoke, testing her sincerity. Only when she saw how slow he was to trust her did she realize how hazardous to their love her request of last night had been. She had not meant to beguile him. Her passions had been as real as his, her request to sail with him an afterthought that surprised even her. But he had not seen it that way. Tears of true regret sprang to her eyes, but still she smiled.

"I have never asked you why you love it so much. Please tell me now."

He began slowly, telling her stories she had already heard, as though still testing her sincerity. He soon warmed to his subject, however, and gradually there came a faraway look on his face, as if he were somewhere out on the ocean searching for whales. Whaling, not war, was the true test of manhood, he declared. Every boy raised on Nantucket knew that. What was an enemy soldier, even one mounted on horseback, even one armed with saber or musket, compared to the mighty whale? Imagine standing on the prow of a twenty-eight-foot whaleboat and plunging a deadly harpoon into the body of a one-hundred-foot leviathan! The man who mounted the back of a whale and slew it was greater than any David who stood apart and flung a stone against his Goliath.

This time, Hannah did not listen with childish amazement or feminine astonishment at his narration. Rather, she began to listen with her heart, reading the passion within him, the passion that had been there all along. Yes, he had told her these stories many times before. But now it was the light in his eyes that told her what words could never explain. Why had she never noticed?

Once, as her father lay ill, he had spoken of his boyhood on the Indiana farm. He had told her about the labor of the plowing and the planting of seeds, the miracle of seeing green life spring forth from the ground, and the satisfaction of a plentiful harvest. The brilliant glow in his eyes had confirmed how much he had missed it, how much he had longed to plunge his hands once again into the soil of his home state. He never should have left the farm in Indiana, he had said, never should have accepted his uncle's bequest. Then there was Jeremiah, with his wholehearted dedication to serving God. Whether he preached or simply spoke of God in conversation, his face was radiant with passion for his calling.

And so it was with Ahab. The whale hunt was his passion. As victory incited the warrior to new battles, the conquest of leviathan lured the whaler back to the sea. It got into his blood. It fed his soul as nothing—not even his wife's most fervent love—ever could.

"Many a man nowadays moves westward across the untamed wilderness of this continent. The oceans of the world are a far greater, far wilder wilderness," he said. "What do the landlubbers go in search of? Land? Riches? Perhaps. But when they have both land and riches, they still forge ahead to scale the next mountain. Every man must engage in the battle of life, girl. If he conquers, what rewards there are. If he is defeated, there's no shame if he's given his best effort. But woe be to the man who surrenders. Worse still, woe be to the man who never tries."

He stared deep into her eyes once more and caressed her cheek. "Ah, Hannah, dost thou understand? I must do this ... or die."

She was quiet for a moment, absorbing this agonizing truth. "Yes," she whispered. "I understand."

"Wilt thou give me leave to go then?"

"You will go whether I let you or not."

"Aye. But wilt thou let me? For thine own sake, wilt thou let me?"

Again she was quiet, searching his eyes for any reprieve from the promise she must give him. But there was none. He would go. She would stay, once again waiting the endless months and years until his return. She would surrender her dreams for his, because she loved him. And, oh, how different her love was from his.

"Yes. I will let you."

He nodded, seeming to comprehend the depth of her sacrifice, and his eyes shone with gratitude and love. He regarded her for several moments, trying in his turn, it seemed, to give her understanding equal to what she had given him. "Thou wilt do well here in my absence, my dear. Thou art well liked already, and no wonder. The women of Nantucket are strong, and thou art like them."

With a sigh, she leaned against his broad chest. Was she truly strong? She did not feel it. If some wonderful magic could have transformed the two of them into a single marble statue locked forever in love's fond embrace, she would have wished it so, for then he could never desert her. But she had given him leave to go. And unlike all his well-meant promises, she would not retract hers.

The *Pequod* was now prepared for its voyage, and the crew was shipped. All that remained was for favorable winds to replace the nor'easter that had continued to pound Nantucket for days. Hannah had always disliked the winds. Now she listened gladly to their incessant howling, treasuring each additional day with Ahab. She hoped that the icy weather would freeze the harbor and prevent any ships from sailing. But at last in late January the harsh winds ceased, milder sailing winds came up, and the sun bore down upon the island with unseasonable warmth. The crew was called together from their homes and rented rooms. They must bring final ship supplies and their own sea chests on board the *Pequod*. What they carried aboard now must last them for three or four years. Of course, if Captain Ahab's greasy luck held out, it might be less time, but one must plan for a long voyage and hope for a short one. The day and hour were set, and all haste was made not to miss the wind and tide.

A few wives and children assembled on the docks to see the ship get under way. Aunt Charity was there to place a copy of Watts in each man's hand as he boarded. Her brother, Captain Bildad, stood by, overseeing last details. Once again answering the call of the sea like his lifelong friend—and keeping watch over his own property—Captain Peleg would serve as first mate to Captain Ahab. It was a fine crew of sturdy Nantucketers, most of whom were already veteran whalers. They knew what they were about. It would be a good voyage.

That noon, Ahab had taken his leave of his son. For a moment, Hannah had seen a blink of regret in his eyes, but it passed all too quickly. As she walked with him toward the ship, she was forced almost to run, for there was an enthusiasm in his long stride that mirrored the feelings of his heart. Eagerness to sail, however, did not prevent him from giving last-minute instructions as they marched down Orange Avenue to Main Street. He expressed his faith in her ability to handle the purse strings at home. All his investments were in the care of his banker at the Pacific Bank of Nantucket, but money would be available for her every need. Mr. Mitchell had his orders regarding the matter. He encouraged her to rely on Abigail and Aunt Charity for household problems.

"When I return, my dear," he added, "thou must not meet me at the docks. Wait, as other captains' wives wait, until the ship is unloaded and I've had my bath and shave. I would not wish thee to endure the stench that accompanies my work."

"That's an order I'm not likely to obey, Captain Ahab." She tried to sound cheerful. "When you return, you will be in my arms as quickly as I can reach you, stench or not."

He chuckled. "Well, then, do as thou wishest. But for my sake, remember that there's nothing quite as troublesome as a flock of hens clucking and pecking about the ship while their husbands try to finish their business."

They had reached their destination. The pilot boat was tethered to the *Pequod*, ready to pull her out beyond the sandbars that enclosed Nantucket Harbor. All that remained was for the captain to board.

Ahab turned and reached down, taking Hannah's face in his hands. "Never think that I love thee any less, Hannah, despite my leaving."

She gazed up into his face with a quivering smile.

He kissed her gently. "I will come back to thee." Then he turned and strode up the gangplank.

In keeping with custom, most wives had not come to the docks. Of those who had come, a few had hastened away as soon as the gangplank was lifted, summoned by urgent work at home or eager to leave the coarse atmosphere. Several younger wives and sweethearts had taken shelter in Captain Bildad's presence, weeping and comforting one another until the ship was out of sight. But it was Hannah who was the last to leave.

As she watched the receding tide, she felt her happiness ebb away with it. How could she live without him? In less than a year, how things had changed for her. All that she had thought her life would be was now a half-forgotten dream. The unknown interval of time until Ahab returned once again stretched before her like a gaping chasm. It almost seemed as if life were not worth living. How did these Nantucket women survive?

Despite the bad language and ill manners of rowdy seamen, she could not comprehend the indifference of those who had not come to the docks to see their husbands away or those who left so hastily while the ship was still in sight. Nor could she release her tears in public, though her own heart ached as much as any of the weeping women's. It must be that each was confronting her burden in her own way.

As the sun dipped behind a cloud, a bitter breeze off the water struck her breast, sending a chill through her. She looked down and saw that her milk had come in, drenching the front of her dress. Poor Timothy must be hungry, she thought absently. Poor orphan child with no father to dandle him on his knee or to teach him to be a little man. The breeze grew stronger and slapped her damp cheeks with an icy hand. She gasped, fully awake from her stupor. As she turned toward home, her eyes swept over the busy Nantucket docks. This island was her world now. She would study it well and find her place in it. And she would learn what it was about these Nantucket women that caused her husband to commend them as he did. But for now, a more important matter demanded her attention.

Lifting her skirts, she raced home to feed her hungry son.

Chapter Fourteen

&

*M*aternal duties kept Hannah busy much of the time. When possible, she attended the book and music clubs hosted by Mrs. Matthew Starbuck, a daughter-in-law of Mrs. Joseph Starbuck. Mrs. Starbuck also persuaded her to join the Society to Assist the Poor. Socializing and doing charitable work in the company of these other women, Hannah began to understand the differences between her various new acquaintances. Those married to ship owners who never went whaling, of course, had greater fortunes than the rest, but it also seemed they had greater peace of mind. Though they might have a son or a brother at sea, the company of their husbands countervailed the many uncertainties of the whalefishery.

Hannah came to recognize the faces of those who bore the greatest personal burden: the whalers' wives. They were for the most part serious, meditative, grim, and lonely. Often she looked into her mirror to see if her face looked that way. Still, though their faces might belie it, most of them were plucky, good-hearted women who had made up their minds to survive despite the hardships and loneliness of their lives.

As she considered this, Hannah could see that Ahab had been right. The women did understand the necessity of what their husbands were doing. Nantucket whalers provided the purest of oils to light the lamps of the world and spermaceti to make candles that burned without smoke. But he had been wrong to think that understanding made the separations easier for either wives or husbands. Even among the captains, most retired from whaling once they had secured enough fortune to care for their families. Few men were as possessed as Ahab was by his profession. And the women? Yes, they were strong, as Ahab had said, but he had never mentioned, perhaps had never seen, that their strength and dauntless spirits cost each and every one of them dearly.

Among them, none was more dauntless than Aunt Charity. Hannah decided that when she grew old she wanted her face to have smiling age lines like Charity's rather than frown lines. But accepting her lot in life with a joyful attitude was not something she could pretend. It must come from within, as it did with her Quaker friend.

Nantucket Quakers were a breed apart from their off-island brothers and sisters. They might cheerfully do business with anyone not of their faith but refuse to speak to a fellow church member who wore a shoe buckle or brass buttons on a coat. A gathering of peace-loving Christians, which had begun amid violent persecution and had flourished for a century and a half, was declining because of infighting. Aunt Charity had no patience with any of it. Her Inner Light, she would say, kept her close to the most basic tenets of the Gospel: charity, kindness, and forgiveness. Hannah noted that, unlike her brother Bildad and his frowning wife Augusta, Aunt Charity had no hint of self-righteousness about her.

Because Kerenhappuch was Timothy's nursemaid, Aunt Charity visited the house on Orange Street daily, dispensing spiritual wisdom to Hannah along with mothering advice. Her appearance was always welcome, especially when the formerly fearless Hannah found herself to be as susceptible to panic as any other new mother. Her son's diaper rash, teething fever, or coughing fits were greeted with great alarm. Although Kerenhappuch reacted with confidence to these events, it took the older woman to reassure Hannah that even in the face of disaster, panic was useless and even injurious.

"Thou must calm thyself, Sister Hannah," Aunt Charity would say. "The child will observe the reaction of his mother and will respond accordingly. Thy Timothy is a calm child, but thou couldest see that change if thou insistist upon thy nervous twitters."

"But how can I stay calm? Sometimes he drinks too greedily and chokes on his milk. Then his face turns blue."

"Did my daughter not show thee? Put him across thy knee and gently pat his back. If this does not help, use thy finger to clear his throat, then blow into his nose and mouth. And of course thou must pray the whole time and trust God. All infants have these little spells, even thee and me when we were small. Yet here we are, all grown up and healthy." She laughed merrily for a moment, then grew serious. "Sister Hannah, ruling thine own spirit is the best mothering thou canst do. Remember, God never makes a mistake. Thou canst trust in that."

Hannah took her words to heart. Although she did not want to be like the somber, frowning women, she did want to be a solid anchor for her son. Aunt Charity had lost two infants before they outgrew their cradle, had lost a husband and two sons to whaling, now endured her last son's long absences at sea, and lived barely above poverty in a tiny, old house. Yet she still faced life with spirit and enthusiasm. Her faith reminded Hannah of her own father's trust in God, but with a difference. Whereas Amos Oldweiler had been a passive participant in his own existence, Charity Coffin attacked life with vigor.

Despite missing her husband, Hannah began to feel like her former self. She found that vigorous daily walks up and down the low hills of Nantucket soon strengthened her body, restored her slender waistline, and flattened her abdomen. Defying the dictates of fashion—and perhaps even community dictates of decency—she found she could dispense with her hated corset, and no one was the wiser, especially when she was wrapped in her shawl. Then, by gently covering and lifting her breasts with soft cotton strips, she could nurse her son and still be comfortable.

In time, it became apparent that she had regained her womanly appeal. While shopping or walking to church, she started to receive more notice than she preferred from some gentlemen of her acquaintance. With her husband gone, she was anxious to maintain a proper reputation in Nantucket's close-knit community. So when Jeremiah began to call on her twice each week, she grew concerned. He had come several times since Timothy's birth, but not with such regularity. Was he still in love with her after all? She was loath to discourage him, but neither would she be like those errant wives who dispelled their loneliness in the company of attentive men, sometimes overnight.

A mild inquiry as to whether he should be with another, more needy parishioner brought her both relief and a chance to laugh at her own vanity. Jeremiah informed her that Ahab had not requested but rather instructed him to visit the house often to be certain all was well. Her husband's trust in both her and her former suitor was a delightful surprise. Surely his experiences as a captain had taught him how to discern human character.

Nor was he alone among whalers in this capacity. Aunt Charity related a story to her of a Nantucket man who hired himself out to sleep in women's homes in case they became frightened during their husbands' absences. To hear that such an arrangement could be acceptable to husbands amazed Hannah. Then she had an opportunity to see the man. He was a peculiar looking individual, rather cloudy of mind but quite strong of body. In addition to providing protection, he performed odd jobs for women. He was as harmless and innocent as a lamb, and Aunt Charity confirmed that no hint of scandal had ever attached itself to him. Likewise, though the young Reverend Harris was as handsome as could be, his sterling character was above reproach, a fact that was obvious to all.

Since the night of her son's birth, Hannah had not commended Kerenhappuch to Jeremiah, but she had not forsaken her matchmaking plans. When Jeremiah visited, she always called for Kerenhappuch to bring the baby for the pastor's inspection. When the nursemaid would enter the room holding the infant, her modesty and shyness coupled with her beauty and competence to create a picture not unlike a madonna and child. Hannah was gratified to see his eyes linger on the girl's face more and more.

Although Kerenhappuch felt her position precluded any right to participate in conversation with her employer and her guest, she did remain in the room, attentive to any need that might arise. By late February, Hannah began to see a new light in Jeremiah's eyes, and a charming bashfulness. He cleared his throat often and seemed more reserved in his conversation.

One day, when he at last had gained courage, he said, "Miss Coffin, I am amazed at your competence with the infant. Where did you learn so much?"

Kerenhappuch glanced shyly at Hannah, then back to the minister. Before now, she had only been required to give simple answers to his polite questions.

"I ... I have always watched the little ones," she said. "New mothers invariably need help. But this is my first real job as a nursemaid, thanks to Mrs. Ahab." She looked again at Hannah, as if she expected no more questions.

"You like children, then?" Jeremiah asked.

Kerenhappuch blushed with pleasure at his continued attention. "Oh, yes. Very much. I would like to become a schoolteacher some day."

"How commendable." He stared at her, smiling, as if he could think of nothing further to say.

Hannah bit her lips to keep from chuckling. As she worked to control herself, she also tried to think of something to say. But Kerenhappuch stood suddenly.

"Oh, he needs a change." She cuddled the baby and fled the room without another word.

Now Hannah laughed out loud. "Well," she said, smiling at Jeremiah.

He grinned sheepishly. "She's ... she's ..."

"Sweet? Charming? Lovely? Enchanting?" Hannah prompted.

"Yes," he whispered.

"So, what will you do now, my friend?" she challenged.

By his next visit, he had decided what to do. Before Kerenhappuch brought the child down from the nursery, he asked Hannah if she would allow the girl to go for a walk with him. "I have spoken to her mother, and she has granted permission."

"Oh, Jeremiah, that's wonderful." She thought for a moment. "You know that Aunt Charity has a very generous heart. Unfortunately, many of her Quaker friends and relatives are not so liberal. Don't begin this courtship lightly, for both mother and daughter may find themselves shunned because of it."

He nodded. "I would never do anything to cause either of them grief. You know that, Hannah."

"Yes, I know." She thought further. "And what will our church members think if you court a Quaker girl instead of one of their own?"

"You're coming late with these questions, Mrs. Ahab," he said, laughing. "You who have plotted this whole affair. Don't you think I've pondered and prayed about this for weeks? For months, in fact? I can't say what anyone else will think or do. I can only ask God to guide me. I will proceed carefully, for her sake and for my own. Perhaps we are not suited for each other after all. Miss Coffin is beautiful and kind, but most important, she is a devout Christian. Still, I will not take anything for granted. She may blush and smile in my presence, but that does not mean she is as interested in me as I am in her."

When Kerenhappuch brought the baby to the parlor, Jeremiah asked if she were well, then fussed over the child as he usually did. As the conversation continued over mundane subjects, Hannah was tempted to take her son back to the nursery and thus provide the young lovers some privacy. But before she could think of a proper excuse, Jeremiah made her proud.

"Miss Coffin, it's an unseasonably lovely day today. I have asked your mother and Mrs. Ahab if I might invite you out for a walk."

"Oh!" The girl blushed with pleasure. "Oh!" she repeated, looking at Hannah in confusion. "May I?"

Hannah reached out for her son. "Why, of course. Give me my son and go fetch your wrap, dear."

The girl placed the baby in Hannah's arms, gave a clumsy, un-Quakerlike curtsey to Jeremiah, then raced to the stairs. Halfway up, she regained her composure and slowed her pace.

Hannah laughed. "Hmm. I don't think there's any problem about mutual interest, Jeremiah. But I was so afraid you might back out that I—"

"Yes, I know. I saw that expression on your face. In fact, I was about to get cold feet. Surely you women don't think courtship is easy for a man, do you? But I thank you for goading me." His face crinkled with amused annoyance. "Oh, Hannah, look at you. You're so pleased with yourself."

"Why, yes, I am. But now it's all up to you."

That spring, romance blossomed on Orange Street like the flowers in Hannah's garden. Jeremiah continued his visits to the Ahab residence. But it was not safeguarding the lady of the house that drew him there, her husband's instructions notwithstanding. Several times a week the young minister could be seen escorting Miss Kerenhappuch Coffin for a short walk about the neighborhood. There were those in both the Quaker meeting and the First Congregational Church who disapproved, and the couple might have avoided criticism if they had kept their love a secret. But neither Jeremiah nor Kerenhappuch could sanction or participate in clandestine behavior. If their courtship could not take place in public, it would not take place at all.

Kerenhappuch might have been put out of her meeting if her uncle, Captain Bildad, had not swayed some fellow members whose livelihoods depended on his wealth. He was certainly not pleased with her choice. And a man of his conservative Quaker breeding could never be accused of defending his niece because of family pride, for such pride would have been a serious sin. Perhaps it was because of the scant number of eligible young Quaker men still in his meeting that he permitted the courtship. After all, he could not allow his niece to become an old maid. Or perhaps it was because the girl was employed by the wife of his own excellent Captain Ahab that he defended her. After all, a ship owner always felt a practical responsibility toward the family of the man on whom his fortunes depended. But, whatever his reason, Bildad spoke, and Kerenhappuch remained in the meeting.

In like manner, Jeremiah received a visit from a group of elders, several of whom had marriageable daughters. Though their church was not as prone as the Quakers to shunning those whom they deemed to have erred, the men did express concern about the object of their pastor's affection. Jeremiah later confided to Hannah that he would just as soon have relived his harrowing fight on the riverboat than to have suffered the elders' interrogations. Yet he had managed to convince them that the young lady was a sincere Christian. And if she decided to join to their church, he would in all probability marry her. Her mother's reputation for good works, from which not a few of them had benefited, provided the final argument against their objections.

After their first walk, the young lady began to lose her shyness, and Jeremiah found her to be more than a charming girl with a pretty face. Her desire to teach children was genuine and came from her own extensive education, typical of the well-taught children of Nantucket. She also had strong opinions about a number of subjects. But like her mother, she would never force those opinions on others and only voiced them when asked. Unlike many of her generation, she felt that as a youth she must bow to the wisdom of those who were older than she, even her young employer. This humility of spirit further endeared her to Jeremiah. But her age also forestalled his proposal of marriage. She was only sixteen, and despite her maturity, he felt that she was too young to take on the responsibilities of marriage. They would wait, he told her, until she turned eighteen. That would give them time to be certain of their affection for each other. Kerenhappuch agreed.

Hannah watched their courtship with delight, but she also could not help comparing it to her own. Both she and Ahab had been surprised by their mutual attraction that had so quickly exploded into love. They had married hastily because of his impending voyage. It could not have happened any other way. Yet she sometimes wondered if things—what things she did not know—might have been different if they had had more patience and restraint. Restraint? No, she thought. She would never wish Ahab to restrain his passionate love for her. She could only wish him back home that they both might enjoy that passion once again. For now, she was glad for Jeremiah's coming happiness. He deserved Kerenhappuch. She would be good for him, be everything he needed. Never for a moment did Hannah regret declining her dear friend's long-ago marriage proposal.

In the meantime, Kerenhappuch was indispensable to Hannah. Under her care, Timothy grew fat and healthy. He was a happy baby who responded to everyone with smiles and laughter. His dark eyes watched every movement as his mother or nursemaid walked about the room. He also adored Abigail. Hannah could not decide whether this was good or bad. It was convenient when Kerenhappuch took her day off, for then Abigail carried the baby around on her hip while she did her housework, talking to him as if he were her own. With difficulty, Hannah concealed her jealousy of this woman who remained an enigma to her.

On more than one occasion, Aunt Charity had mentioned the quiet housekeeper's dependability. True, Hannah agreed. It was remarkable that Abigail had remained a loyal servant to Ahab during all his years at sea, keeping his house like new and never abusing his trust. But who was this brown-skinned woman to Ahab that he should be so loyal to her? Was she now embracing his child because he had not given her one of her own?

Hannah was not so foolish to assume that no other woman had ever claimed his affections, if only for a while. Assuredly none had won his heart for marriage. But then, perhaps when they were young, he could not marry Abigail because she was half Indian. Such a marriage would certainly have been frowned upon then as now. No, that would not answer. Ahab made his decisions apart from the opinions of others. Then perhaps he would not marry her because her father was unknown. Overheard gossip informed Hannah that Abigail's father was thought to have been an errant white whaler who already had a wife. But rather than being a cause of disgrace, this would have made Ahab all the more loyal to her. For despite his reputation and popularity as a superior captain, he often chose to isolate himself and always felt a kinship with outcasts.

As time went by, Hannah grew to regret her jealousy. Why could she not dispense with it once and for all as Ahab had dispensed with his? But then, he at last had understood all about Jeremiah and her. Would she ever have the courage to demand an explanation from her husband about this attractive woman who had always been a part of his life? Until she had an answer, she would have no peace about the matter.

In mid-summer a new neighbor moved in down the street. Young Mrs. Starbuck was expecting a child, and her husband had recently departed on a whaling voyage. His widowed mother had helped to purchase the house so her grandchild could be born in his own home. She now helped her daughter-in-law with the move. Hannah watched for signs that the young woman was settled in. When at last a pineapple appeared on the front door stoop, the neighborhood was alerted that visitors were welcome. Hannah joined Aunt Charity to call on her.

Descended from the Macy family, Mary Starbuck was a true Nantucket girl and a strong Quaker. She wore no buttons or buckles on her clothing, and never went outdoors, even in her own yard, without her bonnet on her head, even in the heat of

summer. But she had a sweet countenance and was fervently religious in the matter of good deeds. Like Aunt Charity, she had
made her peace early with the life to which she had been born.
She and her husband had grown up next door to each other and
had played together like brother and sister. Yet they always had
known that one day they would marry. At twenty, they had
become man and wife and had now been married seven years.
The coming child was not the first one they had anticipated.
Two other little angels lay buried in unmarked graves in the
Quaker graveyard. But Mary was stronger now, and Dr. Gayer
declared that she should have no difficulties this time.

As for Mr. Starbuck, he was a relative of the wealthy Joseph
Starbuck whose daughters-in-law hosted the book and music
socials Hannah so much enjoyed. This branch of the family,
however, did not participate in such worldly activities. Mary was
content to keep house, to perform her works of charity for the
less fortunate, and to watch daily from her roof walk for her
husband's homecoming. Aunt Charity had known Mary since
she was a child and recommended her to Hannah for friendship.

Hannah was not surprised by the typical Quaker plainness of
Mary's home. Her mother-in-law had chosen a house that had
been designed by a humble Quaker merchant. No Greek colon-
nades or window trim adorned the outside, and no carved
balustrades or colorful wallpaper decorated the interior. The
furniture was equally plain, but was built from the best materials.

Hannah often joined her new friend on her roof to watch the
incoming tides bring ships into harbor. Although both their
husbands had been gone only a short time, when their respective
vessels came into sight, each wife wanted to be the first to see it.
Indeed, every ship reaching port was identified before it crossed
the sandbar at the mouth of Nantucket Harbor. News spread

quickly as the harbor bell rang and a flag was unfurled in the town square.

Experienced watchers could tell from the ship's water line and its movement through the harbor waters whether the voyage had been good or poor. A high water line and slow sailing indicated a heavy cargo and a good voyage. If the vessel sat high in the water and sailed easily over the bar, the crew would be frowning as they reached port. There were other signs to watch for, as well. A ship's flag hoisted to the top of the main mast proclaimed safety for all. A half-mast flag reported that there had been deaths.

Despite these outward signs that all could see, everyone involved with each ship hungered for details. Married to the bravest of seafaring men, a Nantucket woman displayed her own fortitude by patiently waiting for her husband to finish his duties, to visit the bath house for bath and shave, and to walk through the door of their home. For the ship captain's wife, news would be brought by young boys not yet old enough to sail. The first one to deliver the news to her earned a silver dollar.

Occasionally there was a woman who would not be satisfied until she laid eyes on her husband, brother, or son. Assured of his safety, she would go home to prepare a welcome feast. Seeing his injuries, she would convey him home for healing. Informed of his demise, she would stoically gather her children and retire to her home or church to mourn in the company of friends and family. A man who had not known his wife was expecting might be presented with a new child, perhaps one already walking and talking. A son might learn of a parent's or a sister's death.

This was the life of the whaling community. Hannah, who had stood apart from it all her life, at last had a compelling reason for participating in the joys and sorrows of her neighbors. Aunt Charity and Mary taught her by example how to rejoice with the fortunate and how to comfort the grieving. The courage and faith of her fellows inspired Hannah, but she wondered if she could be as brave as they were in the face of adversity. Though she tried to dismiss the idea that Ahab could ever have a bad voyage, reality might one day prove otherwise. Aunt Charity advised her to plan as though he would return safely and yet be prepared to accept his not returning at all. A wife best served her husband when she developed her own inner peace, born of a spirit which trusted that God never made a mistake.

Chapter Fifteen

ॐ

Timothy grew quickly. By the end of his first summer, the eight-month-old was already trying to stand, and he was prodigiously inquisitive. More than once as he nursed at Hannah's breast, his sharp baby teeth drew blood as he jerked his head away to investigate a new sound. He always wanted to know what was going on. If left awake in his nursery, he would not cry but rather chatter in loud baby talk, demanding to be a part of whatever was happening in the house. His dark brown eyes were bright and alert, following any action in sight with great concentration. If handed a new toy, he would speak to it in his own language or shake it and shout "Eeeeee!" as if to demand that it explain its purpose for existence. With three doting women at his beck and call, he became a benevolent sultan, bestowing smiles and hugs on his harem when they did his bidding. When they failed to meet his expectations, the tiny tyrant's dark, knitted brow and quivering lower lip compelled them to prompt compliance.

Because Kerenhappuch always attended the Quaker meeting and Sunday was Abigail's day off, Hannah had been taking Timothy to her own church since early spring. Perhaps soothed by the music and by Jeremiah's gentle preaching, the baby had never posed a problem. But as he grew bigger, he began to insist upon standing in Hannah's lap and looking about the congregation. Frowns from nearby worshippers embarrassed the mother, but she would not spank her infant as she had seen others do to their own. However, when her son began to make a running commentary on the pastor's sermons, she took him home, vowing not to return to church until he became more manageable.

Hannah was surprised to discover that she missed attending services. It was not Jeremiah she missed, of course, because he still visited her as Ahab had instructed. Nor did she miss out on his sermons, for he always gave her an abbreviated lesson from the previous Sunday. Rather, it was singing hymns or simply being in the company of other Christians contemplating the wonders of the Almighty. Often she thought of how her father had lived his own faith. She recalled with melancholy yearning the times they had talked of God and how he had once proven to her that she had more faith than she had realized. Many of her old friends in New Bedford had been devoutly religious, but she had not been able to conform to their expectations. Like her son, she had not been able to sit still. Like her father, she would not force her child to sit still either. Just as she had grown up and could now patiently remain seated in her pew, so one day her son would also mature and learn self-control. Aware of the fleeting nature of childhood, she would not hasten that day for anything.

Her conversations with Jeremiah provided more freedom of discussion than her visit with other women. Although many of her new friends were enlightened conversationalists, Hannah felt it best to wait some time before speaking her own opinions too aggressively. Most of these women had known each other all their lives, and, in fact, most were related in one way or another. With Jeremiah, however, she could be herself and could say anything she thought of without fear of censure.

When Kerenhappuch overcame her shyness, she too would venture to put forth an idea. The girl discovered that, unlike Quaker meetings where long silences preceded briefly spoken words of wisdom, Reverend Harris and Mrs. Ahab engaged in lively chats, sometimes interrupting each other and sometimes completing each other's sentences. She learned to speak up.

One day as the discussion turned toward Emerson, she ventured, "Lucretia Mott is an admirer of Mr. Emerson. When she visited the island last year, she caused me to consider some things I have long taken for granted."

Both Hannah and Jeremiah gave her their full attention, and she blushed shyly.

"How interesting," said Hannah. "What did she say?"

"Her most profound statement was, 'Truth for authority, not authority for Truth.'"

The other two looked at her expectantly, but she seemed finished. Jeremiah cleared his throat. "That's very interesting. Do you recall in what context she said it?"

"She was speaking about her conviction which leads her to adhere to the sufficiency of the Inner Light, as should we all … at least in the Friends' way of thinking … resting on the truth she finds there and making that her authority for all her beliefs and actions. I think this is very like what Mr. Emerson has said."

A hint of a frown passed over Jeremiah's face. Hannah could read his thoughts. If Kerenhappuch took up Emerson's Transcendentalism or decided to follow the Hicksite Friends' views that her mother favored, they could never marry. But he would not stifle her as she worked to develop her own beliefs. Rather, he would try to persuade her with loving words.

"I wonder," he said, "how one might know if his thoughts are indeed truth. Do the Scriptures not say that our hearts are deceitful and, therefore, may lead us astray?"

Kerenhappuch nodded. "The Scriptures do indeed say that. But then we must decide whether the Scriptures or the Inner Light is to be our guide to Truth."

Jeremiah listened patiently, but his distress was obvious. Before he could respond, Hannah broke in.

"But I am troubled by the thought that the inner light in one person might differ with that in another. How then does one know what is Truth? If I am not mistaken, in navigation there is a thing called 'true north' which every whaler and seaman must be aware of. With compass and charts, one can find one's way, no matter where he is. If one does not have a compass, one cannot find that true north. Even the most experienced captain must have these external instruments to guide him, no matter how great his experience or how strong his intuition. If that is true for navigating the oceans, how much more so for navigating one's spiritual voyage on this earth."

Jeremiah smiled at her, nodding eagerly. "Yes, one must indeed have a compass. Of course, the only spiritual compass we can safely rely on is the Bible."

"Forgive me, my friends, but I do not believe either of thee understands the nature of the Inner Light. It cannot vary from one person to another. It always speaks Truth to the earnest listener. And Truth is unchanging."

"Indeed," said Hannah, "Truth, by its very nature, is unchanging. It must always agree with itself. Yet this is what convinces me that our source for understanding Truth must be outside of ourselves. Otherwise, every sincere person seeking true knowledge regarding spiritual matters would agree, and we know that this is not so. It is more than obvious by the fighting amongst those called Christians that even the most sincere people sometimes do not agree about the most basic tenets of their faith. Each one believes his own inner light. How can that produce anything but chaos?"

Kerenhappuch agreed. "My mother is deeply grieved by the schism in our two Friends' meetings. To please my Uncle Bildad, we remain in the Orthodox meeting, but Mother's views are not always in agreement with his. Nor are her views always mine."

Jeremiah smiled, and a look of hope brightened his eyes. "I believe it was that great Quaker William Penn who said, 'Men are to be judged by their likeness to Christ, rather than by their notions of Christ.' Do you agree, Miss Coffin?" He would not call her by her first name until their engagement was official.

Kerenhappuch returned a smile. "Yes. Mrs. Mott says that the practical life of a Christian is the best evidence of a sound faith."

It was Hannah's turn to be distressed, but she did not say anything further. Jeremiah and Kerenhappuch had not really come to an agreement about spiritual matters. They both had simply retreated to a safe place of harmony. But if these differences were not resolved soon, they would surely suffer a painful estrangement in the end. Had she made a terrible mistake by bringing them together?

That evening Kerenhappuch asked Hannah to refrain from summoning her when Reverend Harris made his next call. Hannah agreed with reluctance. It seemed to her that confrontation and discussions would solve the lovers' differences. Would they now try to use her as a mediator? Though she longed for them to find happiness together, she felt like a failure as a matchmaker. Her concerns were in vain, for Jeremiah ceased to call.

Kerenhappuch, who was not given to excessive talking, now spoke even less. She did, however, take to reading her Bible every possible moment, when Timothy was asleep or when Hannah took him out for a walk. The girl's lovely face, usually so serene, was now at times marred by a knitted brow or a dark frown. Then, as weeks passed and September neared its close, her former serenity seemed to return. If anything, she was more at peace than ever. On a sunny afternoon as the two women sat on the back lawn with Timothy crawling back and forth between them, she abruptly began to reveal her conclusions from all her reading.

"God is our spiritual True North, is He not, Mrs. Ahab? It is He alone Who is absolute Truth."

Hannah, who had been captivated by her son's persistent attempts to walk, stared at her in surprise. "Why, yes. At least, I believe it would be appropriate to say that."

"Then indeed we must have a compass to direct us to Him, must we not?"

Again Hannah nodded her concurrence.

"I have come to think that we cannot depend upon the Inner Light alone, for our feelings and emotions often interfere with our most pious meditations," Kerenhappuch continued. "Sometimes we are not even aware of that interference. Therefore our decisions and actions become founded on faulty grounds. We end up doing what our human frailties and passions sway us to rather than what God would wisely direct us to."

For some reason, Hannah was reminded of her hasty marriage. She had not planned to marry at all. Yet within a short time, her love and, yes, her passion had compelled her to grasp for a happiness she had feared to lose. She had never prayed about whether she should marry Ahab. She had simply done what her heart demanded. Though she would not wish her marriage undone, she would also not advise others to do the same as she. How wise Kerenhappuch and Jeremiah were to consult God for this most important step in their lives.

Kerenhappuch was accustomed to silences. She allowed Hannah several minutes to consider what she had said before adding, "I am convinced that the Holy Scriptures are indispensable to knowledge and that the Inner Light that I seek must agree with the wisdom written therein, or it is no light at all."

Hannah smiled. "You put me to shame. I have always thought myself very wise. But though I believe in the wisdom of the Scriptures, I neglect to read them or to seek counsel there for my decisions, even though my father lived his entire life guided by his Bible. But now, what will you do with this new conviction? Will you speak to Jeremiah and set his mind at ease?"

Kerenhappuch blushed and an embarrassed smile replaced her serene expression. "Oh, no. If God wishes us to marry, He must draw us together again."

"That doesn't sound like a Nantucket girl," Hannah laughed. "I've heard of more than one who proposed to her beau rather than the other way around. In fact, I was quite assertive in securing my own husband's proposal."

The younger woman nodded soberly. "Yes, and many of them live to regret it when their husbands turn out to be other than they expected. Oh, Mrs. Ahab, I don't mean thee and the captain, of course!"

Hannah suddenly became involved in adjusting her son's clothing. "No, of course you didn't. We're ... we're quite suited to each other."

Hannah's matchmaking instincts were revived by this revealing conversation. She began to scheme how she might lure Jeremiah back for his regular visits. After all, he had promised Ahab he would visit. When October arrived with no appropriate excuse coming to her mind, she nevertheless decided to pay a call on Reverend Harris.

On Sunday afternoon, Hannah set out for Jeremiah's cottage near the church, telling Kerenhappuch that she was going for a walk, despite the gloomy skies above. When she arrived, she found him not at home, but his housekeeper expected him soon.

The woman said that after morning services he had gone to partake of Sunday dinner with Mr. and Mrs. Chase. Hannah waited for two hours before deciding that her mission had been in vain. She stepped outside into a light rain to return home. After walking only one block, she was driven back to the parsonage by an intense shower, arriving at the door just as Jeremiah did.

"Hannah," he cried, pulling her inside, "what on earth brings you here in this weather?"

"It wasn't bad when I came. I've been here for some time waiting for you, and just now was returning home. Where have you been all day?"

The housekeeper brought blankets and hot tea, then helped them remove their damp coats. Wrapped in the blankets, they sat in front of the roaring fireplace to throw off the chill. Jeremiah sat back in his chair and stared gloomily into the fire.

"This is a perfect day for bad news," he said.

"What bad news?"

"Oh, Hannah, everything is going wrong for me. I know that God never makes a mistake, but I wonder if I wouldn't do well to seek a little more of that Inner Light our Quaker friends speak of. Perhaps then I could develop an instinct for—"

"What on earth are you talking about?"

He sighed with exasperation. "I have just spent a very unhappy afternoon at Mr. Chase's house. I was not the only guest. Several of the elders were there to confront me on some issues that have concerned them regarding my pastoral duties."

"But things were going so well for you there. What could have happened?"

"The newness of my being here has worn off, I suppose. I've never faced such obvious disapproval, even from riverboat scalawags."

"How could they possibly disapprove of you? Your theology is in keeping with theirs, is it not?"

"My theology, yes. But it seems that not only my preaching of that theology falls short of their expectations, but apparently I am also entirely too easy on errant church members."

"What nonsense. What did you tell them?"

He shook his head. "I didn't tell them anything. They told me that unless I make some changes, I will be asked to step down."

"Oh, this is unconscionable. The only change they really want you to make is to stop seeing Kerenhappuch. I suppose the lovely Miss Isabel Chase put in an appearance at her uncle's house to assist in reinforcing their persuasion."

He smiled ruefully. "Oh, I doubt that. And though she was there, I suspect from the look in her eyes that Miss Chase's heart is already engaged. As to Kerenhappuch, well, that's already been taken care of, as you may have noticed. Still, I doubt that protesting my … my courtship is truly their motive."

Hannah stared into the fire. She wanted to tell him that the purpose of her visit was to reunite him with his love. But it was past time to nurse her son and her breasts were beginning to feel uncomfortably full. With a flash of inspiration, she said, "I must go home to feed Timothy, but the wind is awfully strong. Would you take me?"

"Of course." He stood quickly and went for their still wet coats.

Hannah grinned with pleasure. He seemed eager to see her safely home, which meant he was eager to see her son's nurse-maid. She had not been forced to actively interfere at all. Her good mood quickly disappeared a few feet from the cottage when a violent gust nearly blew her down.

"We really should stay put, Hannah," yelled Jeremiah above the wind.

"I can't. My baby needs me," she cried.

"All right. We'll make it then."

He grasped her around the waist and held tight as they braced against the pounding gale. More than once, they slipped and fell. More than once they were driven off course by the fury of the storm. Now the wind was tearing shingles from roofs and making a weapon out of anything not tied down. Ships in the harbor were bounced about in the storm surge, their moorings torn loose. The wind came from the east with all the force of a late season hurricane.

Never had Hannah experienced such fear, not for herself, but for her child. What foolish notion had brought her out on a rainy afternoon? Why had she thought to manipulate the affairs of others rather than staying home to care for her precious son? A twenty-minute walk on a clear day had turned into more than an hour of dodging deadly projectiles as they staggered through town against the violent gale. When at last they reached the house on Orange Street, they were welcomed by Abigail and Kerenhappuch and bundled upstairs for dry clothes.

The romance of her friends was far from Hannah's mind as she lay on her bed nursing Timothy. He was fretful as he drank, and his dark eyes reproached her for being so late with his supper. She suspected that the noise of the storm bothered him as much as her negligence, but she vowed never to leave him like that again. Parents had a responsibility to take care of themselves for the sake of their children. If something had happened to her, what would have become of her son?

The hurricane lasted for two days, pounding Nantucket as it had not been pounded in fifty-five years. In most households, all inhabitants stayed downstairs for the duration, for the upper stories bore the brunt of the storm. When the winds finally abated, the landscape was cluttered with chimneys and roof walks that had been torn from nearly forty homes, with pieces flung in every direction. Buildings on the waterfront had been splintered or entirely washed away as water backed up into the harbor, overflowing the wharves to a depth of three feet. Many ships had been damaged, some of them stove and sunk. Inland on the narrow island, several houses and barns were demolished. Embankments had given way, washing everything in their path down toward the sea. Despite all the storm's violence, however, not one person was killed and only one man was injured, breaking his leg as he fell down a slope. And Mary Starbuck was delivered of a healthy baby boy.

Although the Ahab house was on the top of the Orange Street hill, it was in the middle of the block and did not suffer as much damage as many. The trellises in the garden were gone, and several shutters were torn loose, but the chimney was intact, and the roof walk needed only a little repair to make it secure once more.

If there was anything gained from the ordeal, it was the engagement of Jeremiah and Kerenhappuch. While the storm had raged, they had spent the two days in a sanctuary-like refuge. Their chaperones, two reputable women who discreetly permitted their private conversations while assuring that the outside cataclysm did not encourage to uncharacteristic misdeeds the dispirited young lovers within.

Chapter Sixteen

∞

The courage of the Nantucket community was never so evident as in the aftermath of the hurricane. The people came together to clear away the debris and help one another rebuild. Even the two small Quaker meetings demonstrated the charity of their founders, rubbing shoulders with former adversaries as they made renovations in preparation for the coming winter. Due to a scarcity of strong men to handle the physical labor, Jeremiah's congregation soon found cause to forgive his perceived offenses. While the men whose jobs were directly a part of the whalefishery spent their efforts repairing the ships, docks, and shipyards, no man among them did more than Jeremiah to rebuild homes or to ensure the restocking of depleted larders, all the while refusing any payment for his labor.

By spring, however, as memories of the disaster faded, some church members renewed their complaints. They could no longer fault him for his choice of intended wife, for Miss Coffin had been disowned by the Quaker meeting for becoming engaged to a non-member. She now attended services at Jeremiah's church and planned to join it officially upon further study of its doctrines.

The blemish that the elders found in the young minister was his insistence that only the most grievous offenses should result in strong church discipline. In their view, he spoke too often on the love and forgiveness of God and too little on the wages of sin. They seemed to be looking for a fresh incarnation of Jonathan Edwards or Cotton Mather to usher in another Great Awakening. They wanted someone to strike the fear of an angry God into the hearts of their children—especially their whaling sons—so that they might not go astray. Jeremiah was not the man for that job.

To show support for her friend, Hannah began to attend services once again, bringing along her seventeen-month-old son. She and Kerenhappuch had taught him a new game. If they raised one finger to their lips and quietly said "Shh," he was to be quiet. If they sat with hands folded, he was to do the same. Always eager to mimic his mother and nursemaid, Timothy learned to "play church." Nevertheless, Hannah found herself wishing that their pew were near the door for those times when he became bored and began loudly to suggest alternate activities or to make an addendum to the sermon. And he never could understand why he could not go to join his friend who was standing at the front of the room.

As summer approached, it became clear that unless the elders' concerns were addressed and resolved, the congregation would suffer another schism. In a circumstance some years prior, half of the members, wearied by legalistic demands and later drawn to the Unitarian philosophy, had founded the Second Congregational Society. That church, like its begetter, had then locked its doctrine into place and had begun to suppress disagreements.

Jeremiah, though supported by more than half the membership of the First Church, was horrified at the thought of being the cause of a similar division, especially because the difficulties did not concern basic doctrinal beliefs. Meeting privately with the disapproving elders, he agreed to resign his position if he might have one more opportunity to address the flock he had come to love. Reluctantly, they agreed.

On the last Sunday in May, pleasant breezes and the fragrance of flowers outside were a strong contrast to the oppressive pall within the church's sanctuary, where every pew was filled. Hannah sat with her son and Kerenhappuch, watching her friend on the podium. While the congregation sang Watts's "When I Survey the Wondrous Cross," Jeremiah surveyed his congregation. No one seeing the young pastor could have guessed at the sorrow within his heart. As was his custom, he looked about for those who faced particular hardships and silently prayed for them. When the hymn ended, he stepped up to the pulpit and bowed his head to pray again.

Hannah gripped Kerenhappuch's hand in anticipation of his expected self-defense to his unjust accusers. When she glanced at the girl, she was surprised to see a reflection of the peace that Jeremiah's face bore. How could they bear this insufferable treatment with so much serenity? Was this not the time for Jeremiah at last to stand up to these people and scold them soundly for their sinful arrogance? But when he raised his eyes, only love was reflected there, and she could see that he would not.

He began his sermon by reading from his Bible a parable that Jesus had told, the story of the unjust servant who, though he had been forgiven a great debt by his master, refused to forgive a small debt owed to him. Jeremiah did not dwell on the unforgiving servant, nor on his eventual punishment, but rather on the great debt that had been forgiven him.

"So you see," he continued, "it is the mercy of God we are concerned with today. In the Old Testament, we are told of God's chosen people, the Israelites, whom He mercifully rescued from slavery in the land of Egypt, then brought into the

Promised Land, and to whom He gave His commandments, His law. Think of it. Every aspect of the Israelites' lives was controlled by rigid rules of conduct. Was this proof of the mercy of God? Yes, it was. Those righteous laws were given to bring order to God's people in the midst of a chaotic world, a world in which every tribe and nation sought to conquer and destroy those around them. Merciful God was giving His children a land flowing with milk and honey, a land of prosperity wherein they could find peace and happiness. All He required in return was their obedience. Does that seem harsh? Not at all, for disobedience would make them like their wicked neighbors, whose vile and evil practices were an abomination to Him.

"When the children of God failed to keep the law, He mercifully provided sacrifices to atone for their sins so that they might not be cut off from their people or their land. There were sacrifices for every willful sin they might ever commit. But here is an amazing thing: in the book of Leviticus, chapter four, we learn that God even provided sacrifices for unintentional sin, those things done through the frailty of human error, human neglect, human weakness. More than any other, we must look to this provision to see God's generous mercy to His children, and to us. He knows our frame. He remembers that we are dust. The law was given not so that the Israelites, or we, by perfect obedience might become perfect, but rather that we might see how far short of God's perfection we fall.

"Does the law still condemn us? Yes, it does. Does a doctrine of obedience to rules and salvation through good works still seek to bind us today? Absolutely. But, brethren, do not be entangled again in that yoke of bondage. The good news of the Gospel is that Christ has redeemed us from the curse and bondage of the law. He is our sacrifice for sins, intentional and unintentional. He alone is our salvation.

"If we could earn our salvation through good works, by perfect obedience to God's laws, God need never have demonstrated His mercy to us. And Christ our Savior need never have died. The more good works we could manage to do, the greater our right to boast proudly to our brother, 'I am more righteous than you.' But it is not by our deeds of righteousness that He saves us. Rather, it is by His mercy, without which none of us shall ever see God."

Jeremiah stopped and once again surveyed his congregation. He seemed to be deciding what to say next. *Surely now he will tell off these self-righteous people,* Hannah thought.

"How gladly the outside world watches when Christians refuse to solve their differences, for it seems proof to them that our Gospel message is powerless. Let us not be like the unjust servant in failing to forgive the brother who owes us a debt or who has offended us. Through our forgiveness, through our love, we have the power to demonstrate God's mercy to needy sinners."

Jeremiah gripped the sides of the pulpit, sighed deeply, and bowed his head. The room was silent. Even Timothy listened without making a sound. After several moments, the pastor looked up and once again surveyed the room. Tears glistened in his eyes.

"Be not divided, my brethren. Love one another as I ..." he paused. "No, not I. Love one another as Christ has loved you." He paused again and drew in a deep breath. "Thank you for permitting me to be your pastor for these two years. You have greatly enriched my life. May God be with you all."

Unable to say anything else, he picked up his Bible and descended the podium. Then he walked to the pew where his fiancée sat and took her hand. The two of them proceeded to the door of the church, where they stood to greet any who would wish to address them.

The congregation seemed stunned. Although most members had been aware of the elders' complaints, few had expected this sudden resignation of the generally admired young pastor. Hannah, however, picked up her son and marched up the aisle toward the door, vowing never to set foot in the building again.

The following day, the minister of Nantucket's Methodist Episcopal Church performed a simple wedding ceremony for Jeremiah and Kerenhappuch. On Tuesday, the young couple said their good-byes to family and friends, then placed their few belongings on the daily steamer to New Bedford. Hannah and Timothy joined Aunt Charity and an assortment of other relatives on the docks to see them off.

When it was their turn to embrace Kerenhappuch, Hannah and her son both cried. "You taught me how to be a good mother, and you're not even one yourself. At least not yet," Hannah said.

The bride blushed and quickly changed the subject. "Thou hast taught me many things, too, Mrs. Ahab. I shall forever be grateful that thou gavest me my first real job." She glanced shyly at Jeremiah. "And a husband," she added. "Thou wilt always be welcome in our home, wherever we may be. Oh, dear. Let me hold my Timothy one last time, for the next time I see him, he will be too big." She took the boy from Hannah's arms and went to speak to another wellwisher.

Hannah turned to find Jeremiah just as he approached her. She flung herself into his outstretched arms and wept bitterly. "Oh, how can I say good-bye to you? Jeremiah, please stay. Don't you know how much you are loved here? How can we ever do without you?"

Jeremiah held her tightly, and a sob escaped him. "Oh, dear, dear Hannah, my sister and friend. I shall miss you more than you'll ever know. I owe you eternal thanks for the greatest happiness in my life." He stopped, unable to speak without tears.

When he had gained control, he held her away and gazed into her eyes. "Tell Captain Ahab … tell him how much I … respect and admire him. Tell him I … I did my duty as long as I was able. God will surely watch over you now. Besides," he added, trying to lighten this painful moment, "who would dare to harm the wife and child of Captain Ahab?"

Hannah smiled at his brave attempt at levity for only an instant before expelling a weary sigh. "Who ever would have thought when we were children that things would come to this? You're the most tenderhearted, the most generous man in the world, the ablest preacher and pastor. Why …?"

"Let's don't trouble ourselves with 'why.' It's so easy to decide what we think God's plan is. Then when something different happens, we blame God rather than our own faulty concept of Him, proving that we don't know Him at all. We want to know the reason for everything, but He wants us to trust His leading day by day. If He made our paths easy and our lives all happiness and comfort, why would we need to rely on Him? A harder road strengthens our faith." He stopped abruptly and gave her a sheepish grin. "Hmm, I didn't mean to preach a sermon. These are the things I keep telling myself to avoid becoming bitter." He chuckled, then grew serious again. "Oh, Hannah, don't you be bitter on my account."

"How can you expect me not to be?"

He thought for a moment, then chuckled again. "Well, for one thing, you could consider the fortuity of my going back to New Bedford. Why don't I speak to Abel Williams on your behalf and see if he will sell one of Samson's colts to you for your husband. You've been talking about this for a long time. Let me make all the arrangements for you."

She stared at him. "Listen to you. In the midst of your own suffering, you are still ministering to others."

"Shall I do it then?"

She embraced him once again. "Oh, yes, my dear friend and brother. Thank you."

He gave her another brief hug, and the warmth of his masculine embrace made her wish for the comfort of her husband's arms. Then she held her son and waved as the newlyweds boarded the steamer and sailed away. Standing among the other wellwishers, Hannah could not help but think that these Nantucket docks were the scene of far too many sad good-byes.

Chapter Seventeen

છ્

After the departure of her closest friends, Hannah tried to spend more time with Mary Starbuck. In addition to her enjoying the other woman's company, Timothy found baby Isaiah entertaining. But Mary's Quaker meeting preferred its members to socialize among themselves, so Hannah limited their times together to prevent problems for her friend. The more independent Aunt Charity still called, but her visits were short. With her only daughter gone, probably never to return, and her only surviving son at sea, the day of his return unpredictable, she busied herself with additional charitable activities. Hannah might have joined her except that now, without a nursemaid, Timothy demanded all her time. She did not wish to hire someone new, and she left her son with Abigail as seldom as possible.

In a population of nearly ten thousand people, the majority of whom were women whose menfolk were whalers, Hannah had yet to find a kindred spirit. It was not that she disliked the wool carding and knitting parties, the book and music clubs, or the charitable work of the Society to Assist the Poor. And, of course, she did not feel intellectually superior to these well-taught women. Further, as the wife of a successful whaling captain, she found herself in the enviable position of being able to choose her friends from any level of society. She was welcomed in the best of homes because of Ahab's legendary success, a success that had brought him esteem almost to the point of veneration from everyone in the whalefishery. Perhaps that accounted for some wives of more ordinary men being less inclined to seek Hannah's friendship. Yet for some reason, it was those women with whom she felt most comfortable.

Not all ship captains' wives could afford the luxury of developing an extensive social life. Some wives, often those married to younger captains who had not yet earned much money or captains whose greasy luck was minimal, were forced to provide much of their own income. In addition to managing their households, doing chores, raising children, and living like widows in their husbands' absences, many took on the added challenge of running businesses. Centre Street had become known as Petticoat Row, that name being a high compliment to the hardworking women whose shops provided both necessities and luxuries to the community.

Observing all this, Hannah recalled with a laugh the foolish old wives' tale Lila Williams had told her. Nantucket women proved that a woman could use her mind for intellectual and business endeavors and still bear an abundance of healthy children. But for all their hard work, accomplishments, and maintenance of the community in the absence of their menfolk, most of them ultimately deferred to their husbands when they returned home. Hannah could not fault them for it. Her own husband spoke with such authority and from such vast experience that she herself often trusted his judgments more than her own.

In keeping with Ahab's recommendation, Hannah often patronized Ida Stoddard's dry goods store. But her attempts to befriend the other woman had been politely rebuffed for two years. Though Ida was an off-islander like Hannah, and therefore seemed like a good match for friendship, she preferred to keep to herself. When Hannah asked Aunt Charity about Ida, the older woman would only say that it was well known that Captain Stoddard could not be relied upon to do well by his wife. When not working in her store, the woman had always kept to herself, especially when her husband was home between voyages.

Why Ida did not socialize in her spare time was a mystery to Hannah. She had no children. And when Captain Stoddard was home, he did not spend much time at his house on Fair Street or much time sober. Rather, he daily patronized the taverns near the docks, making up for shipboard temperance that Mr. Lyons required of all his captains. But Ahab's suggestion and Aunt Charity's vague words at last made sense to Hannah when she visited the store shortly after the captain's return from the Pacific waters. As a change from her customary upswept hairdo, Ida's long brown tresses hung down, covering her cheeks. And she would not lift her eyes as she helped Hannah make a selection of embroidery thread. It was only when Hannah glanced in the mirror behind the counter that she could see the reflection of a large bruise around Ida's left eye.

"Mrs. Stoddard," she gasped, "whatever happened to you?" She reached across the counter and lifted the woman's chin to study the injury.

Mrs. Stoddard moved back and lowered her head once more. "I fell against the newel post as I was starting upstairs last night. Wasn't that clumsy of me?" She glanced up with a quivering smile, then down again. "Here's your thread. I know your quilt will be lovely when it's all put together. How do you have the patience to embroider all those squares, and with such intricate patterns?"

Hannah gazed at her sadly. She had seen such a bruise just one other time, and that was long ago when her father had explained a black and blue welt on the face of a woman acquaintance. At that time, it had been distressing to Hannah to learn that not every man was as gentle as her father. Now she could see that Captain Stoddard was one of those contemptible men who hit their wives. But what could she, or anyone, do if Ida would not seek help?

"Oh, a stitch here and a stitch there, a little bit every day. Then all the pieces come together. Ida, do you need a friend?" Those last words tumbled out, but Hannah was glad for it.

Ida glanced up once more, tears glistening in her eyes. But as she opened her mouth to speak, the bell on the door jingled, and Mr. Lyons entered the store.

"Mrs. Ahab, how pleasant to see thee. What news of thy husband?"

"No news at all, sir. He's not one to write, and none of the ships that have returned since he sailed had gammed with the *Pequod*." Hannah did not want the attention on herself. But what could she say to Ida now, with Mr. Lyons in the store? She had no need to speak, however, for Mr. Lyons had just noticed Ida's face. In all her life, Hannah had never seen a soft-spoken Quaker gentleman so instantly and completely enraged.

"Ida!" he cried, reaching out toward the woman. Then, mindful of Hannah's presence, he stopped, confused and angry. As he worked to control himself, his eyes filled with compassion, and it seemed that he would have taken her into his arms had Hannah not been there. "Mrs. Stoddard, hast thou ... hast thee fallen again?"

At the gentleness of his tone, Ida began to cry and fled to the storage room at the back of the store. Mr. Lyons followed her, and Hannah was left to ponder the complexity of the situation.

It was clear now that Ahab had encouraged her friendship with Ida so that she could find some way to help her. But how? She would not gossip about what she had seen, nor would she seek information from just anyone. And she certainly could not leave the situation alone, as though it were none of her business. It was time for a visit to Aunt Charity. She found her friend at home in her small, three-room house on Milk Street. She related all she had seen to Charity, then sat back to sip her tea.

"Yes, it's a sad story," the older woman said. "Thou art kind to take an interest. Most people feel that what a man does to his wife is beyond interference or even the law. But there is a higher law Captain Stoddard will answer to one day."

"But isn't there anything we can do now?"

"If I'm not mistaken, Mr. Lyons will do as he has done before. He will get the captain back out to sea on the *Legacy* as soon as possible. I must tell thee that good Mr. Lyons has had a great influence on Ida. She once endured her husband's absences, as well as his homecomings, by the occasional use of opium. I'm sure you know that there are those foolish women here in Nantucket who use it to endure the loneliness and hardships that come from having a husband so often at sea. But Mr. Lyons encouraged Ida to forsake that harmful habit in favor of prayer. As thou well knowest, like most owners, Mr. Lyons feels a responsibility toward the families whose menfolk sail on his ships. With his spiritual encouragement and financial backing, Ida has found the strength to forswear self-destruction and to build her store into the lovely establishment that it is. Unfortunately, when Captain Stoddard is home, she doesn't fare too well. But count on Mr. Lyons. The *Legacy* will soon be out to sea again, and all will be well."

Hannah tried to discern if there was an underlying meaning in Charity's words. But the woman was guileless. Was Hannah the only one who was concerned about the level of Mr. Lyons' care for Ida? She did not have long to consider it. Within a few weeks of her discussion with Aunt Charity, the *Legacy* set sail to go around Cape Horn. A few weeks after Captain Stoddard's departure, Ida shocked the community and lost many of her customers when she performed the scandalous act of filing suit for divorce. Having the testimony of honest men to verify her allegations, she charged Captain Stoddard with bigamy. Her suit was legal, but many felt that she should have quietly endured the shame of her husband's South Seas family, as other whaling women had. But though she would soon be free of her cruel husband, Mrs. Stoddard continued to be censured for other reasons. One week after she filed her suit, Mr. Lyons was disowned by the meeting of Friends. Despite the purity of his friendship with Ida, the elders were certain that the two had broken religious and moral codes. And, indeed, there was no doubt that the two were in love. Hannah could not help but be happy for them. Ida was a good woman. Mr. Lyons was kindness personified. Surely, Hannah reasoned, there was a limit to the cruelty a woman must endure at the hands of her husband.

As the summer wore on, Hannah found her customary solace in cultivating her garden, with her son playing nearby. The trellises had been restored and climbing roses flourished all over them. Whether perennial or annual, every bush and plant bloomed prolifically. Always looking for ways to enhance the landscaping, she decided to add an arbor like the one at her childhood home. But for the time being, no laborers were available to build it.

In addition to her garden, she continued her daily trips to the roof walk to watch for her husband's ship. In late September, she rejoiced with Aunt Charity when twenty-three-year-old Josiah Coffin returned. Aunt Charity prevailed upon her brother Bildad to accompany her to the docks to greet the young man. As with all incoming ships, the first thing families wanted to know was that all had returned safely. Josiah waved vigorously to his mother before returning to his numerous shipboard duties. It was not until he came home three days later that she learned that this had been his final voyage. While any mother would be grateful to know her son would no longer be in such dangerous work, his retirement from the sea came at great cost to his body and to his future.

Taking his turn as lookout aloft in the crow's-nest one day, Josiah had spotted a pod of whales. He had sung out "whale ho" to the crew, then had begun his descent to join in lowering the whale boats. The ship had pitched about in the choppy waters, and a misstep had sent him crashing to the deck below, where his left shoulder had been shattered. Over the many months that the voyage had continued, he had slowly healed. While his strength at last had returned, the mobility of his left arm had not, and he could no longer engage in his trade. It was a sad circumstance for this young harpooner who had worked his way up to third mate, with hopes of one day becoming a captain. Yet, with pious resignation, he accepted God's holy alteration of his own manmade plans.

"God does not take us through deep waters to drown us, but rather to cleanse us," he declared, pleasing his mother far more by his faith than ever he could by financial success.

Profoundly moved by the young man's courage, Hannah hired him to build her arbor and tend to the heavy work around the house. He was also able to manage the care of Samson, the gelded offspring of the Williams's stallion, which was kept at a local stable. Each day Hannah could hear Josiah singing a hymn or respectable sea chantey outside her window as he worked. Like his mother, he had refused to be defeated by the disappointments of life.

Not all homecomings pleased Hannah so well. One morning in late November she went to the kitchen to approve Abigail's menus for the coming week and found that her housekeeper had a guest. He was a tall, well-built man of about thirty years with a deeply tanned complexion, dark hair, and dark eyes. His new clothes, haircut, and shave were those of a whaler just home and cleaned up from a successful voyage. He stood in the kitchen in front of the stove, and as Hannah entered the room, he was lifting a spoon to taste a simmering stew. But rather than be embarrassed by this presumptive behavior, he simply put the spoon down and looked at her with a pleasant and expectant expression. It was Abigail who seemed discomfited, but even she quickly recovered.

"Mrs. Hannah, this is my son, Daniel." She supplied only his first name and offered nothing beyond this brief introduction.

The man smiled and politely nodded. That he did not reach to take her hand indicated his uncertainty as to his rung on Mrs. Ahab's social ladder. It was up to her to inform him. But when she lifted her hand to graciously receive the son of her servant, she almost reeled backward in astonishment. As he reached out and bent forward to place a dignified kiss on her fingertips, his height, his broad shoulders, his handsome brow and dark eyes, even his firm handshake, all were agonizingly familiar to her. So Ahab had given Abigail a son after all!

Hannah had no idea how she masked her horror. But somehow she managed. "How do you do, Daniel? I'm certain your mother is pleased to see you back home safely. Will you be here long between voyages?" These were standard remarks in the whaling community and provided her a safe harbor.

"One never knows," he said. "I'm hoping that my next voyage will coincide with Captain Ahab's. My first was under his command, and there's no finer captain. Since that time, I've longed to sail with him again, but it has never worked out."

Hannah stared at him, nonplused. He was not making any claims on her husband, only expressing his admiration. But then, that was a harmless course of action, for everyone admired Captain Ahab. When she did not respond, he went on.

"My mother tells me that he's been away for almost two years. Since he has a history of short but successful voyages, he's sure to be home soon. Perhaps if I can be patient, it will all work out. But it's difficult for us whalers to stay on shore when there are profits to be made at sea."

During his lengthy discourse, the young man spoke with an unaffectedness that communicated self-assurance. Like Ahab, he had proven himself in his own sphere and therefore could be comfortable wherever he found himself. And, like Ahab, the fire in his eyes as he talked of whaling demonstrated that he was a man with a passion for his profession.

"Well then," Hannah said, "I would suggest that you not pass up any opportunities, for I mean to convey my husband off to Europe upon his return." She was ashamed of her words immediately. They were spoken in spite, with the hope that this pleasant young man would disappear from her life, and Ahab's, forever. Though he may not have understood her intentions, she felt she must make amends.

"If you have no place to stay, you're welcome to one of our guest rooms for as long as you like." *Please God, don't let him accept*, she thought.

"Thank you, Mrs. Ahab. You're very kind. But I have a room already."

Hannah looked at Abigail. The woman's face was a mask, as usual, except perhaps her eyes. Yet the hint of pride therein was maternal, not some sort of triumphant arrogance. Hannah repeated her welcome, then excused herself, ostensibly to tend her son. But Timothy would not be waking from his nap for some time. She was fleeing the room to release the violent emotions she could no longer hide. In the refuge of her bedroom, she closed the door and flung herself on the bed, giving vent at last. Burying her face in a pillow, she sobbed as loudly as she dared. She would not give Abigail any cause for triumph.

So this was how it stood. Ahab had another son. A grown son he could be proud of. One who was following in his footsteps. That was something she dreaded for her own child. Something she would prevent at any cost. Timothy would not be a whaler! But how could she prevent it? In whom could she confide? Who would support her? The women of Nantucket knew what their men were about, Ahab had said. Suffer and grieve though they might, they still undergirded their men, doing whatever it took to manage homes, businesses, and childrearing without complaint. All this for the meager comforts of marriage to a husband who might spend one year in seven at home. It was all too unbearable!

In spite of the turmoil in her mind, Hannah found an unexpected moment of sympathy for Abigail. What kind of life had this woman had, waiting between every voyage for her man to return, yet never being able to claim him as her own? Never being able proudly to parade her child about as the son of the distinguished Captain Ahab, lest all their names be tarnished. How must she have felt after all those years of faithfulness when Ahab had brought home his legal and very young bride? When that bride had given him a son he could publicly acknowledge? Yet Abigail had displayed only tender affection for Timothy and never any jealousy toward her. Why should jealousy consume Hannah when it was womanly empathy she should feel?

What a cruel business this whaling was to its women. Though a ship filled with whale oil might produce evidence of lengthy months and years of seagoing labors, some whalers, such as Captain Stoddard, were known to have spent part of that time producing second families somewhere in the South Pacific. With one family in Nantucket and the other on the shores of a distant island, they could have all the comforts of home wherever they were while their women languished in loneliness. Was her Ahab such a man? Surely not.

She had never seen him display any affection toward Abigail, just a confidential familiarity that was somehow different from his intimacy with Hannah. Despite his professed passion for her, was he simply cold-hearted toward both of them? An unknown foreign rival could not cause the grief that one at home could. While other whalers might keep their two wives separated by half a world of oceans, was Ahab keeping his two women in the same house? No, it was impossible. Yet what other explanation could there be? Daniel looked too much like Ahab. Perhaps this shared son was the cause of Abigail's cool self-assurance. In the face of all the cruel possibilities, Hannah could not fault the woman for it.

When she could weep no more, could think no more, Hannah slept. Waking near sunset, she felt a curious sense of composure that enabled her to further evaluate the situation. Daniel was at least ten years older than she. If Ahab and Abigail had been lovers, his ardor—and perhaps hers as well—had cooled long before Hannah had even been born. They had made the best of things. He had generously provided for this woman and their son, even to giving them both the means of earning their livings. Yet why would he not marry Abigail when she bore him a child? Hannah tried to excuse it, but finding no acceptable justification, she could only look to Abigail's serene acceptance. If she could accept her reduced status, could actually serve her former lover and his wife, who was Hannah to complain? After all, it was she who bore Ahab's name. It was she who shared Ahab's bed ... when he was at home.

Her thoughts were interrupted by a soft tapping on the door. Without waiting for a response, Abigail opened it and brought in a pitcher of warm water for the washstand.

"Mrs. Hannah, are you ill? Timothy has been downstairs these past three hours. He came down all by himself. Daniel is entertaining him now."

Hannah gasped and jumped up from the bed. "Oh, dear Lord. What an awful mother I am." She splashed water on her face and quickly dried it before hastening out the door.

If Abigail was aware of the turmoil her son's appearance had brought upon Hannah, she did not indicate it. She was only appropriately solicitous of her employer's distress that was evidenced by her tear-swollen face. She seemed to believe that weeping wives whose husbands were at sea were best left to themselves to regain control of their emotions.

Daniel visited his mother every day, and Timothy latched onto him with a jolly affection. While Hannah watched closely, Daniel would kneel down on all fours and ride the two-year-old around the parlor. It was clear that the whaler felt comfortable in this house. Had he once lived here? Hannah wondered. But now that Jeremiah was gone, she would not deny her son the influence of the amiable man. Someday, this much-older brother might prove to be a worthy friend to her son. Already he had expressed his care for the household by giving his mother a gun and teaching her how to use it.

"There are too many newcomers on Nantucket Island these days," he said. "This will at least provide some protection should anyone seek to harm any of you. Most criminals are cowards. If they see the gun, they'll flee. Just keep it loaded and keep it where the boy cannot reach it."

Abigail took his advice in stride, but Hannah was filled with gratitude. While Ahab's reputation had always provided protection, some of the rougher newcomers to the island might not know of him. And Daniel's inclusive consideration of the household seemed further evidence of his taking after Ahab.

As the months passed, Daniel, like most whalers, grew restless. Every day he walked to the docks to watch the ships come and go. He often spent his afternoon at a tavern, talking and drinking with fellow whalers. In March, no longer able to resist the lure of the sea, he shipped aboard a whaler that was bound for Greenland.

"It will be a short voyage," he told them in parting. "We should return within the year. Tell my ..."

Abigail lifted her head and arched her eyebrows almost imperceptibly, but it was enough to warn him.

"Tell Captain Ahab that I hope to see him when I return." He lifted the giggling Timothy up into the air and spun him around. "And you, my lad, will sail with me one day when I've become a captain."

Hannah smiled politely. *Not while I live to prevent it*, she thought. "We look forward to your safe return," she said. Then she watched with both relief and sympathy as Abigail and Daniel left for the docks.

Chapter Eighteen

ᔑ

*H*earing the harbor bell ring out one bright morning in late June, Hannah was filled with joy to see the ship she had been waiting for sail into view at the mouth of the harbor. She called to Abigail to watch Timothy, then rushed out her front door. There she was met by a small boy who had run to Captain Ahab's house on Orange Street to confirm the news: the *Pequod* had arrived. He held out his hand for the expected silver dollar.

"Abigail, give him his reward," she cried over her shoulder. Then, ignoring convention as she had warned Ahab she would, she ran down Orange and Main Streets to the docks to greet the ship. Captain Bildad, alerted that his vessel was approaching the camels, appeared on the docks as well, accompanied by Aunt Charity and Josiah. Several other women whose menfolk were on board joined Hannah in Bildad's protective presence on the busy wharf.

The women welcomed Hannah to their ranks with a mixture of sisterly enthusiasm and deference. It was her husband who must answer to all of them, whether the news was good or bad. For this voyage, all signs pointed to good news, as all of Captain Ahab's voyages had in the past.

"Look," cried one woman who knew her ships and whaling. "The masts and sails are new made. They must have lost the others in a storm."

"But, praise God, the flag is at full mast," an old Quaker widow said. She was awaiting the return of her son.

"She looks mighty fine, I'll say," said another woman. "See how she sits gunnel deep. I'll wager it was a good voyage."

"Hurrah for the *Pequod*! Hurrah for Captain Ahab!" cried someone, and a cheer went up from the assembly. Then, as if directed by a conductor, the chorus of voices ceased. Now they all awaited the most important words they would hear. As the camel pontoons floated the ship into the harbor and maneuvered it up to the wharf, a man hung aloft in the rigging.

"All safe!" he cried. "All returned home! Is that my Deborah I see?"

Again, a cheer went up from the crowd as women strained to catch a first glimpse of their loved ones. Hannah's heart felt like it would burst with happiness. Safe! Ahab was safe once again! But as the captain's wife, she must maintain some decorum. Wanting to jump aboard the ship as soon as the gangplank was down, she forced herself to stand back from the throng, forced herself to be dignified. What had Ahab said about hens clucking and pecking about the docks while their husbands tried to finish their business? She would not get in the way, but she would claim that kiss, just as she had warned him, as soon as she could get her hands on him. Already she could smell the rank odor of the ship, but that odor had become familiar to her. What fun it would be to take her husband home and scrub the smell of the sea from him. What fun to tell him that the packet *Merrybourne* was sailing in a month for England, and they would be on board.

There was a giant, grizzled old man on the quarterdeck shouting orders to the men as the camels were disconnected from the *Pequod*. His back was to the dock, but his long gray hair and shaggy clothes could not hide the air of authority in his bearing. Though other men were racing to obey his commands while furtively trying to catch a glimpse of their families, this man's attention was focused on the details on board. Why was he the one giving orders? Hannah wondered. Where was Ahab?

The ship lumbered into place and was anchored. The gang-plank was put over the side, and two young men plunged down it to embrace their wives. The old man above them growled his rage at this offense, and they quickly returned to their onboard duties. Women who had experienced many such homecomings called out greetings to their men, then ran home to prepare a welcome feast. Younger wives wept happy tears.

Hannah searched the crowd for Ahab, to no avail. As she stood on tiptoe, trying to find him, her eyes rested on the old man just as he turned toward her. His full, bushy black beard was streaked with gray, and a stripe of stark white shot through its left side. Above the white was a familiar scar that extended the length of his bronzed face. His shaggy mane of hair could not disguise his noble brow. His piercing eyes met hers, and he gave her a crooked, roguish grin.

"Well, girl, here I am, all safe and sound. Thou hast seen me. Give me a smile, then scud along home and wait till I finish my business," he called.

Hannah did smile. It was her Ahab. But what a toll this voyage had taken. It seemed as if his age had caught up with him at last.

"Not till I claim my kiss," she cried with a giddy laugh. If grayer hair and a few age lines were the only changes in him, she would not complain.

"Begone, woman," he shouted. "We've work to do here."

There was no kindness in his tone, but she ignored that. *My darling Captain Ahab is too used to giving orders*, she thought.

Then, captain's wife or not, she set a bad example by clambering up the gangplank, then up the steps to the quarterdeck. She would have flung herself into his arms had his expression not become threatening.

"Avast!" he roared, lifting his chin and glaring at her.

It was then that she fully saw him. Where once had been two sturdy, powerful legs, there were now only one and a half. His right leg ended above the knee and a thick ivory stick was strapped to the stump. Unable to breathe, Hannah forced her gaze upward to his face. The rage in his eyes died, replaced almost too quickly by a jaunty arrogance.

"Well, girl, what dost thou think of thy husband now? Dismasted ship, dismasted captain. But we both shipped new masts and returned short of thirty months with a hold full of oil. Well, what thinkest thou? Never mind. Thine eyes say it all. Give me that kiss then, and get thee home. I've business to finish here."

With a cry, she rushed into his outstretched arms and held him fast, sobbing with joy and grief.

"There, there," he said roughly, clumsily, as though he had forgotten how to speak to her. "'Tis only a little wound. Nothing to complain about." He held her away and looked into her eyes. "Hast thou nothing to say to me, lass?"

She stared up into his face, loving him more than ever before for his wonderful courage. "Husband, you truly smell terrible," she whispered with a trembling but saucy smile. "Hurry up with your business, then get thyself home so I can scrub thee clean."

"Ha," he cried. "That's my Hannah." He gave her a quick kiss and then lovingly shoved her away. "I'll make short work of it here, thou canst be certain. Now scud along home."

Hannah obeyed. But it seemed as she walked that all sound and motion around her had ceased. Her head ached as her mind tried to grasp what she had just seen. Ahab, her proud, magnificent husband, would not come striding home to her this time, but rather, limping, hobbling. Dismasted, he had said. What a curious description, as though he were a ship that had lost a mast. Surely his legs were, or had been, like the straight, tall, powerful structures that held aloft a ship's sails. His straight, tall, powerful legs had held him far aloft and above other men. How many others could face such a tragic loss with the courage he had just displayed? To lose his leg and still be standing to give orders as his ship sailed into its harbor home.

Hannah could not prevent a random, ugly thought from darting through her mind. Now it was certain he could no longer go whaling. Now he would be hers alone. But what kind of evil heart could be pleased at such a thing? No. No. She wasn't pleased. She felt nothing but horror for his loss. Thank God for his courage, for without it she would have swooned. Was he in pain? Of course. He must be. But what would he expect of her? What would he need? What words could possibly comfort him? She would have to think carefully. How long before the ship was unloaded and all business completed? Two days? Three? Could she gather her courage and wits that quickly? *Dear God, I must not disappoint him!*

Hannah marched to her home on Orange Street, her head held high. If anyone passing spoke to her, she did not know it. Once inside, she leaned against the door, staring into nothingness, unaware of time. But soon Abigail brought Timothy from the kitchen to greet her. The boy embraced his mother's skirt. The mother grasped the housekeeper's hands. The woman stared at her in astonishment.

"Abigail, our Captain Ahab has been injured."

The other woman braced herself for the news.

"He has ... he has l-lost his leg." Hannah trembled as she spoke.

"Ah," Abigail winced.

"He is ... he says that ... I-I think we must ..." Hannah stammered, unable to think clearly.

"Must we fetch him home then?"

Hannah shook her head. "No. It's quite remarkable. He is going about his duties ..." She laughed oddly. "He's quite remarkable. He's got himself a wooden leg. No, I think it's ivory. That's quite remarkable, isn't it? He said he would be home after the unloading and accounting."

"As though nothing had happened?"

"As though nothing had happened."

"Then, Mrs. Hannah, we must treat him no differently than before. Captain Ahab is a proud man. We must not pity him."

Hannah stared into Abigail's eyes. How had she failed to see the strength and wisdom reflected there? "Yes," she whispered. "We must not pity him."

The news of Captain Ahab's courage spread throughout Nantucket long before the *Pequod* could be unloaded. At their counting house, first mate Peleg told his partner Captain Bildad about the extraordinary voyage during which more than one disaster had nearly claimed the ship. Bildad, with proper Quaker reserve, repeated the story to his rival ship owners without the slightest hint of boasting about his captain and crew.

"Friends, the mercy of God looms over Nantucket Harbor today. She looks fit now, but Mr. Peleg tells me this here *Pequod* of ours lost her three masts in a typhoon off the coast of Japan some eighteen months ago. All those three masts pounded against the side of the ship while fore and aft the wild sea broke over them. Yet despite all the terror of Death and Judgment they felt, my good Captain Ahab and first mate Peleg did their duty.

They rigged jury-masts and got themselves to the nearest port, saving all hands. Once the ship was refitted, they struck out to sea again where right off they encountered exceptional blessings, right there off the coast of Japan. Of course, that's when Captain Ahab had his sad little accident. Dismasted by a whale, they say. But he don't seem to mind it much, considering how profitable the voyage was. And that's what we're all about, I think. Do ye not agree?"

And to a man, they agreed. The story of the legendary Captain Ahab was thus advanced to almost mythical proportions. Every ship owner could see that even with his injury, which would have put an end to a lesser man's whaling days, Ahab's greasy good luck had indeed held out. True, he seemed moody and far quieter than he had ever been. But moodiness counted for nothing in this business where profits were king. Far from thinking him unfit for another voyage, every Nantucketer thought him the most excellent whaling man their isle had ever produced.

But for all his wealth, success, and reputation, from the day of his return on the *Pequod*, there was not a woman on Nantucket Island who would have traded places with Hannah.

On the third day, Hannah paced the parlor, checking out the front window from time to time to see if Ahab was on his way home. To her dismay, he had sent that morning for Abigail. The housekeeper had been surprised as well. But Hannah had set aside her own disappointment and reminded her they had agreed that following his orders was the best way to help him. When she finally looked out the window and saw him walking up Orange Street, Abigail beside him, her heart felt near to breaking. He was striding, after all. He barely had his land legs after a thirty-month voyage. Indeed, one of those legs was an ivory stand-in for the original. Yet he was striding toward his home with his head

held high. Though his pace was shortened, there was no change
in his noble bearing from when, on two legs of flesh, he had last
traversed this same street.

Once inside the house with the door closed behind him,
however, he stopped, covered his face with his hands, and shuddered violently. Abigail stood close beside him in case he
faltered. Hannah watched, her face a pleasant mask. She had
braced herself for this moment. When at last he looked up and
saw her, he held his arms out and forced a smile.

"What? No greeting for thy returning husband?"

She ran to embrace him, trying to express her eagerness
without knocking him off balance. But he had mastered his new
appendage and stood firm, even lifting her off the floor as he
returned her embrace. She buried her face in his chest, savoring
the fragrance of soap and shave cream that emanated from him.
But as he set her down, she looked up with a start. His hair had
been cut, his beard trimmed and shaved to its former chin-
curtain shape, and his clothes were new.

"Ahab," she cried with chagrin. "I was to scrub the sea from
you this time. Why didn't you let me?"

"I'm a rich man, my dear. Should my wife perform such a lowly
task?" He took her hand and drew her toward the north parlor.
As he walked across the hardwood floor, his ivory leg tried to slip
from beneath him, but he quickly gained control.

"Abigail," he said gruffly. "See to this floor. Perhaps some
carpet—"

"Aye, Captain," the housekeeper said. "We have a man who's
able to fix it." She then returned to her duties.

He took his chair by the fireplace, with his unbending right leg
stretched out before him. Then he pulled out his pipe and a new
pouch of tobacco from his coat pocket. Hannah would have sat

on his lap according to their old custom, but she feared to hurt him. If he noticed her hesitation, he did not mention it.

"And what of the boy?" he asked.

"He's napping."

"Good. Good. Sit down, girl. Let's get acquainted." He filled his pipe and lit it. "What hast thou done with thyself these past thirty months?"

Breathing in the lovely aroma of his cherry tobacco, Hannah gazed at her husband, loving him with all her heart. It was true that the voyage had aged him, that there were lines … no, true wrinkles … where none had been before. But coupled with his gray-streaked hair and sun-bronzed complexion, they made him look even more distinguished and handsomer than ever before.

"Well, speak up, girl. Don't just sit there." He hardly looked at her as he spoke.

Now she understood. He was testing her. He may have embraced her on the ship and at the door, but he would hold her at arms' length until certain that his injury did not repulse her. And until he was certain, he would not tempt himself by looking at her.

"Captain Ahab, you have been at sea entirely too long. I have not been a girl for some time. Look at me. I am a woman. And I am so pleased …" her voice broke slightly, "so pleased to have my dear husband at home once again."

He looked up sharply, then his face softened. "Aye, I can see that. It's good to be home."

Against her will, tears of confusion sprang to her eyes. Why would he not respond to her as before? Had his love changed? No, she must not think that. He needed time to adjust. But she needed something too. She stood and walked to his chair, took his pipe and set it on the side table, then patted his left thigh.

"My darling, it's been so long. May I sit on your knee?" she whispered.

He scowled. "If thou must. Aye, have a seat."

She sat on his whole leg and nestled into his arms, forcing him to embrace her. If her weight caused him pain, he did not reveal it. Gradually, his cool façade melted, and he regarded her with interest.

"Thou lookest well, Hannah. Thy color is good, and thou seem'st to be strong."

"Oh, I'm very well, now that you are home." Now she permitted her tears to fall, certain all would soon be well with him.

He allowed her to rest in his arms, but ignored the tears. They held each other for several moments until a soft, whimpering sound caught their attention from across the room. There in the parlor door stood Timothy, his tiny hands clasped together and his eyes wide with anxious confusion.

"There he is," roared Ahab with a hearty laugh.

"Come here, my darling," cried Hannah. "Look who's here. Come see your Papa. I've told you all about him. Come, dear."

After the briefest hesitation, the boy ran across the room. Hannah stood and lifted him to his father's lap. He no longer hesitated, but hugged the great gray bear who now held him so tightly.

"Ah, my son, thou hast given me great joy by this reception. Oftimes whaling fathers return to young children who run in terror, having seen few men in their lives. My dear, I received thy letter concerning the departure of our good friend, Reverend Harris. It was my hope that he would ward off that fear of men in our son. Yet thou hast done well, as usual. He fears me not."

Though he seemed not to notice, Hannah knew her smile was strained. This was not the time for confrontation. But she must explain, or he would think later she was keeping something from him.

"Abigail's son Daniel was here for several months. He was a great playmate for Timothy."

"Ah, good man, that Daniel." Ahab still inspected his son, who in turn inspected him.

"Yes, he seemed so. He expressed a desire to see you. But like you, he was eager for another whaling voyage. He sailed just three months ago." She could not keep the shrillness from her tone.

He glanced up sharply, but only replied, "Mmm'h'mm."

Her gaze fell beneath his stare. She would not argue with him now. But when she looked up again, he was staring past her, as though into a void. A strange, almost haunted expression was in his eyes. She must cheer him somehow.

"Abigail is roasting mutton for our supper. I'm sure after thirty months of dried meat, you'll appreciate something fresh. She's also prepared some apple pudding."

"Mm'h'mm," he said again. Then, responding to the tiny hand that reached up to caress his cheek, he sighed. "How good it is to be home."

Hannah checked her sleeping son one last time before joining Ahab in their bedroom. The boy had taken to his father without hesitation, playing with Ahab's watch, his coat buttons, and his beard. With the child between them, they had passed a pleasant evening. She had treasured the expression on her husband's face as he fell in love with their son. She had watched with pleasure as he ate Abigail's welcome home feast. And she had agonized behind her smile as he considered carrying the boy up to bed, then reluctantly handed him to her, uncertain of his ability to keep his balance on the stairs. Now the greatest test of her strength would come. She had practiced in her mind for three days for this moment, wishing it did not have to happen, yet knowing it was the door to their future together. If she had the courage to view his wound without dismay, all would be well with them. If she faltered, all might be lost.

She entered their bedroom and placed her candlestick on the bedside table, then looked around to find him in the dimly lit chamber. He sat on a chair in the sitting room staring at the floor. An oil lamp cast shadows that seemed to exaggerate the dark features of his face. He was a savage Norse deity, Thor in fierce repose, a god, yet wounded, and his suffering wounded her as well. She blinked away threatening tears. He had removed his coat and dropped it nearby. As she came near, he did not move. She knelt beside him, bending in front of his face until he focused on her.

"Hello, my love," she whispered.

He grunted and seemed to come to himself. "Um, hum. I was just thinking how I've forgot how to sleep in a bed after so long in my hammock. I'd best sleep in the spare room so thou wilt not be disturbed by my tossing about."

She took his hand and kissed it, then laid it against her cheek. "I had plans for this night that cannot be done alone." She gazed into his eyes and smiled.

He retrieved his hand and looked away. "No. No. It's been a long day for thee. Thou must be tired …"

She took his hand again and pressed it to her breast. "No, my love. Not tired at all."

He pulled it back, then bent to rebuckle his one shoe. "I must go to the bank early tomorrow and see to my accounts. Is the spare bed made up?"

Moving on her knees in front of him, Hannah placed a hand on each of his thighs. "Either now or later I must see your injury, husband. Let it be now."

"No!" he growled, fixing on her his angriest glare. He gripped her shoulders and would have moved her away, but she dug her fingers into his thighs and glared back. He trembled with rage, grinding his teeth. "Hannah!" he snarled.

"Ahab," she whispered.

The fury in his eyes died slowly, replaced by a wild bewilderment, then tormented confusion, at last profound grief. "Aye. Look at it then."

He released the strap that secured the ivory stick to his stump. Carefully setting the ivory piece on the floor beside him, he pulled up the shortened pant leg and inspected his injury before glancing up at her. "Well, there it is. A pretty piece of work, eh?"

The lower leg had been sheared away just above the knee, leaving no bendable joint. The ragged purple wound had not entirely healed, but the skin had been stitched together over the end of the bone, and it was healing without serious infection.

"Ummm." Hannah disguised her horror with a throaty moan. When she could speak without a sob, she said, "Mr. Peleg did good work here. I must remember to commend him." She gently caressed the scar, then gazed up into his troubled face with a faint smile. He must see that she was not repulsed, that she loved and admired him as before. She bent and kissed the wound, then gazed up at him. "How brave you are, my darling husband. How very, very brave."

He had the look of a lost child. "He stared me right in the eye as he struck me, Hannah. Right in the eye."

"Who?"

"The white whale. The cursed white whale. In near to forty years of whaling, I've never seen a bigger rogue of a beast than he. Moby Dick. That's what they call him. He's the one that took off my leg. Stared me right in the eye and dared to strike me. Aye, that was Moby Dick, none other."

The whale has a name? she thought. "Did you kill it?"

"What?"

"Did you kill the whale?"

"Kill him? Kill him? No, the blasted beast got away. He already had a dozen harpoons in him, and now he's got one of mine. But still he lives and swims freely about the seven seas while I must hobble about on an ivory pole." His eyes began to grow wild and distant again.

"Well, cursed be the nasty creature," she said pertly, trying to pull him back to the present. "But then, it's only a dumb beast. I hope whoever kills it marks the barrels of oil so we can know when we burn it in our lamps. That would be sweet revenge."

"Revenge. Aye, revenge." His softly spoken words seemed to roll around the corners of the room like distant thunder.

Hannah bit her lip. She had passed the test of her mettle, but now there was something else to set in order. She pulled the shortened pant leg down over his stump. Looking up into his eyes once more, she pressed close to him and encircled his waist with her arms. He cast his troubled gaze on her and absently caressed her hair.

"Will you not give me a kiss, my love?" she whispered.

"Hm? A kiss?"

"Yes. If you've forgotten how, let me show you." She stood up, smiling. She took his face in her hands, brushed his lips with hers, then stared into his eyes again. When he blinked with consternation, she pressed her lips against his, kissing him with all the pent-up passion of their too-long separation. Slowly he began to respond, and with a sudden jolt, he grabbed her about the waist and pulled her down to his lap.

"Ah, Hannah," he growled lustily. "My God, how I've missed thee!"

Chapter Nineteen

ℰℬ

*B*y summer of 1843, when the *Pequod* returned to its home port, the profits of the previous year had been tallied, revealing that 1842 had been the most profitable year the whole of the whalefishery had ever experienced. As the world's whaling capital, Nantucket was at the height of her prosperity. Yet there were other events that had marked that same year in the history of the island.

In 1842, the elder Mrs. Starbuck had died, leaving behind a proud legacy. She was survived by her husband Joseph, along with their three sons, four daughters, and twenty-seven grandchildren, who continued in their parents' tradition of community involvement and improvement.

In 1842, Nantucket's internationally known astronomer William Mitchell had correctly predicted the coming of a comet, which the islanders had viewed with awe for several evenings in March.

In 1842, Peter Ewer built the camels, pontoon boats to carry ships across the sandbar at the mouth of Nantucket harbor.

And in September 1842, Hannah's husband had lost a leg while whaling off the coast of Japan.

When the *Pequod* returned in June 1843, it was only one of eighty-six whaling ships that called Nantucket home. Every ship had a captain and a crew of more than thirty men. With nearly three thousand Nantucketers sailing the world in the dangerous work of hunting for whales, tales of tragedy were common on the island. Mutinies against overbearing captains, storms that dashed ships to destruction, whaleboats full of men dragged beneath the waves by their enraged prey, diseases that infected the crews in foreign ports, and individual accidents such as a crippling or fatal fall from the rigging ... all these took their toll on the men who made their living from the sea.

Hearing that a whaleman had been incapacitated by a serious injury was not a new circumstance for the people of the island. With inherent Nantucket fortitude, a man in such straits resigned himself to some alternate form of employment. If he had labored before the mast, he might find himself doomed to a life-time of financial difficulties. If he had been an officer and had managed to save an adequate fortune, he could live out his days in comfort. Either way, he found cause to be grateful, for after all, he still had his life. Most likely, he had a loving family who welcomed him home, all of them thanking God that he had survived yet another voyage.

Though every whaling wife lived with the constant awareness that her husband could be injured or killed or perhaps even may have been dead for years while she had continued to pray for him, she could never fully prepare herself for the actual occur-rence. Hannah was no different. She had feared it, had dismissed it, had forgotten it because of her husband's extraor-dinary good fortune. But now that he was indeed wounded, deeply wounded, every fiber of her being was alive with antici-pation for his needs. Did he want his breakfast in bed? Did he still like roast beef on Sundays, with apple pie for dessert? Would he like to sit with her in their new arbor so nicely built by Josiah Coffin, who himself was recently retired from the sea?

She did not mention Josiah's injury nor the faith with which he had accepted it. Indeed, in every way, she sought to consider her husband's feelings before speaking.

She recalled the delight Ahab had taken in bringing her a gift on his previous voyage. Should she ask if he had brought a gift this time? Perhaps he had been injured before finding something appropriate. No, she would not ask. Yet if he had brought a gift and she did not show interest, would she seem indifferent to his efforts on her behalf? Then there was her gift for him. Should she present it to him? What if he found it too difficult to ride the spirited Samson with just one leg? Would that plunge him into despair?

The only thing she was certain of was his enjoyment of their son. With newly installed carpet runners throughout the house to prevent his slipping, he carried the boy about on his shoulders, telling him stories that were fully appreciated though not at all understood by the two-and-a-half-year-old. Timothy's giggles and Ahab's hearty laugh could be heard in every room.

It had not taken the child long to discover his father's unusual leg. With seeming indifference to his loss, Ahab allowed Timothy to inspect the ivory appendage, telling him that not everyone had the advantage of being able to remove a leg whenever he wanted. With the adaptability typical of children, the boy quickly grew accustomed to it and ceased to find it interesting.

From the morning after his return home, Ahab had resumed his daily walks. On the days when Hannah accompanied him, she was no longer forced to run to keep up with his lengthy stride. Even Timothy could keep pace with his father. Yet now, as before, Ahab took great pride in parading his beautiful young wife and their child around the town. He expressed interest in all the changes in his homeport, especially the new camels doing their duty at the mouth of the harbor. During all their daily rounds, he never complained, though sometimes Hannah could see him grimace in pain as he walked. If she inquired about his discomfort, however, he would dismiss her inquiries with a grunt and an impatient wave of his hand.

He had been home several days when he disappeared after dinner, then came back downstairs to the parlor carrying two gifts. He gave one to Timothy: a round wooden ball, carved by an islander off the coast of Japan, and painted with the features of a gruff old man. Ahab twisted the ball, separating it into two parts, revealing another ball, this one painted with a woman's smiling face. The second ball opened to reveal a third, which was painted with the features of a sweet, small boy. He set the balls on the floor, lining them in a row in descending sizes. Timothy sat on the floor to figure out just how it had all been done.

To Hannah, Ahab presented a Swiss music box with a dancing couple on top that turned in circles as a Strauss waltz played in bell-like tones. Pleased at the lovely gift and certain that this was his promise that one day they would dance again, despite his injury, she decided she would give him the gelding on the morrow. He seemed inclined to lightheartedness, so she permitted herself the pleasure of teasing him.

"I could not see the purpose of buying you a gift, husband," she said, all the while playing the little music box. "After all, when last you returned from a voyage, I gave you a gold coin for good luck, yet you left it at home." Immediately, she regretted her words.

"Ah," he cried. "I forgot the gold coin." Then he stared past her, and his face took on a dismal expression. It was not until Timothy handed him several mismatched pieces of his puzzle that Ahab's attention returned to the happy parlor scene with his family.

That night Ahab began to talk in his sleep, cursing and mumbling unintelligible words, sometimes even shouting. Once, he sat up suddenly and clutched for his right leg, pawing at the sheets in desperation when he could not find it. Hannah could only watch, her heart aching, for he seemed not to be awake. In the morning he did not mention it, but Hannah reported the incident to Abigail.

From the moment they had shared the news of Ahab's loss, an unspoken bond had formed between the two women. All concerns about the housekeeper's prior attachment to her husband were set aside in this new circumstance. For Abigail's part, she seemed to view her Mrs. Hannah with new respect. With a look or a nod, they were learning together how to understand and adapt to his disability without hurting his pride. After breakfast, when Ahab went to the bank, Hannah sought out Abigail in the kitchen.

"Shall I give him the horse? Will he think it a cruel joke?"

Abigail considered the question for a moment. "It is never good to hide things from the captain. He will learn of it sooner or later. It's best to give it to him as though nothing had happened."

Thus advised, Hannah sent her to find Josiah and give him instructions to brush and saddle Samson and bring him to the house. When Ahab returned, she greeted him with affection and invited him to sit with her in the arbor.

"Later, perhaps, my dear." He brushed past her and took his seat by the parlor's cold fireplace.

"Well, at least look out the dining room window to see ... to see the new roses. I've had wonderful luck with them this year."

"Later." His tone showed his disinterest, and he involved himself with his pipe. She was at a loss as to how to proceed. Eventually, the horse would nicker or whinny, drawing Ahab's attention, but she so much wanted him to see the handsome beast before hearing it. Perhaps if she teased and annoyed him, he would do as she had asked. She sat in her chair facing him, sighed aloud, stared at him, and smiled.

He returned her look with a frown. "What is it that thou wanted, wife?"

She rested her chin on her hand. "Just to be with you, my darling."

Before, he might have responded with a laugh or an invitation to sit on his knee. Today he scowled. "Begone, girl. Go tend thy son. Don't stare at me as if I were—"

"He's napping." She interrupted before he could say any more. "I have a gift for you. It's in the back yard."

He started. "A gift?" he asked gruffly.

The puzzled look on his face seemed to explain it all. *He's used to being the benefactor*, she thought. *He never expects to receive surprises.*

"Yes. If you don't wish to see it now, I'll send it away until you're ready."

"Um, um," he said. "Very well. If it will please thee, I will see it now."

His dismembered leg had no knee joint to bend, which greatly inhibited his agility. Once seated, he found it difficult to stand. Hannah hesitated between protecting his pride and rushing to his aid. But her revelation of the gift had softened his mood.

"Well, girl, give me a hand. We'll go out and have a look at … those roses."

She stood beside him while he labored to pull himself upright. He grasped her shoulder as little as possible as he endeavored to gain his balance. Though it was clear from his grim expression that the morning walk had taken its toll on his wounded stump, he gamely walked through the house to the back door. Once outside, he stared at the horse for a moment without comprehension.

"Mmm'h'mm," he said at last. "A fine horse. Very handsome."

She gazed up into his eyes. "He's not just any horse, my darling. Do you recall our ride together through New Bedford the day after we met? This is Miss Peach's colt, the son of that fine stallion you rode, born that very same day. Samson. Do you recall him? This is Samson, too."

"Mmm. Yes, I recall what a fine stallion the sire was. So they gelded the son, did they?" He gave a soft grunt. "Thou hast given me an appropriate gift."

"Oh, do you think so? I'm so glad." But then she caught his meaning and could think of no way to correct her words. "Josiah has kept him in good condition. Do you want to ride him now?"

"No." His tone had only a slight edge to it. "Another time." After that, he never sent for the horse, nor did he mention it.

Ahab's moods had always been unpredictable, but Hannah had never feared to challenge him. Since his return, however, she felt it best to avoid disputes. In time, she was certain, he would become accustomed to his loss and would adjust his life and his moods to accommodate it. As the days went by, however, he seemed to grow more moody than ever. She could never predict what might set him off nor could she appease him once the damage was done.

For the most part, Hannah did not blame herself for his changes, though in trying to please him, she often thought she fell short. She struggled to walk the tenuous path between doing too much and doing too little. Sometimes he chatted with her about the latest news in town. Sometimes it seemed that he did not even remember her existence. She was as affectionate as ever, yet after his first night at home, he had not slept with his arm around her as he had in years before. It seemed to her that he was happy only when playing with his son or when he sat reading while the boy amused himself nearby.

In time, however, even the charms of his innocent child ceased to hold his attention. Awake, he seemed lost in his own thoughts. Asleep, he seemed tossed about on the waves of his dreams. Sometimes as he sat reading by the fireside, he would unconsciously reach down, as if to scratch his missing leg. At the touch of the hard, dead ivory, he would come to himself sharply, and his face would cloud with confusion and stifled rage.

Only when he ventured forth on his daily walks did he come near to being his old self. Oh, a little less likely to be in a good humor than before, perhaps even a little more moody, some of his old friends said. And grieved about his loss, of course. That was to be expected. Better a moody good captain than a cheerful one who's incompetent, all agreed. But, though Hannah was proud of his reputation as a good captain, it was she who had to live with his moods.

Although Ahab was well read and used as many biblical allusions in his conversation as any of their religious acquaintances, she had never seen him read a Bible. The only times she had seen him touch the large family Bible her father had bequeathed to them was when he signed it on their wedding day and when he wrote their son's name in it. So she was greatly surprised when he began to read the heavy volume voraciously. In his chair before the upstairs sitting room fireplace, he searched it, often late into the night, as though he were in pursuit of some great truth written therein. How pleased her father would be, she thought. Amos Oldweiler had worried even more than Jeremiah about the state of Ahab's soul.

Occasionally he would burst forth with an exclamation about his reading. "Aha, where is the justice in that?" he might say. Or

"The hand of God weighs too heavily on this just man." Another time, he uttered, "But I would not have treated him thus."

Because his tone was so indignant, almost to the point of rage, Hannah never inquired about the passages he was reading. Surely he would reason it out, as he always had. Yet if she heard a common theme in his outbursts, it seemed to be his concern with equity in judgment. Was he thinking of his own brushes with death? Was he reconsidering some of his own judgments while shipboard? She had heard several stories of murderous mutinies against overbearing captains. So arduous was the business of whaling, so needful that a crew be kept obediently on task, that many a God-fearing captain on land became "God Almighty of the quarter-deck" at sea. Yet stern as he may be, even severe, Captain Ahab had never been known to be unjust. It was one of the many things that Hannah loved about him.

In time, he began to have more complete conversations with himself as he read. "Types, the preachers call them. Types! But types are like a pasteboard mask. The question is, what's behind them? What's in the layer just below? Methinks there is an unjust force striking from behind the mask, striking deliberately … striking me! By God, then, I'll strike the mask! I'll break through to the true power! Then we'll see justice." Another time, he muttered, "Weights and balances, eh? Well, two can play that game. I have weighed God in the balance and found Him wanting."

Then, "Ah, Job, thou didst not suffer as I have suffered. From any loss, any illness a man may recover. Possessions can be regained. Another child can be born. But can a man grow another leg to replace the one so unjustly torn from him? God rightly asketh thee, Can man draw out Leviathan? Canst thou fill his skin with barbed irons? For surely in thy day, man could not. But I have defeated a thousand leviathans and even today my iron is lodged in Moby Dick's accursed white hide. If this is the test of God's strength, then perhaps the Almighty can be defeated after all!"

It was when she heard him speak those words that Hannah began to be afraid for him. Was he losing his grip on reality, he who had always been so rational? She did not need to inform Abigail of her alarms, for the older woman had observed his turmoil for herself. Neither could Hannah call upon any of her friends, even the stalwart Aunt Charity, lest she besmirch her husband's name. Though she wrote of his injury to Jeremiah and Kerenhappuch, she said only that his distress over the accident continued unabated.

By August, as the first anniversary of his encounter with the white whale neared, his agitation increased. He was as cordial as ever—even more so—to outsiders, yet often seemed unaware of his family. It was as though, within the refuge of his home, everything and everyone were merely furniture. He moved all his navigational instruments and charts into the little-used south parlor, put a lock on the door, and began spending his evenings there by himself. The room would now be his study. He began sleeping in one of the spare bedrooms, telling Hannah that the circles under her eyes proved what he had said from the first: they were disturbing each other's sleep and would do best to sleep alone.

After several nights of crying herself to sleep over this new arrangement, Hannah decided that she had been at fault. Somehow, he had felt her fear of his torments and thought she had ceased to desire him. She was grieved to have disappointed him and resolved to make amends. Bathed and perfumed, she donned a fresh nightgown, brushed her long auburn locks over her shoulder, and waited until he came past her door. Hearing him enter his bedroom, she waited a few more moments, then walked down the hallway and tapped on his door.

"Hmmp. What is it?" He did not open the door.

"My darling, I only wish to say goodnight," she said.

"Goodnight."

"But may I not come in and kiss you?"

He did not respond.

"Ahab—"

The door was jerked open, and he stood towering above her, glowering at her savagely. "What dost thou want, woman?"

An icy chill filled her breast. She could not speak, could only stare at him in dismay. Was his love for her truly dead? The dim light from her candle seemed to magnify the dark glare on his face. With sinking heart, she shook her head.

"I'm sorry. Go back to bed."

But as she turned to leave him, she felt his hand gently touch her arm. Turning back, she saw pain in his eyes.

"Come to my bed," she whispered. "Hold me once again, as you used to do."

He looked beyond her into the darkened hallway and groaned. "I cannot."

She stepped close to him so he would smell the fragrance of her perfume and feel the softness of her hair. After a moment, he pulled her close, almost absently, and brushed her forehead with a kiss.

"I cannot," he repeated. "Perhaps after ... yes, after the task has been completed ..."

"What task?"

He looked at her sharply, then softened again. "Turn in to thine own berth, my dear. Thou wilt sleep better without me."

She did as he instructed. But he had been wrong about her sleeping. She wept late into the night, and in the morning, dark circles appeared under her eyes.

Chapter Twenty

ॐ

*H*annah refused to succumb to despair. Somehow she would reach her wounded husband, no matter how long it took. Somehow she must find a way to comprehend what he was feeling. She regretted that she had not met more whalers as she was growing up. Her father had sheltered her from every part of the whalefishery except the company of other owners' daughters and wives. He could not have known that his daughter would one day need greater human understanding than this limited preparation had given her. Her closest examples of masculine behavior were her father and Jeremiah. When these two men had suffered their losses, they had accepted them without complaint. Hannah sometimes thought they had been far too passive. Ahab, on the other hand, had not. To Hannah, his fiery spirit was one of his most admirable qualities. But surely his rage against God was inappropriate. Many other whalers had been severely wounded, even to the point of losing arms and legs. Yet, grateful to be alive, most of them had adjusted to their disabilities. In time, would Ahab adjust too? What could she do to help him?

He had not seemed willing to tell her about the accident, so she had not pressed him. Other than his claim that the whale had maliciously struck him, he had said nothing more. Perhaps Captain Peleg would be willing to relate the whole experience to her. She would visit him, if she could do so without Ahab knowing of it. But her concern that he might forbid her to go out without reporting her itinerary to him was unnecessary. Each day after breakfast, Ahab now took little notice of her. He would disappear behind his study door, locking himself in to prevent intrusion. Needing no explanation for her errand, Hannah left her son with Abigail and went in search of Peleg.

It was a warm morning in August, the kind of day when flowers were in full bloom and the gentle Nantucket breezes could lift the soul and lighten the step. Despite the balmy weather, Hannah would rather have been some other place beside on her way to visit the old captain. Like Bildad, he used words to his own advantage, and she was not certain those words were always accurate. But who else could relate the story of Ahab's disaster? Somehow she must discover clues for helping Ahab recover without maligning his reputation.

Carrying one of Abigail's delicious apple pies, she walked to the north end of Orange Street, then turned west on Main. One block beyond the three brick mansions of the Starbuck brothers lived Captain Peleg. Though he could often be found at the docks or in the taverns where he traded stories with his fellow whalers, this day Hannah found him at home.

"Mrs. Ahab, what an honor. To what do I owe the pleasure of thy visit?" Peleg's eyes were on the pie as he escorted her into his parlor. But giving her no chance to answer, he continued. "How is thy husband, our excellent Captain Ahab? I saw him only yesterday at the shipyard as we surveyed the refitting of the *Pequod*. As he is a part owner of the ship, thou wilt be happy to know that the work progresses agreeably."

"He is well, thank you, sir. And you look well too." Hannah offered him the pie, which he quickly accepted.

"Thank you, ma'am. What extraordinary kindness. Shall we have some now?"

"None for me, thank you. But please go ahead."

He set the dessert on a sideboard in the adjoining dining room and served himself a large slice, and then returned to sit across from her in the parlor and took a hearty bite.

"Ah, delicious. An old bachelor like me rarely has such a privilege as to enjoy pie this good. Especially not on a voyage."

Hannah nodded, eager to pursue her quest. "Yes, that's what my husband says. And you both seem to have recovered from this last voyage, difficult as it was. Storms and injuries certainly abounded this time, didn't they?"

"Oh, nothing but trifles, nothing but trifles. I could tell thee of much worse …" He stopped, frowning with embarrassment. "Of course, thy husband suffered far more than the rest of us on account of that accursed whale that refused to … But he has taken it well, dost thou not think so?"

"Yes, his courage is astounding. He thinks so little of his injury that he won't even tell me how it happened. I know he must have been tremendously brave. But as well you know, my husband is also modest. Since he refuses to boast about his own heroics, perhaps you will do it for him. I've heard it said you're the best storyteller on Nantucket." She smiled at Captain Peleg.

The old bachelor, who could stare down the throat of Jonah's whale without flinching, reddened beneath his weathered brown hide, making obvious his unabashed pleasure at her request.

"Well, my dear girl, I'd be happy to, though I give warning, it may frighten thee."

"As long as my husband is safe at home, I have nothing to fear about the incident."

Peleg gave her a paternal smile. "Ah, Mrs. Ahab, what a sweet girl thou art, and so bravely resigned to thy husband's loss. And oh, our good Captain Ahab, what a grand, god-like man he is. The best captain out of Nantucket, and far above the common man for courage. Though I've been a captain for years myself, I gladly shipped as his mate once again for this last voyage for the trust I have in him. Last voyage! Aye, it was my last voyage, for I am too old to sail again. We're the same age, thy husband and I, but not all of us have held up as well as Captain Ahab. I do recall one old captain some forty years ago who was about the same age when he …" He stopped. "But that's another tale."

"I would love to hear it another time, sir. But for now, I must apologize for neglecting to thank you the moment I saw you for your amazing treatment of my husband's injury. You sewed the wound with the skill of a trained surgeon. If you had not, if a less experienced man had attended the wound, he surely would not be up and about as he is. Perhaps he would not even have survived. How can I ever thank you enough?"

Peleg glowed with pleasure over her praise. "Nothing at all, my dear girl, nothing at all. It was simply a matter of seeing what needed to be done, then doing it. Anyone else in my place would have done the same. Thine own husband has done many such surgeries."

She nodded. "Still, I thank you, sir. Now, please tell me exactly what happened and what you did to save my husband."

He chuckled and cleared his throat, then became serious, as was appropriate for the tale he was about relate. Focusing on the wall above Hannah's head, the gray-haired old salt seemed to be looking back through time and space to the scene of Ahab's tragedy.

"Well, to begin with," he drawled, "we lay somewhere off the coast of Japan shortly after the *Pequod* had lost her three masts overboard in a gale. There we managed to make land at a small port—secret-like, of course, for Japan is still officially closed to

American vessels, blast 'em. I beg thy pardon, ma'am. I must remember whom I speak with. Anyhow, we cuts new masts and puts them up in place of the original ones, then sets out again in pursuance of the business we'd come for. We was in full pursuit of a rogue whale, and the captain he lowered with the rest of us. Aye, he did. Dost thou know, girl, that his lance is known as the keenest and the surest out of all Nantucket? And he's not one to shirk his duty. Not Captain Ahab.

"Now I must tell thee that this whale is a beast of legend, a great white whale so well known amongst the whalefishery as to have a name. Moby Dick he's called, and he's a monstrous brute of uncommon bulk with a peculiar snow-white wrinkled forehead and a high white hump, almost like a pyramid. By these signs, and the grove of spears planted in his flanks, he reveals his identity to one and all. He seemeth to have a thirst for human blood, they say. Aye, more than a few fatalities have attended his chase. Such panic does he strike that few hunters are willing to encounter the perils of his jaw. Another captain might have steered clear of 'em, but not our Captain Ahab, no sir. He would put an end to the beast once and for all, and render him down to oil and a candlestick."

By this point, Captain Peleg was fully engrossed in his tale and seemed unaware of her. Hannah pulled her handkerchief from her sleeve and gripped it, trying not to twist it as his narrative became more alarming. How like Ahab to pursue his quarry so fearlessly.

"We was in full pursuit of him, with all boats lowered. Three boats was already stove around him, and the men from those boats was thrashing about, swimming for all their souls' worth to reach the safety of the *Pequod*. That's when our Captain Ahab jumped into the fray. He grabs the first thing he sees, a line-knife, a mere six-inch blade, and stabs for the heart of the beast. And then it was that Moby Dick sliced off Ahab's leg, just as if he was taking a bite of some mother's Sunday roast beef."

So powerful was Peleg's description, so lost in his tale was Hannah that she vividly envisioned the violent, tragic moment of her husband's wounding.

"Oh, merciful God!" she cried.

At her words, Captain Peleg returned to the present. "My dear lady, forgive me. Thou shouldest not be hearing this. It is too much for thee."

Hannah dabbed at her tears with her handkerchief and forced a smile. She must gain control, must hear all of his story.

"No, no, please. Go on. You have not told me how you saved my husband's life."

He seemed pleased that she was acknowledging his heroism.

"Very well, then, though I take no delight in giving thee despair."

"No, of course not. Please continue."

"We swore off the whale and hauled the captain back to the *Pequod* as quick as we could. I did my best to stitch the flesh together around the bloody bone. I've done more than one such operation in my day, but in all my trips 'round Cape Horn, this was the cleanest cut I ever did see. The captain, he took it as well as could be expected. But he was in such pain as to make him unable to give orders for a few days."

"Only a few days?"

"Well, no. It was more like weeks. Months, if truth be told."

"Was he ... was he ... rational during this time?"

Peleg started at the question and gave Hannah a penetrating, almost glaring stare.

"What is it thou askest me, my girl?"

She must not put Ahab in a bad light, but she must understand what had happened. It was apparent that, like many whalers who lived most of their lives at sea, Peleg was not accustomed to parlaying with women. Perhaps he was concerned that she might encourage her husband to bring suit against the primary owners of the *Pequod* because of the severe loss he had suffered while earning great wealth for them. To reassure Peleg, she gave him a sweet, sad smile and an innocent gaze.

"What did my brave husband say about his injury?"

His expression relaxed. "He may have been a bit delirious for some time. Not long."

"No doubt. Captain Ahab is a very strong man, both in mind and in body. Did he ... did he simply lie in his hammock after you attended his wound?"

He sighed, looking back through time once again. "No, ma'am. I wish I could say that he did. But no, he did not. He thrashed about so severely due to the pain that we was forced to lash him to the hammock and keep two strong men with him at all times. Thou wilt be glad to know that for all the months of our voyage home, I was rarely away from his side."

"That gives me great comfort, Captain Peleg." *Dear God, why could I not have been there to console him?*

He grinned. "Glad to, glad to, ma'am. After all, as captain he had looked out for all of us. And thou canst see by his condition now that he is as good as new, despite the raving—"

"Raving?" Hannah felt her chest tighten.

"Well, not raving so much. That's a strong word. Yet perhaps it's the right word after all."

"Do you recall what he said?"

"The words, thou meanest? Oh, very well do I remember. Alarming words, blasphemous words! And not a one I would say in a lady's presence." He stopped, reconsidering once more. "But thou must take nothing from that, Mrs. Ahab. Any man wounded as he was would rave madly, even the most godly sort.

Shortly, as we sailed homeward, he came to himself and seemed to leave his delirium behind him as we rounded Cape Horn. Fitted with the first of his ivory legs by our ship's able carpenter, he came forth from his cabin and took command once more, all in his usual calm and able manner. And, ah, how we all did thank God that frightful madness, I mean, delirium was gone."

While Hannah had listened to Peleg's story, she had tried to keep from showing how it was affecting her. Now that it was over, she felt exhausted.

"Then you have seen none of his former illness since that time?"

"Why, no, ma'am. Not at all. Oh, I would say he's a bit moody from time to time, as thou mayest have seen, but there's nothing to that. And naturally grieved for his loss, of course, as any of us would be. But Ahab is Ahab, my dear girl, and there's still an abundance of fire left in him. Make no mistake, he is and always was the best captain Nantucket has ever made. I say that without shame, though I've been a captain myself. And there's not a man amongst us owners who would hesitate at shipping him again. That's why we keep him apprised of the refitting of the *Pequod*."

What nonsense. He cannot possibly go whaling again.

"I don't imagine there's really any need. If he wishes to go to sea again, I hope to pack him off for a nice tour of Europe."

Peleg chuckled paternally. "Ah, the sweet and idle dreams of young girls ..."

She would not permit his tone to dismay her. "Captain Peleg, thank you so much for taking such good care of my husband. And thank you for telling me all about his courage ... and yours. Will you do me one last favor? Don't mention to my husband that I visited you. He truly is so modest about his exploits. And, of course, I know he has not wished to alarm me with these details of his ... his misfortune."

"Not a word, my girl, not a word."

Now she knew all the horrid details of Ahab's accident. Yet it seemed to her that he was living two lives. To his whaling associates, his understandable moodiness did not overshadow his intellectual brilliance nor his ability to master a ship. And he must be masking his pain in their company as well. They had seen neither the agony that each step caused him nor the evidence of his inner torments that erupted in the sanctuary of his home. Just as she had hidden from Peleg the nature of her concerns about Ahab, Ahab was concealing from others the depth of his rage over his injury. Still, her understanding did not show her how to help him.

In early September, a letter from Jeremiah arrived, addressed to both Hannah and Ahab and responding to her news of Ahab's misfortune. After returning to New Bedford for several months, Jeremiah and Kerenhappuch had next moved to Boston, where they had established a mission for seamen. After ministering to many men, such as Ahab, who had suffered devastating losses while whaling, the young pastor did not speak lightly when he observed "our trials are meant to bring us closer to God." He wrote of some men who had found other satisfying work on land after such injuries. He recommended the services of a doctor in the Boston area who had devised an artificial leg far superior to any previously created. The invention was said to be more comfortable and made walking easier than any of its predecessors. He regretted that he could not visit them, but since Kerenhappuch would soon be due for her confinement, he would not leave her until the child was born.

Hannah devoured every word, imagining the comforting tones of Jeremiah's voice. It was the last paragraph, however, that she treasured above all.

"Fitted with one of Dr. Brace's limbs, Captain Ahab, you should be able to enjoy your long-awaited European travels in comfort. I hope to hear soon that you and Mrs. Ahab are enjoying the historic points of interest about the Mediterranean."

Since his homecoming, Hannah had not suggested travel to Ahab. How could she ask him to walk around viewing the sights of Europe if every step caused him unbearable suffering? She could not be so selfish. If the idea came from Jeremiah, however, Ahab might decide it was worth the effort. Further, the news of the artificial leg gave her hope. Before his tragedy, he had walked with sure-footed dignity. It was difficult to see him reduced to hobbling about on an awkward ivory pole. Jeremiah's suggestion might move him to acquire something more suitable. In any event, she reasoned, Ahab deserved a rest from his long, hard life of whaling. If he could be made comfortable, the trip would provide a distraction from his injury and perhaps even peace for his anguished soul.

"Come sit with me by the fire, my dear," she said that night after supper. "Let me read Jeremiah's letter to you."

"I've not forgot how to read. Give me the letter. I'll read it when I'm ready."

"But—"

"Give me the letter, girl, or leave it where it sits. It makes no difference to me." He pushed himself up from the table and walked toward his study. Before he reached the dining room door, Hannah drew the letter from her pocket and thrust it at him.

"At least have the courtesy to read it," she snapped.

He stopped short and glared at her for a moment. "Very well." He snatched the letter from her hand and resumed his trek to the study, where he closed and locked the door.

His cross tone had hurt her, but at least he would read the missive. Perhaps it would encourage him as it had her, and he would be more open to discussion on the morrow. To her regret, the following day he was as distant as before.

Chapter Twenty-One

ॐ

As Timothy approached his third birthday, he resembled his father more and more. In addition to his rapid growth, he was an inquisitive child. It required the constant efforts of both Hannah and Abigail to keep him from injury, whether from inspecting boiling pots on the stove or finding his way up to the roof walk. When they told him no, he might give prompt obedience to their orders, but then he would test their sincerity by going back to the forbidden activity. When they took a warning step toward him, he would scoot away and begin to explore other territories. He tested their boundaries but was never defiant.

Hannah had hoped that once Ahab returned from his voyage, he would involve himself in raising their son. She had watched with joy as they had taken to each other and had spent hours together. Though she did not care for Ahab's telling Timothy sea stories, she was grateful for their immediate bond. After the newness of Ahab's return had worn off, however, father and son seemed to go their separate ways. Seated amidst his toys that cluttered a corner of the parlor, the boy would cast an adoring glance at the dark giant as he disappeared into the locked study, then would resume his play. It had only taken one order from Ahab, delivered in his sternest captain's voice, and the chastened child avoided the study door and the hallway leading to it.

For his part, Ahab had become so preoccupied by his work that he seemed to have forgotten he had a wife and a son. When he did emerge from the study, his dark brow was furrowed, and often he was muttering to himself. If Hannah tried to talk to him at these times, he would cut her off and either leave the house or go upstairs to his room. Hannah had long indulged Timothy in allowing him to keep some of his favorite toys downstairs so that he could play nearby as she read or worked on her embroidery. When it was time for his nap or his supper, they had made a game of his stowing every block or ball in the wooden toy box— dubbed his sea chest—which Josiah had built for him. Now, seeing his father disregard his mother, the child began to ignore her instructions as well. When she scolded him, he obeyed but seemed to copy his father's defiant glare.

A serious confrontation was fast approaching, of that she was certain. Ahab's support would be vital when it arrived. But because he seemed to avoid spending time with her, she had not been able to bring up the subject. So she depended on words of wisdom from other, more experienced mothers. Aunt Charity had raised three sons and a daughter, and her words of advice were frequently on Hannah's mind: be calm, be firm, persuade the child when possible, and as a last resort, apply a switch to the well-padded place that God had provided. It was natural, advised the older woman, for a child to seek his own way. It was the parents' responsibility to guide him to God's way.

"The child does not truly want to win, my dear," Aunt Charity had said. "He knows the boundaries are good, and he feels safe within them. It is his human nature that forces him to push against thine authority."

Remembering her own childhood and the way her permissive father had often been forced to save her from disaster, Hannah realized that she must gain the upper hand and teach her son obedience in order to keep him safe. Their current conflict was over the toy box. One evening, when Abigail announced that Timothy's supper was ready in the kitchen, Hannah put down her embroidery and smiled at her son.

"Your supper's ready, Timothy. Time to stow your toys," she chirped. "Hurry. Let's pick them all up."

He was engrossed in taking his painted balls apart and setting them in a row. When she spoke, he ignored her.

"Timothy," she said in a quiet but firm voice, "you must mind me. It's time to put your toys away."

He glanced at her out of the corner of his eye, then went back to his play.

"Timothy," Hannah stood and folded her arms. "Put away your toys."

His eyes were wide, his lower lip trembled, and he gripped his toy. "No," he whispered.

"What?"

Now he stared at her fully, his eyes snapping with defiance. "No!"

"Timothy!"

"No! No!" He jumped up, clutching the balls to his chest.

"You will put that in your toy box." Hannah took a step toward him.

"No! No! Papa!" he cried, and ran toward the closed study door.

"Timothy, don't!" She tried to grab him as he scooted past her.

He spun around in front of the study, holding one ball over his head as though he would throw it at her. His eyes were wide with fear, and he trembled at his own audacity. Yet he would not relent.

For a moment, Hannah puckered her lips to keep from laughing. He was so small and his weapon was so impotent that his childish threat held no power. But for him it was the supreme test of his courage. Yet, just as Aunt Charity had said, she could see in his eyes that he did not truly want to win. For his own good, it was time for her to show him who was in charge. She marched toward him.

"Noooo! Papa!" Then he let out an ear-piercing scream.

The study door jerked open, and Ahab stood in the doorway. "Belay that noise!" he roared. Startled, Timothy dropped the three balls on the floor. Six pieces scattered in six different directions. As Ahab took a step toward the boy, his ivory leg struck and shattered one rounded shell, and he almost plunged headlong to the floor. With a violent oath, he grasped at the wall to keep from falling. His balance regained, he pursued his tiny tormentor into the parlor and raised his hand to strike. Hannah dashed to thrust herself between her husband and son before his blow descended.

"No!" she cried, shielding the boy even as Ahab's hand struck the side of her head. For a moment, all she could see were pinpoints of white on black. All she could hear was a piercing whine that seemed to cut through her head. Gasping for breath, she found herself on the floor, clutching her terrified son. Ahab stood over them, trembling, his eyes wild with rage. He seemed to be struggling to regain himself, but Hannah could not take a chance that he would.

"If you wish for me to be frightened of you, then you've succeeded," she whispered. "Just don't hit the child."

"Oh, my God!" With a groan, Ahab covered his face with his hands and tried to drop to his knees beside them. His half-leg, with its ivory attachment, did not bend as his whole leg did, and he landed clumsily on his buttocks on the floor. His anger renewed, he swore. He shuddered violently, again trying to regain control. Then he stared at Hannah and Timothy, who both returned his stare with wide, fright-filled eyes. Ahab grabbed the two of them into his arms, pouring out unintelligible words of distress. Hannah held fast to her son, unable to think straight.

"Hannah, Hannah, I would not hurt thee nor the boy. Ye see how it is with me. I must have my way clear. Give me the child. He must see that his father is not a monster." He pulled the whimpering boy from her arms and kissed him again and again.

Her ear and face stung where his large hand had struck her. She reached up to touch her cheek, and his attention was drawn to the growing welt.

"Curse me, curse me," he said, touching her with a trembling hand. "Thy lovely, gentle face …"

She tried not to draw back, lest he become enraged again. His touch—always dear to her before—now burned both her flesh and her spirit. She moved away, took her son in her arms, and stood up. It would take Ahab a few moments to stand. By then, she could have the boy in the nursery. Or should she flee the house entirely? She could make it to the door. Was it madness to remain in the presence of this rage?

"I'll put him to bed," she found herself saying. Thus committed, she hurried out of the room and up the stairs, leaving her husband seated on the parlor floor, there to regain his dignity in solitude.

Halfway up the staircase, she paused, arrested by a movement in the dark hallway below. There stood Abigail, flattened against the wall. The pistol Daniel had given her was in her hand. Hannah stared at her, trying to understand what she meant to do. Abigail jerked her head toward the top of the staircase, ordering Hannah to continue upstairs. Obediently, she fled to the nursery and closed the door.

"Sorry, Mama," whimpered Timothy. "I'm sorry. I love you." He patted her face as she bent down to dress him for bed.

Though the touch of his tiny hand was gentle, it stung her face and renewed the pain that now pounded throughout her head. She took deep breaths and tried to think clearly. Despite her pain and tears, she must smooth things over for her son.

"I love you too, darling" she whispered.

"I was bad. I hurt you and Papa."

Hannah shook her head, making her pain worse. "No, no, sweetheart. Well, yes, you disobeyed Mama. You must obey when I tell you to put your toys away. But Papa was not angry with you. He was angry about something else. He didn't mean to ... didn't mean to ..." She could not finish her sentence.

"I love you, Mama. I love Papa." He looped his arms around her neck and hugged tightly.

Nausea surged through her, and she gasped for breath. "To bed, my darling," she whispered. "We love you too."

The gentle tap on the door sounded like thunder, the click of the door latch like hailstones on glass. Hannah jerked about, fearing to see Ahab. It was Abigail with a tray of food for Timothy.

"He mustn't go to bed without his supper," she said. "Here, Mrs. Hannah, let me finish. You sit there in the rocker." She handed Hannah a damp cloth. "Put this on your face."

Hannah obeyed. At first, the coolness of the cloth stung her skin, but soon the pain in her head began to subside. Now, horror at her husband's violent behavior and a sense of her own vulnerability overwhelmed her. What was she to do?

As she watched Abigail feed the hungry boy and clean him up for bed, she could see how tenderly the woman treated him. She loved him as if he were her own. She had brought out the pistol and would have done whatever was necessary to keep Ahab from hurting him. Hannah was grateful for that. The thought that Ahab might have harmed his son was beyond her comprehension. He had struck at the child. He had struck her instead. Was he insane? Or had she somehow deserved to be struck?

Timothy was ready for bed. The women kissed him good-night and watched while he fell asleep. Then Abigail turned her attention to Hannah. "He will forget everything by tomorrow. Children forget quickly. You must allow me to tend your injury, Mrs. Hannah."

"I'm afraid to leave him—"

"Captain Ahab has retired to his room."

"Did he speak to you?"

"No. He only spoke …" She frowned and dropped her gaze. "He was angry with himself, only with himself."

Tears scalded Hannah's eyes and flowed down her cheeks. He had not meant to hurt either of them. It was his injury that made him act this way. But how much more could they be expected to endure?

Abigail led her to her bedroom. Rather than allowing Hannah to dress for bed, however, Abigail sat her in a chair by the fireplace and started a fire. After freshening the damp cloth with cool water, she seated herself across from Hannah and began to ask her questions.

"What street did you live on in New Bedford?"

"Why do you ask?"

"I was in New Bedford once. The most beautiful homes were being built on Country Street."

"No, it was County Street. My father's uncle built his home there. It is where I was born and where I grew up."

"Tell me about your father."

Despite the soothing effect of the cool cloth, Hannah's head ached, and she still felt nauseated. All she wanted was to sleep.

She lay her head against the back of her chair, only a little curious about Abigail's uncharacteristic questioning.

"Mrs. Hannah." Abigail was kneeling in front of her now, touching her face. "Open your eyes, Mrs. Hannah. Look at me."

"Why are you tormenting me? Let me sleep."

Abigail gently shook her. "No. Not yet. If you sleep now … It's not good to sleep when your head hurts this way. Stay awake just a while longer. Talk to me. I know it will be difficult, but you must stay awake to get well. It is for your son, Mrs. Hannah."

Hannah stared at Abigail. Her face was lined with concern, even fear. A new respect for this brown-skinned woman surged up inside Hannah. If she had been willing to shoot the man she loved for Timothy's sake, she could be trusted. Hannah took a deep breath, struggling against the sleep that tried to envelop her.

"My father was a kind and gentle man. He had a charming little smile. When I was naughty, he never raised his voice or scolded me. But the sadness in his eyes could break my heart …"

Chapter Twenty-Two

∞

*W*hen Hannah awoke, the sun was shining through the window. She sat up in alarm as memories of last night's horror tumbled through her mind. She must go to her son, must make sure he was safe. But as she tried to put her feet on the floor, the room seemed to turn, and she sank back against the pillows. Staring at the ceiling, she tried to think.

Abigail had forced Hannah to talk, telling every story she could remember about her father, her childhood years, the way she had met Ahab, the books she had read, anything to keep her awake. Several times Abigail had gone down to the kitchen to freshen the cool compress. At last, after the mantel clock had chimed two in the morning, she had allowed Hannah to go to bed. Abigail's nursing was unlike anything Hannah had ever heard of, but it had helped. Although she was dizzy and could still hear a dull pounding in her ears, the pain had subsided, and she no longer felt nauseated. But where was Timothy?

Hannah rolled over on her stomach and swung her feet off the bed, then lowered herself to the floor. She crawled to her wardrobe, hoping somehow to dress herself. Her reflection in the large oval mirror on the wardrobe door startled her for a moment. Her long auburn hair was disheveled, her face was pale, and dark circles hung under her eyes. On her right cheek, almost hidden by her abundant hair, was a bluish-purple bruise. Her right ear was swollen. If she wore her hair just so, the bruises could be covered, she thought. At least her eye was not blackened by the blow, as Mrs. Stoddard's had been after Captain Stoddard had struck her. No one ever had to know that Captain Ahab had also struck his wife.

With that thought, Hannah slumped against the wardrobe and wept. What had their lives come to that he would behave as he had last night? All the strength and energy that Ahab exerted to kill a whale had been unleashed against their tiny, helpless son. If he had struck Timothy instead of her, the boy surely would have died. Fear gripped her heart. Where was Timothy now? She must not rest until she found him. Crawling back to the bed, she pulled herself up just as Abigail entered the room.

"Mrs. Hannah," she said, "let me help you. How do you feel?"

"Put her in the chair," another voice ordered. Hannah glanced up. It was Tishtega. "Sit here," the woman ordered, taking Hannah's arm and, along with Abigail, helping her to a chair.

"Where's my son?" Hannah asked Abigail. "Where's Timothy?"

The other two women traded a look. "He is well ... and safe," Abigail said.

Tishtega gently touched Hannah's bruises, probing to see how far they extended above the hairline. Then she took Hannah's chin in hand and held up one finger of the other hand. "Look here." She slowly moved the finger up and down and from side to side, not allowing Hannah to move her head. At last she seemed satisfied. "You are strong, Mrs. Ahab. You must be up and about for a while, rest a little, then walk about the house again. It is a fair day outside. Go out and enjoy your garden. This will heal soon."

Hannah gave her a slight nod. "Thank you, Tishtega." She reached for her purse on the nearby table, but the woman waved it away.

"To help you is to repay an old debt."

After the midwife had gone, Abigail helped Hannah wash and dress. She selected Hannah's sea green dress, helped her put it on, and fussed over fastening its bows and buttons. She sat Hannah at her dressing table and brushed her hair to one side in a loose bun that covered the bruises. She found a green ribbon in Hannah's drawer and secured it in the thick roll of hair with a hairpin. Then she scrutinized her work in the dressing table mirror.

"You look lovely, Mrs. Hannah. Shall I fix you some breakfast?"

Hannah turned around and stared into her eyes. "Abigail, where is Timothy?"

Abigail sighed. "His father took him out right after breakfast. I think they went down to the docks."

"Ah, how could you have let him do that?" Hannah tried to stand, but she moved too quickly and was forced to sit down again. "Why?"

"Captain Ahab was ... was ... he was well this morning, Mrs. Hannah. He was jolly, in fact. He had me dress the boy and even put a sweater on him himself. They both were laughing as they went out." Her every word and look was an apology. "How could I have stopped him?" she whispered.

Hannah gazed at her for a moment, noticing for the first time how many silver strands coursed through her raven hair. "Yes. I know. No one ever stops Ahab from doing as he wishes, do they?"

"Let me help you downstairs," Abigail said. "You need to eat."

They were halfway down the staircase when Ahab barged in the front door, his son in one arm and several bundles in the other. Father and son were laughing together over some private joke, just as they had when Ahab had first come home. Hannah froze, her eyes meeting Ahab's. He stared at her, examining her face. His brow was knit with concern.

"Mama!" squealed Timothy, struggling to get down from his father's arms. Safely on the floor, he dashed up the stairs and hugged her skirts. "Mama, we bought you a surprise! We bought you a—"

"Hush, boy," Ahab laughed, but his eyes were dark. "Don't give it away. Come down, my dear. See what we brought thee. Thy son is a great shopper. We visited every shop on Petticoat Row. Mrs. Stoddard sends her greetings to thee. Come down, girl … eh, wife. Abigail, bring her down."

Untangling himself from her skirts, Timothy bounded down the stairs and hopped around in circles. "Presents, presents, presents!" he squealed. In his excitement, he collided with Ahab's ivory leg, almost knocking him down.

"Timothy, watch out," Hannah cried, hurrying down to avert disaster.

Ahab forced a laugh. "There, there. No harm done. I've got my balance. Come along now, let's have a look at what we've got here."

As Hannah reached the bottom of the stairs, Ahab reached out to her with his free hand. She pretended not to see it, but followed her son, who had scampered into the parlor and was plumping the pillows on the divan.

"Mama, sit here," he commanded.

How like his father. Giving orders already. "Aye, my little captain. If you'll come sit on my lap."

"No, no," said Ahab. "We have something else to put on thy lap. First mate Timothy, step forward." The boy giggled and ran to him. "Arms forward." The boy held out his tiny hands, and Ahab placed a small, wrapped box in them. Timothy ran to Hannah.

"Here." His eager eyes danced as he thrust the box at her then lounged against her knees to help her remove paper and string. He tore off the box lid and pulled out an ivory comb decorated with scrimshaw. "Let me." He reached up to place the adornment in her hair.

"Ow!" She tried not to wince, but he had hit a tender spot. "I'll do it," she said, endeavoring to laugh away her cry of pain. With trembling hands, she gently worked the comb into her thick hair. "How does this look?" she asked her son.

"Pretty," he cried.

"Lovely," said Ahab.

She stared up at her husband and saw the sorrow in his eyes, even as he smiled. She took Timothy's face in her hands and kissed him. "Thank you, my darling, for my beautiful present."

"Now Papa's," the boy said.

Again, Hannah looked up at Ahab. There was a little of the son in the father at that moment: unsure of himself, vulnerable, so much wanting to please her. Tears stung her eyes as she gave him a quivering, expectant smile.

"This gift is far overdue, my dear." From behind his back, he pulled a slender brown package tied with string.

Hannah tried to unwrap it, but her hands trembled, and the twine tangled into a hopeless knot. "Oh, dear. Now look what I've done."

"Mama," said Timothy with an impatient giggle. "Let me."

"No. Allow me," said Ahab. With difficulty, he sat down beside her on the divan and pulled out his folding knife. As he reached to cut the twine, his rough hands brushed her soft one. Without meaning to, she pulled her hand away. A sigh escaped him as he cut the string and unwrapped the package. Inside was a white lace parasol with baleen ribs and a carved ivory handle and stem. "To replace the one thou lost as we sailed to

Nantucket," he said quietly. "It will restore thy lovely ivory complexion." He started to touch her face, then changed his mind, putting his hand down before she could pull away from him again.

"Thank you. It's very nice," she whispered. She would not tell him that she had decided long ago that parasols were a mark of vanity, not to mention a nuisance.

"Mrs. Hannah," Abigail said, "it's time for Master Timothy's dinner. May I take him to the kitchen?"

"Yes," Ahab said. "He's had a busy morning. Scud along, boy."

Timothy took the housekeeper's hand and skipped along beside her as they left the room. Hannah felt her chest tighten. She did not feel well enough for a confrontation.

Ahab put his arm around her and pulled her close. He kissed her hair just above the ivory comb. "Thou hast never been more lovely, my dear. This dress becomes thee as none other does." He sighed again. "Methinks I've been far too busy these days. It's true that I've much work to do, but I must not neglect my family while I am on shore. Wilt thou attend the lecture with me at the Atheneum tomorrow evening? A professor of archeology will be speaking about recent discoveries in Egypt. It should prove interesting."

Hannah struggled to keep up with the flurry of feelings and thoughts that swept through her as he spoke. His embrace had never been more tender, but she was wary of trusting him. Yet, though he did not say he was sorry for last night, his actions seemed to show it. She wanted to forgive him. But what work was he doing? What did he mean "while I am on shore"? Was he planning a trip? Surely not another whaling voyage. But if he wanted to hear the lecturer on Egyptian antiquities, perhaps he planned, at last, to take her on a tour of the world. But why would such plans require him to lock himself in his study? Why would they cause him such violent moodiness?

"Hannah, art thou ill?" He held her away and stared into her eyes with concern.

She gave a breathless laugh. "No. I haven't eaten today."

His laugh was hearty. "Then, my dear, thou must be fed. Let it not be said that Captain Ahab's wife goes hungry."

As he stood, Hannah marveled at his strength. Though he had difficulty sitting down with his former grace, he had adjusted to rising on his whole leg alone, using the ivory appendage only for balance. Her heart pulsed with admiration for his courage. But as she stood to join him and was overcome by dizziness, she could not gain her own balance as easily. He grasped her as she started to fall forward and pulled her close, lowering them both back down on the divan with a clumsy thump.

"Sit a while longer, my dear. Abigail will tell us when dinner is served."

She tried once again to take comfort in the strength of his embrace as she always had before he struck her. But though she might forgive him, was she foolish to trust him again? Despite his tender tone, he seemed like a stranger to her. Still, when he sensed her hesitation, he became all the more attentive.

"Rest thy head on me." He gently pressed her head against his chest and kissed her forehead. A small sob escaped her. "Shhh. All is well," he whispered. "There will be no more difficulties. I swear it to thee on my life." He brushed away her tears and kissed her cheek. She gazed up, allowing herself to believe him and hoping that her smile told him so. His eyes seemed to reveal his gratitude. He brushed her lips with his, then lingered there, kissing first with tenderness, then with passion. She responded in kind. He reached out to pull her body against his, but stopped abruptly and sat back against the divan.

"This will not do." He stared out the window. "There will be time enough for it later."

Hannah laughed. Her face was flushed with pleasure. "Of course. Tonight."

He looked at her sharply, but was quick to soften his expression. "Mmm'h'mm." He seemed to struggle with his thoughts for a moment. At last he spoke with what seemed to Hannah too much cheer. "My dear, dost thou like the parasol? Would there be another gift that thou wouldest prefer?"

Surprised at his sudden change of mood, she tried to respond with good cheer as well. "Oh, no. It's lovely. Thank you, my darling."

"Ah, thy words tell a different story from thy eyes. What is it that thou wishest? I will buy it without delay."

"What I want cannot be bought, husband." She reached up and caressed his leathery cheek, gazing into his eyes with tenderness. "I would like for you to sit with me in the parlor after supper each evening—just for one hour—as we used to do. Then you can go to your study and work as late as you like on your sea charts."

He frowned. "Is that all? Is there nothing else I can give thee?"

"You can take Timothy and me along for your daily walks, as you did when you first returned from this last voyage."

He was beginning to smile. "Thou wishest only to have my company? Ah, the sweetness of thy requests warms my heart, my dear. But is there no other gift I can give thee?"

She gave him a coy smile, cuddled close, and whispered in his ear, "You can give me a daughter."

"Humph!" he cried, pulling away with mock indignity. "Thou art an insatiable creature, wife. Is not one child sufficient to keep thee busy?"

"Is one whale sufficient for a voyage?" she shot back.

"Ah!" he cried. "One whale! One whale? Yes, if it be the White Whale, it is sufficient!"

His eyes blazed, and his fists were clenched. Hannah gasped and pulled away from him. He quickly softened. "Never mind. It will be done soon enough. I will give thee an hour each evening. And I will take thee out for a walk, thee and the boy, each day. All of Nantucket must see what a fine family Captain Ahab has."

Chapter Twenty-Three

✥

A hab was true to his word. That evening, he sat in the parlor with Hannah for one hour, smoking his pipe while she worked on her quilt. The next morning, he permitted Timothy and her to accompany him on his daily walk about town. Having mastered the use of his artificial leg, he was now required to slow his pace so they could keep up with him. He hailed old acquaintances, admired new babies, complimented young whalers on the beauty of their sweethearts, and insisted on buying a toy for Timothy at Mrs. Stoddard's dry goods store. Hannah breathed a silent prayer of thanks as she observed that his steps did not seem to cause him as much pain as before, even at the end of their walk.

That evening, he took her to the lecture at the Atheneum. Hannah was fascinated by the professor of Egyptian antiquities as he spoke of his upcoming trip to examine the sites Napoleon had plundered. How she longed to join his expedition. But Ahab was unimpressed by the man. As they left the library lecture hall, he remarked that it was not the man who expounded on the findings of others who was worthy of adulation but rather the man who charted his own course and made his own discoveries.

"Even searching out treasures buried at ancient sites is a simple task," he added. "To trace the paths of an adversary that roams the seven seas, that is a remarkable feat. Yet it can be done."

Hannah could not think of any appropriate response. But then, he seemed to be speaking only to himself, as he often did these days. For the moment, all her efforts were needed to keep up with him as he strode up Orange Street toward their home. Since he had declined an invitation to the social to be given for the professor at Mrs. Matthew Starbuck's house, she hoped that he would sit with her by the fire to further discuss the lecture. Though he did not think much of the professor, perhaps she could find a way to suggest that they, too, travel to Egypt to discover its wonders for themselves. Once they arrived home, however, he seemed to feel he had completed his duty to her, for he disappeared behind his study door.

As the autumn weather grew colder, their daily walks grew shorter, and they seldom walked through the residential neighborhoods. Ahab preferred to visit the docks and see what ships had come in or to patronize the stores on Main Street where whaling supplies were sold. Hannah noticed that the store-owners and clerks were quick to give him their attention, even if another customer had come into the establishment before them. This deference to her husband both embarrassed her and made her proud. All Nantucket seemed to honor him and to value his opinions.

Would the camels improve Nantucket's whaling trade and reconfirm the island as the whaling capital of the world? Ahab declared that the camels were a remarkable invention and that, having tried one voyage out of New Bedford himself, he would henceforth recommend sailing only from Nantucket.

Did he think the price of oil would go up or down this year? Ahab viewed the success of the previous year as a sign that profits would continue to rise, voicing the familiar local adage, "Nantucket oil lights all the world!"

Was this brand of rope or that type of cask superior to any other? Ahab's stamp of approval on a product ensured that every store would carry it and every ship's owner would give it a try.

As Ahab's wife, Hannah received similar esteem from the women merchants of Petticoat Row, as well as from all the other whaling wives. Even the three daughters-in-law of the wealthy Joseph Starbuck never failed to include Mrs. Ahab on their guest lists. The socials given at their three brick homes on upper Main Street were the most prestigious on the island. But, though Hannah found their company pleasant, she still preferred a humbler branch of the prolific Starbuck clan.

Mary Starbuck's husband had returned home in August from a good voyage, during which he had sailed as first mate on one of his uncle's ships. Since his uncle had praised his leadership abilities, he had hoped to be named captain on his next voyage. But his uncle had more captains than ships, so young Mr. Starbuck decided to seek other opportunities. He approached Captain Bildad and Captain Peleg about the *Pequod*, now being refitted at the shipyard on Brant Point. The old ship owners promised to keep him in mind. Mr. Starbuck appeared to be in a happy frame of mind when he and his family met up with the Ahabs as they all walked down Orange Street.

The two women introduced their respective husbands, with Hannah exclaiming, "It's hard to believe that you both are born and bred Nantucketers, but you've never met."

"That's the whaler's life, my dear, what with all the coming and going," Ahab said. "Mr. Starbuck, how d'ye do?"

"I am well, thank'ee, Captain Ahab. It's a true pleasure to meet thee, sir," the young man said. "Thy reputation precedes thee."

"Likewise, sir." Ahab shook his hand. "Thy uncle commends thee to all who will listen."

Mr. Starbuck gave a sober nod. A modest Quaker, he would not indulge in sinful pride. But this acknowledgment from Captain Ahab clearly pleased him. "Tell me, sir, thy last voyage was on the *Pequod*, was it not?"

"Aye."

"And she's a worthy vessel, is she not?"

"Aye, that she is." Ahab eyed him with interest.

Mr. Starbuck nodded again. "I'd like to sail on her next voyage out. Wouldest thou recommend it?"

"A good ship always needs a good first mate."

Disappointment flickered in the younger man's eyes, but only for an instant. He straightened his shoulders and gave Ahab a nod of respect. "Aye, and a good captain as well." He reached out to shake Ahab's hand again before the two families parted company.

Hannah and Mary embraced, promising to bring their sons together for play some day soon. Two-year-old Isaiah Starbuck tried to hug Timothy, but the older boy reached out to shake his hand, and both boys giggled.

Despite all the pleasantries, Hannah left the encounter with uneasy thoughts. How could Mary stand by and watch her husband plan another voyage so soon after he returned? And what had the exchange of compliments between the men meant? Ahab could not go whaling again—could he?

By the end of October, her apprehensions became reality. Ahab no longer accepted invitations to socials or lectures. Although he continued to sit with Hannah by the fire, he seemed to struggle against his own impatience, then retreated to his study as soon as the promised hour had elapsed. Each night, she tried to find subjects to interest him, but he only gave her brief answers. She decided to set aside her quilting and to read to him. He puffed on his pipe, nodded from time to time, but found nothing worthy of comment.

In everything of importance, he seemed to move away from her once again. He would not return to share her bed. He abandoned intimate conversation and treated her with detached courtesy. And now, with each failed attempt to restore their intellectual dialogue, her spirits dipped lower. He was going whaling again. She was sure of it. But what good would it do to confront him? Captain Peleg had called her "resigned." No. She was not resigned. She would not let Ahab go without a fight. Yet he must not know that she was fighting. But what could she do to win him?

After several days of contemplation, she decided that for every step he took away from her, she would take two steps toward him. She would read to him, then ply him with questions about the reading. When he responded, she would praise his wisdom. She would embrace him and tell him how much she depended on his strength. She would caress him and show him how much she desired him.

In the daytime, she would keep Timothy near him that he might be captivated by the boy's brightness. After she put their son to bed, she would draw Ahab to the nursery to view the sleeping child. If the sight of his dark lashes against his cherubic cheeks did not melt the father's heart, what more could she do? Yet, even then, she would not give up.

On a cold evening in early November, she wrapped her shawl around her and picked up a small volume of sonnets. "Shall I read to you?" she asked Ahab.

He lit his pipe and grunted his assent.

"Ah, this is poetry: 'Being your slave, what should I do but tend / Upon the hours and times of your desire? / I have no precious time at all to spend, / Nor services to do till you require.' Hmm. 'Being your slave ...'" She smiled at him, but he looked away. Hannah threw off her shawl and went to his chair. "It's been too long since I've sat on your lap, Captain Ahab. Get thyself comfortable, because I'm going to set me down."

"Dost thou seek to annoy me, wife?"

"Yes, I do." She laughed. "It's only for an hour. Now, make room for me." Settling herself on his lap, she opened the book again. "Here's another poem: 'Thou art tyrannous, so as thou art, / As those whose beauties proudly make them cruel; / For well thou know'st to my dear doting heart / Thou are the fairest and most precious jewel ...'" She whispered the last line into his ear.

He clamped his teeth on his pipe, and it seemed to Hannah that he was making an effort not to smile.

"Very well, if we must read Shakespeare, give it to me." He took the book and turned to another sonnet. "'No longer mourn for me when I am dead / Then you shall hear the surly sullen bell / Give warning to the world that I am fled / From this vile world with vilest worms to dwell ... / O, if, I say, you look upon this verse/ When I, perhaps, compounded am with clay, / Do not so much as my poor name rehearse, / but let your love even with my life decay.'"

She hid her face in his shoulder to keep from crying at his reading. How could she have thought to outsmart him? Now he would indeed be annoyed by the tears he himself had brought to her eyes. "Why did you read such a sad poem when I'm telling you how much I love you?" she muttered.

"Thou makest much ado about nothing, my dear," he quipped.

She glared at him. "My love is nothing to you?"

"Hannah, don't be difficult."

"Ahab, don't be difficult." She laid her head against him again and played with the buttons on his suit coat. He shifted uncomfortably. She slid her hand into his coat, feeling through his shirt the power of his chest. "Don't be difficult, husband," she repeated in a whisper. She gazed up into his eyes and smiled, then nibbled at his lips with hers.

He began to return her kisses, but then turned his head and stared into the fire, holding her away. "No, Hannah. Thou must not tempt me this way."

"Tempt you?" She gave a short laugh. "I'm your wife."

"Thou art Circe," he said lightly. "Thou wouldst keep Odysseus from his labors."

"You're thinking of the labors of Hercules. And, for your information, Odysseus returned to Penelope and with Penelope he *stayed*."

"Ha! Good answer. My dear, thou hast entertained me long enough this evening. I must get to my work." He put her off his lap and stood to go to his study.

Hannah was discouraged for only a moment. On reflection, she decided that he had weakened a little, as evidenced by his bantering with her. Tomorrow she would be cheerful with him and would make certain he played with Timothy. And then, perhaps, if all went well, tomorrow night he would find her in his bed, where she would do all she could to remind him of their wedding night.

Her plans came to naught. The following day, a bitter wind kept her at home nursing Timothy's sniffles. Ahab took his usual walk without them and stayed out all day. When he sat with her after supper, he read the *Inquirer*, grunting short responses to her attempts at conversation. Then, instead of going to the study, he put on his greatcoat and walked out into the night. He did not return until long after she had fallen asleep.

She would not give up, despite his deflection of her efforts. She instructed Abigail to prepare his favorite foods. He countered the instructions, saying that long years at sea had inclined his tastes toward plainer foods. She sent Timothy to ask his father's help with a toy puzzle. He patted the boy's head and sent him back to her, saying mothers had more patience than fathers with such things. She asked him to sit with Timothy and her for a daguerreotype. He stated that he would not have his likeness spread abroad for any fool to ogle, but that she and the boy could pose for the portrait if they pleased. When she framed the finished daguerreotype and placed it beside his bed, he moved it to a table in her sitting room. At last, she decided to accost him in bed. If he could not be won through his heart, perhaps he could be won through passion.

Chapter Twenty-Four

છ

*H*annah had come to the conclusion that Ahab was detaching himself from his family to avoid the pain of his departure, whenever it was to be. He had not brought it up because he wished to forestall her tears as long as possible. She must let him know that she knew. She must assure him that she understood. No, not understood, but at least accepted his decision to sail again. She would have to act quickly. If he told her of the voyage, he might close the subject. If she asked him about it, perhaps he would open up to her. Perhaps he would lower the shield he seemed to have placed over his heart to keep her and their son out.

He had begun to shave minutes off their evening time together until it was now a scant half-hour. In that time, he would give her only a few minutes to chat about their son's latest accomplishments or to inform him about a recent birth, betrothal, or death before he retreated behind the pages of the *Inquirer*. Any concerns she expressed about the latest childhood illness or the rising prices of dry goods brought from him a simple remedy or a brief assurance that his financial resources would see them through any period of inflation. Each abrupt answer reinforced her decision to confront him.

"Captain Macy had a good voyage," she remarked one evening as soon as he had taken his chair by the fire.

"Aye." He filled his pipe and lit it, then fussed with the newspaper on his lap.

"Mrs. Macy was quite pleased to see how well her son proved himself. She had worried about his sailing with his father, but Simon showed himself to be up to the task, they say."

"Mmm'h'mm."

"It must have been difficult for Captain Macy not to show partiality to his son for all that time."

He stared into the fire.

"I saw from the roof walk that the *Pequod* is in the harbor. Is she fit to sail now?"

He looked up sharply, frowning at her.

"When will you sail?" No amount of preparation could have kept her voice from breaking as she spoke. But she smiled at him, hoping that her eyes revealed her acceptance of the inevitable, despite the tears.

His frown softened. "Late December, if all goes well. I've sent for some special ... eh, supplies, and not all of them have arrived."

She nodded and stared down at her quilt. Her heart felt as if it would burst, but she must not let him see her distress. "Have you a crew yet?"

"Some have shipped."

"Mr. Starbuck?"

"Aye. First mate."

"Mary will be proud to have her husband sail with you. And Aunt Charity will be pleased that you're taking her brother's ship out again. The profits from her investment in your last voyage enabled her to purchase a stove."

"Mmm'h'mm."

"Well, my dear, I suppose you must get to your charts. A captain must be well-prepared for his voyage."

He raised his eyebrows and stared at her for a moment. "Aye." He tapped his pipe into the ashtray and set aside his unread paper. As he stood to leave, he came to her chair and caressed her face. "Thou art a good woman, Hannah."

She gripped his hand and kissed it, savoring his gentle touch. Then she released him, lest he think she was trying to detain him. "Go now," she whispered.

His eyes showed his gratitude, and her heart warmed. As he walked toward the study, his buoyant posture revealed that she had cheered him. In another hour, she would go to his bed and wait for him there. She would entreat him to give her a daughter, or at least to try. With all the understanding she had heaped upon him, how could he refuse her this one consolation to his absence? Then, if she pleased him well enough, perhaps he would decide that Mr. Starbuck would make a suitable captain for this voyage of the *Pequod*.

She must go to his room at just the right moment. He did not retire at a regular time each night. If she went there too soon, she might fall asleep in his bed, and he would sleep in another room. If she waited too long, he might be there already and send her away.

When he had been in the study for a short while, she went upstairs. After checking to be certain her son was sleeping comfortably, she walked down the hallway toward her room. For a moment, she thought she heard a muffled sound. She looked down the hall. The sound seemed to come from the small bedroom just beyond Ahab's, the room with a door to the outside staircase. Icy fear seemed to freeze her heart. Had someone crept up those outside stairs, broken the lock, and entered their home? She tiptoed nearer. A low cacophony of unintelligible words confirmed her suspicions. And there was more than one! She turned to tiptoe back to the nursery, but the floor creaked beneath her. She stopped. The voices stopped. There was a sinister laugh. She ran to the nursery door, spinning around just as the other door opened. She nearly swooned at the sight of a dark Asian man dressed in black standing at the end of the hallway. He was flanked by others of his race, how many she did not know. Maternal instinct roared up inside and revived her. With arms outspread, she flung her back against the nursery door.

"Ahab!" she screamed. "Help! Murderers! Ahab, save us—"

"Avast, woman! Belay that shrieking," thundered Ahab from below. "Thou'lt wake the dead!" He lumbered up the stairs at a casual pace while she stared in horror, first at him and then at the savages who had invaded her home. Abigail appeared behind him, dressed in nightclothes, with her pistol in hand. Ahab glanced back at her.

"Put that away," he ordered. She obeyed with reluctance. When he reached the top of the stairs, he took in the scene, then confronted Hannah. "Now, what's this noise about?"

She stared at him, unable to speak, unable to stop her violent trembling.

Ahab, however, looked calmly at the three men standing in the hallway. With a jerk of his head, he ordered them to retreat back to their room. They complied, murmuring in a foreign tongue and laughing among themselves. The one who seemed to be the leader glanced back at Hannah and gave her a leering smile before he closed the bedroom door, his solitary tooth gleaming at her like a threatening fang.

"Dear God, Ahab, who are those savages?" Hannah croaked. "What are they doing in our home?"

He lifted his chin and glared at her. "Be careful whom thou callest a savage, girl. They are honest whaling men waiting for work. When no one would give them a room because of their race, I gave them leave to sleep here. Wouldest thou, with rooms to spare, deny shelter to a man in winter because of the color of his skin? I'd say that would be the mark of a savage."

"Ah," she cried. "But could you not have told me?"

"Could you not have told *me*?" Abigail stood at the top of the stairs. Her eyes blazed as she stared at Ahab.

Ahab looked from one to the other. He straightened his shoulders and cocked his head defiantly. "Must I answer to women now? Leave me to my work." He started to go back down the stairs but was arrested by the sound of the nursery door latch.

"Mama ..." Timothy stood in the doorway rubbing his eyes and clutching the whaler rag doll Abigail had made for him. "Mama." He reached for Hannah, and she pulled him up into her arms.

"Now look what thou hast done. Thy hysteria has wakened the boy. Go back to bed, shipmate." Ahab struggled to keep his tone light as he spoke to his son.

"No!" Hannah said. "He will not sleep up here with those men in this house."

"Is this mutiny, woman?" Again he tried to speak lightly, but there was a growl in his voice. "Where will he sleep then, for the men will stay?"

Mutiny? Hannah glared at him. She would not play word games over this. "I will take him down to Mary Starbuck's. Come, darling, let's get your clothes."

"Avast!" shouted Ahab. "Thou'lt do no such thing. Wouldest thou shame me before my first mate, that my wife does not feel safe in my house? Look. Thou hast frightened the boy."

Timothy clung to her, his eyes wide as he watched his parents argue over him.

"Give him to me." Abigail reached for him. "He can sleep in my room."

"Yes, and so will I." Hannah started toward the stairs.

Again, Ahab looked from one to the other. "Avast. There's no need. I'll nail the door shut so they cannot come out this way. Yet I must have access ..." He stopped. "Tomorrow I'll put a bar on the door myself. No need to bother Josiah. I still know how to use hammer and saw. That way, we can open it, but they cannot. And then, if need be, we can use the room while they are out." He started down the stairs as if the matter were settled. Hannah and Abigail followed close behind him.

Hannah had not been into the small parlor since Ahab had turned it into his study. She grimaced when she saw her elegant furniture shoved aside to accommodate a massive, rough-hewn table upon which his navigational instruments and a large wrinkled roll of yellowish sea charts were spread. As she entered the room, he turned around and glared at her.

"I'll do as I said. Dost thou not trust me? No, thy eyes tell me thou dost not. Well, then, I'll go nail the door shut for tonight. Will that suit thee? Look, thy son is going back to sleep on thy shoulder. Wouldest thou have me waken him with the noise of pounding? Put him back in the nursery. He will be safe."

Hannah returned his glare. "We'll wait down here until you've finished securing the door."

He heaved a great sigh of annoyance. "Woman, thou art too much trouble." But he sat in a chair and dug in his toolbox for hammer and nails.

Hannah took Timothy and sat down on the steps outside the study door. She would not move from there until Ahab kept his word. She glanced up at Abigail for support.

Sorrow lined the woman's face, and she seemed to struggle with indecision. At last she entered the study, knelt beside Ahab, and took his hands.

"What dost thou want?" He glared at her and tried to pull away.

"No." Abigail gripped his hands firmly. "You must listen. Since the night we two were born, what have I ever asked of you except to make a home for you? When you, an old man, brought me your young bride, I gladly served her as I serve you. And your son. I love him as I love my own. Now I ask something of you, and you must grant it. I beg you, Ahab, don't abandon your child as your father and mine abandoned us. This voyage is madness, and you know it. Would you leave your child to be an orphan, your wife a widow?"

"Avast!" he cried. "What's all this talk? Ahab always returns, and with a full cargo of oil!"

"Do you think I don't know what you're about with those men up there?"

"Avast, I said." He stood, almost knocking Abigail to the floor. "Go to thy kitchen, woman. I'll have no more of this nonsense. This voyage is no different from any other."

Abigail stood slowly, shaking her head. "You cannot hide it from me. I know you too well." She walked through the study door and gave Hannah a sorrowful look. "I have done what I could for him, Mrs. Hannah. Now we must see to the boy's safety."

"The boy is safe, I tell thee. I'll have no more of this bilge from either of ye," Ahab muttered as he lumbered past them and up the stairs, carrying the necessary tools for his task.

Hannah reached out one hand to Abigail, inviting her to sit beside her on the stairs. Trying not to waken her son, she slipped one arm around the older woman's waist and laid her head on her shoulder. "My sister, my sister," she whispered through her tears. "Why did he never tell me? Why didn't you.—?"

"He has always protected me. My mother and his were not the same. I am only an old Gay Head Indian and a servant. Who cares who my parents were? And like my mother, I was not married to the father of my child." She paused, glancing at Hannah with an almost vulnerable expression. "I have never told you my last name. It is Moontalk. It is the name my mother gave me for the pretty words my father spoke when he came to her at night." She then lifted her chin with dignity. "The ways of my mother's people are different from those of the white man. To our people, there was no shame in her being the second wife of the white whaler. And I felt no shame in giving my love to Daniel's father when we were not permitted to marry. Under Ahab's protection, who would dare condemn me for it? You see how all Nantucket stands in awe of him, even the wealthiest ship owners. He is Ahab. His very name is legend."

Hannah nodded, her heart welling up with a new and deep affection for this remarkable woman. Then, glancing up the stairs, she sighed. This night had revealed too many things for her to grasp. What had Abigail just said? Ahab's name was "legend." With that Gay Head inflection, it almost sounded like "legion." With a shudder, Hannah thought of the Bible story of a demoniac healed by Jesus Christ. When the Lord had asked the tormented man his name, the demons within him had answered, "Our name is Legion, for we are many." How many demons were tormenting Ahab that he could not hear the voices of those who loved him? How could he bring some of those very demons into his home to afflict his wife and child—and his sister? How unlike him to fail to protect those in his care.

"His goodness to you and Daniel does not surprise me. He is so generous, so wise, most of the time. Why must he go whaling again? Why can he not ..."

Abigail patted her hand. "He's always had something broken inside, Mrs. Hannah. Though my heart ached for his emptiness, I have never fully understood it. When he brought me his young bride, when I saw that you truly were all the good things he had written to me, I thought his happiness with you would mend him. But I guess he was too old to change. Then losing his leg that way, it just seemed to set him off. You know how he never lets a thing go until he's mastered it. He won't rest till he's got his revenge on that whale."

"Revenge? Against a dumb beast that was just trying to escape being killed?" Hannah shook her head, recalling with dismay how she herself had suggested revenge. But she had spoken in jest, never dreaming he was planning to do it. "Do you think he can actually find one certain whale in all the oceans of the world?"

Abigail gave her a wry look. "If there's one man who can, it's our Ahab."

Hannah studied her face, then nodded. "Yes. Yes, I believe he can. I believe he will." She was cheered by that thought and another. "Abigail, please do something for me."

"Anything, Mrs. Hannah."

"Please just call me Hannah. Don't you realize that through Ahab we are sisters?"

Abigail looked away. When she looked back, tears glistened in her eyes. "I will, but only when we are alone."

Hannah nodded her understanding. Then they both jumped at the sudden sound of Ahab's hammer on the bedroom door. He must have spent several minutes explaining to his "guests" what he was doing. "Shhh," she said to Timothy as he shifted in her arms. She glanced up the staircase. "I don't want to sleep up there," she whispered. "And I certainly won't take my son …"

Abigail shook her head. "It won't do to defy him. You sleep in the nursery with Timothy. I'll put a mattress in the hallway and sleep there with my gun. With Ahab and me between them and the nursery, you need have no fear. Besides, they would not dare harm Ahab's wife and child."

With reluctance, Hannah agreed.

"Mrs. …" Abigail stopped and smiled briefly, trying out her new role. "Hannah, we must not mention any of this to anyone, not even your friends Mrs. Charity or Mrs. Mary Starbuck. I know that they … all of Nantucket, I mean … I know they watched Ahab after he came back to see how he took his loss. He never let on to them about the white whale."

"Yes, you're right. It wouldn't do to talk about it. In any event, he never lets his investors down. This voyage will be as successful as all the others. If he comes across the creature who … who hurt him, he'll kill it this time and sell its oil for a tidy profit."

Abigail stared at her with a frown, then nodded slowly. "Yes. That's it. He will have a good voyage. As always."

"I only wish he would be satisfied to stay at home. We already have all the wealth we could ever need."

Ahab came back down the stairs, and the women went up. As she brushed past him, Hannah hoped there would be no further confrontations. He seemed just as willing to ignore her. But that only added to her disappointment, for she longed for him to take her in his arms. When she had trembled in terror at the appearance of the strange men, when she had desperately wanted to feel his protection, he had turned on her and sided with the source of her fear. How quickly his mood had changed from earlier in the evening when he had been thankful for her understanding, when he had called her good. Would she never again hear such kind words from him? Never enjoy the comfort of his strong arms around her? Oh, but she must not succumb to despair. She was certain that he would have a good voyage, as always. Abigail thought so too.

But if she truly believed it, what was this feeling of dread she could not shake off?

Chapter Twenty-Five

❧

By late November, Ahab had removed himself from all society that did not have to do with his coming voyage. Even Bildad and Peleg, having once again signed him as captain, did not feel that they needed to seek his company. In the business of whaling, they all knew what they were about. Aware of Ahab's preferences, the two owners had the responsibility of signing the crew and supplying the vessel with all the necessary stores. The captain would assume command when it was time for the *Pequod* to set sail.

With the exception of his daily walks, which he now took late in the evening, Ahab could be found in his study or in the small work shed behind his house. However, he was not often sought. As Ahab had withdrawn from the community, the community had withdrawn from him as well. Since his first voyage at eighteen, he had seldom been on shore and even then had never been one to socialize extensively. Further, all of Hannah's friends seemed to understand that she would prefer to devote her time to her husband before he sailed.

She would have indeed preferred to spend time with him, but he had little time for her. Other than supper, he took his meals behind the closed parlor doors. To make the best of their short time together, she now permitted Timothy to sit at the dining

room table with them, for only in their son's presence could she
see any softening in Ahab's dismal moodiness.

"Thou must mind thy mother when I am gone, boy," Ahab
would say each evening. He would lean toward his son with a
glowering expression and add, "I don't want to hear of any
disobedience during my absence."

"Aye, sir," Timothy would lisp in his childish voice, giving his
father a solemn salute. Then he would giggle at their game, and
Ahab's expression would relax almost to a smile.

Ahab might then remark to Hannah about the weather or
some whaling ship's recent arrival. She might return with a question about something insignificant regarding his own upcoming
voyage. His reply would be concise. She would nod with understanding. It became a ritual. Yet these were the happiest
moments of Hannah's days. Her heart aching with love, she
would gaze at his handsome, tortured face.

Each night, he visited the bedroom where the whalers slept,
then barred the door from the hallway and retired to his own
room. To set Hannah's mind at ease, he had explained that, if
they appeared evil to her, it was because she was not used to
foreigners, especially those from Asia. He assured her that these
Chinese men were among the strongest and most courageous of
all whalers. Their fierce looks need not frighten her, he added,
for their true fierceness came to life only in pursuit of whales.
Despite these assurances, Abigail still slept in the hallway with
her loaded gun beside her, and Hannah slept in the nursery,
haunted by sinister dreams.

Even in daylight, the specter of evil crept into her mind. She
imagined that one of the strange men might climb up to the roof
some night, enter the house through the roof walk, and steal
away her son. Each night, she secured the bolt on the roof walk
door. She imagined that Ahab might decide to provide supper for

the men in her dining room and that she would be forced to endure the leering stares of Fedallah, their leader. She breathed a prayer of thanks each evening when only her small family gathered at table.

Then one night in early December, she was wakened by shouts and pounding from within the whalers' bedroom.

"Miz Captain, you come quick. Hurry!" shouted Fedallah.

Both Abigail and Hannah rushed to Ahab's room to waken him, but he was not there.

"Miz Captain, Captain is hurt. Come quick!" The shouts and pounding continued.

"Where is Ahab? Did he come back in after his walk?" Hannah asked Abigail.

"I don't know." Abigail stared at the bolted door, her brow knit with indecision.

"Dare we trust them? What if they've done something ... what if they've—"

"Hush. Don't think that. We must see what they have to say. Let me get my gun." She quickly retrieved the weapon and cocked it, then nodded to Hannah to lift the bolt.

As soon as it was removed, Fedallah flung open the door. "You see, Captain hurt." Ahab lay senseless on one the whalers' cots, his lower body covered with blood.

"Oh, you horrid beast!" Hannah flung herself down beside Ahab and glared up at the man. "What did you do to him?"

"No, Miz Captain. I didn't. We came back tonight and Captain, he lying outside back yard. Dead leg stick here." He pointed to Ahab's groin.

Only then did she see that the ivory leg was shattered. One of the men held the bloody, broken piece that had pierced him.

"Lift him and carry him to the bed in his room," ordered Abigail.

"No, we keep him this bed." Fedallah said.

"No!" Abigail lifted the cocked pistol and pointed it at his face. "Put him in his own bed. You." She nodded at one of the men. "You go get the Indian midwife Tishtega. You know where she lives. On Fair Street. Go, and be quick, or Fedallah will die."

The man looked at his leader. Fedallah said something in their tongue and jerked his head toward the outside door. The man ran to obey.

"Now put him in his own bed," Abigail said again.

Fedallah glared at her, trying to back her down. She took a step toward him. He growled his surrender, then ordered his men to carry the unconscious Ahab into the next room. Hannah tried to help with the lifting, but Abigail pulled her out of the way.

"Hannah, you must go to the kitchen and get water and clean rags. And bring some ice from the water pail on the back stoop."

"No, I must stay—"

"Listen to me. They are afraid of me but not of you. We don't know what they will do if I leave. If Ahab is moved again, he may bleed to death. Now, be quick and get the water, my sister. We have little time to save him."

Hannah ran to obey. By the time she returned, Abigail had chased the men out and bolted the door. She had also removed Ahab's clothing, unstrapped the broken ivory leg, then covered him partially with a sheet. Above his right thigh, the jagged wound oozed dark blood. Hannah gulped in a deep breath to keep from swooning at the sight.

"It's deep, but the bleeding has slowed," Abigail said. "I don't think the ivory pierced anything vital, but Tishtega will know. We must wash him and keep his head cool."

Hannah plunged a cloth into the pan of water, squeezed it, and gently washed the blood from around the wound. Ahab stirred, moaning, but he did not regain consciousness. Abigail put a cool, damp cloth to his brow and searched his head and body for further injury. Satisfied that there was only one wound, she inspected it again.

"No splinters," she said.

Hannah now gave herself leave to shudder and to wipe her tear-stained face. "What could have happened? Do you think Fedallah was telling the truth, that none of them knows what happened?"

Abigail shook her head. "I don't know. I think if they wanted to kill him, they would have chosen a different way. Besides, it doesn't make sense for them to kill him. He's their benefactor."

Ahab moaned again and began to mutter unintelligible words. Hannah moved close to his face.

"My darling, I'm here. We've sent for Tishtega. We're going to take care of you."

More than an hour passed before Fedallah once again banged on the bolted bedroom door. "Miz Captain, woman here. You open door."

Abigail once again cocked the pistol while Hannah opened the door. Tishtega strode through the passage carrying a large leather satchel.

"Where is he?" she asked.

Hannah took her arm to lead her to Ahab, but Fedallah stepped into the hallway and tried to block her.

"I work for Captain. I take care of Captain. This woman is woman doctor. I am man doctor."

"You're not a doctor at all," Hannah said. "Now go back to your ... to that room."

"I take care of Captain," Fedallah repeated. He motioned to the other men, now four in number, and they quickly stepped into the hallway to back him up. "You go do woman's work. I take care of Captain."

"You will not," shouted Hannah. "Now get out." She glared at him, trying despite her trembling to appear firm. She felt Abigail and Tishtega flanking her, and grew bolder. "Get out, I say. I'll run you clear out of the house if you don't leave this minute."

Fedallah's eyes darted from one to the other. He lifted his chin and glared at them with contempt. "You have him now. But I will have him one day." A hideous grin broke his face, revealing his one fanglike tooth. Seeming to revel in Hannah's rage, he gave a low, sinister laugh. "I will have him one day. You see." He jerked his head toward the door, and his men retreated.

As soon as they had left the hallway, Hannah pulled the door shut and bolted it. When she turned around, Tishtega and Abigail had already gone to the other bedroom and were bent over Ahab, tending his wound.

"The wound is deep, but it is only in the flesh. Nothing vital was struck," Tishtega said, confirming Abigail's diagnosis. As she pulled various items from her leather bag, the only things Hannah could identify were honey, black tea, and vinegar. But there were numerous herbs and liquids from which Tishtega began to prepare a compound in a small porcelain bowl. "You cleaned it well. Now bring me hot water to mix the poultice." Abigail complied, and soon Tishtega was applying a sweet-smelling plaster to Ahab's wound. "Now we must wait for his body to fight the sickness that will come."

The three women took turns watching over him throughout the night. Hannah would not have left his side at all if the other two had not convinced her that her son would need her the next day as much as, if not more than, her husband. During her vigil, she sat near the bed, applying fresh cloths and kisses to his forehead from time to time. When he mumbled vague sounds, she bent close but was unable to distinguish any meaningful words. When he threw off his covers, she tugged them back into place, hoping he could somehow feel despite his unconsciousness the tender touch of her caress. *He will surely forego this voyage,* she thought. *He cannot recover in time to sail as planned.* Her heart ached over his suffering, but she could not keep from rejoicing over the good that would result from it.

She surrendered her post to Abigail for several hours only to be wakened by a call for help. Ahab had become delirious. He was shouting obscenities and thrashing about in the bed. With difficulty, Abigail had prevented his knocking over the lamp burning on the bedside table. Hannah and Tishtega rushed to help restrain him. But for all the strength of the two older women, he would not be subdued. He tried to get out of the bed, but without his ivory leg, he could not gain his balance or take a step. Falling back on the bed, he continued to curse and to flail his arms about senselessly.

"Miz Captain," Fedallah called through the bolted door. "Miz Captain, you need help. I have rope to tie him down."

Hannah dodged her husband's fist and tried to hold his arm. "Tishtega, what shall we do?"

"Get the rope," Tishtega said. "But don't let them in here."

Hannah rushed to the door, unbolted it, and tried to grab the rope from Fedallah.

He jerked it back. "You need man's help." He strode through the door to Ahab's room and, with much struggle, they all worked to tie the rope securely around both Ahab and the bed without harming the patient. Despite being unconscious, Ahab seemed to realize he was bound. He ceased to fight and fell into a deep sleep. Fedallah stood back and surveyed the group of women with a haughty grin.

"You need man's help," he repeated.

"You can go now," Hannah said to Fedallah.

"I go." He glared at her. "But I be near, always near." His wicked laugh echoed through the door of his room after Tishtega had bolted it.

In the midst of the ordeal, Hannah had been removed from her emotions. Now that it was over, she shook violently, then grabbed a chamber pot from the nearby washstand and vomited until her head ached. Abigail washed away the residue that ran down Hannah's chin and helped her to a chair. Hannah tried to give her a grateful smile.

"Until that man came into my home, I never knew the meaning of true evil."

Chapter Twenty-Six

ಐ

Ahab sat in his bed staring out the window in moody silence. He had rejected his breakfast, had rebuffed Hannah when she offered to shave him, and had forbidden Timothy to come into his room. In the week since his accident, he had said little and had refused to answer questions about how his injury had happened. Though his fever had not entirely abated, the minor infection had been extracted by the poultice, so Tishtega had gone back to her own home. When she called to inspect the wound, he grumbled that she had poked at him enough and was no longer needed. Until the wound had further healed, however, he would not be able to attach one of his ivory legs. He was forced to remain in bed. Hannah and Abigail tended his needs as much as he would allow, his terse orders revealing how he despised his inescapable dependence on them.

After much discussion on the potential danger of the five men now residing in the outer bedroom, the women decided that they were not an immediate threat. The whalers seemed to have accepted their position, for Fedallah no longer tried to interfere with Ahab's care, and little noise came from beyond the bolted door. Hannah refused to be responsible for any of their needs, but Ahab seemed not to notice. How they fed themselves or dealt with other necessities, she did not know or care.

Although Hannah still slept in the nursery, Abigail had returned to her own room near the kitchen. Each evening, Hannah would sit by Ahab's bed and work on her quilt until he fell asleep, or pretended to. They had no conversation. But, having given up her delusion that his injury would prevent him from sailing, she insisted on staying by his side as long as he was home.

In the dim candlelight, she would often gaze at him until he returned a glare or turned his back to her. After he fell asleep, she would continue to watch him for a few moments before retiring. She longed to caress his face and smooth out the harsh wrinkles that, even in his sleep, so deeply creased his brow. His hair was now iron gray, with the solitary streak still blazing through it like a white-hot fire. The scar that sliced down his face seemed paler than before, set as it was against skin so often burned by the sun that its bronze color never faded. He seemed like Zeus to her, both in his god-like appearance and in his fearsome inapproachability. Yet she loved him still, and all the more so, for the unabated suffering in his soul. Oh, that her love might heal that suffering. But he would not allow it.

On a rainy, blustery day in the third week of December, Captain Peleg came to visit, but Ahab would not see him. Hannah informed the captain that her husband was sleeping off a mild fever that he had had for several days. Would Captain Peleg care to leave a message? Yes, indeed, the man replied. Weather permitting, the *Pequod* would be ready to sail by Christmas Day. The ship's larder was nearly filled. The last item to go into the hold would be numerous casks of Nantucket water, that nectar of the island that was far superior to any other liquid on the planet. An excellent crew had been signed, and it lacked only one more competent harpooner and one or two more oarsmen. There was no want of possibilities, however, for every day whalers from off-island arrived who sought to ship from

Nantucket. Captain Bildad's brother-in-law Mr. Stubb would be second mate, having just returned from another voyage. Mr. Flask was signed as third mate. Assuming that Hannah would be as pleased as her husband about the steady progress of the preparations, Captain Peleg reaffirmed his trust in him, stating that he and his partner were eager to see Captain Ahab and the *Pequod* embark on another successful voyage.

The news cheered Ahab. He began to eat more often and allowed Hannah to bring him his shaving tools. While she steadied the bowl of hot water and held a mirror in place, he shaved the sides of his face, his chin, and his upper lip, then trimmed his beard down to the jaw line, after his accustomed fashion. He even permitted her to touch his clean-shaven cheeks, but only for a moment.

Shortly after Peleg's visit, a package was delivered by one of the errand boys who roamed the streets of Nantucket looking for work. Little black Pip would not surrender the parcel to anyone but Captain Ahab. To Hannah's surprise, Ahab consented. Once he was admitted to the upstairs bedroom, the boy placed the bundle on the bed as if presenting a jeweled gift box to a mighty potentate.

"Ah, the last of my needs for the voyage," cried Ahab. "Well done, boy. Hannah, fetch him a coin, for he has brought the last, best news."

"Sir, if you please," said the child, "I don't want no coin."

Ahab stared at him. "Indeed! But thou hast done me a great service. I must repay thee. What wilt thou have, then, if not a coin?"

"Sir, if you please, I beg to ship on the *Pequod* with you, sir. It be the dream of every Nantucket boy to ship with Cap'n Ahab, sir. I like hard work. And I can sing and play a little music on my tambourine when the men grow sea-weary. Won't you let me ship with you, sir?"

Ahab scrutinized him. "The dream of every Nantucket boy, thou sayest? But thou art not from Nantucket. Thy dialect betrayeth thee."

"No, sir. I'm from Tolland County, Connecticut, but my family got tooken down to Alabama a few years back. Then Mr. Douglass, he bring me back up north. Now Miz Swain, she let me sleep in her shed."

"Well, then, my boy, no more sheds for thee. Thou mayest tell Captain Bildad that Ahab gives thee leave to ship on the *Pequod.*"

"Thank you, Cap'n, sir. You won't be sorry. Pip will be there when you need him."

After seeing the happy child out, Hannah returned to Ahab's room. As she had watched his kind treatment of the other boy, she had longed for him to remember his own son. She would confront him, would insist that he see Timothy. But he was busy examining the contents of the box. Though he talked to her, he did not seem truly aware of her.

"See here, Hannah. These are stubs from the steel shoes of racing horses, the hardest steel ever wrought by a blacksmith. Aye, there's no harder metal on the face of the earth."

"Horseshoe stubs? Are you planning to ride Samson before you go?"

He stared at her as though she were a stranger. "Ride? Ride? The only thing I'll be riding is the back of a white ..." He stopped and scowled at her. "Bring me the leather bag from my sea chest, the bag that's empty."

She went to the study and found in the chest the small rusty-looking leather bag. It had long ago lost the fragrance of a freshly tanned hide, and now smelled of its many voyages on the seven seas. Though much used, it still was strong enough to serve Ahab's purpose. He deposited the horseshoe stubs in it and pulled the drawstring tight, securing it with what appeared to Hannah to be an intricate seaman's knot.

"Why don't you teach Timothy that knot, or at least a simple one, before you go?"

"Hmm? Who?" He frowned at her.

"Timothy has missed you terribly, my dear. Won't you please let him sit here on your bed and learn to tie a knot or two from his papa? Tomorrow is his birthday, you know."

He stared out the window, seeming to consider it. *Please, God,* she thought, *make him say yes.*

"Aye. I could do that. Here, take this." He thrust the leather bag at her. "Put it in my sea chest. Then bring the boy and two lengths of rope. Let him try his hand at his father's trade."

So long had it been since Timothy had been permitted to see his father that he threw his arms around Ahab and giggled with glee. Ahab seemed merely to endure the embrace. Hannah sat by, working on her quilt and keeping her tears at bay. Though Ahab would not allow himself to express his love for the boy, there were moments when she could see he felt it. With Timothy facing him, he would demonstrate a simple knot, then watch as the boy tried to do the same. His dark eyes would soften as his son's tiny fingers worked the thinner cord, each time failing to match Ahab's example. At last, Timothy grew impatient.

"Can't." He held up his tangled cord to Ahab.

"Never say 'can't,' boy. Thou canst do it. Let's try this." Ahab pulled Timothy up on his lap and faced him toward the foot of the bed. Then he reached over the boy's shoulders to tie the knot. Leaning back against his father's chest, the child watched carefully, then took the rope. Ahab guided his hands through the procedure.

"Cross ends, go under, loop over, under, through," Ahab said. "Now do it solo, lad."

Timothy's brow was knit with concentration as he worked to remember the maneuver. "Cross ends, go unner, go over, unner, froo. Mama, look. I did it."

"Yes, you did. That's wonderful."

At the catch in her voice, Ahab frowned. He set Timothy off his lap. "Enough for one day. Get to thy nursery, boy."

"No, Papa. More knots."

"Scud away, shipmate," Ahab growled.

Timothy was too young to hide his disappointment. As he climbed off the bed, his lower lip quivered. "Aye, sir."

"Darling," Hannah said, "run down to the kitchen and tell Abigail I said you could have a ginger cookie."

The child's eyes lit up, and he scampered away to seize this special privilege.

Hannah glanced at her still scowling husband, then quickly looked down at her quilt. Would he dismiss her too? When she looked back up at him, he was still frowning at her, but with concern. Her heart seemed to skip a beat, and she gave him a tentative smile.

"Thou hast become too thin, Hannah. Thou must eat to keep up thy health ... for the boy's sake."

She nodded, then attempted levity. "Aye, sir."

His look of concern hardened into a scowl, and he turned toward the window. She stared back down at her quilting. At least he had not sent her away. What would he have done if she had said what burned in her breast? *Stay home, Ahab, stay home ... for your son's sake.*

"Fetch my dead leg."

Hannah jumped, startled by both his sudden command and the enthusiasm in his voice. "What?"

"Fetch the leg, girl, and be quick about it. I'm ready to walk again."

Chapter Twenty-Seven

ଚଚ

The shipboard carpenter who had fashioned several artificial legs for Ahab from the jawbone of a sperm whale had also created a leather strap with which to attach them to his stump. If one leg broke or became unreliable, another would slip in and attach to the strap as a replacement. Ahab's striding about the cobblestoned streets of Nantucket had worn out some of the legs. His accident had put an end to another. But there was one sturdy appendage remaining, and Hannah rushed to retrieve it from the study. After the accident, she had wiped the leather strap clean with oil and stored it in a drawer in Ahab's room. Now, putting the two parts together, she brought them to him and stood by to help as she was needed.

Ahab strapped on the leg, then swung both legs over the side of the bed. Leaning on Hannah, he stood on his living leg. Despite his lengthy stay in bed, it stood firmly beneath him. He shifted his weight to the other limb, testing before trusting it. He winced and uttered an oath.

"It's too soon, my dear. Please rest a little longer." Hannah tried to steer him back down on the bed. Putting her hand to his face she frowned. "Look. You're warm. You still have a fever."

"No." He shoved her away and leaned on the ivory leg again. "The fever is nothing. I've rested too much already." He took a tentative step, then another, pressing his hand against the wound in his groin. "The leg holds fast. The wound will heal in time."

Within a matter of hours, he regained his balance and forsook his bed. Once again, he pored over his yellowed charts and examined his instruments. Once again, he parlayed with the Chinese whalers each night before retiring. He no longer welcomed Hannah's presence during the day, although he permitted her to sit in his room for a short time each evening. She persuaded him to continue Timothy's lessons in knot tying. These brief moments of togetherness for father and son gave her great happiness. That is, until she came to his room one afternoon and found Fedallah working the ropes with them.

The man cast a sidelong look Hannah's way, then turned back to Timothy. "You like to go with father on ship? You go whaling with us?"

"Aye, I do. Papa, can I go with you?" Timothy's eyes were bright with excitement at the prospect of such an adventure.

Before Ahab could answer, Hannah swept into the room and snatched up her son. "Time for your nap, my darling." She would not allow herself to shudder, would not allow Fedallah to gloat over her.

"Aye," said Ahab. "Run along, boy. We'll have our last lesson tomorrow, for I sail the day after."

"I want to go with Papa," Timothy said as Hannah carried him away to the nursery.

"Of course, you do, my darling. But not until you are older. You have many knots to learn before you can be of use on a whaling voyage." *No, no! I'll never let you be a whaler!*

Pleased at the prospect of future adventures, the boy laid his head on her shoulder with a happy sigh and, once in bed, was soon fast asleep.

In deference to Hannah, Ahab permitted Abigail to prepare a Christmas Eve feast. He sat with his wife and son for one last meal before going to his ship. Once again, he leaned toward Timothy and gave instructions.

"Thou must mind thy mother while I am gone. I won't look kindly on disobedience during my absence."

"Aye, Papa." Timothy raised one tiny hand in a salute, then laughed at their game.

Ahab also gave his last orders to Hannah. She must teach the boy to read soon, for he must have his education before his first voyage. She would do well to take the boy to the mainland, perhaps for a visit with her friends in Boston, Reverend Harris and his bride, when the weather was pleasant. She must put on a few more pounds to ensure her good health. More meat and potatoes should do the job. And, oh, yes, he had almost forgot: pleased with her household money-managing skill, he had signed a power of attorney and left it, along with his will, with Mr. Mitchell at the bank. She would now be responsible for keeping his fortune intact, and he had no fear that she would do just that.

This last order sat on her heart like a portent of tragedy. Mention of his will was dreadful enough, but why would she need a power of attorney? Of course, it was well known that women often lost everything when their husbands died without giving them legal control of their estates. But Mr. Mitchell's integrity was indisputable. During Ahab's last voyage, the banker had handled things very well for them. Moreover, Ahab had never really taught her about finance and investments. Why would he wish to leave his money in her care unless he did not expect to return? No. No. She would not think it.

After Ahab had given Timothy a goodnight kiss, Abigail took the boy to bed. Hannah tried to draw Ahab to the hearthside for one last evening together, but he lumbered toward the study. She pursued him, grasping his arm before he could disappear behind a locked door. He stopped but would not look at her.

"We've enjoyed our share of time, girl." He spoke in an offhand manner, as though he would dismiss her. "I must be certain everything is stowed in my sea chest."

"Don't forget the gold coin ... for good luck."

He stared at her, and she gave him a tentative smile.

His eyes narrowed. "Aye. That has not been forgot. It's here in my pocket."

"And that vial of Nantucket sand from the harbor to remind you of the home where your loved ones await you?"

He patted his vest pocket. "Here, as always. Now get thee to bed. Tomorrow thou wilt be free of thy husband. Many a Nantucket woman rejoices to see her husband gone a-whaling so that she may rule the house again."

"I'm not a Nantucket woman."

He glanced at her, then away. "Aye. So thou hast said before."

Hannah tried to move into his line of vision, but he turned. "I have a gift for you," she said. "Something to remind you of me when you're half a world away."

"I have all I need."

"But you've seen the quilt I've been making all this time. Surely you knew it was for you."

"I've no need of a quilt. Fine cloth is spoiled by sea air."

"I made it of the strongest cotton I could buy."

He frowned and took a step toward the study. "Keep it on my bed for my return."

She sighed. "Very well. But will you not take the daguerreotype of Timothy and me with you?"

"Hast thou no understanding, woman? My quarters are small. I don't need more things to clutter it."

Hannah gulped back a sob. "Very well, then. Good-bye, my darling. I will pray every day for your safe voyage." She would have flung herself into his arms, but her words had sounded too much like a dismissal. He entered the study and closed and locked the door.

Hannah tucked the covers around her sleeping son, then snuffed out her candle and slipped beneath the blankets on her bed. The weather had cleared, and the moon now shone through the window above her, making the whole room appear like a dream scene. Her body ached for rest, but she blew away the sleepy mist that crept into her head. When would he leave? Would he kiss her good-bye after all? Surely he could not leave her this way. She opened her eyes at a sound in the hallway. The moon had shifted, and its blue light now rested on her.

She had slept!

Had he gone?

His thud-thump gait halted outside the nursery door, and the door was gently opened. With effort, he moved quietly toward Timothy's crib, pausing there to gaze at the child in the dim light. He reached down and caressed the boy's cheek. Hannah could see in his profile the tender expression of his love, and hot tears rolled down her cheek. She would tell their son every day how much his father loved him.

But even as she thought it, her heart ached. Would he leave without a farewell for her? As he turned, she closed her eyes so as not to accost him. With a great sigh, Ahab moved toward her, reaching down to touch her cheek too. A new flood of tears betrayed her, and his hand stopped.

"Weeping as thou sleepest?"

Her hand reached up to clasp his, and she started to rise.

"No," he murmured. "There's no need—"

"But I must." She stood, gazed up into his eyes, and placed her hand on his chest. "Is there nothing left in you for me ... or for our son? Is it all hatred in here?"

He stared into her eyes. "The moonlight reflects in thy lovely eyes, my dear. Thy matchless beauty, thy pale cheeks, like an ivory goddess thou drawest me as thou didst long ago when my heart was first spliced to thine. All too easily, thou might bewitch me ... if I let thee."

"Oh, then let me bewitch you. Oh, my darling, say that I can. Say that I have done so. Say that you will not go. Stay with me and with our son. I beg you, Ahab, stay home." She breathed out that last word with all the longing and persuasion that burned in her heart.

He turned away and stared out the window, his eyes on some unseen vision. "Would that I could do so." His voice seemed to echo hauntingly throughout the small room. "Yet before me lies a path laid with rails of iron, and I am compelled to that path by forces thou knowest not, forces that thou canst not understand."

"Ah, but I do, my love. You must go and kill your whale."

He started, aware of her once more. "Whale? Am I permitted only one? 'Twould be a beggarly harvest."

"I know what you are about, Ahab. In all the seven seas, there is only one whale you are seeking."

He lifted his chin and arched his brows severely, but her steady returning gaze softened him. "Give me thy blessing, then, and I'll be about my task."

"I do bless you, and pray you Godspeed."

He began to move away, but she grasped his hand, pressing it to her lips and kissing it violently. His arms encircled her waist, and he pulled her against his breast, as though he would kiss her, yet he did not. She saw fear in his eyes, fear that if he succumbed to her kisses, she would hold him, that she would break his resolve.

"Stay with me," she whispered.

His look hardened. She sighed.

"Then go. Go kill your horrid whale. You will never be mine again until you do. But hear me, Ahab, you are to come back home to me, and to your son. Is that understood?"

He stared into her eyes again, and then smiled his half-smile, the smile she had not seen in many months, the smile that made her knees go weak. Still, she stood firm.

"Go!"

He nodded curtly. "Aye. I will." He glanced toward the crib. "See to the boy."

"Aye. I will."

Then he was gone. And as the thud-thump of his steps echoed down the staircase, she lay on her bed and wept bitterly until dawn.

The *Pequod* was set to sail at high tide, which would come at noon. But unlike other voyages, when Hannah had watched until her husband's vessel was no longer in sight, she could not find the energy even to climb to the roof walk to observe his departure that cold Christmas Day. Instead, she lay in bed and prayed, until she convinced herself that Aunt Charity's generous distribution of Gospel tracts to the crew and, most of all, the presence of pious, praying Mr. Starbuck ensured a safe voyage for them all.

Ahab would return to her. He always had. He always would. He always would!

Chapter Twenty-Eight

ဆာ

Abigail would not be satisfied until she had cleaned the now empty whalers' room, scouring the walls, floors, and ceiling to remove the taint of evil they had brought into the house. She burned the bedding and curtains, then hired Josiah Coffin and the stepson he had acquired when he married Widow Fry to give the room a fresh coat of paint. The project seemed to heal an ache inside Abigail, for after it was completed, she was her old self again.

Hannah took comfort in cleaning Ahab's room herself. Though she was reluctant to destroy the lingering aroma of his pipe tobacco, common sense prevailed. She removed the bedding and had it washed. With loving hands, she dusted each item that he had used and placed the quilt she had made for him on the bed. She was tempted to sleep where he had slept for the past five months, as if to fill the space he had left and to breathe in the air he had breathed out would bring him close to her once more. Instead, she moved back into the master suite.

Timothy fussed to join her, for he missed her in his room, and he missed his father. Unlike the adults, he was too young to devise a ritual that would help alleviate the loneliness his father's absence created. Hannah might have given in and permitted him to sleep with her except for Abigail's intervention.

"He must learn to quiet his own heart in such times as these," the older woman said. "Perhaps if you removed the infant crib and put in a new berth all his own, he might see that it's time to put away baby things."

Hannah took her advice and asked her son if he was ready to surrender the crib. His response was enthusiastic. Mother and son began by shopping for a bed and ended up redecorating the whole room—with some help. Josiah found an old ship's berth from a captain's quarters and refurbished it to make a bed. At Mrs. Stoddard's dry goods store, Timothy chose pictures of whaling scenes for his walls. Hannah embroidered squares of ships, anchors, and whales and sewed them together to make a colorful quilt. Aunt Charity made curtains from sailcloth. Daniel returned from his voyage with a gift for Timothy that provided the finishing touch: a scrimshaw model of a whaling ship much like the *Pequod*, complete with three ivory masts, intricate twine rigging, and canvas sails.

The child was delighted with his renewed accommodations. But as Hannah surveyed the room, she wondered at her own cross purposes. She was desperate that Timothy should not follow his father's trade. Yet here she was, joining the Nantucket conspiracy to turn her gentle son into a whaler.

In April, Hannah redesigned her garden. With Josiah's help, she dug out the perennials, replacing them with straight hedges and pathways that formed a geometric design. In the center of the design, she placed a fountain in the form of a spouting whale. Then, in the beds beside the rock pathways, she replanted her roses and hydrangeas and pruned her lilac bushes.

As summer arrived, her days became routine. Before the sun grew hot, she worked in her garden. Mid-morning she gave Timothy his reading lessons, as Ahab had instructed. In the afternoon, she received visitors or attended socials in other homes. For supper, she sat at table with her household, which now included Abigail and Daniel. Each night as she put her son to bed, they prayed together for the safety of their beloved husband and father, along with his crew. Timothy always added a special request for the safety of Isaiah's papa, Mr. Starbuck.

Daniel provided education as well as diversion for Timothy. He continued his knot-tying lessons and took him down to the docks or to the shipyards on Brant Point to teach him all about ships. In June, Daniel bundled the whole family up in a horse cart and drove them to the sheep shearing at Miacomet Pond. Hannah and Abigail happily agreed to the trip, knowing his purpose was not so much to entertain them as to give himself an opportunity to dance with a certain Miss Chase.

Taking Timothy along to hide his own shyness, Daniel sauntered around the crowds of celebrants near the pond until he spotted the young lady. At the same moment, she chanced to turn and see him and his young charge. She offered a confection to Timothy, then, as if surprised to see Daniel, offered him some too. The boy was soon back with his mother and aunt, and Daniel and Miss Chase could be seen doing a merry jig on the dance floor. The young lady's uncle did not protest. In the tradition of Nantucket, Daniel's hazy lineage was overridden by his prodigious success as a whaler. By early July, the couple was engaged.

In late July, Mary Starbuck gave birth to a daughter. As soon as Mary was able, she wrote to Mr. Starbuck about the happy event. She had not told him of her suspicions about her condition before he sailed, for it would not do to have him worry that she might lose another child or die herself in childbirth. Now that they had another healthy baby, she could write to him about Jemima, who had been born with dark eyes and a full head of blond hair, like all the famous Nantucket beauties.

Isaiah and Timothy found the baby to be an endless source of interest, and Mary told Hannah that Timothy was the only other child beside Isaiah whom she could trust not to pinch the baby when mother's back was turned. Hannah was pleased with the report of her son's gentleness. She admired the lively infant along with her son. But after visiting the Starbuck home, she sometimes cried herself to sleep, longing for a daughter. With two children to claim his heart, perhaps Ahab would not have gone a-whaling again. Or perhaps, with two children as consolation, she could somehow endure his absence.

At the end of summer, Hannah learned that Mrs. Stoddard had been granted her divorce. Although her dry goods store was almost entirely shunned by that time, except for a few friends such as Hannah and Aunt Charity, Ida no longer required the support it had provided. Social shunning did not prevent Mr. Lyons' success in the whaling business. Even when it was discovered that Captain Stoddard had sold the *Legacy* in Chile and was living with his other wife on some remote island, Mr. Lyons was not dismayed. The loss of that one ship was not worth counting when compared to the joy of his gaining the gentle Ida as his wife. At the risk of her own reputation, Hannah often invited the couple to dinner.

When Ahab had been gone a year, and Timothy had just turned four years old, Isabel Chase and Daniel Moontalk were married in Hannah's parlor. They moved in with Isabel's widowed mother near Siasconset village at the east end of Nantucket Island. The following month, Daniel left on another voyage, this time as captain of the *Marker*, which belonged to Isabel's uncle, Mr. Chase. Once again, Abigail and Hannah did their spring cleaning early in order to cope with their loved one's departure. By February, Abigail learned that she would be a grandmother.

That same month, Hannah attended a meeting at the Unitarian Church and heard some thoughts of the famous Nantucketer Lucretia Mott. Although at first Hannah did not grasp everything the woman said, she was amazed to observe James Mott sitting quietly, supporting his wife and permitting, no, encouraging her to be the spokesperson for their cause. As Hannah listened, more of Mrs. Mott's remarks began to make sense, especially as she encouraged women's suffrage. All the strident remarks made by Miss Applegate to her schoolgirls did not have the persuasive quality of this Quaker woman's gentle reasoning.

If the idea of women voting seemed too advanced, Mrs. Mott declared, or if women had been made to feel they did not have the mind for discernment, then let the women of Nantucket serve as an example of feminine intelligence in its highest form. Was it not the women of Nantucket who managed the community in their husbands' absences? Was it not the women of Nantucket who kept accounts for shops and counting houses alike, all the while running their own homes smoothly as well? Was it not the women who taught school and prepared the next generation for adulthood? Have no fear, then, that women can just as wisely, if not more so, decide on political policy or decide on who should hold leadership positions. In time, Mrs. Mott asserted, both men and women would grow accustomed to the idea, accept it, and, yes, even welcome it.

Hannah found the lecture enlightening. After meditating on several points, she wrote her thoughts to Ahab, with the hope that he would find these new ideas worthy of response. After all, he had always boasted about the women of Nantucket. Despite the fact that he had never taught her much about financial management, he had demonstrated his trust in her ability to manage their finances in his absence. And so she wrote him her questions: What did he think of Mrs. Mott's position on women voting? What did he think of Mr. Mott's acquiescence to his wife? Would he think his own wife capable of intelligent voting? And what did he think of women holding public office? She wrote with a hopeful heart, praying more for any response he might send rather than his agreement on Mrs. Mott's ideas.

Indeed, every month since the *Pequod* had sailed, Hannah had sent a letter to Ahab on whatever whaler was setting out to go around Cape Horn, giving him all the news of Nantucket and the rest of the country. Each day, she watched the incoming ships from her roof walk in hopes that it carried a letter he had sent to her. But of course he had not sent one. Not only was Ahab not given to writing either good news or bad, but more letters were lost than received throughout the whole whalefishery. What letters were received sometimes came years after they had been sent. Ahab had only received one of her letters on his last voyage, though she had sent one out every month then as now. Still, she would watch and hope, for her only alternative was to give in to despair.

One bright April morning, as she gave lessons to Timothy in his room, Abigail summoned her to receive a caller. Her visitor stood staring out the front window. He was a tall, muscular man with long, sun-bleached blond hair; a thick, full, red beard; and the tanned and weathered complexion of a seaman. He appeared to be in his mid-thirties. Despite his somber black attire—a style broken only by the ivory buttons on his coat and gleaming brass buckles on his boots—he looked like a Viking warrior. As she entered, he turned to her, his face lit by a guileless smile and his clear gray eyes filled with gentleness.

Hannah's heart seemed to stop. Despite his smile, there was a look of sorrow in those eyes. What could it mean? Surely if she was to receive bad news, Captain Bildad would have come himself.

"Mrs. Ahab, how good to see you," he said.

"Sir?"

A frown knit his brow and his smile vanished. "Forgive me. Please allow me first to offer my condolences in the loss of your father. It is a loss for all of us, for he was truly a good man. He has been greatly missed to this day."

"Thank you, sir." Hannah stared in confusion, certain she had never seen him. What Nantucket whaler would have known her father and only now had heard of his death?

"I sailed into New Bedford three weeks ago, and after unloading the ship and securing the cargo, I spent some time solving the riddle of where you might be found. Please believe that I have come as soon as I was able."

Hannah continued to stare at him. "I don't understand. Why should you trouble yourself—"

"Ah." He smiled again. "Of course. We met only once, and I was clean-shaven then. You can't be expected to remember me. I'm Captain David Lazarus. I've just brought the *Hannah Rose* safely home to New Bedford. It was a successful voyage."

"Oh!" Hannah dropped into a chair. "Oh, my dear Captain Lazarus, we were told that the ship had sunk, that you all had perished. Dear Lord, it's been … why, it's been seven years since you sailed." She stared at him for a moment. "Forgive my manners. I'm just so startled by … Please sit down. Oh, Captain Lazarus, your wife and child!"

He dropped down on the divan, staring at the floor, and cleared his throat. "Yes … "

"I'm so very sorry. Did you just hear?"

He nodded.

Hannah gazed at him through her tears. "You understand that, thinking the *Hannah Rose* lost, we never sent you word of it. Oh, dear sir, the smallpox epidemic of thirty-nine was the worst our region has ever seen. It devastated New Bedford. So many died. Eliza thought you were dead. She thought she would see you in heaven ..."

He nodded and cleared his throat again. "And I thought I was coming home to give her everything she had ever wanted. To think she and my little Lizzie have been gone six years. This business of whaling is cruel, indeed." He wiped his eyes, unashamed of his tears. "Forgive me. I should not speak ill of the business that provides for us ... for you. I understand your husband is in the Pacific now. I'm sure you ..."

With a shrug of resignation, Hannah sighed. "There is no amount of money that can ever repay me for the years of his absence."

"Ah. Then, I am loath to bring up that subject, but I must have your instructions."

"Instructions?"

"About the disposal of the cargo of the *Hannah Rose*. I have the oil, more than thirty-seven hundred barrels, and more than twelve thousand pounds of ivory stored in a New Bedford warehouse. If you like, I will act as your agent and do whatever you wish with it. The ship is being refitted at the dry dock. I'll be happy to help you find another captain, for I'll not go out again."

Hannah gave a short laugh. "It was a good voyage, wasn't it?"

"Yes, ma'am." He glanced about the room, then looked back at her with gentle smile. "Not to take anything away from your husband, Mrs. Ahab, but now you're a wealthy woman in your own right."

"Then you are now financially secure as well, Captain."

He shrugged. "As you said, no amount of money makes up for the absence of loved ones."

"Yes," she whispered. "Well, do as you think best with the cargo, Captain. My husband and my father had complete faith in you, and that satisfies me. I'm sure the crew is eager to receive their wages. Did you lose anyone?"

"One by desertion, three in … accidents."

"Then please take care of the widows and mothers. I know you will do what's right." She thought for a moment. "But, Captain, if you have plans other than sailing, will it not inconvenience you to complete this business for me?"

He shook his head. "I have no definite plans for the present. After all is completed, I may travel to Boston to visit my brother. He has a large family and a humble occupation, ministering to seamen in a mission there. It may be that I can assist him in some way."

"How generous of you." Hannah gave him a gentle smile of encouragement, for the pain in his eyes still revealed great suffering at the loss of his family.

The thumping sound of childish feet plunging down the staircase caught their attention. "Mother, I've finished practicing my letters. May I go to Isaiah's for a gam?" Timothy ran into the room waving his writing slate. Then he saw their visitor. "Oh, excuse me, sir." He straightened up and reached out to shake the man's hand.

"Timothy, this is Captain Lazarus. Captain, this is my son, Timothy."

"Master Timothy." Captain Lazarus stood and shook his hand. The captain's expression revealed that he was both amused by the boy's mature manners and touched by his childish beauty. As he sat back down, Timothy climbed onto the divan beside him and leaned against him as though he were an old friend. Moved by this winsome gesture, the man drew him to his lap and tousled his hair.

"What a fine boy you are, young man."

"Thank you, sir. Do you know my father?"

"Yes, I'm proud to say that I do. He's a fine, no, a great captain."

Timothy seemed pleased with that report. He would have got down and gone to his playmate. But the captain, having lost his own child, seemed to search for some excuse to detain him.

"Show me what you've written. Ah, these are well-formed letters. You're very young to do so well, my boy. Tell me, what have you been learning in Sabbath School?"

Timothy looked puzzled for a moment. "I don't know." He glanced at his mother, then back at the captain. "I don't go to Sabbath School, but my friend Isaiah does."

The captain struggled not to frown. "Then you'd best run along and ask Isaiah to share his lessons with you."

Timothy gave him a crooked smile and jumped down. "Mother, may I go?"

"Yes, my darling. Be back home for dinner."

"Aye, ma'am." He started toward the front door, then turned back. "I'm pleased to meet you, sir."

Captain Lazarus nodded. "My pleasure, sir." The door slammed loudly, and the captain turned to Hannah, his face glowing with pleasure. "What a wonderful child, Mrs. Ahab."

She stared down at her hands, certain that her face betrayed her annoyance over his question to Timothy. "Yes, he is."

"Forgive me, please, but I must say this. Your dear father would be sad to know his grandson is receiving no religious training."

Hannah lifted her chin and stared at him. "Thank you, sir. My husband and I—"

"You and your husband had your religious training. It was yours to believe or reject. Surely you must give your son the same opportunity. How could we endure adversity and suffering without God?"

Captain Lazarus spoke with such feeling that Hannah could no longer take offense. Surely it was his grief that was speaking.

"That is true, Captain. We could never endure suffering without God's help. But please don't think I've abandoned Him because I have left the church. My son and I pray every night for my husband's safe return." At least, she was teaching Timothy to say the right words, even when her own prayers felt empty.

Still Captain Lazarus frowned, so she added, "I promise to consider your words with regard to his training."

He stared down at the floor for a moment, shaking his head. "Forgive me."

"Please don't apologize. I understand."

He cleared his throat. "About the *Hannah Rose*, what shall I do with her?"

Hannah gave a little shrug. "Why, sell it, of course."

Chapter Twenty-Nine

ഇ

She stood on the front stoop, watching down Orange Street. The tall, dark figure strode nearer, his eyes set on her, his long legs quickly covering the distance. He was the most magnificent man she had ever seen. Now she was in his arms, laughing and crying at the same time. And he was laughing, too. *Hannah, my Hannah. I will never leave thee again. Come away with me. Let us sail away to see the world, my darling wife.* He lifted her above him, and she seemed to fly like a seagull, the wild Atlantic wind whipping over her face until she lost her breath. She looked at him, but he had turned away from her. *Ahab, Ahab, help me. I can't breathe,* she cried, but he was gone.

Hannah struggled to awaken, to catch her breath, but a weight seemed to press on her chest. It was the third time she'd had the dream in as many days, but this time, it ended differently. The first two times, he gazed into her eyes and told her how he longed to sit with her once again by the fireside, with the boy nearby. This time he turned away in the dream as he had in life, and she seemed to lose her breath. Awake, she was enveloped by a feeling of deep melancholy. *Ahab, my dear, beloved Ahab …*

She staggered to the window to close it, but a fresh burst of the crisp night air swept the room and refreshed her. As she began to breathe normally again, she gazed at the twinkling diamonds spread across the black velvet of the late autumn sky and wondered what constellation Ahab might be viewing that night. *What a foolish dream*, she told herself. She closed the window and lay on her bed again. But as she drifted back to sleep, her melancholy lingered.

Before dawn Hannah awoke thinking of her father. So sweet was his memory, she curled up in her bed, imagining herself seated once again upon his lap as he prayed. Oh, how he could pray. Never for himself, no matter how ill he became. Always for others, no matter how small their need. Unlike her recent prayers, which seemed to bounce off the ceiling with ghostly resonance, Papa's always seemed to be answered.

What would he pray for her now? For Ahab's safe return, of course. For Timothy to grow up strong and wise. And, oh, yes, that his grandson would become a Christian.

But what would he pray for her? Perhaps that she would know how to be the wife Ahab needed in his suffering. For surely, when Ahab returned, his quest complete, he would stay with her and their son. Would she ever be able to make her husband happy?

"Dearest Papa," she whispered, "Tell me what I need to know, what I need to do. Do you see how I still need my father's wisdom?"

My Father's wisdom. The words echoed back and penetrated into Hannah's soul. She had prayed, hoping the fervency of her request would bring the answer she sought. But something was missing. Something Papa once told her.

"Ah, yes, I see."

She slipped from beneath the covers and knelt beside the bed, her heart so warm she barely felt the floor's winter-like chill.

"Our Father, which art in heaven." She paused, lifted her eyes upward in the dark room, and smiled at the One Who is Light. "My Father in heaven, unto Thee alone do I lift my prayers. Two things only do I ask. Strengthen my faith in Thee, and grant me wisdom to be the wife and mother Thou wouldest have me be."

A long-forgotten peace flooded her soul, and she knew her prayers would be answered. As her papa once told her, her faith was stronger than she realized.

It was November 1845, and Ahab had been gone almost two years. By late the following spring, Hannah might reasonably hope to see the *Pequod* being carried over the bar by the camels. After all, Ahab's voyages rarely took longer than two and a half years. No matter what the weather, each time the harbor bell rang, Hannah and her son climbed to the roof walk to look through their telescope to see if it was his ship that was coming over the bar.

Timothy was nearing five now, but he was almost as tall as a seven-year-old. His long legs were strong and well formed. His dark eyes and black hair were reminiscent of his father's, and his crooked smile could melt Hannah's heart just as Ahab's had always done. Yet, despite her doting, he was unspoiled. Seeing his character and maturity, many a whaling captain offered to ship him as a cabin boy in another five years. All Nantucket assumed he would follow in his father's work.

It was on a February morning in 1846 that the Nantucket whaler *Delight* limped into Nantucket harbor, not needing the camels to lift her over the bar. Viewing it from their roof walk, Timothy pointed out to his mother that just by watching how high the ship sat in the water he could tell she had not had a good voyage. And that was even before he saw the ship's flag flying at half-mast or the shattered, white ribs and splintered planks of what had once been a whaleboat hanging in the shears. Proud of his keen eye, Hannah nonetheless felt a surge of pity for the ship captain's wife and whatever new widows and orphans had been made by the ship's disaster. Though she might not know any of them, she must inquire if any of the women had been left destitute, then help out where she was able. Aunt Charity would know best who required assistance. With these thoughts fresh in her mind, she was glad to receive her friend that afternoon, along with Captain Bildad.

"Aunt Charity, how good to see you. Captain Bildad, please sit down. I see the *Delight* has returned with bad news. I hope the captain survived. Please tell me how I can help."

Looking more sincere and sorrowful than Hannah had ever seen him, Bildad remained standing. He started to speak, then cleared his throat and deferred to his sister. Charity heaved a great sigh and pulled Hannah into her arms.

"My dear child, the bad news is not only about the *Delight*."

"Ah." Hannah's legs would not support her. As she began to fall, Bildad and Charity caught her, then lowered her to the divan. Charity sat beside her and once again wrapped her arms around her.

Bildad stood by the window and regarded her gravely. "The captain has brought news that the *Pequod* is reported to have sunk. He received word of it from another ship, a New Bedford vessel that passed him as they both sailed up from Cape Horn."

"Then it may only be a rumor? My father's ship, the *Hannah Rose*, was thought to have been lost in thirty-eight, yet it returned safely just last year."

"I would gladly believe it to be a rumor if the captain of the *Delight* had not gammed with Ahab only days before my ship is said to have gone down." There was a harshness in his tone and, though Charity frowned at him, he continued. "He reports that thy husband insisted on pursuing a great white whale, the very same one that had just destroyed his own whaleboats and killed his men. Now the captain of the New Bedford ship confirms that my *Pequod* was stove and sunk by the same rogue whale. That's enough for me to file a claim for the insurance."

"Bildad!" Charity exclaimed.

At the mention of the white whale, Hannah grew faint. "It's true then," she whispered. "He did it. He pursued it and killed them all."

"What's this thou sayest?" Bildad eyed her carefully. "Who pursued—"

"Shh!" Charity said.

Hannah stared back at Bildad. "My husband … Mr. Starbuck … your own brother-in-law, Mr. Stubb … all dead? All?"

"The report is that there may have been one survivor, a crewman. If he is still alive, he will be aboard the *Rachel* with Captain Gardiner, for that's the ship that happened on the remnants of the sinking. Of course, one would not expect them to return until they fill their hold, so it may be some time before we find out for certain if he lives."

Charity patted Hannah's hand. "My dear, permit me to pray with thee—"

"No! No!" Hannah cried. "He is not dead. He cannot be! Ahab never fails! He cannot … he must not …" She fell into Charity's arms and wept.

"Mother!" Timothy rushed into the room and flung himself at her knees, crying at her distress. "Mother, what's the matter?"

Hannah struggled to pull herself upright. She touched her son's cheeks and brushed away his tears. "Oh, my dear child, my poor dear orphan child …"

All her denials would not bring him back. He was truly dead. But unlike her father, he had left her no empty shell upon which she could bestow good-bye kisses. There would be no coffin, no burial, and no gravesite to visit. No place where she might go to scold him for his willfulness that had brought so much heartache and pain to those who loved him. All she could do was weep and hold fast to her son.

Timothy bore his loss with Nantucket stoicism, learned by observing countless islanders who had grieved before him. In his premature baptism into the waters of adult suffering, he instinctively sought to bring comfort not only to Hannah, but to Mary Starbuck and Isaiah as well. And, while not a day of his young life had passed without his mother or someone else in the whaling community praising Ahab to the boy, his own memories were dim. He, too, longed for something tangible to remind him of the great man who had been his father.

"Johnny Macy and his mother often put flowers on Mr. Macy's grave in the north cemetery. Could we not put a gravestone there too, to remember my father?" he asked only a few days after they had learned of Ahab's death.

Hannah gazed at her son, willing herself to be what he needed. She must not abandon him, either by succumbing to despair or by dying. Abigail had once told her that Ahab's mother had surrendered to hopelessness after her husband had been lost at sea. When Ahab had been born shortly after that calamity, she had refused to improve her mental state and had died when he was only a year old. The old Gay Head midwife, Tistig, had for some time taken care of the infant, decrying his evil name but declaring that it would one day prove to be prophetic. It was Tistig who passed the story to her daughter, the mother of Tishtega ... and of Abigail.

"Yes, my darling, we can erect a monument to your dear father and to all the men who died on the *Pequod*. What a wise little man you are. Come, we'll go to the stonemason's right now, this very day."

Chapter Thirty

෨

The April breeze swept over the graveyard as the warmth of the afternoon sun melted the last of the snow hidden behind the gravestones. A wrought iron fence outlined the place where Ahab's mother had been buried fifty-seven years before. There was one empty plot beside her. Hannah and Timothy watched while the stonemason and his workmen manipulated ropes and pulleys to lift the heavy monument down from their wagon, erecting it at last onto the designated spot. It was a black marble pillar, two and a half feet by one, set in a white granite base, and almost as tall as the man whom it memorialized.

"Is that satisfactory, Mrs. Ahab?" the stonemason asked.

"Yes, thank you."

"Will you need a ride back to the church now?"

"No, thank you. My son and I would like to stay here a while."

"As you wish, ma'am."

The men removed all their equipment, working quietly, reverently, as though they hoped not to disturb the grieving ... or the dead. Their job completed, they guided their horse-drawn wagon out of the graveyard and turned back toward town.

After they had gone, Hannah stepped through the narrow gate of the grave enclosure. She touched the shiny marble. Then with a sudden sob, she embraced it and pressed her cheek against its cold surface. Oh, how she longed to hold in her arms the one whose name was carved there. She gave a bitter laugh. It was indeed like embracing him, though not as she wished. For the frigid marble was as unresponsive to her as Ahab's breast had been the last time she held him.

She glanced at Timothy. He had grown restless while the men had worked. A large black butterfly had caught his attention, and he ran between the grave markers to catch it. Absently, Hannah wondered at the single streak of white that arched across one of the insect's wings. She had never seen a butterfly marked like that.

Turning back to the memorial, she breathed out a painful sigh. Now that she was here, far away from her stoic Nantucket neighbors who frowned upon outward displays of anguish, now that she had her tangible reminder of Ahab, now that she had no one to answer to but herself, she could pour out all the grief that had been locked away, tearing at her heart these past months.

"Oh, Ahab, I miss you so much. But then, I was always missing you, wasn't I? We shared happiness, yes, but for such a brief time. Oh, my darling, my dearest love, why did you go away? I know that you loved me. Your eyes declared your passion for me even when you tried to hide it and would no longer speak the words to me."

A wave of anger surged through her breast. "Now, husband, what about our son—this dear boy who looks so much like you? Why couldn't his bright, worshipping eyes put an end to your awful pride? I know why. Because you would not allow it. You would have your way—your revenge—as though by killing a whale, you could punish God for maiming your perfect body and scarring your proud soul. What does that pride accomplish for you now? What does it accomplish for me? Don't you realize how my arms ache to hold you? Yet all I have is your name to trace with my fingertips. Look at me, proud husband! See how Ahab's wife is reduced to seeking consolation in stone as hard as your heart!"

She moved her fingers across the shiny black surface.

This Monument Erected in Memory of
Captain Ahab
of Nantucket, Aged 58 years,
Who perished with his ship, the *Pequod*,
In the South Pacific Ocean
November 27, 1845.
All hands lost save one.
Committed to Merciful God
By his loving wife and son.

"Somehow, I should have known you were gone. That terrible dream I had, the dream when you came to me then turned away, was that the night you died, the very hour when you sank beneath the waves? Perhaps the very moment your breath departed was the moment when I awoke, unable to breathe. In some insane way, I believe it to be true. So now the last cord of our heart connection is severed, and it was you who severed it. It is you who are lost.

"Because of our love, I always thought I knew you, Ahab. But perhaps I didn't, after all. I don't think anyone did. That was by your choice, by your own pride and self-sufficiency. You cut your-self off from the rest of humanity, like a remote, Olympian god. Oh, yes, you were a god-like man. Even the most pious Nantucketer would agree. And perhaps that was your undoing, for you would have no other gods before you!" A sob escaped her. "Oh, my darling, why could you not see that the One Who truly is God is loving and kind and that He always had his arms open to comfort you in your suffering?"

As tears ran down her cheeks, she covered her face and shook her head, as if to make this scene of sorrow disappear. Yet when she opened her eyes once more, the monument still stood before her. With a sigh of exasperation, she thumped her fists against the black marble. Slowly, her fingers uncurled, and she once again caressed the letters of his name.

"And so, good-bye, my darling. Good-bye. You told me I am strong, so I will be strong. You told me I would do well in your absence, so I will do well. And, yes ..." She gave a short, bitter laugh. "Yes, my whaling husband, I will decide our son's future ... and my own. You see, I've become a Nantucket woman, after all. But I would trade all my empty days of independence to spend an hour in your strong arms, to smell the sweet fragrance of your pipe, to gaze up into your dark eyes, to hear your deep voice, to feel your touch ... Oh, Ahab! How could you destroy our happiness, our very lives, this way?"

"Mother, who are you talking to?" Unable to catch the butterfly, Timothy had abandoned his chase and now encircled her waist with his arms, staring up into her face with concern. Reaching up, he brushed away her tears, as he often had in the last two months.

She held him close. "I am scolding your papa, my dear. It was so cruel of him to go off and die." His eyes clouded in confusion. Regretting her words, she caressed his face. "Never mind, my darling. I'm talking foolishness because I miss him, and I'm so very sad."

At a distant sound, he looked over his shoulder. "Listen, Mother, the bell is tolling. May we go to the church now?"

"I suppose we must."

"And may we come here again?"

Hannah surveyed the monument once more. Now that it was a reality, it proved a poor substitute. But it was all they had.

"Yes, as often as you like." She took his hand, and they began their walk to the First Congregational Church a half mile away.

"The *Rachel* is a fine ship, Mother. Do you think Captain Gardiner would allow me to be his cabin boy one day?"

Hannah did not answer him. She could not explain to a child that Captain Gardiner had returned to Nantucket a broken man. His own young son had been lost because of the same whale that killed Ahab. Now that his ship had returned home, he would never sail again.

No, my son, you'll not be a cabin boy for Captain Gardiner or for any other. For soon I will take you far from this place that so callously sends her children off to die. We'll visit Jeremiah and his family in Boston. We'll go to London, then perhaps to Egypt. You'll have the finest tutors, go to the finest schools. You will learn of God's love, and you will learn to love life. My son will not be a whaler!

When the *Rachel* had arrived in port the day before, she had brought a full cargo of whale oil. She also had brought the single survivor from the *Pequod* disaster. He had been plucked from the sea some days after all his shipmates had drowned. He had been asked to recount his tale to the community of what had occurred on that fatal voyage. There was already concern, and much disbelief, over a report from the *Rachel*'s crew that Captain Ahab had refused to help Captain Gardiner find his lost crewmembers—and his young son. Once Hannah would have rejected the idea that her fearless husband could have denied aid to a fellow whaler. But what would the witness say?

It seemed all Nantucket had crowded into the island's largest church. When Hannah walked in with her son, many people acknowledged her with solemn nods. She took her place beside Bildad and Charity in the front row. Charity grasped Hannah's hand and caressed Timothy's cheek. Captain Peleg was seated across the aisle, with the Gardiner family next to him. In the back stood Abigail and Tishtega with arms entwined, supporting each other.

After a few moments, the pastor entered the sanctuary, accompanied by a whaler who appeared to be in his late twenties. The young man removed his hat to uncover sandy brown hair. His skin was tanned but not yet weathered like that of older whalers.

Though the pastor pointed to the pulpit, the man refused to ascend the podium, choosing instead to remain close to those gathered to hear his tale. Whispers ceased as he pulled up a chair and stared out upon the congregation. His face had a haunted look about it, a look of dread at some unseen terror. Still, wisdom beyond his years illuminated his eyes. He scanned the crowd, taking in each face and trying to comprehend the grief each heart must be feeling. His gaze came at last to Hannah, and it seemed by his compassionate stare that he knew she was his late captain's widow. Perhaps he saw a semblance of Ahab's visage in the boy who sat beside her.

Not a sound was heard in the room for many minutes until at last, with weary voice, he began.

"Call me Ishmael …"

Branching Out

ဆာ

Herman Melville's Moby Dick begins where Ahab's Bride ends. This is not, however, the end of the story for Hannah Ahab. She and her son must now go on, with choices to make that will shape the rest of their lives. Hannah started out as a naïve young woman, and is now worldly-wise from her experiences. The power of a story such as this is the reader's ability to live the experiences of the characters. Hopefully, you have enjoyed walking with Hannah and meeting her friends Jeremiah, Kerenhappuch, and, of course, Captain Ahab.

Reflect on the following questions as you continue your journey with Ahab's Bride.

1. How do you think Hannah's spiritual life would have progressed had she married Jeremiah instead of Ahab?

2. Hannah told Jeremiah, "I don't believe in perhaps. I believe in planning." How important are our plans to God? Does God want us to plan our future?

3. Hannah declines Ahab's offer to "tell frightening tales of my encounters with ferocious cannibals or deadly pirates." She explains, "How then shall I ask such a frivolous question to

obtain an amusing and artificial fright, when what I truly feel is gratitude toward all our brave whalers?" Who are the "brave whalers" of today? Do we honor them, or use their experiences for our entertainment?

4. Hannah tells Jeremiah, "I am examining what I believe, but surely that is no sin. If I don't question what I am taught, how can I claim it as my own?" Is Hannah correct to question the beliefs she was taught growing up? Does God permit our questions?

5. To Hannah, praying was as natural as breathing. She had questions—not about God, but about religion and the church. Would you agree with Hannah's father that she did "have a faith after all"?

6. Jeremiah preaches a sermon wherein he encourages the congregation, many of whom are leaving soon on whaling ventures, to either follow self-serving Saul, or follow humble, God-serving Joshua. Which of these two are you following now?

7. Hannah had to quickly learn to manage not only her new household, but also the business affairs for her father. How do you think this affected her view of the need to rely upon God?

8. Hannah asks Ahab if there will "ever be a time when you listen to what I want? A time when you honor my requests?" Ahab answers, "Aye. When thou hast seen enough of life to make wise decisions." Do you think this was a fair response from Ahab? How would you have reacted if you were in Hannah's position?

9. Jeremiah was rebuked by the elders of his church for not being stern enough with those who do not obey the church's laws and traditions. In his final sermon, he says, "How gladly the outside world watches when Christians refuse to solve their differences, for it seems proof to them that our Gospel message is powerless." How do you react to other believers who may not exercise their as you think they should? Do you agree with Jeremiah that Christians who refuse to resolve their problems show a powerless Gospel?

10. What is the significance of Hannah changing her prayer from "Our Father, which are in heaven" to "My father in heaven"?